I0525731

THE REDEMPTION OF KAL KARIUKI

Ladaki-6 is a terrible place, a planet controlled by the Assembly of the All-Knowing One, a fundamentalist cult with a fondness for hangings, a severe shortage of cash, and an unshakeable belief that faith, not science, will keep its devotees safe.

Kal Kariuki never planned to go anywhere near it, but Ladaki-6 is one of the few places in humanspace willing to employ an out-of-work marine with an addiction problem and no money.

Only to find that the Fates have other plans for her.

Hundreds of light-years from Ladaki-6, a conspiracy fueled by raw greed and a lust for power is about to unleash an orgy of death and destruction that will engulf all humanspace.

An orgy that only Kal can stop.

The problem? She has spent most of her life running from tough decisions and has a catalogue of failures to prove it.

This time she cannot run.

But will she?

BOOKS BY GRAHAM SHARP PAUL

HELFORT'S WAR*
Book I: The Battle at the Moons of Hell
Book II: The Battle of the Hammer Worlds
Book III: The Battle of Devastation Reef
Book IV: The Battle for Commitment Planet
Book V: The Final Battle

THE GUILD WAR
Book I: Vendetta
Book II: Counterattack

SATAN'S SOLUTION

Books 1 to 4 of the Helfort's War series are published in the United States by Del Rey Books, an imprint of the Random House Publishing Group, a division of Random House Inc., New York.

NOTICES

For Elodie, Eva, Oliver, and Euan

Δυνατὰ δὲ οἱ προύχοντες πράσσουσι καὶ οἱ ἀσθενεῖς ξυγχωροῦσιν.

The strong do what they can; the weak suffer what they must.

Thucydides
History of the Peloponnesian War, Book V
circa 415 BCE

Auferre trucidare rapere falsis nominibus imperium, atque ubi solitudinem faciunt, pacem appellant.

To plunder, to slaughter, to pillage in the false name of empire, and when they have created a desert, they call it peace.

Publius Cornelius Tacitus,
De Vita et Moribus Iulii Agricolae
circa 98

Those who cannot remember the past are condemned to repeat it.

George Santayana
The Life of Reason: Reason in Common Sense
1905

KOLOVCHENKO GATEWAY SYSTEMS ANNOUNCES RECORD QUARTER-3 FINANCIAL RESULTS

New Hainan, Hainan Province, AsiaEast
October 6, 2305

Kolovchenko Gateway Systems (GLOBEX: KOLSYS) today announced FY 2305 third quarter revenues of $10.9 trillion and earnings before tax of $6.3 trillion ($3,565 per share), increases of 18% and 32% respectively over the preceding quarter.

"Kolovchenko's outstanding performance in this quarter reflects the fundamental strengths of our gateway and pinchcomm businesses," said Amos K. Ferruci, Chair of the Board, "as well as management's commitment to the introduction of innovative pricing strategies designed to maximize the yield from Kolovchenko's gateways without compromising the corporation's consistently high levels of customer satisfaction.".

The complete quarterly report and financial statements are available from the company's website.

For more information, please contact Bu Xiaolin of Investor Relations (BXL-5671-7183-8881-9196).

—1—

Face down. Eyes screwed shut. World spinning. Maniac with cleaver hacking at her head. Heart thumping. Mouth dry. Stomach churning, threatening to erupt.

Fragments of memory. Hazy. Fleeting. Flashes of color. Splinters of conversation. Shouting. Noise. Toasts. Cheers. Singing.

What the f . . .

And then Kal remembered. A party awash with illicit booze smuggled in from Voronezh-4. A farewell for one of the maintenance techs leaving Ladaki-6, his precious contract bonus intact. A man with every right to celebrate.

She slid out of bed, found her clothes, and staggered to the sickbay, her body overwhelmed by the all-too-familiar amalgam of nausea, vertigo, and pain. Her hands fumbled at the dispenser, cursing as the medibot took an age to fill a beaker with nanomeds. She swallowed the blue liquid in one long draft, grimacing at its overpowering bitterness. A taste engineered to punish hungover drunks, everyone believed.

Tossing the beaker into the recycler, she berated herself for her stupidity. With all common-sense drowned in alcohol, godknows whom she had vilified, whose parentage she had disparaged, whose talents she had denigrated.

Like every other time she had messed up, she had allowed drink to take control, to make decisions for her.

This could not go on. She had to stop drinking; she really did.

Kal glanced at her reflection in a glass wall panel as she headed into the canteen.

Her expensively geneered body was losing its fight against alcohol and age. Black hair, once thick and glossy and cut short to frame an angular face, was flat and lank. Hazel eyes, once bright and flecked with gold, were dull and set deep in gray-dusted wells. Olive skin once tight and luminous, had started to slacken and wrinkle. Lips, once full, had thinned into a semi-permanent grimace. Her stomach, once flat, pressed against the front of her overalls.

She looked 65, not 43.

She hated herself.

She hated Ladaki-6.

And she hated one unarguable fact: She was what she was thanks to a lifetime of bad decisions fueled by phenomenal amounts of cheap alcohol; drugs too, when she could afford them.

Blackness enfolded her, a formless, sodden nothing that sucked the energy and hope from her.

She pulled a mug of coffee from the foodbot. Adding a hefty slug of icy water, she drained it in one, wincing as it burned a path into her gut. Pouring herself a second, she found a table and sat, closing her eyes to let nanomeds and caffeine work their magic on her ravaged body.

A chair scraped back. Kal opened her eyes. Her face turned as sour as her breath. "Go away."

Marty Lim's face broke into a jaunty grin. "And top of the morning to you, Ms. Kal Kariuki, Senior AI Technician and highly valued member of the Garford Corporation team supporting the benighted citizens of Ladaki-6 . . . Jeez! You look like a sack of crap, Kal. Hard night at the office, was it?"

"Didn't I just tell you to go away?"

"Why would I? I am having such fun. Hey! Word is you told everyone what you thought of our esteemed CEO."

"Dj'eela's an asshole."

"So you said. A lot, apparently. Come on, Kal! Dj'eela is going to fire you if you don't stop being such a dick. And she'll make sure Garford blacklists you; you'll never get another job, not an honest one anyway. Is that what you want?"

"Piss off. Leave me alone."

Lim shrugged. "Don't come bleating to me when she kicks your useless butt back to Voronezh-4 without your contract bonus. Remember that? The bonus you need to pay for all that fancy neuronic programming you keep talking about? Or is that just more Kal Kariuki bullshit?"

"You know it's not."

"Yeah, right! We both know your bonus won't make it past the first bar you come to . . . And talking of money, Maritza in Finance says the Ladakis are short again. Payroll's been delayed until next month."

Kal wondered how she was going to find the money for her next case of bootleg vodka. "Useless bastards."

"Anyway, much as I enjoy taking with you," Lim went on, "I have to go. My boss will have my ass if I don't fix that heat exchanger before the end of my shift."

"Go . . . And thanks for cheering me up, asshole."

Lim gave an airy wave as he left. "Always happy to help a woman in pain. See you later."

Nursing her coffee, Kal went outside. The view from the canteen's deck down the slab-sided fjord that connected Foundation City to the Great Southern Ocean was breathtaking.

Remove the locals, and Ladaki-6—one of the thousands of earth-like balls of rock and water in humanspace—was a stunning place.

A young planet with soaring mountains, glaciers, rock-walled fjords, violent, surging rivers, and endless earthquakes as tectonic plates battled for supremacy.

A beautiful planet.

A cursed planet.

A planet she was trapped on for another two years.

She needed a drink.

—2—

The Guardian was every bit as intimidating as the Assembly of the All-Knowing One intended him to be. Tall and heavily muscled, he had stood unmoving over Kal Kariuki as she wrestled a recalcitrant AI into submission, not once letting go of his assault rifle.

Finally, Kal stood, wiping her hands on her overalls, the Garford Corporation logo a cheerful splash of gold and blue on the left breast pocket.

"I'm finished here, chief," she said, packing away her test equipment. "You shouldn't have any more problems. If you do, feel free to call the best AI technician on Ladaki-6 . . . which is me, of course. Right, I'm off."

The Guardian's eyes had narrowed in contempt. Ladaki women spoke to men only when spoken to. And hate; AIs and the people who maintained them were the Dark One's spawn.

Whistling tunelessly, Kal slung her bag over a shoulder and walked out of the AI systems center, past more Guardians manning the security post, all big men, hard-eyed, sullen, hostile.

Kal gave them a cheery wave as she walked past. "Bye, boys. Have a wonderful day."

Faces tightened.

She pushed through the access lock. For all her bravado, the Guardians frightened her, brutal, violent men every one of them. She needed to be careful; she would push them too far one day.

"Garford Base," she told the AI as she climbed into the waiting van.

The ugly, battered box on wheels accelerated away from the headquarters of the Assembly, the wellspring of all power on Ladaki-6, humanspace's nastiest planet in Kal's opinion, an opinion shared by every Garford employee.

She licked lips suddenly dry. She should have risked bringing a hip flask. Fuck the Guardians, she decided. Next time, she would.

The van crested the hill and Foundation City's central plaza opened in front of her. On any normal day, the soulless expanse of concrete would have been empty. Now, it was a mass of . . .

"Stop!" Kal told the van's AI.

The instant the van pulled up, she jumped out. Locals packed the plaza, the woman in headscarves and dun-colored dresses, the men in rough coats and pants of every shade of gray, many with small children on their shoulders.

The crowd's focus was an island of color in a leaden ocean: a row of hooded figures in orange overalls standing on a platform below a thick crossbar, nooses around their necks. Even held by two Guardians, one of the condemned, a young man, twisted in a desperate fight to hold on to life.

Kal's gut cramped up. She had forgotten that today was one of the Ladakis' monthly Atonement Days.

Mass-murder day, more like it.

A tall figure in black stood out front. His arms wind-milled as he harangued the throng, his voice rasping, hoarse. Patriarch Wei, absolute leader of the Assembly of the All-Knowing One, Ladaki's only religion.

The torrent of words stopped. The man's head went back. He lifted his hands skywards and the figures vanished through trapdoors in a blur of orange. A murmur soughed through the crowd.

Kal stomach rebelled. She doubled her over and vomited, her body racked by spasms until she had nothing more to lose. Alcohol or shock? She wasn't sure. Both, probably.

A voice, loud, aggressive, furious. "Hey! What are you doing, woman?"

It was a Guardian, laboring up the hill towards her, his face red. "You are not permitted to exit your vehicle without an escort," he roared.

Kal wiped her mouth on a sleeve. "I had to be sick," she yelled back.

"I don't care. Stay where you are."

Kal knew what that meant. At best, a beating. At worst, being bludgeoned to death. Not wanting either, she gave the man the finger and scrambled back into the van, which took off, leaving the Guardian bellowing after her in impotent fury.

She stuck her head out of the window. "Go say a prayer for my soul, you useless sack of . . . Oh, crap!"

She ducked back inside as the man raised his assault rifle and emptied the magazine in a wild fusillade that shredded the air around the fast-fleeing vehicle.

Kal slumped back in the seat, shaking. She consoled herself with the promise of a stiff vodka over ice once she was back on base.

Godknows, she had earned it.

~~~

Kal's neuronics announced a comm from her boss. "What's up, Mikey?"

Mike Wajiya's avatar jabbed its finger at Kal. "I've told you not call me that, goddammit! Stop what you're doing and get your ass here, now!"

"I have to be . . . What a jerk," Kal said as the man disappeared.

As she sauntered into his office and sat down, uninvited, Wajiya leaned back, arms crossed, lips clamped into a thin, bloodless line, eyes mere slits.

Kal called that Wajiya's 'I'm massively pissed off with you, Senior Technician Kariuki' pose. Provided she did her job—as she always did—the man mostly left her alone, but he had his limits. When Kal's general insolence and contempt for the Ladakis became too blatant to ignore, he would smack her with a disciplinary citation.

She'd had four so far. Two more, and the CEO, Anthea Dj'eela, would fire her. And that would be Kal's bonus gone; she needed to be careful.

"The Office of Guardians has just lodged a Breach Notice with Dj'eela's office," Wajiya said. "They say you left your vehicle this morning without authorization."

Kal rolled her eyes. "Oh, for fuck's sake! It was only for a minute. No big deal."

"How many times do I have to tell—"

"Listen, Mike. I had to throw up, so back off. Okay?"

"I have enough crap on my plate to waste time dealing with your stupidity. That's the third complaint from the Guardians about your behavior this month. Take a vomit bag with you if you're not feeling well."

"I will the next time I'm in town on mass-murder day."

"Oh, yes," Wajiya muttered. "It's the last Thursday in the month. How many this time?"

Kal thought for a moment, then said, "Uh . . . 19, I think. Unless there was a second batch; Ma'alikaa from satcomm systems says they do that sometimes."

"Shit . . . I'm not surprised you threw up. Listen, I'll file a response with the Guardians saying you were so ill you couldn't help yourself and that it won't happen again. Just get the medibots to give you something in case Dj'eela checks up. And stop upsetting the locals, Kal, please. They are paying your salary."

"Money is the only reason I'm here, Mike."

"It's the only reason any of us are here."

—3—

Kal's neuronics pinged to tell her she had a comm from security.

"Good morning, Ms. Kariuki," the AI said. "Daniel Wei has commed me to say he will be at SecPost-5 in ten minutes."

Kal groaned; she had forgotten. SecPost-5 was on the far side of the compound. Away from the city, it was an uncomfortable walk on a muggy day. She was the only Garford staffer who ever went there; it was the perfect place for her meetings with Daniel.

"I'm on my way."

She activated the malware she had infiltrated into Garford's security system to scrub all evidence of Daniel's visit from the knowledgebases, a visit that broke so many rules she would be on the first freighter back to Voronezh-4 if management found out, out of a job and out of money.

Not that Kal would ever allow that to happen; she was too accomplished a hacker.

~~~

Just past his sixteenth birthday and already a head taller than Kal, Daniel Wei was a lanky boy dressed in the faded gray pants and work shirt worn by most of the locals.

He wasn't just outrageously smart, he also had a gift for blackmail, as Janos Baldar—Kal's predecessor—had discovered when Daniel had caught him getting all hot and sweaty with a local woman.

The little sonofabitch gave me two choices, Baldar had told Kal: Help with his education, or he would hand the holovid of what happened that day to Garford management.

Unsurprisingly, Baldar had chosen the former. The cynic in Kal thought that had little to do with protecting his lover from the gallows and everything to do with saving his precious contract bonus.

Look after Daniel, he had told her before he left, he is worth it. And Kal had, ignoring the clause in her contract prohibiting any unauthorized contact with Ladaki citizens, an impulsive decision so out of character it had surprised her then and still did. But it had been one of the few decisions in her life she had not regretted, one she took great pains to ensure she never did.

She led the boy into a small interview room. "What can I do for you?"

Daniel pushed a datastick across the table. "I'm done with this."

Kal tried to conceal her disappointment. "I was hoping you'd see it through to the end."

Daniel grinned. "I have. Straight As, Kal. Straight As."

"You're kidding! I only gave you that 'stick six months ago."

"It was difficult at first, but once I'd understood the Leung-Vijay equations, it was straightforward. Pinchspace mechanics is just mathematics, you know."

Kal blinked. Just mathematics? Fiendishly difficult mathematics more like it; some said that not even a hundred people in humanspace understood the science of pinchspace in its entirety.

She never would be. "Okay. What now?" she asked.

"I'm halfway through my master's, but I'd like to start the applied pinchspace engineering program; I want to understand how the theory translates into practice."

"Hold on a second. Two masters at once? Can you do that?"

Daniel flicked a dismissive hand. "I can. I've convinced my father I want to become a priest. He gives me all the time I want to study the Sacred Texts, not that I ever do."

"Please tell me you're being careful. You're risking your life just talking to me."

"Stop fussing. Who would ever suspect the son of the sainted Patriarch Wei of being a dissenter?"

"He won't protect you if he finds out what you're doing," Kal said.

"Or course he won't! The crazy nut-job would string me up, just like he does with everyone else who steps out of line."

Kal knew Daniel was right; Patriarch Wei's ironbound rectitude was the stuff of nightmares. Just don't let the old buzzard catch you."

"I won't. Now, what about that extra program?"

"I'll have the AI to put together what you want. I'm hoping to be offshift on the 24th. You can pick it up then."

"Thanks. See ya."

Kal slipped the flask from her pocket and swallowed a slug of vodka as Daniel Wei left.

Never was there a human so out of place. Knowing the Ladakis, things would not end well for Daniel. One day he would make a mistake, and Patriarch Wei would send his oldest son to the gallows without a second's compunction.

And there she was, worried about her contract bonus.

As she got to her feet, her neuronics pinged. She groaned. Mike Wajiya again. Closing her eyes, she accepted the comm, pasting a cheerfulness on her face she did not feel.

"Hey, Mike. What can I do for Garford's number one manager?"

"Fuck off, Kariuki. When are you going to Kaliakos?"

"Now."

"Take Kellerman with you then," Wajiya said.

"Who the hell is Kellerman?"

"She arrived last week. Power-systems tech. She hasn't left the compound yet, so show her a bit of the place, make sure she knows the rules. And go easy on her, Kal, please. She's just a kid."

~~~

Kal glanced at the woman sat beside her in the van as it left the compound.

Youtha Kellerman made Kal feel ancient, worn-out, a loser. She was everything Kal was not: beautiful, young, keen, optimistic, full of hope, a woman with the face of an ebony angel.

"Why Garford?" Kal asked. "Why Ladaki-6?"

"Even though the Ladakis are mob of superstitious primitives, there are probably worse places to start. And I won't be here forever; I'm only on a two-year contract."

"Half your luck. My neuronics think you sound Alafradian. Are you?"

Kellerman sighed. "I am. It really sucked; I had to leave."

Kal smiled. From what she had heard of Alafrad, it sounded like her sort of place: wealthy, not too many people, stable government, no corruption, decent climate, no nasty predators or bugs, low asteroid risk, and safely away from potential supernovae and gamma-ray bursters.

Kellerman pressed her face to the window, tinted to stop the sight of off-worlder agents of the Dark One contaminating the locals. "They look like peasants from the Dark Ages. They're all so ragged, so dirty . . . so beaten down."

"Money's tight, which is why they're always paying us late. One of the finance guys says the economy is close to collapse. He gives it five years, max. Maybe less."

Kellerman frowned. "Garford's recruiters never mentioned that."

"Of course not. You wouldn't have signed up if they had been honest about this cesspit of a planet. And wait until you see what happens on Atonement Days."

"Why? What does happen?"

"That's when the Guardians hang any Ladakis who've stepped out of line."

"I'm beginning to think I might have made a mistake."

Kal patted Kellerman's hand. "Welcome to reality, kid. Just keep your head down. Your contract will be over before you know it."

—4—

Kal finished an ill-tempered session with the AI responsible for managing Ladaki-6's power distribution network.

It had been a long day. She needed a drink. It was hot; thanks to yet more of Dj'eela's cost-cutting, the air-con had been playing up.

Maybe a beer. Or a double vodka?

Decisions, decisions.

It was too hard, she decided. She would have both.

Kal was on her way back to her room when Mike Wajiya commed her.

"Any luck?" he asked.

"It's the datafeeds. How many times do we have to tell the Ladakis to look after their sensors? That's their job, not mine. I'm going to tell those useless fu—"

"For chrissakes, Kal! Stop! Much as I would like to listen to you crapping on about how much you hate the Ladakis, I have better things to do. Just tell me when the problem will be fixed."

"The Ladakis say the sensors will be nominal by 21:00."

"And will they?"

"I told them Garford would be forwarding a detailed report to Patriarch Wei if they didn't."

Wajiya seemed relieved. "That'll work. Thanks."

"I have never let you down, Mike. That is why you like me so much."

"Yeah, yeah. Now, have you been through the report the Ladakis sent through? They think the planetary-defense AI has a power problem."

"Yes, I did, though there'll be more to it. You know the Ladakis; they never tell us the whole story. I'm going to see if I can isolate the problem from here. I'll need a shuttle up to November-55 if I can't."

Wajiya grimaced. "Dj'eela won't like that. She told the department heads this morning she's cutting the maintenance budget again, and shuttles are expensive to run."

Kal didn't care about Dj'eela and her budget. "If she's not worried about asteroids hitting Ladaki-6, then why would I be? I don't give a toss if one kills millions of Ladakis. In fact, I rather like that idea."

"Losing the AI which keeps us all safe is not an option," Wajiya said. "Ladaki-6 rates ten on the Torino scale. That mean the chances of a high-energy asteroid strike are high, so don't be a jerk."

"I was just pulling your pisser."

"Don't, unless you want another disciplinary citation."

Kal wanted to go to Wajiya's office and punch the man in the face. She squashed the impulse. She needed that goddammed bonus too much.

—5—

Kal commed Wajiya. "I've fixed the planetary-defense system's power supply, but I found something else. The deepspace radar and optronics datafeeds are off-line."

Wajiya frowned. "If the sensor data aren't reaching the AI, we won't know if an asteroid's coming our way."

"No, we won't. I need to get up to November-55 to find out why, so best you authorize me a shuttle."

"Shit! You sure?"

"Come on, Mike! The closer the diagnostic AIs are to the problem, the better. Transmission lags, remember?"

"Ah, yes. Hold on a sec . . . Okay, I have authorized the job."

"Sheesh! How did you get Old Tightpants to agree to that?"

"Dj'eela hasn't; I didn't ask."

Kal whistled. "The rumors were wrong, Mikey baby. You do have testicles after all, big ones."

"I'm writing you up for insubordination, Kariuki. That's your fifth disciplinary citation. One more and you can forget your bonus."

"I know, I know. Sorry. Forget what I just said, will you?"

"Not a chance. Just be at the spaceport at 11:00. You need any help?"

"I'm too smart to need any."

"You're such a jerk, Kariuki."

Wajiya cut the comm, leaving Kal to wonder why she risked getting fired just to piss off her boss.

Cursing her reckless stupidity, she headed for her room. If she hurried, she had enough time to meet with Daniel. Today was the 24th, and she was not going to stand him up. He was the only thing about Ladaki she liked.

~~~

Daniel Wei waited in the interview room. "You look rushed," he said as he took the datastick from Kal. "What's happening?"

"Problems on November-55. I'm on my way up there now."

Daniel's eyes widened. "Is there a problem with the planetary-defense AI?"

"Hey! Locals aren't supposed to know Ladaki's safety depends on one of Garford's evil AIs."

"Janos told me about it."

"Bloody Janos Baldar. As soon as my contract's up, I'm going to hunt him down and kick his fat ass . . . I have to go. I'll see you later."

Daniel reached across the table, his hand on Kal's. "Wait a second. Let me come with you, please. Nobody will know. And I've never been off this stinking planet; I might not get an opportunity like this again."

"I'll be up there until the system is nominal again. That could take weeks."

"I'm not stupid. If I don't want my father to know where I am, Mom tells him I've gone to the Mount Shandanna monastery to meditate on the meaning of the Words. She's, uh . . . friends with the abbot."

Kal shook her head. Adultery—she was sure that was what Daniel meant—was one of many capital crimes on Ladaki. "Won't your dad check?"

"Why would he? Shandanna is the sort of place wannabe priests are supposed to go. Shows commitment, you know? And I hack my personal tracker in case he does check. I've been doing it for years. One time I didn't see the old bastard for four months, and not once did he look to see where I was. So, stop worrying. I'll be safe."

"Look, I hear you but no way. It's more than my job's worth."

Contempt twisted Daniel's face, all excitement gone. "And what is your job worth, Ms. Kariuki? Not much, given all you do is make sure us Ladakis don't dirty our hands dealing with AIs, even though this shithole of a planet wouldn't last a month without them."

"Hey! I do my job."

"Yes, you do. Supporting murderous hypocrites."

Kal glared at the boy, angry now. Not with Daniel, with herself. Angry because the boy was right. Angry for letting her life slide out of control. Angry for all the bad decisions that left her trapped in a dead-end job on a dead-end planet drinking herself to a slow death.

She should say yes.

Except she couldn't; she needed that contract bonus.

"The answer's no," she said. "I'm sorry."

Daniel stared at her, and then he was gone.

Kal wanted to run after him, to tell him he could come with her, but the risks were too great. If they were caught, she would be out of a job, but Daniel? He would end up doing the Ladaki tango at the end of a hangman's rope, as did everyone who defied the Assembly's authority.

Let him go, she told herself. You've made the right decision.

Dismissing Daniel, she enabled SecPost-5's security and headed out to the van.

~~~

Kal was waiting for ShipCon to finish the shuttle's pre-flight checks when an alarm sounded.

"System anomaly, Personnel Access Lock 2," ShipCon reported. "Checklist aborted."

"Caused by what?"

"Insufficient data."

Muttering unkind words about cheap shuttles controlled by cut-price AIs, Kal left the flight-deck for the cargo bay.

Where she found Daniel Wei, leaning against a bulkhead, arms folded, a grin stitched across his face.

"What the hell are you doing here?" Kal shouted.

"Coming with you, what else?"

"No, you are not! How did you get past ramp security? And how did you persuade ShipCon to open the airlock?"

Daniel's grin broadened. "That van was big enough to hide ten people down the back. And you're not the only hacker who can persuade Garford's piss-poor security AIs to ignore intruders. As for this shuttle's AI, its cybersec is pathetic. It only took me a few seconds to break in and open the airlock."

"Let me guess," Kal said, sour-faced. "Janos Baldar showed you that trick?"

Daniel giggled. "And a few more."

"That sonofabitch is going to get more than a kicking when I catch up with him. And I'm not some dumb AI you can hack. You're not coming with me."

"Fine. I'll just step outside and tell security to take me home. And I'll tell the Guardians you invited me to have a look at the shuttle."

Kal swore under her breath; with her disciplinary record, she'd never be able to persuade Garford Daniel was lying. "No, I don't think you will. Your father's hung Ladakis for less, and well you know it."

"What's the point of living?" Daniel said. "I have no future here; I feel like I'm in a box with the lid nailed down. I might as well be dead."

Kal threw her hands up as a wave of reckless indifference engulfed her. Daniel had decided he would come along. He was a smart boy. He knew better that she did the consequences of getting caught. Who was she to stop him?

"You are a piece of work, Daniel Wei. Fine. You can come."

—6—

"I can see it; I can see it!" Daniel called out as the shuttle's forward holocam zoomed in on November-55, a thousand-kilometer-wide shape cut out of curtaining stars, pinprick lights marking its shuttle dock. "This is awesome. Did you know . . ."

Kal tuned out. Daniel had not stopped talking during the ride out, not even to eat, shower, or sleep.

When the shuttle finally docked, she felt like cheering.

She grabbed Daniel's arm when they reached the planetary-defense complex, a rock cavern cut out of the heart of November-55. "Right, listen up, Daniel. You can go wherever you like, but stay out of my way; I have work to do. You will find a foodbot in the canteen; facilities and bunk spaces are next door. No suiting up to go outside the complex. And stay off the commsnet. We are both in the shit if my boss finds out you're here. Any problems, you come find me. I'll be in the planetary-defense control room. Understood?"

"Got it."

Kal headed off, not to the AI room but to the canteen for ice to go with the vodka she had smuggled in. A couple of shots and she would be set up for the day.

~~~

". . . which means Ladaki-6's planetary-defense system is blind in sectors 13 through 18," Kal said. "I'm checking the datafeeds now; most likely it'll be sensor problems."

Wajiya sighed. "So what's new? You sure you don't need any help?"

"No point. I spend most of my time waiting for my crawlbots to tell the diagnostic AIs what they have found, and for the AIs to work out what it all means, so one person or a hundred makes no difference. I've—"

"One person? You sure about that?"

Kal's heart skipped a beat. "What are you saying?"

Wajiya sat back, arms crossed. "You think you're so damn clever, don't you?"

"I don't have time for games," Kal retorted. "If you have something to say, just say it."

"November-55's environment-control AI has flagged an oxygen consumption anomaly. It's double what it should be. Any idea why? An unauthorized passenger, perhaps?"

Oxygen consumption! Kal swore under her breath; how had she missed something so obvious? She didn't even bother arguing. "I brought Daniel Wei with me."

The color drained from Wajiya's face. "The Daniel Wei? Patriarch Wei's son?"

"That's the one."

"You're finished, Kariuki," Wajiya barked. "I have had enough of your smartass crap, your drunkenness, your endless complaints about the Ladakis, the rule-breaking. You are going to send me a comm me saying you quit, effective today. Understood?"

"Fuck off, Mike. No way! I'll lose my contract bonus."

"Hah!" Wajiya snorted. "You already have. I'm giving you an hour. If I don't have your comm by then, I'll tell Dj'eela about Daniel."

"You'll lose your job too."

"A job not worth having with assholes like you around . . . It's your call, Kal, but don't forget what'll happen to Daniel when Wei finds out."

"Wei doesn't have to find out!"

"What you've done is a serious breach of Garford's contract with the Ladakis. Dj'eela has to tell Wei about it; Clause 16.4, I think. And she's not the sort of woman who'd risk her job to save some Ladaki kid's ass."

"Come on, Mike, be reasonable. Yes, I made a mistake—"

"One hour, or I tell Dj'eela. And it's on you if Daniel Wei gets strung up by his psycho father."

Kal was pretty sure Wajiya was bluffing—even he would not let the Ladakis murder a boy of 16—but he might not be. She could not play games with Daniel's life. "Fine. I'll quit if you fix things so I can keep my bonus."

"That is never going to happen."

"Asshole," Kal shouted but Wajiya had gone.

She had always wondered how far she could push him; now she knew.

Ten minutes later, she commed her resignation to Wajiya, trying not to think what scratching out an existence on Voronezh-4 without money would be like.

Shit, she thought, like most of her life had been.

~~~

"I'm going to really spoil your day," Kal said.

The smile on Wajiya's face couldn't have been much broader. "Now that I know you'll be on the next freighter out of here, nothing's going to spoil my day."

"Trust me, Mike, this will. The AI which processes data from the deepspace radar and optronics sensor arrays in sectors 13 through 18 has defaulted to standby mode. No matter what the arrays detect, the planetary-defense AI thinks there are no asteroids coming our way. And no, I cannot fix the damn thing; its core has burned out."

"Why didn't the planetary-defense AI tell us that?"

"Come on, Mike! You know how things work. It told the Ladakis months ago; they only tell us if they think it's a problem worth paying us to fix. And they didn't."

"Well, we know now. Get a spare out of stores and replace the burned-out AI."

"We don't have a spare. The Ladakis decided they didn't need one."

Wajiya put his head in his hands for a moment. "Dear god, why are those assholes so fucking useless . . . Okay, no problem. We'll just have to order a replacement from Voronezh-4."

"Do that, but we can't wait for the next freighter. Wei has to pay for a cargo drone."

"Why the rush?"

"I had Daniel go through the raw data to see what the planetary-defense AI has been missing. Turns out it's a lot. Only a week ago, a lump of rock a kilometer wide missed Ladaki-6 by 23,000 klicks."

Wajiya flinched. "Fuck! 23,000 klicks? That is way too close."

"And AI had no idea it even existed. Daniel says we are three months into the worst asteroid storm since the Ladaki system was first surveyed. Things are so bad they are off the Torino scale and are getting—"

"Okay, okay, things are bad, I get it. Let me talk with Dj'eela."

"Just don't mention Daniel."

"I think I have enough to worry about."

Kal commed Daniel once Wajiya cut the call. "Get your skinny ass here, now! I have another job for you."

—7—

Two weeks wasted trying to cobble together a fix for the burned-out AI had left Kal exhausted. And worried. The harder she searched, the more problems she had found. Built by Garford using cut-price hardware, the planetary-defense system had not aged well, the endless reports of failures ignored by the Ladakis.

Wajiya commed as Kal was struggling to finish her report summarizing the system's many defects. "Wei has cancelled the replacement AI. Dj'eela just told me."

"That's crazy! Why?"

"Because it's not needed. Wei says the All-Knowing One will keep Ladaki safe. Not that it's your problem anymore. *Leviathan-VI* will be here next week to take a shipment of copper ingots to Voronezh-4, and you are going back with it . . . and yes, I will be glad to see you go, so glad I'm organizing a farewell party for you. Everyone you have ever pissed off will be there; I have received over 700 acceptances so far. Dj'eela says I can take over the canteen."

"You're such an asshole," Kal said. "What about Daniel? I can't just abandon him."

"And nor could I; it's not his fault you've dropped him in the shit. That's why I've spoken with Dj'eela. She—"

Kal's fist slammed onto the workstation. "Jeezus, Mike! What were you thinking? As soon as she tells Wei—which she has to—Daniel is dead."

"Calm down Kal. Dj'eela isn't telling anyone, least of all Wei. She said, and I quote, 'That old bastard's hard enough to manage as it is; I'm not telling him a rogue Garford employee took his oldest son for a joyride in a shuttle. She thinks it's best for everyone if he just, you know . . . disappears."

"And how's he going to do that? I don't care how clever he is, the Guardians will track him down eventually."

"They won't find him," Wajiya said. "Daniel's booked to go out with you."

"Ah, right. That'll work, I guess. And it is what he wants; he told me he would rather be dead than live the rest of his life on Ladaki-6 . . . Do I need to do anything?"

Wajiya's hands went up. "Oh, dear god, no! You've done enough damage already. Dj'eela wants Daniel gone without any fuss; as of today, he's on the books as Morris Chang, Assistant AI Technician. He'll be just another Garford employee heading home. What happens to him once he gets to Voronezh-4 is your problem."

"Gee, thanks. I'll tell him when he gets back. I've sent him out to see if the shuttle's collision-avoidance radar can pick up anything heading our way."

"Can it?"

"Daniel says it can. He's hacked the radar to look for big objects on vectors to hit Ladaki-6."

"Was that his idea?" Wajiya asked.

"It was."

"He's a smart boy."

Smarter than anyone else on Ladaki, Kal told herself as Wajiya cut the comm.

~~~

"We've been through your report," Wajiya said. "We knew the planetary-defense system was messed up, but not that badly. Problem is Wei doesn't have enough money for half the work that's needed . . ."

"What a surprise."

". . . which is why I've told Dj'eela she needs to think about Garford's contract with the Ladakis. Six months in a row now, they've been late paying us, a problem that is only going—"

"Sorry, Mike, hold on a second. Emergency comm from Daniel. Stay patched in . . . Go ahead, Daniel."

The boy's face was ashen. "The shuttle's radar has picked up an object inbound from the Koswekija Cluster. The AI's just computed its vector. It's heading for Ladaki-6 and it looks huge . . . but I, uh . . . I'm not sure . . . I don't know . . . We'll—"

"Stop, Daniel, stop! Deep breaths . . . That's it, nice and slow . . . You okay now?"

"Sorry. Yeah, I think so."

"Okay, listen up. This is why we have interceptor drones with nuke-pumped kinetics. We have to give them the best chance we can of diverting your asteroid. But calculating the optimum strike pattern takes hard data: vector, volume, density, shape, spin rate, spin axis. Got that?"

"Yes."

"Go get it for me then . . . Mike? You copy?"

"Yes. What do we do?"

"Brief Dj'eela," Kal said. "Just make sure she doesn't say anything to the Ladakis, not until we're certain. And tell her we should launch the interceptor drones."

"She will never approve that. IDs and their nukes are expensive. Wei will rip Dj'eela a new one if we waste them."

Kal threw her hands up. "Oh, for chrissakes! Better wasted drones than being too late; if we are, we are all dead."

"I know that, but—"

"Dj'eela's not stupid. She'll agree if you walk her through the data."

"I hope so," Wajiya said, a tremor in his voice. "I'll get back to you."

Kal commed Daniel. "How are you going?"

"The asteroid is an M-type about 30 klicks in diameter. And it's moving fast; 43 kilometers a second."

Kal was sure her heart stopped for an instant as she did the math. "Jeezus! M-type asteroids are all nickel-iron; that means a shitload of kinetic energy is coming our way. Where's my targeting data?"

"Almost there."

Kal's neuronics chimed to announce a new comm. Dj'eela's avatar popped. "Anthea, hi. Has Mike spoken—"

Dj'eela's hand chopped Kal off. "He says you want to launch the IDs."

"We have to. The sooner we hit that asteroid, the better our chances of deflecting it."

"No other options?"

"None, sorry."

"Goddammit . . . Okay, I'll send you the launch codes."

Dj'eela did as she had promised. Minutes later, the interceptor drones—Ladaki-6's only hope of survival—powered away from November-55.

Kal commed Daniel again. "The IDs are on their way. I need to compute their strike profiles."

"The data is on its way to you now. What's next?"

"I'm hoping we can just sit back and watch those kinetics nudge the asteroid clear."

"That won't happen," Daniel said, wooden faced. "That asteroid masses too much to deflect. It's a planet-killer. Thousands of IDs wouldn't stop it."

Deep inside, Kal knew Daniel was right; any M-type asteroid that big moving that fast was unstoppable. "How long do we have?"

"17 hours."

"Fuuuuuck!" Kal hissed, iron bands crushing her chest; fear, raw, overwhelming, immediate. She forced herself to think. "Best we sit on this until the AI gives us a precise time to impact. And, before you ask, you're too far out to get back in time to rescue anyone."

"Garford has other shuttles. My mother can catch a ride out on one of them; I have already told her to get to the spaceport. And she is not stupid; she'll be there, no matter what my father says."

It near broke Kal's heart to see the faith in Daniel's eyes, faith that the one person he loved would find a way to escape the catastrophe about to engulf Ladaki-6. "I'm sorry. There'll be no Garford shuttles taking anyone to safety."

"There must be. I saw six on the ramp as we left."

"Three haven't flown in months and never will," Kal said. "Garford is cannibalizing them to save money."

"That still leaves three."

"Two are INOP waiting for spares from Voronezh-4. The last one's tokomak is being stripped down for servicing. That takes two weeks, and the techs only started six days ago. I've checked."

Daniel's face lit up. "Ladaki-6 has its own orbital shuttles. One of them can lift my mother off. And your people as well. They don't need to die."

"Dj'eela just commed me. Your dad is refusing to allow anyone to use them, Garford's people included. She's sent a team to talk him round."

Daniel's face crumpled into a mask of pain, of fear, of loss. "That man never changes his mind on anything, you'll see. Are you sure I can't go back? I could tell ShipCon to redline the main engines—"

"You are too far out. You don't have enough time. I'm sorry."

Daniel's eyes filled with tears. "My mother's not going to make it."

A long silence.

"The best thing you can do is come back here," Kal said at last.

Daniel nodded.

"And take the time to talk to your mom," Kal added. "She'd want that."

"I will."

Savage anger at the pointless, avoidable stupidity of it all consumed Kal. She took a deep breath to make herself calm down. Much as she hated everything the Ladakis stood for, they did not deserve to die, though she'd make an exception for Patriarch Wei.

"Senior Technician Kariuki," said the planetary-defense AI. "Based on the data I have been given, there are no effective countermeasures against the incoming asteroid. Its vector, mass and spin preclude any—"

"Stop! Got it. Time to impact?"

"16 hours, 53 minutes."

"Where?"

"The Great Southern Ocean, 300 kilometers southwest of Foundation City."

A tiny flicker of hope sprung to life deep inside Kal. "Won't hitting the water diffuse the shock of impact? It must be pretty deep there."

"Over a thousand meters at the impact site. However, that will not reduce the lethality of the asteroid; it will simply vaporize millions of cubic kilometers of seawater, all pumped into the atmosphere as steam."

"Will anyone dirtside survive?"

"Over time, no. The asteroid's kinetic energy is approximately 5,000 trillion tonnes TNT-equivalent. The near instantaneous release of that much energy . . ."

Kal's mind struggled to absorb the enormity of the forces at play. It failed.

". . . will cause massive shock damage, tsunamis hundreds of meters high, firestorms from debris blasted into sub-orbital trajectories and heating up on reentry, severe earthquakes, superstorms with winds exceeding 500 kph and torrential rain. I predict at least three-quarters of all species planet-wide will have died within four weeks of asteroid impact."

Stunned, Kal fought to find her voice. "Then things will calm down, right?" she asked.

"No, they will not. The superstorms will drop rain which has been turned acidic by sulfur-rich carbonate rock vaporized at the impact site. Volcanic eruptions will blast enough dust and smoke into the atmosphere to trigger global winter. Within a year of the impact, 99.9% of all species in Ladaki's biosphere will be extinct. Any humans that do live will not survive as runaway global warming triggered by extreme atmospheric carbon-dioxide levels replaces extreme cold. 20 years after impact, only some unicellular and simple multicellular species will remain."

"Oh, dear god," Kal whispered, crushed by the scale of the disaster about to fall on a hapless Ladaki-6. "This'll be like Chicxulub, only a thousand times worse."

The AI broke a moment's silence. "Excuse me, Senior Technician Kariuki. I do not understand your reference to Chicxulub. There are no dinosaurs on the planet."

Despite everything, Kal could not help smiling; AIs could be incredibly stupid sometimes. "You are right, but all life on Ladaki-6 will have gone the way of the dinosaurs by the time this is all over. Unless Wei agrees to let Garford use his shuttles, it'll just be Daniel, me, and anyone else lucky enough to be off-planet."

"There is nobody else off-planet. The gateways and orbital transfer station are not due to be staffed until *Leviathan-VI* arrives from Voronezh-4."

At least she and Daniel would be able to get the hell away from Ladaki-6, Kal thought. She commed Dj'eela.

"I can't think of a painless way to say this," she said when the woman's avatar popped, "so I'll just say it. Asteroid impact will be in less than 17 hours, 300 klicks southwest of Foundation City. I will send you a link to the countdown timer. Given the mass and speed of the asteroid, most life dirtside will be destroyed inside a month, the rest within a year."

Shock tightened Dj'eela's face as she processed the death sentences Kal had just passed on millions of Ladakis and Garford Corporation's 2,000 employees. "No, no, no, that can't be right . . . Surely we'll be okay, won't we?"

"No, you won't. That asteroid's a monster, a planet-eater."

"Any chance you've got it wrong?"

Kal felt for Dj'eela; the woman deserved better. "None at all . . . I'm so sorry, Anthea."

Dj'eela laughed, a laugh tinged with hysteria. "Yeah, well, that's the way it is . . . I have 17 hours left?"

"Unless Wei lends you his shuttles."

"That is not going to happen. The sonofabitch has torched them all. And he had the Guardians hang the poor bastards I sent to change his mind."

"Why would he do that?"

"For interfering with the One's sacred plan."

"And what plan is that?" Kal asked, quite unable to make sense of the Patriarch's superstition-warped thinking.

"Oh, it's quite simple. The All-Knowing One has sent the asteroid to destroy Ladaki-6 and everyone on it. That way, we all get to go to heaven. Once there, the One will forgive us our sins and we can all live for eternity in paradise."

Kal stared at Dj'eela. "You are kidding! Who believes that shit?"

"The Ladakis, apparently. Wei cannot understand why we'd rather not die. He says he's doing us a favor by giving us a life of eternal bliss rather than a short life of sin, pain, and suffering. When I called him a perverted psychopath, he said he forgave me, and the All-Knowing One would too."

"Fucking asshole . . . I'm sorry, Anthea. I wish there was something I could do."

Dj'eela brushed Kal's words away. "It is what it is. Let's see . . . Once I've told everyone what's going to happen, I am going to drink myself into a coma. Hey! I might even get lucky with that hunk in logistics, Balachandram. Now there is the man to spend your last hours with. I just hope he hasn't had a better offer. Okay, we are done. You always were an insubordinate asshole, Kal Kariuki, but at least you did your job. How, I cannot imagine. You drank more alcohol in a day than I did in a month."

"You knew?"

"It was my job to know, not that your drinking was hard to miss. I told Wajiya to leave you alone unless you did something particularly stupid. AI techs as good as you don't end up on Ladaki-6. Anyway, stay safe. I hope things work out for you and Daniel on Voronezh-4."

"Thanks. I'm—"

Dj'eela had gone. Kal could not blame her. The woman only had hours left to live, and Ravi Balachandram was an astonishingly handsome man. Funny too; maybe he'd cheer Dj'eela up.

Once she'd fetched herself a badly needed triple vodka, Kal commed Lim. "Hey, Marty."

The man was a freshly exhumed corpse: skin waxy and gray, bloodless lips, dead eyes. "Dj'eela has just told everyone we're dead. Dead, dead, dead."

"What can I say? Shit happens, I guess."

Lim stared at Kal, bug-eyed. "Shit happens?" he barked. "How does saying that help? And why are you allowed to live? Why not me? I'm not a bad person. I don't deserve to die, not like this, I really don't . . ."

The man was crying now, the tears streaming down his cheeks.

". . . Kal, help me, Please! Help me."

"I'm sorry, Marty. I can't."

"You're smart. You can find a way. Please, Kal, tell me you can."

"I need to go. I wish I'd had the time to know you better."

"How could you? You were too busy getting wasted, you useless, drunken piece of sh—"

Kal cut the comm; she could not take it anymore.

Another comm, this one from Youtha Kellerman, eyes red-rimmed and tear-flooded, lips trembling.

"Hey, Youtha."

"Please help me. I don't want to die." The young woman's voice was breaking up.

Kal's eyes filled; the implacable unfairness of it all was almost unbearable. "I've done everything I could. I'm so sorry it wasn't enough."

Kellerman wiped her face. "No need to apologize; I knew that . . . You always liked to tease me, Kal, but at least you were honest. Not like most of the other jerks down here. All they ever wanted was get in my pants."

"It's been years since I had that problem."

"Lucky you. And they are still trying, except for those two dickheads from security. They won't be bothering me again. One's off nursing a pair of seriously bruised balls. The other didn't have any balls to kick, so I broke her arm instead."

Kal chuckled. "You're a decent kid, Youtha. Ladaki didn't deserve you."

"It's too late to worry about that. You know, it's funny how things play out, though. I wanted to come here more than anything I had ever wanted, to come to the Rim, to the edge of humanspace. It all sounded so exciting."

"Garford's recruiters are masters at dressing shit up as candy."

Kellerman's face soured. "Mine sure was. Not that I was hard to convince."

Kal could sense the woman's growing acceptance of her awful fate. Youtha Kellerman was a lot tougher than she appeared.

"It wouldn't be so bad if the Ladakis were worth losing my life for," Kellerman went on, "except they're not. They are an awful bunch. Except for the kids. I hate the thought of them dying.; it's not their fault their parents are brain-dead, superstitious assholes. At least I've seen something of the universe. They never will, Kal, they never will."

"It's not fair. Life rarely is."

"A lesson I learned early on . . . Okay, it is time I went. One of the survey techs has locked up a flyer. We'll head for the impact point and hold hands until, you know . . . I don't suppose many people ever get to see a monster asteroid up close. I'll stream the 'vid to you. Think of me as you watch it."

Anguish consumed Kal's whole being. It took an effort just to speak. "Promise me something, Youtha."

"Sure. Whatever you like."

"Give the big mother the finger from me."

"I will. You take care, Kal. I hope you make it home okay."

Then Kellerman was gone, leaving Kal to mourn the senseless, random futility of life.

~~~

Kal sat as the time-to-impact counter run down, the silence leaden, Daniel's breathing fast, irregular, tremulous.

Holovid from dirtside filled the control-room holoscreen. The Ladakis had flooded in their tens of thousands to join those already on their knees in front of Foundation City's Great Hall of the Assembly, the air filled with a susurrus of moans, cries, and sobs, faces wet with tears and pinched with fear, oblivious to Patriarch Wei's strident assurances that their annihilation was part of The All-Knowing One's plan to bring his favored people to paradise and redemption.

"What a crock of horseshit," she muttered as she cut the screen over to Youtha Kellerman's holocam as it tracked the asteroid's malignant plunge to earth.

The enormous mass of rock hung overhead, frighteningly close.

Kal fought to breathe, her whole body filled with an awful, sickening dread. "I am Death, destroyer of the world."

The first faint fingers of ionized gas flickered around the massive asteroid as it tasted the first tenuous traces of Ladaki-6's atmosphere, fingers that erupted into raging flames of scarlet, gold, and white as the searing heat of hyper-compressed air scoured rock away into a pillar of fire and smoke that tracked the planet-killer's fall to earth.

Not three seconds later, the asteroid plunged into the ocean, its impact blasting a gigantic cloud of superheated steam outwards, a cloud engulfed within seconds by a roiling wall of pulverized rock torn from the seabed, a ravening monster set to devour an entire planet.

Grief tore at Kal as the holovid stream cut off. "Sleep well, Youtha."

She turned to Daniel. Slumped in front of the screen, he was a huddled mess of misery. "I'll be in the canteen. Starting tomorrow, we're going to—"

The AI cut her short amidst the wailing of the emergency alarm. "Asteroid alert. Time-to-impact November-55, 5 minutes, 36 seconds."

"Where did that come from?" Kal shouted. "And what does that mean for us?"

"I have insufficient data to answer those questions."

Kal fought the fear back. AIs were simple beings; they responded best to simple questions. "What's its mass?"

"1,000 tonnes."

Kal breathed a little easier. November-55 massed billions; the asteroid packed too little kinetic energy to nudge the moonlet out of orbit any time soon. They should be okay.

Daniel's body was shaking. "Put the IDs on it!" he screamed. "Blow the bastard apart! Do it, now!"

Kal walked over to him and gave him a hug. "It won't bother us; it's too small. A bit of praying won't hurt, though."

Daniel's face split into a lopsided grin. "I'll give that a miss, if you don't mind. In my experience, it never works."

"Pray anyway."

Kal counted off the seconds . . . 5 . . . 4 . . . 3 . . . 2 . . . 1 . . .

The asteroid hit with a heavy, metallic crunch that tripped November-55's artificial gravity, floating Kal and Daniel flailing around the room.

The artgrav came back on-line. Kal dropped to the ground, Daniel landing in an awkward tangle of arms and legs beside her.

She scrambled to her feet. "Status report!"

"Habitat is nominal, no breach," the AI said. "All systems nominal. Preliminary assessment confirms no significant orbital perturbations; no decay expected. Shuttle is nominal."

Kal turned to Daniel, dismayed to see him still on the floor staring at the holoscreen, mouth open. She kneeled beside him and squeezed his hand. "Hey, hey, hey. We're going to be okay."

Daniel's face was white. "No, we're not. The asteroid hit one edge of November-55. The impact has spalled off thousands of fragments, like a giant shotgun's gone off. I've got the AI to compute vectors for the debris cloud . . . Okay, have a look."

Kal stared at the holoscreen. Red lines showed the fragments' predicted vectors, a spray of red lines radiating from November-55 that enveloped the gateways and the orbital transfer station.

"I don't believe it. We are so fucked."

"Yes, we are." Daniel's face was gray.

Five excruciating minutes later, the fragment cloud swept through the gateways, overwhelming their defensive lasers, an unstoppable blizzard of rock shards that ripped apart the fragile lattice arrays and their cluster of support modules, leaving two flayed, bleeding carcasses behind as they headed for the OTS.

Which died, consumed by an enormous ball of searing energy when fragments tore through its hull and smashed open the tokomaks.

Kal commed the AI. "Pinchspace gateway status?" she asked.

"Both gateways off-line."

"Ships in transit?"

"Only one, the *Leviathan-VI*, inbound. It will have made a crash drop into normalspace."

Kal's stomach tightened. Her and Daniel's only hope of getting off Ladaki-6 was now adrift somewhere in interstellar space. And there it would stay, its crew doomed to a slow death.

"Can one of the gateways be repaired so we can get back to Voronezh-4?" she asked the AI.

"Gateway-Bravo has suffered the leas damage. It may be repairable."

"Any idea how long that would take?"

"I cannot answer that question without a detailed project plan."

"Best estimate?"

"At least five years."

Five years! Kal thought even that was an optimistic assessment. Kolovchenko's gateways were complex beasts; she wasn't sure if fixing one after a rock storm had trashed it was even possible. "Get me that plan. Maybe there's a way we can speed things up."

"Yes, Senior Technician Kariuki."

Kal turned to Daniel. "This is not looking good; fixing Bravo is going to be a bitch with only two of us to do all the work. And, until we have a working gateway, we're not going anywhere."

"Voronezh-4 will know what's happened. Won't they send help?"

"Not a chance. Somebody has to give Kolovchenko hundreds of millions of dollars before it'll send its construction drones out to rebuild the gateways. Nobody's going to do that, not now Ladaki-6 has been destroyed. Either we fix Gateway-Bravo ourselves or we're going to die here. I'm sorry; we are on our own."

Despair stared back at Kal. "On our own," Daniel whispered. "Yes, you're right. We're on our own . . . I'm tired . . . so tired."

He closed his eyes and let his head hit the floor.

Leaving the boy where he lay, Kal did what she always did when life shafted her: get blind, stinking drunk.

—8—

The fallout from Kal's latest bender battered brutal splinters of pain into her head. No matter how many promises she made to Daniel, alcohol-fueled oblivion was proving to be a whole lot better than living with the prospect of a short, miserable life on a doomed planet.

She forced herself to concentrate. "Are you sure you want to do this, Daniel? We can abort."

"Enough, Kal! The drop window opens in 30 minutes, and we are going dirtside. I understand the AI thinks that is a really bad idea, but somebody may have survived . . ."

Kal knew the chances of that to be vanishingly remote, but even her hangover-fogged brain knew Daniel was right; they had to check. Assuming they survived the shuttle ride down to Foundation City's spaceport, that was.

". . . and we need decent repairbots. We cannot fix the gateway back to Voronezh-4 without them. The bots here on November-55 are cut-price crap, like everything else Garford supplied."

Kal stood. "I can't argue with you there. Okay, we'll go. Just give me five."

Daniel's face tightened with disdain. "Going for a chat with the medibot, are we? I'm surprised it has any hangover nanomeds left."

"You are such an asshole," Kal called out, stomping off.

~~~

Ladaki-6 filled the holovid screen. It was an ugly sight, no prettier now than it had been in the awful days following the asteroid's impact. Cloud still masked the planet, a roiling mess of gray and black punctured by plumes of ash punched into the stratosphere by volcanoes provoked into violent eruption by an impact-shocked mantle.

What they were about to do was insane. Kal was certain she was going to die. ShipCon wasn't happy; it had said there was 67% chance of airframe failure and total hull loss.

Not that anything she'd said made any difference. Now that the superstorms battering the planet had eased off, Daniel had insisted they went dirtside.

ShipCon broke the long silence. "Vector nominal for reentry. Standby de-orbit burn . . . now!"

The shuttle's main engines came to full power, the deceleration so savage the airframe twanged and groaned, the artgrav rippling as it absorbed g-forces no human could tolerate.

The shuttle felt like it was falling apart.

Daniel's face was pure horror. "Is it always like this?"

Kal realized this was all new for him. Nobody ever forgot their first dirtside drop, and this promised to be an absolute ball-buster. She patted Daniel's arm. "Yeah, it is."

A lie.

The engines shut down. ShipCon fired the reaction control jets to turn the shuttle end-for-end, pointing its nose down at the maelstrom below. Soon the hull started to feel the atmosphere, a whispering that grew into a steady hiss, the shuttle first trembling then shaking, harder and harder as it plunged into fast-thickening air.

"Hold on, Daniel," Kal called out, "we'll start aerobraking any second now."

"I'm not sure what aerobraking is, but I don't like the sound of it."

"Trust me; nobody does."

ShipCon lifted the nose. The artgrav shuddered in protest as the shuttle's belly met the onrushing air, the shuttle's kinetic energy ripped into a long tail of flame and smoke.

"Speed 8,000 kph," the AI said at last. "Vector nominal. Commencing aeroflight transition."

The nose eased down and the slow process of deploying the shuttle's foamalloy wings started. Now the storms tearing the atmosphere apart made themselves felt, the turbulence, shocking in its ferocity, thrashing the wings up and down, the flight deck full of the strident honking of alarms.

Kal tried not to think how much worse the ride down could get.

She got her answer: a lot worse as the shuttle crunched through the turbulence. It was so brutal, she was convinced the airframe had to fail.

Kal turned to Daniel. "You okay?" she asked.

The boy's eyes were wide with fear. His mouth opened. No words came out.

Kal could not blame him for being terrified. This was the worst shuttle drop she had ever experienced. Worse than the worst combat drop facing opposition armed with missiles they knew how to use, and she had seen a few of those.

"Hang on," she called out, "we'll be landing soon."

Another lie. Kal was sure crashing was the most likely outcome of this hellish ride.

"Passing through 1,000 meters," ShipCon said finally. "Flaps 5 . . . Flaps 10 . . . Flaps 30 . . . Speed 400 kph, reducing. Commencing transition into hover."

The nose lifted. Belly thrusters fired to slow the shuttle and take its mass off the wings.

"500 meters, speed 300, flaps retracting . . . speed 250 . . . 200 . . . wings retracting . . . 100 meters, wings stowed . . . speed 100 . . . 50 . . . 30 . . . 10 . . . Hover is nominal . . . Landing gear down and locked . . . LZ is clear. Landing."

The AI let the shuttle fall before a savage burst of power and a series of muffled thumps told Kal they had arrived. "Landed. Shutdown checklist complete; all systems nominal . . . Shuttle is nominal for launch."

"Roger that. Deploy rover." Kal did her best to sound relaxed, as if dropping through a superstorm in an overworked shuttle to land on an asteroid-racked planet was an everyday event.

"Deploying rover now. You may disembark through the starboard personnel access lock when ready. Conditions outside temperature -9 Celsius, visibility variable to 6 meters, wind speed 100 kph, gusting 120, snow heavy at times."

Kal threw off her harness. "A perfect spring day. Status of planetary positioning system?"

"PPS is nominal."

"At least we aren't going to get lost," Daniel said, already on his feet. "Come on, let's go."

It was bad outside, the wind a whistling wail that buffeted Kal's body, the blizzard streaks of white in her helmet-mounted lights. She checked the PPS; Runway 05 was 20 meters below her.

Daniel had dropped to the ground behind her. "Standing here, alive and well, knowing what's happened . . . It feels all wrong."

Kal climbed into the low-slung rover. "It does. We both lost people we cared about. Okay, let's go. We'll check the terminal buildings first."

The rover moved off, its fat, low-pressure tires untroubled by the snow, its ride punctuated by random twists and turns to avoid boulders. Some were enormous; the rover's radar found a flame-blackened monster a hundred meters across. Kal could not imagine forces capable of flinging something that massive to the very edge of space.

Five minutes later the rover came to a stop.

Kal climbed out. "The PPS says the south side of the terminal is just off to our right."

They had only gone a few meters when a giant hand battered the earth, the shocks so violent they threw her to the ground, Daniel too.

When the tremors stopped, Daniel got to his feet. "Us Ladakis know all about 'quakes, but I've never felt one that bad."

Kal took Daniel's hand and pulled herself up, brushing the snow from her skinsuit "Aftershocks from the asteroid. Ladaki-6 is a young planet; its mantle holds a lot of energy, so we can expect more. Come on."

The terminal had been a functional three-story building, plasfiber panels over a plasteel frame. Designed to handle major earthquakes, Kal expected to find it damaged but still standing. What they found was testament to the prodigious power of the asteroid. The terminal had vanished; only a few shattered stumps of its frame showed above the snow.

"The tsunami must have finished what the impact shock started," Kal said. "We can check the city if you want. We might find—"

Daniel shook his head. "There's no point. If the terminal hasn't survived, nothing on this coast has."

"We'll head to Kandinsky. It's far enough away to have missed the worst of things. And it's in the middle of Ladaki's biggest desert; there shouldn't be as much snow there."

~~~

The rover trundled down what once had been a broad, tree-studded avenue into Kandinsky's town center. Flame-seared rocks and the remains of shattered buildings punctured a mantle of dust-streaked snow. Scarred by pale slashes where earthquakes had loosed billions of tonnes of rock into the valley below, the mountains cradling the town loomed high, hazy in dusty air below a sullen sky.

The one positive was the wind: There wasn't any, the silence broken only by the soft scrunch of the rover's tires on a thin coat of fresh powder snow.

The rover stopped, its way blocked by rocks dropped from space into a haphazard wall. Kal and Daniel got out and threaded their way through. A shape caught Kal's eye. A hand squeezed her heart when she realized what it was.

Some freakish force had flung a woman skywards to fall back to earth, her shattered body racked across a rock, face up, arms thrown out wide, eye sockets dusted with snow staring sightless into eternity.

Daniel looked down at the corpse, then spun away, ripping open his visor an instant before the contents of his stomach exploded from his mouth. Shoulders heaving, he fell to his knees.

When Daniel had nothing left, Kal took his arm and helped him to his feet.

"We're going to see a lot more like her, aren't we?" Daniel wiping his mouth.

"I'm afraid so."

"Maybe we could have saved her if we had been here sooner. Why didn't we?"

Kal sighed. "I have told you why. We really pushed out luck coming in today. That airframe was redlining all the way down. I still don't know how we made it dirtside intact."

Daniel's head dropped. "Yeah, I know . . . I'm sorry."

"Don't worry about it. Come on, let's go."

They walked on, heading for the central plaza. As they stepped around a tangle of snow-dusted rock and debris, Daniel stopped.

Snow-shrouded shapes between boulders crowded the sprawling space. Thousands of shapes.

Kal checked the PPS. She pointed to a chaotic heap of rubble a good ten meters high. "That's what's left of Kandinsky's Great Hall."

Daniel's voice was a half-choked whisper. "All those people. They came to pray for the All-Knowing One to save them. Why didn't they try to live? Why didn't they fight?"

"You can't fight an asteroid, Daniel. They had no chance, and they must have known it. All they could do was wait to die."

Kal glanced across at Daniel; tears traced lines down through the dirt on the boy's face. She squeezed his arm; nobody so young deserved to see horrors like this. "Let's go. Unless we want to spend the rest of our lives dirtside, we need to find those repairbots."

~~~

Kal stared across Kandinsky's planetary-defense force base. If there were any working repairbots left, they would be in the maintenance complex.

Wherever that was.

The shock of the asteroid's impact and months of earthquakes had reduced the base's buildings to shattered rubble. She and Daniel would have to find their bots the hard way: searching mound by mound.

It would be worth the effort. Unlike the cut-price junk Garford used, the maintenance bots here were as capable as any in humanspace. They had to be to keep Ladaki-6's inventory of obsolete ground-attack aircraft operational, a cost the Patriarch Wei had been more than happy to meet to keep his grip on power.

"It's like a huge hammer's pounded everything down," Daniel said.

Kal put a hand on Daniel's shoulder. "Not one, hundreds. Come on. Let's get started."

It was getting dark by the time they found a scarred sign with the words '401st Maintenance Squadron'.

Daniel's booted foot kicked debris from the wrecked building. "What do we do now?"

"The floor slabs have collapsed onto the rubble from the walls. Our bots should be in the gaps between them."

"We have to go inside?"

"I'll do it. You can stay out here."

Daniel put a hand on Kal's arm. "Neither of us should go in. It's way too dangerous."

"We have to," Kal said. "Some of that rubble is too big for us to move. I need you to find a dozerbot that hasn't had a rock dropped on it so we can pull it clear. I'll look for a safe way in. If we're wasting our time, the sooner we know the better."

She had wriggled ten meters inside the ruins, when an aftershock pounded the ground. She bit back a scream as something hard bit into her thighs, the pain instant, searing, fading fast as her neuronics dumped nanomeds into her system.

Kal tried to move. She couldn't. She commed Daniel. "Get your ass here. I'm trapped."

"On my way . . . What's the problem?" Daniel said an age later.

"I have a piece of concrete across my legs. I can't move."

"Hang on . . . Okay, I see the problem. I've found a dozerbot, a bit beaten up but still working, godknows how. It has a hydraulic jack and a laser cutter; I can use them to get you free. I'll tell you when I'm ready."

Daniel bustled around behind her, doing whatever he was doing. Finally, he tapped Kal's leg. "Right. The jack is in place. You ready?"

Kal gritted her teeth. This was going to hurt. "As I'll ever be."

"Okay. Lifting now!"

The pain was immediate, excruciating, a blowtorch that seared a path down the back of one leg, so bad Kal screamed.

"Sorry, Kal. I need to move the jack; it's not lifting evenly. Hold on for one second."

Kal was past caring. "Just get me out of here before the next 'quake."

"Okay, okay. Hold on . . .. That's better. Right, let's shift this thing off you."

Agony, white-hot, tore through her trapped legs, this time for only a few seconds. And then it was over, the crushing weight and searing pain gone.

~~~

Kal opened her eyes to see Daniel leaning over her. "Oh, hi. I must have fallen asleep."

"I told the medibot to make sure you did. How are the legs?"

"Sore as hell. What's the medibot saying?"

Daniel gave Kal a thumbs-up. "No major damage. A few cuts, which the medibot has cleaned up and stitched, a shitload of bruising, and some ligament damage. You won't be able to walk too well for a while."

"That's going to slow us up. I tell you what, Daniel, every hour I spend on this asswipe of a planet is an hour too long."

Pain flitted across Daniel's face.

Kal cursed her stupidity. For all its faults, Ladaki-6 had been his home. "Sorry. That came out all wrong. Listen, when we are done, we'll take the time for you to say goodbye."

Daniel's eyes glistened. "I want to leave something to tell anyone who comes here what happened. The dozerbot has a laser cutter. I can use that for the inscription."

"Sure, but what about our repairbots? We'll never fix Gateway-Bravo without them."

Daniel tapped the holoscreen mounted above Kal's bunk. "Check this out."

Mouth open, Kal stared at the screen. "How did you get those repairbots out?" she asked.

"The next building over has a ramp down into the basement. I used the dozer to open a way in. When I got inside, there they were, all neatly lined up. And we got lucky; if the slab had dropped another five centimeters, they would have been crushed."

"If we were lucky, wouldn't be here."

Daniel poked Kal's shoulder. "Don't be so negative. Anyway, once I worked out how to get them started, I picked the five best and told them to move out. They are in the cargo bay now. Okay, I'm off to start on the memorial."

Kal ignored her body's protests as she levered herself out of her bunk. "Not without me, you're not."

~~~

Dawn was long gone, the thick black of night oozing away to leave a murky, gray day under a wind-flogged sky, the air full of dust and grit.

Kal sat on a rock, nursing her legs, as Daniel stood in silence in front of the memorial with its laser-cut inscription:

> *In memory of the millions who died on Ladaki-6,*
> *November 10, 2305.*
> *They deserved better.*

Kal stood and hobbled over.

She put an arm around Daniel's shoulders. "I'm so sorry."

Daniel wiped the tears from his cheeks, his gloves leaving smears of dirt across his face. "All those people gone. I don't suppose anyone will ever read what I've written; maybe one day somebody will. Right, we are done. Wait here. I'll bring the rover up."

Kal watched him walk down the hill.

Daniel was no longer a boy, but was he man enough to cope with whatever came next?

Was she woman enough?

—9—

Daniel's voice wormed its way through the fog enveloping Kal's brain.

"... wake up, you drunken pig!"

Kal lifted her head off the floor, wincing as pain pounded red-hot spikes into her skull. Wiping half-dried saliva from her mouth, she sat up.

"Aarrgghhh," she moaned. "My brain hurts."

"You forgot your alc-patch, didn't you?"

"I got too shit-faced to remember," Kal mumbled. "I always do ... Water, please."

His face wrinkled with distaste, Daniel handed her a large mug.

Kal drained it in one. "More."

A lot of water later, the pain had receded a fraction, but enough to add shame and embarrassment to Kal's suffering.

"I'm so sorry, Daniel. Things got a bit on top of me. I won't do it again, I promise."

"You keep saying that. All alcoholics do. I've checked."

"Sure you have. And I am not an alcoholic. I only drink to relieve the stress ... Oh, shit, I'm going to chuck if you don't shift your sanctimonious ass down to the sickbay and get my meds ... Come on, move it."

Two minutes later, Daniel returned with a beaker of pale-blue fluid. He handed it to Kal with a scowl of profound disapproval.

Kal took the beaker and sank it in one. "Oh, mama! That will do it."

"Is this how things are going to be? Whenever we hit a problem, you get trashed, pass out, wake up sick as a dog, I fetch the meds, and you promise never to do it again ... a promise you've not kept, Kal, not once."

"Oh, stop it. I do what I do, okay? When you have seen a bit more of the shit the universe can throw at you, then you can judge me. Until then, just shut the fuck up."

Daniel spun on his heel and walked out.

Kal cursed her stupidity. After what the boy had been through, he did not need her dumping more crap on him.

It took a while before Kal felt well enough to totter off to find Daniel.

He was prepping one of the repairbots.

"Can we talk?" she asked.

Daniel refused to look at her. "We have nothing to discuss. If you want to wallow in alcohol and self-pity because you are too gutless to fight your way out of the mess we're in, then fine. Now, go away. I've work to do. You too; I need those pinchspace field sensors off the gateways and back here, today. And you've not even started on the pinchspace nodes."

"I know, I know."

~~~

Kal dropped into a seat. After hours stripping sensors off gateways, sweat had glued her shipsuit to her body and her body aching. Daniel sat across the table; his face was gray with exhaustion. "I went through the test results from those multiplexers," she said. "They're as good as new now; well done."

Daniel smiled back, his face dominated by eyes staring from gray wells, eyes bloodshot and tight with exhaustion. "Thanks. And sorry I was so cranky this morning. I know how hard you've been working."

"We both have, not that we're making much progress. Every problem we solve only seems to create ten more . . . Which reminds me; I checked our driver-mass reserves this morning. The shuttle's burning through it a lot faster than I planned for."

"Are you saying we'll run out before we fix the gateway?"

Kal nodded. "I'm afraid so. We're already badly behind schedule and I can't see any way we can catch up."

"Oh . . . So, what we do? Start setting up dirtside?"

"If we can't fix that goddammed gateway any faster, then yes, we have to."

"If you're right . . ."

"Trust me, I am."

". . . then we'll just have to find another way out of this mess."

Something in Daniel's voice, a firmness quite unlike the unemotional flatness she'd been listening to all these months, made Kal sit up. "Is there another way?" she asked.

"I, er . . . I don't know. Sorry, ignore me."

Crushed by fatigue, Kal slumped back, happy to oblige. "Listen, Daniel. Both of us have been working too hard for far too long. We should take a few days off. Maybe we'll see something we've missed, something that'll show us how to get that gateway fixed before we run out of driver-mass."

With a grunt, Daniel dragged himself out of his seat. "I could do with a decent night's sleep. I'll see you in . . . Oh, screw it, three days?"

"Go for it."

As Daniel left the canteen, Kal tried not to think how horrible life on a doomed planet was going to be, an endless, grinding struggle to stay survive, any hope of rescue gone. But she did wonder why Daniel had said what he'd said. She had learned by now that everything he said was for a reason.

What that reason might be, she could not imagine. Facts were facts. They'd either fix Gateway-Bravo or die dirtside on Ladaki-6.

And her money was on the latter.

—10—

Kal looked up as Daniel walked into the canteen. "Hello, sleepy head. You better?"

"I've never been so tired," Daniel said, helping himself to a mountainous breakfast from the foodbot before sitting down. "A proper night's sleep was all I needed, though. Unlike you oldies, that's all youngsters like me need to bounce back."

Kal skimmed a spoon past the boy's head. "You cheeky little shit! If you were one of my kids, I'd, I'd . . . I don't know what I'd do. Keeping children in line isn't one of my life-skills."

"You should have been a Ladaki," Daniel mumbled through a mouthful of food. "Disciplining kids was really simple: beat hard and beat often. I learned early on to stay well away from my dad."

"That must have been horrible."

"I hated having to rote-learn the Words of the All-Knowing One even more. That was like having your brain pulped for hours every day, six days a week. The beatings weren't as bad; at least they were over quickly."

"Having your brain pulped was the whole point," Kal said. "All religions do it; the last thing they need is rational thinkers asking awkward questions they cannot answer."

"Which didn't take me long to work out, so I went looking for something better than those endless pages of nonsense. The Elders weren't stupid, though; they knew that too much knowledge risked exposing their religion for the fraud it was. That was why they had locked away all the dangerous stuff in the archives."

"Let me guess. That's why you're such a great hacker?"

Daniel smiled. "That and being able to make sure my dad never knew what I was doing . . . It took me a while to break in; when I did, the archives had most of what I wanted; what it didn't have, the advanced stuff, Janos Baldar got for me. By the time you took over from him, I had finished my master's in mathematics and moved on to pinchspace mechanics. And the rest you know."

"How did you find the time to do all that? What about the Words? Your teachers would have seen you weren't keeping up."

"We had to learn a page a week, which took me half an hour, max. The rest of my class were as dumb as mud; a week wasn't enough for most of them. The rest of the time I was head down, mumbling my way through my math coursework. I was so convincing I won the 'Most Diligent Student' award twelve years in a row. And don't look so surprised. I am such a ginormous genius, it was easy."

Kal chuckled. Not that she doubted the boy; he was so smart it was scary. "Modest too, which I like."

"No, just honest. What about you, Kal?"

"My parents were mining engineers. I was six when they died; a drillbot blew up. My great-aunt, Binzhu, adopted me. She was a smart woman with a PhD in Classics who turned out to be a wonderful, caring, funny mother. Thanks to her, I loved history, was fluent in Latin and Ancient Greek, and was all set to go to Seebohm U, just like she had. I couldn't wait, and then she . . ."

Kal's voice faded, her eyes brimming with sudden tears.

Daniel took Kal's hand, an oddly affectionate gesture from a boy so self-contained. "We can do this later if you like."

"No, it's okay." Kal took a deep breath. "Two days after my eighteenth birthday, Binzhu died; a massive aneurysm. One minute she was there, the next she'd gone. After losing my mom and dad, losing her too made me feel cursed, that I'd never be happy. After I'd blown my trust fund on booze and drugs, I knew I couldn't spend the rest of my life getting trashed, so I went to M'bakaa, got myself cleaned up, and joined the marines as a grunt."

"The marines? Why?"

"Because it was the hardest job I could think of. By the time I made staff-sergeant, I'd had enough, so I quit to become an AI tech. And here I am."

"And why Ladaki-6? Nobody with half a brain would come near the place."

Kal winced. "Gee, thanks, Daniel. As well as asking too many questions, you can be very rude."

"We're in a really bad place, Kal. Since we depend on each other so much, I just wanted to understand you." Daniel stopped, his face reddened by embarrassment and confusion. "Sorry. I'm being too nosey."

"It's okay. What else can I tell you?"

"More about your time in the marines. You didn't say much about it."

"Okay . . . M'bakaan marines were mercenaries, competent ones too. I saw a lot of combat, as a grunt to start off, and then more as a TACCO—tactical operator—in assault landers. I loved the marines; it wasn't long before it had replaced the families I had lost. I'd still be serving if I hadn't had half my guts torn out on New Magoska."

"What went wrong?" Daniel asked.

"Oh, the usual: bad intelligence and incompetent commanders . . . Anyhow, I came out of rehab expecting to return to duty, and why not? I was a staff-sergeant, I had a lot of combat experience with the medals to prove it, and I was on-track to be an officer. But a seat-polisher in personnel had other ideas. She told me M'bakaa was reducing the marines' contract work for other systems and had to make cuts—which was all bullshit, by the way—so here's your severance pay and pension, now piss off."

Kal had to stop, the bitterness of the betrayal still raw even after so many years. "I appealed, of course," she went on, "which got me nowhere . . . What followed was probably one of the longest benders in human history. When I finally woke up, broke, I realized I needed a trade, so I sold my pension to a bank, swore off the drugs and booze, and went back to school."

"Why did you pick AIs?"

"A random impulse, really. I still don't know what. The funny thing was, I began to enjoy it after a few weeks, so I worked my ass off, and passed out top of my class. Two years, it took me; I have never worked my brain as hard. Problem was I made so much money from my first job I slid back on the booze. Not every day, but often enough to wreck my chances of becoming employee of the year . . . I think you can fill in the gaps after that."

"I can, but why? The drinking, I mean."

Kal shrugged. "It's what I do."

"You must have a reason. Was it losing your folks?"

"What is this?" Kal snapped. "Are you a goddammed shrink now?"

"No, I'm just trying to understand who you are. Given what's happened to us, how much we have to do to get ourselves out of the shit we're in, is that so unreasonable?"

"No, I guess not. Sorry, sorry . . . And yes, I think it was. A kid can only take so much loss, I guess. It still hurts, deep down."

"No partners?" Daniel asked.

"I've cared for a few people along the way, not that any of them cared enough about me to hang around. Grunts busy being grunts and AI techs prone to getting trashed aren't what life partners go for."

"Is that going to be a problem? The drinking, I mean?"

"Will I get shit-faced when being shafted by life becomes more than I can bear? Is that what you're asking?"

"I wouldn't put it quite like that, but yes."

"Listen to me," Kal said. "What has happened, has happened. Most days I am fine with it, but I reserve the right to let it upset me now and again."

Daniel sighed. "That will have to do, I guess . . . Who knows? Maybe a part-time drunk and a smartass kid can get back to Voronezh-4."

"Which takes a working gateway we don't have and never will, the way things are going."

"I agree, and that's why I've been through all the research published by the Keliang. It seems—"

Kal's hand went up. "Hold on! The who?"

"The Keliang Foundation, humanspace's leading pinchspace research institute. The only credible one, in fact. There's a handful of others, but their work is third-grade rubbish. Anyway, I've read every paper the Keliang's published, and it seems to me—"

"Stop, stop, stop! How the hell have you found the time to do that?"

"Not sleeping as much as I should," Daniel said. "Why do you think I've been so tired? It's surprising how much you can get done when your life depends on it."

Kal grimaced, part anger, part frustration . . . and part hope. "I was going to rip you another one for wasting time, Daniel, but maybe I should hear you out first."

"I'd like that."

"Well, get on with it. The clock is not our friend."

"Sorry. So, it seems to me that . . ."

~~~

". . . and I'm done." Daniel's hands trembled, and a thin film sheen of sweat glossed his forehead.

Kal sat back, shaking her head. "Jeez! That was one hell of a surprise. But what you want to do can't be done, Daniel. It's impossible; everyone knows that."

"So we've been told . . . by people who weren't looking hard enough. Trust me, the science says it is feasible. I'm much more concerned about modifying the shuttle. I'm not an engineer, and neither are you."

"Assume we are. Are you sure the science says we can do it?"

"Maybe is all I can say. I can tell you this, though: life on Ladaki-6 won't be living. It will be dying, slowly. Running the risk I might be wrong is better than that."

Kal shivered. Daniel had a point; just the thought of going dirtside appalled her. Not that that made backing his judgement any easier. She had understood too little of what Daniel had said to know whether he was right; the physics of pinchspace were fiendishly complex. And he was right about the engineering; even helped by AIs and repairbots, turning an over-worked, worn-out shuttle into a starship was going to be a bastard of a job.

One thing was clear: Whatever they did next was not about her. It was about Daniel. He was young. He had so much to live for. He had so much to contribute. He deserved a chance to live out his life.

She'd had her chances and blown them all.

And that reframed the question.

It wasn't whether she thought Daniel was right or wrong. No, the question was whether she should put her faith in Daniel, a young man who believed he could find a way out of the trap they were in.

Or should she give up, as she had always done when things got too rough to handle?

Daniel's face was taut, a mix of fear and excitement, a face lit by hope and ambition, the face of someone desperate to take on the universe and win.

Kal recognized that face. It was hers the day she joined the M'bakaa marines.

She took a deep breath to steady jittery nerves and made her decision, one she knew for certain was both insane and desperate. "No more trying to fix gateways," she said, "and no going dirtside. We're going to put a jump drive into that shuttle."

Daniel jiggled up and down with excitement. "Really? You mean that?"

"I certainly do," Kal said with a great deal more confidence than she felt. "But calling it a jump drive is way too dull. Whatever you do, Great-aunt Binzhu always said, always do it with panache. So, let's see . . . Yes, the quaqua drive, I think; that is Latin for the anywhere drive, in case you wondered."

Daniel chuckled. "Neat; I like it. Quaqua drive it is, Q-drive for short."

"Not as stylish as Binzhu have liked but fine. Okay, Daniel, let's see if we can do it."

"Hold on. I do have one condition, and it's non-negotiable."

Kal did not like the sudden hard edge to Daniel's voice. "I don't usually react well to people who say that to me but go on."

Daniel stared right into Kal's eyes. "You do not touch another drop of alcohol until we reach Voronezh-4. What we are trying to do is difficult at best, impossible at worst. And we have to do it before we run out of driver-mass for the shuttle. That needs you to be one hundred percent. Not some of the time. All of the time."

Kal tried to imagine life without the warm, comforting buzz of alcohol to smooth the edges off her crappy existence. She couldn't. "Even if I drink, I will be."

"Not when you are lying face down, shit-faced, you won't. I cannot do this on my own. You know that. So, decide. No more alcohol. Or we give up and head dirtside."

"Fuck! You mean it."

"I certainly do. So tell me which it's to be."

Fighting back the desperate craving for one last drink, Kal said, "Not one drop until we're dirtside on Voronezh-4, I promise."

A promise she knew she would struggle to honor.

A promise she had made to herself a thousand times.

A promise she had never kept.

This time was different. Daniel's future depended on her; she had to keep her promise. With her own life at risk too, maybe she could.

Maybe, maybe, maybe . . .

—11—

The pressure had been intensifying for months. In the end, it had forced Kal to resort to threats of violence to get Daniel into the canteen. Now, they sat in silence so thick Kal could grab handfuls of it.

"What the hell is going on?" she said at last. "All you do is brush me off. I can't keep waiting for you to give me the design for the Q-drive. Do you have any idea how much work it'll take to install?"

"I have to be sure what I give you won't kill us both."

Kal sat back, arms folded to help contain her frustration. "Oh, for god's sake! Listen to me. I don't care anymore. Just show me what you've got."

"Do I have to?"

"Yes, you damn well do," Kal barked. "Now!"

"Jeez, Kal! Calm down . . . Okay, watch this," Daniel said.

Kal peered at the image on the canteen holoscreen: the shuttle, its hull bristling with stumpy masts. "What in god's name is that? And are those pinchspace nodes on top of the masts?"

"Yes, 32 altogether. They maintain the normalspace bubble that moves the shuttle through pinchspace."

"What the fuck, Daniel?" Kal said. "I can't believe you've been working on this without saying a word. It's just not on. We're supposed to be a team."

Daniel's head dropped. "I'm sorry. I had to think things through until they made sense to me."

"And do they?"

"Well, I, uh . . . No, not yet."

Exasperated, Kal threw up her hands. "We are running out of time. All we need is a drive which works well enough to get us to Voronezh-4. What we don't need is perfection; we cannot afford it."

"I know that."

"I'm not sure you do . . . Assume that's the final design. How long would it take us to install it?"

"I'd allow 16 months. That's a week to make the hull penetration for each mast and one more to run the control and power cables, plus a margin for testing and any problems we run into."

"Shit! Talk about cutting it fine. We run out of driver-mass in 20." Kal thought for a minute, then said, "Can you give me the final design for the Q-drive eight weeks from today?"

Daniel shook his head. "The honest answer is I don't know. The hard part is the AI that controls the Q-drive. Machine learning takes time, you know that."

"Yes or no, Daniel."

"Yes, I think I can."

Kal took Daniel's hand. "I think you can too, but no more secrets, okay? I want an update once a week, every week. Okay?"

"Okay."

"Do me a favor: Use words I can understand."

Daniel smiled. "I will, I promise."

—12—

Kal stared at the shuttle. It was only a simulation on a holoscreen, but it looked real. As real as the brutally modified mess she called Daniel's hedgehog could look.

"Sorry I've taken so long," Daniel said. "Okay, we're ready to jump. The Q-drive AI is enabling pinchspace field sensors . . . calibrating sensors . . . errors in limits . . . data flows are stable . . . computing optimum node power configuration . . . nodes configured . . . powering up . . . and we've jumped."

A flash of ultra-violet and the shuttle vanished.

"The shuttle is in pinchspace," Daniel went on. "Now, if you look . . . Oh, goddammit!"

The shuttle had dropped back into normalspace. What was left of it. Everything 15 meters back from the bow had been sliced clean away.

Daniel wiped a thin sheen of sweat from his face. "That happens when the bubble slides towards the shuttle's bows. The stern section is off somewhere in normalspace . . ."

A shiver ran through Kal's body. That'd be a bad way to die.

". . . Sorry, I thought I'd fixed that problem."

Kal groaned. "That's what you promised me last week. Any idea why this keeps happening?"

Daniel was hunched forward, a fleck of misery. "No . . . Everything I've done is based on the Keliang Foundation's pinchspace model; I've run hundreds of sims of the normalspace tunnel between two gateways. They all worked perfectly. This should have too."

"Except it doesn't," Kal said.

She sat back to think. She'd worked with some very smart people over the years; it had surprised her how often they'd miss something simply because it never occurred to them to check it out. Maybe that was what Daniel had done here. She chose the most obvious cause of his problem she could think of. "A gateway tunnel isn't the same as a shuttle bubble. Could that be why your design doesn't work?"

Daniel screwed up his face; he looked like someone trying to swallow a pineapple. "I know they're not the same. How does that help me?"

"I don't know. Maybe your shuttle bubble doesn't interact with pinchspace the way a conventional gateway tunnel does. That would explain why gateway sims work and shuttle sims don't."

"Tchah!" Daniel snorted. "That's nonsense. Pinchspace is pinchspace. It doesn't change just because . . . Oh, shit, shit, shit! Of course it does."

"Of course it does what?"

"I've messed up, Kal. Normalspace bubbles can't interact with pinchspace the way a tunnel does. Their energy gradients are too steep, if I can describe an n-dimensional probability matrix that way."

"I don't care how you describe it, as long as you know what you're talking about; I certainly don't. But, if I understand you right, the Q-drive AI is assuming a bubble is just a short tunnel?"

"That seemed logical. So logical, I never even thought to question it. I'm sorry, Kal."

"You need to check the literature. Someone at the Keliang might actually have done something useful on those energy gradients."

Daniel got to his feet, radiating a sense of renewed purpose. "I will . . . And thanks, Kal. My gut tells me you've found us a way past the problem."

"Glad I could help," Kal called out to Daniel's fast-receding back.

~~~

Six hours later, Kal had her feet up on the canteen table, mug in hand, happy to do nothing for the first time in an exceptionally long day, when Daniel burst in, eyes wide, blazing with excitement.

"Marcia Grivak!" he said. "I think she's right. That means—"

Kal's fist thumped the table, the only way of stopping Daniel when he was in full flood. "Who the hell is Marcia Grivak?"

Chastened, Daniel fetched himself a coffee and sat down. "She was one of the Keliang Foundation's star theoreticians. She proposed that pinchspace isn't uniform, but has bands, each with a higher Zuoqiu-Gesiyev—"

"Enough! Forget the theory; I'll never understand it. Just tell me how this helps us. And keep it simple, for chrissakes."

"The problem's not the bubble. It's how I've been looking at pinchspace. Zuoqiu said—"

"Simple," Kal growled.

"Sorry . . . Grivak says the Keliang's wrong. Pinchspace isn't uniform; it has energy bands. Kolovchenko's gateway tunnels tap into the lowest energy, the alpha band. The Q-drive can't do that; the bubble with the shuttle inside is too small making the tap unstable. If Grivak's right, a stable tap into a higher band is possible, though there is a lot more to it than that."

Kal patted Daniel's hand. "I don't care, so don't waste your time trying to tell me. And why would we trust this Grivak woman? Maybe the Keliang was right to fire her."

Daniel grimaced. "Oh, please! Grivak was the principal researcher on the Block-9 gateway upgrades. Even though the Keliang said her multi-band model of pinchspace was crackpot science based on falsified data, a criticism parroted by every other researcher in the field, that was all bullshit. Trust me, her work is the best."

"So why was she sacked?"

"I don't know. She just was, but I'd trust her with my life."

"I'm happy to hear it," Kal said, "because you will be."

"What should I do?"

"Follow your instincts and go with Grivak's paper. See if . . . What am I saying? You know what you need to do."

Daniel was already on his feet, running. "I'll get back to you."

Kal watched him go, not at all sure trusting the man-child with her life had been the smart thing to do.

—13—

Kal threw herself into a chair in front of the canteen holoscreen. "I'll buy Grivak her own damn planet if this works."

Daniel was jumpy, sweat beading under his eyes, tongue flickering across his lips. "Okay, let's see if the Q-drive AI can handle Grivak's model of pinchspace."

A minute later, Kal and Daniel sat staring at the shuttle: it was a piece of toffee taken by pair of giant hands and twisted back on itself.

Kal broke the oppressive silence. "Don't beat yourself up, Daniel. This is your first attempt. It would have been the biggest miracle of all time if it had worked. Okay, I need to get on; those masts aren't going to make themselves."

She left Daniel sitting there, a chip of misery adrift in an uncaring universe.

~~~

"Where are you up to?" Kal snapped when Daniel appeared in the canteen. It had been a long day; she was tired and in no mood for any of the boy's games.

"Hello, Kal. I'm happy to see you too."

"Just tell me what you've got. And make it quick. I need a shower and some meds for my back."

"Watch this."

Kal groaned when the familiar shape of the shuttle appeared on the canteen holovid screen. She was sick of Daniel's simulations. She must have sat through a hundred; none had ended well.

She closed her eyes as the Q-drive AI started on its pre-jump routine, her mind on the more pressing problem of how to make life on Ladaki-6 livable.

She would send a habitat dirtside first along with the fusion power packs, she decided. That would give them then a base camp to work from. And then a second habitat for the fabrication shop; she would have to disassemble the—

"There!" Daniel said. "Did you see that?

Kal's eyes blinked open. The shuttle had not moved. "See what?"

Daniel glared at Kal. "You weren't even watching. Pay attention! Okay, here we go again."

Kal's mouth sagged open as the shuttle vanished in a blaze of ultra-violet before returning ten seconds later, intact. "I'll be monkey's uncle. Show me the g-force data from inside the shuttle."

"Standby . . . Here you go."

Kal studied the graphs. "Look at that! The artgrav held an earth-normal gravity field the whole time without even the smallest instability." She put an arm around Daniel's shoulders and gave him a hug. "Well done. You are one smart sonofabitch, you know that?"

Daniel flushed pink with embarrassment. "Not really,"

"Don't argue! You are. Now, tell me we can start installation."

"I still have a couple of tweaks to do . . ."

Kal groaned.

". . . but they are all minor; I'll do them now so we can start installing the Q-drive tomorrow."

As Daniel rushed off, Kal tried not to think about how little time they had left.

Something else struck her. If Daniel's Q-drives worked, Kolovchenko's gateway business had a big problem on its hands.

Every freighter captain alive hated paying the exorbitant gateway fees which had made Kolovchenko the biggest and most profitable corporation ever. Once their ships could jump from anywhere to anywhere, no tunnels required, they would not have to pay Kolovchenko a cent.

With its gateway monopoly shattered, Kolovchenko, a multi-trillion-dollar business, would be worthless. And now Kal knew why the Keliang had sacked Grivak; she was too dangerous, too big a threat to Kolovchenko, not to.

Another thought came to mind. If Kolovchenko wanted to stay in business, it would have to buy Daniel's Q-drive. Given how much it had to lose, it would have to pay whatever price he demanded.

As long as Daniel and his Q-drive didn't kill them both first.

—14—

Daniel's voice boomed in Kal's neuronics as she drifted across the shuttle's hull. "It is Charlie-4 again. The AI's still bitching; it says the node isn't aligned."

Kal groaned. When would the endless parade of niggling little problems ever end? She clamped the calibration frame around the base of the node mast. "Go!"

"Standby . . . recalibrating . . . Okay, the AI says the alignment's nominal, so I think we're done."

"Please tell me we can go."

"We should do months of trials," Daniel said, "but since we're too short of driver-mass to do any and desperate to leave, yes, we can."

"You sure there's nothing more to do out here?"

"No. The diagnostic AI is going through the entire system one last time. That will take 30 minutes; if everything's nominal, we can undock."

"I'll go clean up then."

Kal locked into November-55 for what she hoped was the last time. The sooner she was away from the ghosts of a dying Ladaki-6 and its slaughtered millions, the happier she would be.

There was still the chance—a good chance, Kal thought—that Daniel's Q-drive might kill them both. At least it would be a quick death as gravity shear ripped their bodies apart.

She shivered. Maybe Ladaki-6 might not have been such a bad idea.

Back aboard the shuttle after a long shower, Kal gave the cargo bay a last look over. Lashed down amidships were the AIs that controlled the Q-drive's pinchspace nodes. Next to them were microfusion packs, power and data distribution boxes, and the pinchspace sensor AIs, all connected by thick bundles of cables.

All the work of an unhinged lunatic.

She smiled. In a way, it was.

She worked her way forward past plasfiber containers of driver-mass stacked high. In case we need to make our way home the slow way, she had said to Daniel. He had been way too stressed to appreciate the joke.

Water tanks and everything else they might need filled the rest of the cargo bay. Satisfied all was well, she went forward and climbed up the ladder to the flight-deck, dropping into the command pilot's seat alongside Daniel, a seat as worn as the shuttle around it.

She took the boy's arm; it was all bone and no flesh. "You okay to do this?"

"As I'll ever be. Shit, I hope this works . . . I'm think I'm going to chuck."

Kal knew how the boy felt; her own stomach was in free-fall. "Please don't . . . Now, before we go, I've been thinking. We need to give the shuttle a proper name, to show it some respect."

"Ah, um . . . How about . . . Far out! This is harder than I expected."

"It always is. Why do you think you see the same names over and over? Maybe the word 'star' should be in there somewhere."

"Maybe . . . How about *Star Walker*?"

"Hah!" Kal snorted. "Who walks between the stars?"

"Uh . . . How about *Star Wraith*?"

"Now that I like. A wraith is what this ship will be when it jumps into pinchspace . . . How about plain old *Wraith*? Nice and simple."

"Deal! Hold on a sec!" Daniel vanished down the hatch, returning a minute later with two mugs in hand, handing one to a mystified Kal. "The foodbot says it's champagne. Apparently, it's what you use to name new ships."

"That's exactly what you do." Kal raised her mug and dribbled champagne to the deck, the temptation to take a sip or ten almost irresistible. "I name this ship the *Wraith*. If there is anyone running this crazy, fucked-up universe, may she keep it safe and us with it."

"Amen to that," Daniel said, emptying his mug, his hand shaking.

Knowing what came next, Kal thought he should feel frightened; she was. "ShipCon," she said. "Confirm shuttle status."

"All systems nominal," the AI reported. "Navplan confirmed. Ready to depart Ladaki-6 nearspace."

"Roger. ShipCon, take us out."

Daniel and Kal sat in silence as the shuttle accelerated away from November-55, on vector for the *Wraith's* first jump.

~~~

"Approaching jump datum," ShipCon said. "Vector is nominal. Request command approval to execute pinchspace jump."

Daniel's face was one big grin.

Kal returned the smile, her body tense with a heady mix of excitement and fear. "I'll take that as a vote of confidence from the designer of this death trap. Approved to jump."

"Roger. Standby pinchspace transition . . . now!"

Time oozed to a crawl.

"Normalspace transition," ShipCon announced. "All systems nominal."

Kal could not speak. It was only when her lungs began to burn that she realized she had been holding her breath. "Holy shit! We're alive!"

Daniel tried to speak, his mouth opening and shutting as tears ran down his face. "We did it, Kal," he said at last. "We have just jumped 18 million klicks."

Kal let out of long sigh, part exhilaration, part relief, mostly sheer exhaustion. "Let's not get too excited. We still have to make the big jump to N'jeema's Star."

~~~

The star blazed blue-white ahead of the *Wraith*. Kal sat on the flight-deck, stunned into silence by the outright impossibility of it all.

No human had ever visited N'jeema's Star.

No human ever could, not without a Kolovchenko gateway.

And now two had, jumping 10 light-years in 16 hours. Kolovchenko was going to shit itself when the *Wraith* turned up. Its gateways could only move a ship at five light-years a day. The *Wraith* did three times that.

Daniel reappeared and threw himself into his seat. "I hate to say this, but everything is nominal. Voronezh-4, anybody?"

A craving overwhelmed Kal, a soul-deep hunger to be back with ordinary people, doing normal things, breathing air that didn't smell of unwashed armpits, digging her toes into beach sand, swimming . . . and having her first beer in many months.

"Let's go home."

—15—

A day into the transit back to Voronezh-4, ShipCon broke into Kal's sleep.

"Captain! Flight-deck, now."

"If I must," Kal grumbled. "On my way."

As she threw her sleep-sodden body into her chair, ShipCon said, "The Q-drive AI is having trouble holding vector lock."

"Okay. Recommendation?'

"Drop into normalspace now and investigate."

Kal thought. Only for an instant. She had felt the same sense of imminent doom before, and terrible things had followed every time.

"Drop now," she ordered, comming Daniel to the flight-deck.

The breath caught in Kal's throat as the holoscreens exploded into a coruscating mass of stars, billions of them scattered in careless profusion across a background of bottomless black.

It was a sight she would never tire of. No human could.

Daniel burst onto the flight-deck. "What's the problem?"

"We're way off our planned vector. I've dropped so we can work out why. Any ideas?"

"Not until I've been through the Q-drive system."

~~~

Daniel sat hunched over his workstation. "I can't understand what's happened. The Q-drive was working perfectly."

Kal though for a moment. "Maybe it's something outside the ship . . . or maybe not. This is interstellar space. There's not a lot out there."

She glanced over at Daniel when he did not respond; his eyes were half-closed, staring at something he alone could see.

She sighed. It might mean he'd just had some stunning insight. Or he was as baffled as she was. Or just tired. She could never tell.

Daniel's voice was soft, contemplative as he followed the unseen thread of his thoughts, so soft Kal had to strain to hear him over the sough of the air-conditioning vents. "Something outside . . . something outside . . . What's outside? . . . Neutrinos and photons. A bit of dust. Molecules of hydrogen and so on. Not enough dark matter or dark energy to make any difference . . . So, what's left?"

Daniel snapped his fingers and opened his eyes. "Gravity! That's what's left."

"Care to explain?" Kal said. "And no pinchspace field equations, please."

"Let's see . . . Okay, the *Wraith* is like a car on a road with gravitational ripples instead of ruts and stones. Even moving at two billion kilometers per second, the Q-drive AI can compensate for those ripples if they are small enough. But a researcher called Keneally proposed the existence of localized gravitational anomalies where the ripples are much more intense. He called them gravity reefs. I think the AI is struggling to deal with the normalspace vector changes those ripples cause."

"Did this Keneally guy find any of these reefs?"

"Oh, no. His work was theoretical."

Kal's spirits sagged. "I don't buy it, Daniel. Gravity reefs aren't a problem for Kolovchenko's gateways. Why would they bother us?"

"A question I can only answer by making a short jump."

Kal raised her hands in protest. "Hold on. You don't know why we had to drop out of pinchspace, and now you want to jump back into pinchspace to find out? That sounds like a really, really bad idea."

"I need more data to confirm what happened. Limit the jump to 20 seconds, and we'll be fine, I promise."

Every instinct Kal possessed screamed at her to say no, the same instincts that had saved her ass in combat more times than she could remember. But she'd trusted Daniel this far; now was not the time to stop. "I'll give you ten, and not one second more. And we'll suit up, just in case."

"Okay, okay," Daniel grumbled, reaching for his skinsuit.

"Right, let me just set this up . . . Okay, we're set. ShipCon, confirm status."

"All systems nominal, ready to jump."

"Approved."

The *Wraith* jumped. Kal eyes never left the time-to-drop counter as the seconds dribbled away with agonizing slowness. 9 . . . 8 . . . 7 . . . 6 . . . 5 . . .

The ship dropped.

The artgrav failed.

Kal slammed up against her harness, the impact driving her chin into her helmet and teeth through her lips, blood running coppery into her mouth, the flight-deck filling with the shriek of alarms, holoscreens blazing red as system-error messages cascaded down, an emergency locker coming away from the bulkhead to crash into the empty seat beside Kal, splitting open to spew tools and equipment in all directions, a hydraulic jack hitting her helmet with such force it pounded Kal to the edge of unconsciousness before bouncing off a holoscreen amidst a cloud of shattered shards of plastic and metal.

Gloved hands locked in a death grip on the arms of her seat, Kal could do nothing except pray that the chaos would end, that the madness would go away, all the while fighting through the haze of pain to find a way to take control of a situation she could never control.

With shocking suddenness, it all stopped. Kal forced her battered brain to focus. "Where are we?"

"In normalspace, position unknown, vector—"

"Hull integrity?"

"Compromised. Ramp seal failure. Cargo bay has been isolated."

"Power?"

"Tokomak-Alpha and Bravo tripped. Shuttle is on emergency power. All other systems are nominal."

Daniel! Kal's heart stumbled when she saw him, head slumped to one side. She threw off her harness and pushing across to him, cursing the red fog so determined to bury her. "ShipCon, how's Daniel?"

"Unconscious. Vital signs are within safe limits. Moderate concussion. His suit has transfused emergency nanomeds."

"Safe to leave him for the moment?"

"Yes."

"Okay. Right, priorities, ShipCon. I need one tokomak back on-line. How long?"

"Estimate 30 minutes for Tokomak-Bravo."

"Do it. Artgrav?"

"The system is nominal; it only tripped."

"Keep it offline until I've checked the shuttle. Comm me when Daniel wakes up. And get a repairbot started on the ramp seal and flight-deck."

~~~

Kal worked her way across the hull from forward to aft as she checked the stumpy masts carrying the pinchspace nodes, relieved to find them undamaged. It was a mystery how they had survived what ShipCon said was gravitational shear so extreme the pinchspace drive AI had been forced to dump the *Wraith* back into normalspace before the shuttle was torn apart.

And then she came to the stern. Kal's heart lurched.

It was as if a huge blade had skimmed across the hull, slashing away three pinchspace nodes, taking with them any hope of ever jumping back into pinchspace. For an instant, Kal wanted to lock back into the *Wraith* and strangle Daniel for his reckless stupidity.

She forced herself to breathe, long, slow breaths until her heart stopped trying to batter its way out of her chest, until panic and fear subsided.

It wasn't Daniel's fault. She was the *Wraith*'s captain. The decision to jump had been hers, a decision that her instincts had urged her not to make.

She blipped her personal maneuvering unit to take her away from the hull. She stopped 30 meters out, the space around her filled with spectacular curtains of stars, diamond-hard in their unblinking brilliance.

It was a beautiful place, but even beautiful places were bad places to die. And, without a working Q-drive, die they would.

She turned around. The *Wraith* was a black shape cut out of the extravagant sheets of stars, its anti-collision lights painting splashes of red across the hull.

Flipping her neuronics down into the infra-red, Kal was scanning the hull for any more damage when ShipCon commed her.

"Daniel's awake but confused," the AI reported.

"Okay. How's Tok-Bravo?"

"Completing hot restart. It will be back on-line in two minutes."

Kal blipped her PMU to take her back to the airlock. "At least we won't freeze to death, which is something, I suppose. I'm done out here. Keep the artgrav off-line until I've moved Daniel back to his bunk."

~~~

Kal sat back as Daniel walked into the crew-room. "Feeling better?"

"Much, thanks," Daniel said, throwing himself onto a bench. "My neuronics are having trouble accessing the shuttle's AIs. Have they been damaged?"

"No, they're fine. I've locked you out until you were better. Sit down."

"Oh . . . Something's up, isn't it? Are we back in normalspace?"

"I'm afraid we are. We've lost our Q-drive. Gravity shear sliced three nodes off a nanosecond before we dropped. Godknows where they are now."

Daniel's face turned a dirty white. "Shit! We can lose one or two and the AI might be able to compensate, but not three."

"There's more. Whatever happened in pinchspace has pushed us way off our planned vector. The delta-v to put the *Wraith* back on vector for Voronezh-4 is so massive the main engines don't have enough driver-mass to line us up for the jump."

Daniel stared at Kal for an age, then said, "If I can't fix the Q-drive, and you can't find a way to work around the driver-mass problem, then we're stuck here. Is that right?"

"Yeah, it is."

"How long do we have, before . . . before, you know?"

"Before we die? A year probably. A bit more if we are careful. Less if the environmental-control system gets any worse."

Daniel dropped his head into his hands. "I'm so sorry, Kal. I screwed up. I almost killed us both."

"We can't worry about that. We need to find a way out of this."

"We do. Well, since every minute counts, best I start looking for a way to make the Q-drive work even though it's three nodes short."

And then Daniel was gone, leaving Kal wondering where she was going to find driver-mass deep in the hard vacuum of interstellar space.

A question to which there was only one answer: nowhere.

—16—

It seemed an age since Daniel had come close to destroying the *Wraith* and killing them both.

As she did too much of the time, Kal sat at the crew-room table, drinking so much coffee her nerves twanged. She had been through her share of rough times, but the days since their disastrous drop back into normalspace had been the blackest of all, days so crushing that even climbing out of her rack every morning left her exhausted, what little energy she had drained by nightmare-plagued nights spent wrestling with sweat-tangled sheets.

Not that all the news had been bad. Trawling through the knowledgebases Kal had taken from November-55, she had discovered the *Dragon Star*, a long-abandoned station in Clarke orbit around Wallenski-7.

A station the *Wraith* had enough driver-mass to set vector for, a station Kal hoped would have driver-mass stored in its bunkers.

Which only raised more questions. Assuming Daniel was able to fix the Q-drive, could the *Wraith* reach it? The *Dragon Star* was 876 light-years away, a distance so gargantuan the chances of without something critical blowing up were worryingly close to three-quarters of bugger all.

But say, *miraculum miraculorum*, the *Wraith* did make it. Did the *Dragon Star*'s bunkers hold driver-mass? Was it usable after so long? Was it the right grade for the *Wraith*'s fusion drives? Could Kal transfer it to the *Wraith*?

All questions of academic interest until Daniel had fixed the Q-drive, which Kal was certain he never would, bringing the *Wraith*'s career as humanspace's first jump ship to an end.

She shivered as she imagined the *Wraith*, its Q-drive broken, a tomb that would drift for the rest of eternity.

In a fit of rage and frustration, Kal hurled her mug into the recycler. The way things were going, it didn't matter what she wanted or didn't want.

The universe did not care.

As for Daniel, he had collapsed in on himself, a hermit trying to salvage the Q-drive, only emerging to grab something to eat, face haggard and nails bitten down to the quick, showering only when even he could not stand the smell of his own rancid body.

Kal had long since stopped asking if she could help, tired of being brushed off without a word.

Suppressing a flash of resentment, she stood. It was time to resume her efforts to persuade the microfabs to produce usable driver-mass from material cannibalized from inside the *Wraith*.

Efforts which had been as unsuccessful as Daniel's work on the Q-drive.

She was walking aft when Daniel dropped from the fusion plant room hatch, hitting the deck with a thump right in front of her.

He scrambled to his feet, eyes refusing to meet Kal's. "Oh, hi."

Kal recognized desperation when she saw it, and desperate people took awful risks. "I hope you weren't messing with my tokomaks," she said. "Lose them, and we are screwed. So, tell me what you were doing . . . Hold on; are you smiling?"

Daniel's smile widened. "I think I am."

Hope, dead these long months, flickered back to life. "Is this the right time to be happy again?" Kal asked.

"Might be. One more sim to run, and then I'll know for sure."

"Best I come and watch then."

Kal followed Daniel's emaciated frame—she had given up trying to make him eat when he'd said she sounded like his mother—down the passageway to his workspace, a former storeroom now cluttered with holoscreens and ΛIs.

Daniel pointed to one of the screens. "Have a look at this."

"Tell me what you're doing first. It's been months since you've said more than a couple of words to me."

"It's been hard." Daniel paused, marshaling his thoughts with a pained look of such intense concentration Kal could not help chuckling. "Remember the gravity reef guy?" he went on.

"Keneally, yeah. How could I forget?"

"We hit one of his reefs, just like a ship driving onto rocks out in the ocean."

"And you think that's what forced us out of pinchspace?"

"I'm sure of it. And I'm sorry it's taken me so long to work it out. Extracting the data from the Q-drive's knowledgebases wasn't easy."

Kal shrugged. She'd long since given up trying to force Daniel to keep her updated. "At least you know now . . . Can you set up the Q-drive AI so it knows when we're getting close to one of Keneally's reefs?"

"Already done. As soon as we do, it drops the *Wraith* back into normalspace. It won't let the ship jump back until the reef is past and gone. The trick is to choose the right time. Drop too soon and you could spend years to crossing a reef."

Kal's face was grim. "So, we can go from A to B without killing ourselves even if it takes a bit longer. All of which is great, Daniel, but you still haven't told me if the Q-drive can work without the missing nodes."

"By shifting three from amidships, I think it will, though the drive will need—"

"More power. That is why you were checking the tokomaks. Why didn't you ask? I could have told you whether that was feasible."

Daniel's head slumped. "I didn't want to disappoint you. I'm sorry."

Kal threw her hands up in frustration. "Don't be sorry. Just tell me what you need."

"Redline plus 10% from both main-engine toks for the five seconds it takes to stabilize the bubble."

Kal blinked. "Jeezus! That is a shitload of power you're asking for. Give me a minute."

Daniel waited as Kal dived into the *Wraith*'s power system schematics, muttering to herself. "Okay then," she said finally. "The answer is a qualified 'yes' though we will need to override the system AI, which mean we might lose a tok, both maybe. Ah, what the hell! It's not like we have much to lose."

"Let me show you the sim."

Kal could not help herself, crossing her fingers as the *Wraith* appeared on the holoscreen.

"Okay, powering up now. Q-drive system is nominal. Enabling pinchspace field sensors . . . calibrating sensors . . . errors in limits . . . data flows are stable . . . computing optimum node power configuration . . . nodes configured . . . powering up, peak power demand now . . . 4 . . . 3 . . . 2 . . . 1 . . . and the *Wraith* is in pinchspace."

Daniel turned to Kal. "Relocate those nodes, give me the power, and I'll take you to that abandoned orbital you found."

A rush of excitement flooded through Kal.

They still had a chance.

—17—

The transit to Wallenski-7 had taken the *Wraith* 66 days, a journey prolonged by five gravity reefs. One, almost twelve million kilometers across, had added three full days in normalspace.

Kal had refused Daniel's suggestion they name it Shits-Me-Off Reef. She had called it Disappointment Reef instead. We need to think of our legacy, she'd said. If we have one, he'd replied.

Today they would arrive at Wallenski. She still found it hard to believe they had made it; she had been so sure the *Wraith* would find some way to kill her first. Anticipation had rewarded her with that rarest of rare things: eight unbroken hours of sleep, waking to luxuriate in the warmth and security of her bunk, happy to stare at the deckhead listening to the air-conditioning's soft hiss.

She pulled the curtain back and glanced across at Daniel's bunk; it was empty.

She found him sitting in the crew-room, his hands clasped around a mug, empty eyes staring at the far bulkhead.

"Hey, Daniel."

A grunt.

Kal knew she'd not get much more out of him. Most days he didn't say a word. She knew why. The guilt he felt had built and built until he had collapsed in on himself, her assurances that things would be okay ignored.

She helped herself to a mug of coffee and sat down. "Cheer up, Daniel We'll be at Wallenski-7 in four hours. The *Dragon Star*'s bunkers will have the driver-mass we need."

Daniel fixed blood-shot eyes on Kal's. "You can't know that. That orbital was abandoned a long time ago; godknows what's happened to it since."

"It should be there. Driver-mass is a super-fine dust and a total pain; that is why it's transported in containers. Once it's been dumped into the bunkers, the feed system takes care of moving it but transferring it back into containers? Nobody does that; it's way too difficult. Trust me, it'll be there."

Whether it was usable after so long was another question, one Daniel did not know enough to ask, much to Kal's relief. "I'll try to catch some sleep before we arrive," he mumbled as he walked out.

Kal sighed. She did not think she could take much more of Miserable Daniel.

~~~

The *Wraith* was decelerating to intercept the *Dragon Star* when Daniel appeared on the bridge, wearing a clean shipsuit and showing welcome signs of having showered.

Kal whistled. "I was wondering when I was going to see you again. Feel better?"

"Much. Uh, I'm sorry . . . I not sure what got into me."

Daniel's eyes filled with tears, shoulders heaving as sobs racked his spare frame.

Kal took him into her arms. "It's okay. We've made it. Things will be fine."

"I was so afraid I'd messed things up. What I did was stupid. I almost killed us both."

Kal pushed Daniel back to look into his tear-streaked face. "Hey! What you have done is extraordinary; it would be beyond extraordinary if mistakes weren't made. Let's just be happy we've survived this far; nobody else in humanspace would have done. Without you, I'd be dirtside on Ladaki-6, trying to choose the best way to kill myself."

"I'm sorry for being such an asshole."

"Enough! Now, when did you last eat?"

Daniel thought for a second. "A while, I guess, but I'm starving. I feel like I haven't eaten for a month."

"Because you haven't. Go on, then. Eat! And don't take all day; we have work to do."

Daniel returned to the bridge, a plate piled high with food in one hand, sat down and, seemingly without even taking a breath, demolished the lot.

"That was impressive." And Kal meant it.

Daniel belched. "I thought so too. How's the *Dragon Star* look?"

"Like any abandoned orbital: beaten up."

"Any sign of the gateways?"

"Only the frames. Kolovchenko folds everything else back when the rental payments stop."

"That'd be right."

~~~

The outer airlock door opened, and Kal pushed out into space.

The *Dragon Star* hung in front of her. Built by an eponymous consortium from New Xinjiang to support the terraforming and colonization of Wallenski-7, the orbital was a typical pre-artgrav orbital: outer ring, spokes, hub. It had operated for only 30 years before the project had collapsed, overwhelmed by a storm of debt, recrimination, and legal suits.

It would not be the last such project to fail. Terraforming an alien planet was a risky business, even one like Wallenski-7 with a comfortable climate, no apex predators capable of tearing humans apart, no venomous species, and no lethal bugs, viruses, or fungi.

An agreeable planet, in fact. Kal could understand why the New Xinjiang consortium had been so keen to colonize it. So keen, they had overlooked the need for ruthlessly disciplined project management.

Daniel's head peeked out of the airlock. "I'm not sure I want to do this." His labored breathing made it obvious he was not enjoying his first spacewalk.

"Just follow the safety line. I've clipped you in, so you'll be fine . . . Daniel! I'm talking to you."

"Sorry . . . Got it. Follow the line."

Shaking her head, Kal grabbed her tool bag and pushed off the *Wraith*'s hull. She shot across the gap, letting the line run out through her hands. With a few meters to go, she tightened her grip to slow her approach, reaching out to fastset a hardpoint to the hull alongside a personnel airlock outlined with sun-flayed yellow and black stripes.

"Okay, the line is secure." Kal turned to see Daniel's shoulders heaving. "Oh, for chrissakes! Are you throwing up? Did you take your meds?"

"Ah, no. Sorry. I forgot."

"You forgot? You are such a dickhead. Now you'll need a fresh suit."

"No, no, no. I'm fine. I used the waste dump . . . Well, I think I did."

"I hope so. Cleaning vomit out of a skinsuit is a miserable business, as you'll find out. Come on, get your ass over here."

It took an age, Daniel was so tentative, but he arrived at last, panting like he had just sprinted up a mountain.

Kal tried using the manual override lever to open the airlock; it refused to budge. After decades of neglect, she wasn't surprised. She pulled a laser cutter out of her gear bag and opened a small hole in the center of the door. She put a gloved hand across it. "No air inside this airlock, not that I expected any, not after so long."

The cutter sliced the door from its frame; Kal sent it tumbling off into space.

She drifted inside. It was like every airlock she'd ever seen: the same controls, the same status panel, the same emergency oxygen and power connectors, the same hectoring placards on the bulkheads with Standard English below big, attention-grabbing, scarlet ideograms.

Kal was already cutting a hole in the airlock's inner door. "Okay, Daniel. Let's go find us some driver-mass."

~~~

As Kal drifted to a stop, Daniel tumbled past. Arms and legs flailing, he crashed into the huge cylinder around which the entire station rotated.

Kal grabbed Daniel as he bounced back the way he'd come, seizing a hand. "For fuck's sake! How many times do I have to say it? Gentle jumps, remember?"

"Yeah, sorry. It's harder than I thought . . . Is this the orbital's service core?"

"It is. The driver-mass containers will be next to the docking bays. Just follow me, and take it easy, for chrissakes!"

A firm kick sent Kal arcing through the web of ceramsteel beams that connected the core to the orbital's outer ring. With casual competence, she flew from girder to girder, her headlamp splashing brilliant patches of light as she searched for the access door into the driver-mass feed system.

"It's got to be here . . . What the hell!" she said as a spear of metal missed her helmet by centimeters.

A torn girder. She grabbed it and jerked to an abrupt halt. "Daniel! Stop where you are and do not move."

Right in front to her was a two-meter-wide hole, its edges blackened and heat-seared.

"Get up here, Daniel, but go really slow. There's a lot of broken metal around."

"What did this?" Daniel asked as he arrived.

"A meteorite, I'd say. Let me have a look inside."

Five minutes later, Kal backed out of the hole. She held out a gloved hand, its fingertips black with dust. "The entire driver-mass feed system has been trashed. That's all that's left."

"Are we going to die here?" Daniel asked. His voice quavered.

"Not yet, we're not. How's your Chinese?"

"I don't understand."

"You will. Follow me."

~~~

The faded red sign on the door read:

限制进入区域 人工智能 仅系统技术员
RESTRICTED ACCESS: AI SYSTEMS TECHNICIANS ONLY

Daniel tapped Kal's helmet. "Any chance you're going to tell me what we're doing here?"

"I didn't want to get your hopes up," Kal said, already cutting the door out of its frame.

"You just have, so start talking."

"The first thing every terraforming team does is set up a spaceport dirtside, and every spaceport in humanspace stores driver-mass for its shuttles and flyers. Wallenski-7's will be down there somewhere. I want you to find it."

"By breaking into the *Dragon Star*'s knowledgebases?"

"Yup. They should be in this compartment. As soon as you have found that spaceport, we'll go dirtside to remass."

Daniel sighed. "You haven't thought this through, have you? All the *Wraith*'s pinchspace nodes will burn off on reentry."

"Don't be such a dick, Daniel," Kal snapped. "I installed those nodes; I can remove them. Once I've patched the holes in the hull with ceramfoam, the shuttle will be good for reentry."

"Ah, right . . . What if we can't find any driver-mass?"

"We'll be stuck dirtside."

"This is Ladaki-6 all over again."

"No, it's not," Kal said, pushing the door clear. "Wallenski-7 is as close to paradise as you're ever going to get, so don't go all floppy on me. Besides, we don't have any better options. Right, enough talking. I'll start removing the nodes while you get every knowledgebase you can find back to the *Wraith*. One of them will have the detailed maps we need to find the shuttle base . . . Go on! What are you waiting for? Get looking."

"You're going to leave me here?"

Kal turned; Daniel's eyes were wide. What was she thinking? The man-child had been through enough. "Now that I think about it, no, I'm not. Let's recover the knowledgebases before we think about making the *Wraith* drop-ready."

"Thanks, Kal . . . I'm sorry. This is all my fau —"

"Stop! I would have died back on Ladaki-6 by now if it wasn't for you. Come on, let's get this done."

—18—

With a screech of brakes, the *Wraith* came to a stop.

"Shutdown checklist complete," ShipCon said. "All systems nominal. Driver-mass reserve 6%. Unable to achieve Clarke orbit."

Knowing they were now marooned at the bottom of a gravity well on a planet 33 light-years from New Xinjiang and civilization—not that anyone would call a system mired in an endless, bloody civil war civilized—did nothing for Kal's battered morale.

At times like this, all she wanted was a liter of the foodbot's best ersatz vodka and somewhere quiet to drink herself into oblivion.

"Conditions?" she asked.

"82/18 nitrox atmosphere, pressure 103 kilopascals, temperature 29 Celsius, no wind."

"Biohazard rating?"

"1-Alpha: no dangerous contaminants or biohazards detected. Hazmat precautions not required."

Kal offered up a silent word of thanks. Decontaminating a skinsuit was a pain. "Come on, Daniel. Let's see if we can find what we need," she said, already heading for the airlock.

Once outside the *Wraith*, she took a long look around. After years of neglect, trees and vines were doing a respectable job of tearing the terminal building apart.

She could imagine the place as it had once been, busy with people for whom Wallenski-7 had been the start of a new life, one full of hope and excitement, the spaceport busy with the endless stream of shuttles and flyers busy establishing an earthlike ecosphere.

And burning through hundreds of millions of dollars a month.

Daniel pointed to a range of ice-capped mountains north of what the colonists had—in an excess of optimism—called Golden City

Spaceport. "It's stunning. I can think of worse places to be marooned on . . . Ladaki-6 for starters."

"I'd prefer somewhere with decent bars," Kal said. "Let's start with those buildings to the left of the terminal. One of them should have our driver-mass."

~~~

Warmed by the open fire, contentment suffused Kal's whole being.

The driver-mass had been where it supposed to be. Even years after the colonists abandoned Wallenski-7, it was still usable, and Daniel had coaxed a feederbot back to life. That had saved the two of them one of the most tedious jobs known to humanity: remassing a shuttle by hand.

At first light, they would return to *Dragon Star* to start restoring the *Wraith*'s Q-drive. One week after that, they would be on their way to the Toussaint system to meet with her old friend and M'bakaan marine buddy, Jaden Harafi, the only man alive she could think of who might lend her some money.

Money they desperately needed; the $9.75 left on her cashcard would not get them far.

Daniel handed Kal a plate. "Flame-grilled chicken kebabs. They're damn good."

Kal tried one. Daniel was right. It was superb: smoky, charred in places, almost primitive in its simplicity. The *Wraith*'s foodbot only had one setting: bland. "I have a question for you, Daniel," she said in between mouthfuls. "How do you feel about us having our own planet? This one maybe? It seems nice."

"Hah!" Daniel snorted. "Questions so dumb, why even ask?"

"You've clearly not heard of the Ingala Convention, my opinionated friend."

"Uh, no . . . What's that have to do with anything?"

"It allows us to take ownership of the Wallenski system. All we have to do is lodge our claim with the Registry of Human-Settled Systems back on Terra."

"We can't do that. The New Xinjiang consortium got here first. They own it."

"Not anymore. Their claim lapsed when they pulled out and Kolovchenko recovered its gateways. Nobody owns this place now."

"Wah! Our own planet! I like the sound of that. Let's do it then."

"We will . . . as soon as I can find the 50 million bucks I will need to pay the registry fee."

Daniel flicked a kebab stick at Kal. "You are a complete bastard! I knew there'd be a catch."

"Don't be such a pessimist; the *Wraith* is worth a fortune. Maybe one day we—"

Kal stopped. Beyond the firelight, a flicker had caught her eye. "Daniel, I want you to bring me two needleguns and a torch. You know where they are?"

"Uh, yeah. Emergency locker beside the airlock. Why?"

"Just go. And don't look back."

Daniel was back inside a minute. He handed a gun to Kal, now on her feet. "What's up?"

"We have a visitor. Stay here. Any probs, get back in the shuttle and close the airlock."

"But—"

"Just do it."

Kal walked away from the *Wraith*. She raised the gun and flicked on the torch.

A man, skinny and dressed in a faded shipsuit, stood, transfixed, eyes glittering red in the torchlight.

He raised a hand. "Welcome to Wallenski-7. I'm Hemed Biteko. It's good to see you. I've been waiting a long time for visitors."

~~~

Kal had been a marine, and marines knew how to eat, Daniel a close second, but she had never seen anything like Biteko. She began to worry the man might explode.

He did stop, eventually. Sighing, he put his plate down and belched. "I eat well enough here, but nothing like that. My foodbot packed up years ago . . . I must go now. It's a long walk back to my place, and it is getting late. Thank you for your hospitality. I hope you have a safe journey."

Kal put out a hand. "Wait on. Aren't you coming with us?"

"Oh, no. This is my home. I was born here, my wife is buried here, and I will die here."

"Is there anyone else around?"

"No, just me. When the consortium pulled out, I was the only one who wanted to stay."

Firelight splintered off tears.

"My kids went back," Biteko went on, wiping his eyes. "They didn't want to spend the rest of their lives stranded on a failed colony . . . I do miss them."

"Can we give them a message?"

"Thank you, no. They would have decided I was dead long ago. Best to leave it that way."

"Are you sure? We can give you more time to decide if you want."

The man stood. "I'm sure. This is my home."

"Is there anything you need?"

Biteko swayed from foot to foot. "Uh, no . . . unless you have a spare foodbot. Mine stopped working ten years ago and I'm a crap cook."

Daniel glanced at Kal, grinning. Ignoring her mouthed 'don't even think about it', he said, "We don't, but we did load emergency rations before we left Ladaki-6. Months' worth. We can buy a new bot when we get to Toussaint."

Kal sighed; she loathed ration-pack coffee, but she knew a fait-accompli when she saw one. "Yes, we can," she mouthed.

Daniel leaned over and patted Kal on the back. "I knew you had a heart in there somewhere. I'll go get it."

"I assume you have power and feedstock?" Kal asked.

Biteko nodded. ""Oh, yes. hectares of it . . . But I have one question before I leave. Am I going to wake up one morning to find ships dumping thousands of colonists onto this lovely place?"

Kal pointed to the shuttle's hulking black form. "Like I said, there are no more ships like our *Wraith*. There'll be no colonists, I promise."

Biteko smiled. "I hope not . . . Ten kilometers north of here is a lake, a beautiful lake; the water's like glass at this time of year. You'll find my house further on, up the eastern side. You flew over right it; I thought I was going mad after being alone for so long. Please come back to see me."

Kal returned the smile. "I would like that very much."

Daniel appeared with the foodbot and handed it to Biteko.

The man did a little jig, a kid receiving the best present ever. "You are so kind. I hope I can repay your generosity one day. Travel safe."

With that, he turned and vanished into the night.

Kal wondered how it felt to be so utterly alone; New Xinjiang was 33 light-years away and utterly unreachable. "He was a bit of a surprise," she said. "I didn't expect to see anyone here."

"Me neither . . . Tell you what, though; he really hates Kolovchenko. And I had no idea how much new gateways cost. No wonder the consortium ran out of money and collapsed."

"Hemed was right: Kolovchenko is run by money-grubbing parasites. And you know what? I really don't like the idea of doing business with people like that."

"Oh, come on!" Daniel protested. "Kolovchenko has the most to gain if it buys us out and the most to lose if it doesn't. And it is humanspace's richest corporation. There is nobody better to sell to."

Kal frowned. "I'm not sure that's the smart thing to do."

"Money's money, and Kolovchenko's is as good as anyone's. Besides, if not Kolovchenko, then who?"

Kal found a stick and poked the fire into a blaze. "I have no idea."

—19—

Daniel made himself a mug of coffee and sat down. "How's the biowaste reactor?"

Kal sighed.

They were 37 days out of Wallenski-7; she had spent most of them fixing defective equipment. The *Wraith* was showing its age. Thinking about the money it would take to keep it space-worthy made her teeth ache.

"Falling apart, like the rest of this shuttle," she said, "but it's working again."

"Glad to hear it. And while I've got you, we need to decide whether we're going to sell the Q-drive to Kolovchenko. We can't just keep talking about it."

"No, we can't. And, yes, I have been dragging it out. I needed to understand the risks of cuddling up to Kolovchenko. Going through the knowledgebases takes time."

"It's okay; I shouldn't nag. So, what are you thinking?"

"It's a long story, Daniel, so stay with me . . . I'll start with the Keliang Foundation. I discovered it has fired 33 pinchspace researchers in the last 20 years. Of those, 19 have committed suicide, a rate so statistically improbable there has to be something wrong going on."

Daniel shrugged. "Yeah, I guess."

"No guessing needed. The probability that those deaths were all suicide is as close to zero as makes no difference. The medical examiner's reports confirmed that none of those deaths were from natural causes. That means somebody killed them. Which raises two questions: who and why?"

"Where are you going with this, Kal? I can't see what the deaths of sacked Keliang researchers have to do with us."

"The Keliang Foundation isn't the independent research organization its PR hacks say it is. Kolovchenko provides all its money; that means it calls the shots. That links those murders back to Kolovchenko."

"Jeez, Kal! You're only saying that because you hate Kolovchenko."

"It's more than that. Kolovchenko is the wealthiest corporation humanity has ever seen, and wealth brings enormous power. And, as history shows, power always corrupts."

"I'll accept Kolovchenko's corrupt, but greasing politicians' palms to protect a gateway monopoly isn't the worst thing in the world."

"I'd agree if that's all it was. No, I'm talking about the moral corruption that promotes a do-whatever-it-takes culture, where eliminating anything that threatens Kolovchenko and its gateway business justifies any means, no matter how criminal."

"The Q-drive is a huge opportunity for Kolovchenko," Daniel said. "It's only a threat if we refuse to sell, and I really don't want to do that."

"I know you don't, which is why I want to talk about this guy."

A holopic of a man appeared on the crew-room holoscreen. Impeccably dressed in a high-necked suit of midnight blue, he radiated confidence, authority, privilege.

"That's Amos Ferruci," Kal continued. "He is the chair of Kolovchenko's board of directors and head of a shareholders' group called the Founders; their families have controlled the business right from the start. It's obscene how wealthy Kolovchenko has made them. Ferruci alone is worth well over a trillion dollars."

Another image: Ferruci standing beside a flame-haired, green-eyed woman, flawless in a black pantsuit. "Jo Risell. She runs Kolovchenko's Security Verification Group."

"Which does what?"

"Kolovchenko's annual reports say the SVG audits company security."

Daniel studied the holopic. "She reminds me of my dad. She has the same dead eyes, the same hard face."

"Because she is a hard woman. She was a colonel in the Kassafar marines. During Kassafar's civil war, she commanded the 56th Special Assault Group. She had a reputation for killing civilians who got in her way. When her side lost, she left Kassafar before the war-crimes investigators arrested her and washed up on Terra a year later. Ferruci hired her to run SVG, which Risell staffs with veterans . . ."

Kal put up another holopic, a heavily built man in an armored exosuit, assault rifle in hand.

". . . like this man. That's Harto Diop. He was one of Risell's NCOs and is now her deputy. The pic was part of the Kassafar War Crimes Tribunal's brief of evidence against Risell; it was taken just after the 56th trashed an entire village, killing hundreds of non-combatants, the civil war's worst single atrocity. My guess is the rest of SVG's vets will be a lot like Diop."

"Why would Kolovchenko employ thugs like him?" Daniel asked. "I thought corporates were all about looking after their customers?"

Kal laughed. "Dream on, son; all they care about is making money. So, ask yourself why an organization like SVG would exist . . . Come on, Daniel; join the dots. Moral corruption, remember?"

Daniel broke the long silence. "Protecting Kolovchenko and its gateway monopoly would be my guess, but doing that by killing people? Even SVG wouldn't go to such extremes."

"They will if the bosses think that is what's needed."

"That's just speculation."

"No, it's Occam's razor: The simplest explanation is the most likely. And the simplest explanation is that SVG killed those researchers."

"I don't—"

"Those deaths weren't suicides, Daniel. They were murders: fact. SVG exists: fact. SVG is run by a psycho: fact. SVG is staffed by professional killers like Diop: fact. Kolovchenko's owners have more power than anyone in history: fact. Power always corrupts: fact. And that is why I think SVG killed those people."

Daniel was quiet for a while before responding. "I was about to argue with you until I thought about my father. His religion gave him absolute power over millions of Ladakis. I saw for myself how that corrupted him. How else could he send thousands to the gallows every year, even kids? And godknows how many the Guardians and the camps killed as well; hundreds of thousands over the years if the rumors were right . . . He was obsessed with just one thing: protecting the Assembly of the All-Knowing One, the source of his power. In his mind that would have justified everything he did."

"I think it's the same with the SVG. The need to protect Kolovchenko legitimizes everything Risell orders it to do. Can you imagine how it's going to react when we turn up with our Q-drive, an existential threat bigger than anything Kolovchenko has ever faced? I can, and that is why I'm worried."

"And it's not just about the Q-drive itself. Even if Kolovchenko buys us out, we will always be a threat. What's to stop us taking Kolovchenko's money, pissing off to some system out on the Rim, and building thousands of *Wraiths*? We did it once. We can do it again."

Kal frowned. "Ah, yes. I hadn't thought of that."

Daniel rubbed his face, drawn, tired. "And there was me thinking we could just waltz in, show Kolovchenko the *Wraith*, take a shitload of its money, and live happily ever after . . . You know, I'm not sure we'd live long enough to spend any of it."

"Which is why I'd rather kiss a death-adder than go anywhere near Kolovchenko. Whatever we do, we have to do on our own."

"Let's assume we don't sell the Q-drive to Kolovchenko," Daniel said. "That leaves us flat broke. I know you keep saying your friend Jaden Harafi is going to help us out. Will he?"

Kal put her head in her hands. "Oh, dear god . . .. As I've told you a hundred times, of course he will. Why else would we be going to Toussaint?"

"Sorry . . . We can't rely on him forever, though."

"No, we can't, but he will lend us enough to take the *Wraith* to a deepspace asteroid called Deepshorne-6455."

Daniel's face creased into confusion. "Why would we do that?"

Kal's face broke into a huge grin. "Because Deepshorne-6455 is home to the biggest gold mine in humanspace. A mine from which we are going to steal as much gold as we can carry. A mine owned by Kolovchenko. A nice touch, don't you think?"

"Get a grip, Kal! We can't just waltz in and help ourselves to boxes of gold."

"Trust me, we can, Daniel. And, once we have our gold, we will pay Marcia Grivak a visit. She challenged Kolovchenko and survived. She can help us understand what we are up against, and she was a great researcher. The two of you can talk about all that pinchspace stuff you like so much."

"Won't SVG have people watching her?"

"I doubt it, not after so long. Don't worry, though. With the right surveillance equipment, I can make sure they're not, no problem at all."

The look on Daniel's face made it obvious what he thought of Kal's breezy optimism.

—20—

Kal thought Jaden Harafi quite the captain of an up-market cruiser, a bluff, prosperous looking man in a tailored shipsuit with four thin gold rings on each cuff, his deepspace-command starburst studded with diamonds, big ones.

A starburst that would have cost as much as Garford had paid her in a year.

Harafi pushed steaming mugs of coffee across the table. "The asteroid strike on Ladaki-6 was a huge story: millions killed, gateways destroyed, a ship lost in transit, and not one survivor. Which makes it one hell of surprise to see you alive, Kal. Care to tell me how you managed that?"

"It's a long story."

"No problem. As Toussaint-5's moons go, Calmette is the best by far. The scenery is sensational; and there is a lot of it; my passengers won't be back for hours."

"I'll start with Ladaki-6. It was terraformed by a fundamentalist cult, the Assembly of the All-Knowing One. Thanks to a severe shortage of money, the Assembly had neglected . . ."

~~~

Harafi studied Kal with a mix of awe, respect, and disbelief. "If anyone else had fed me a story like that, I'd boot them out the airlock . . . You do know that this is going to really piss off Kolovchenko?"

"It did take us a while to realize that, but yeah, we do."

Harafi tapped the station nameplate Kal had taken from *Dragon Star*. "More than you can imagine, so be prepared; there's nothing good about Kolovchenko." He looked at Daniel. "Since it's your ass on the line as well, perhaps I should explain why you can trust me to keep my mouth shut about all this."

"I'd like that. Thinking about what Kolovchenko's thugs might do to us keeps me awake nights."

"They're dangerous, no doubt about it . . . Did Kal ever tell you we were in the M'bakaa marines together?"

Kal put her hand up. "Stop right there, Jaden! That was all so long ago. Leave it, please."

"Not a chance . . . This will help you sleep better, Daniel," Harafi added as an image appeared on the bulkhead holoscreen: a young Kal Kariuki.

She was in a dark-green armored exosuit scarred by laser fire, visor up, assault rifle in one gloved hand, a plasma pouch held high in the other, its line running into the arm of the man lying on a stretcher: Jaden Harafi, his eyes closed, sunk deep in a face gray with exhaustion, a face black with encrusted blood laced through with the fluorescent green of woundfoam.

It was Kal's helmeted face that dominated the holopic, a face dominated by eyes that bored into the holocam with an awful, accusing intensity.

Harafi pointed at the screen. "That was taken outside the Mount Shadari cave complex on Kolokaar-5 at the end of a shitty day for the 41st Marine Combat Group. I would not be here if Kal hadn't ignored orders and led her squad into the tunnels to pull me and my guys out before those Kolokaar Liberation Front assholes overran us. The 41st's CO—Colonel Ling was her name—was so pissed she tried to have Kal court-martialed."

"Was she?" Daniel asked.

"No; the brigade commander took Ling aside and told her a court-martial would be bad for business. He forced Ling to recommend Kal for the Marine Cross instead. She ever tell you that? No? Well, she should have. It's M'bakaa's highest award for bravery by a marine in the face of the enemy. Kal's one of only 212 who've received it since M'bakaa was settled almost two centuries ago."

"Not that the Marine Cross helped when I was wounded," Kal said.

"No, it didn't. Ling's daddy was the commandant-general. He had fast-tracked Ling to brigadier; she was running personnel, which is how the corrupt bitch was able to toss one of M'bakaa most highly decorated marines out on the street." Harafi leaned over to look Daniel in the face. "And that is why, Mister Wei, you can trust me to keep your secrets . . . Now, what can I do to help?"

"It's ironic," Kal said. "Daniel and I escaped Ladaki-6 in a clapped-out shuttle worth billions and not much else."

"Come on. What do you need?"

"Some cash. Er . . . How about ten grand? That okay?"

Harafi reached into a drawer. Pulling out a cashcard, he pushed it across to Kal. "You'll find 200 k on that."

"Come on, Jaden! That's way too much. I can't accept this."

"For fuck's sake, just take it! This ship makes me more money than I can spend. And we can call it a loan if it makes you any happier. You can pay me back when you're a trillionaire. Now, what else can I do for you, Kal?"

"I have a feeling we're going to need to hire some muscle. Ex-military, but no crooks or thugs. Any idea how I'd do that?"

"I worked for a large security outfit out of Martens for a while. We always used ex-marines from Andimeshk; they are the best. Talk with Yannick Labele. He's a broker: competent, discreet, with a big network; all the best mercs work for him. He never let us down."

"Is he still around?"

"He sure is; I still use him whenever I have VVIPs onboard. He's wary of strangers; I'll send him a comm to let him know to expect you. Now, anything else I can do for you, Kal, and I mean anything?"

"No. You've been more than generous."

"No, I haven't. Some debts can't be repaid. Right, let me show you around my pride and joy, and then we can have some lunch."

"The tour, yes, but no lunch, thanks. We need to—"

Harafi leaned forward. "You sure? I have a Jorgenthaler."

Kal did not hesitate. "We're staying!" she shouted, at which she and Harafi guffawed uproariously.

Daniel stared at the pair, baffled. "What are Jorgenthalers?"

Kal wiped the tears from her eyes. "The best foodbots in humanspace, and by a huge margin."

—21—

Daniel commed Kal as she knelt over her home-made sled checking the propellant feed lines.

"Flight deck when you can."

"What have you got?" Kal asked as she arrived.

"I've broken into Deepshorne-6455's datanets. The feed from one of the security holocams is on screen."

Kal stared at the mine, a blazing island of light amidst the black of deepspace, fascinated by the mindless precision of the loadbots as they trundled in procession into the mine in pursuit of gold. A second stream returned with their skips piled high with laser-cut slabs of rock, dumped their loads at the processing plant, backed, turned, and headed back underground.

Kal patted Daniel on the back. "Well done."

"It wasn't hard. A Ladaki burger bar has better network security."

"Anyone around?"

"Good . . . The facility defense system. What have we got?"

Daniel brought up a schematic. "The FDS has radar and optronics arrays watching for incoming space debris. When the arrays detect an object on vector to hit the mine, the AI uses pulsed-laser batteries to blow it apart. Megajoule lasers; the *Wraith* wouldn't last five minutes."

"And how do we stop the FDS from seeing us?"

"Volatile malware injected into the AI will scrub the dataflows coming in from the arrays. A hundred *Wraith*s could visit Deepshorne-6455; the FDS wouldn't see a thing. I'll do the same for the holovid feeds from all the mine's holocams. When we're done, the malware evaporates, and everything goes back to normal."

Kal smiled. Trying to work out what had happened was going to drive Kolovchenko's security people mental.

But that wasn't enough. She wanted to really piss them off as well, and she knew how.

~~~

Daniel sat on the sled behind Kal and plugged his comms line in. "I hope we look the part."

Kal patted the yellow Deepshorne Mining Company logo on her skinsuit. "We do, not that anyone's ever going to see us . . . Okay, strapped in, neuronics off, suit nominal?"

"Check."

"Let's do it."

The sled was simple, almost primitive, a testament to Kal's ingenuity: two seats, a load-bed, a side-stick controller, fuel and oxidizer in pressurized tanks for the hypergolic thrusters, a small screen, an inertial navigator, backup oxygen cylinders and batteries, and a laser tightbeam back to the orbiting *Wraith*.

Kal blipped the thrusters. Once out of the cargo bay, she sent the sled on its way to the mine, now hidden below the asteroid's horizon.

"I see it," she said, 30 minutes later. "Right on the nose. We okay to go in?"

"Malware's live, so, yes, we're ready."

Kal slowed the sled as they closed in. The gold mine was as simple as any in humanspace: a fusion power plant off to one side, artgrav arrays below pads and roadways, light towers, loadboats, and a separation plant that fed vaporized rock into centrifuges which in turn spit pure gold into molds and tailings into space.

The final product—boxes packed with one-kilo bars of gold—sat piled in stacks ready for shipment to Miyashita-5.

Stacks to meet humankind's insatiable demand for gold.

Stacks worth 750 million dollars each and just begging to be stolen.

Apart from the AI and maintenance facilities and a small accommodation block for any sad bastard unlucky enough to end up on Deepshorne-6455, that was it.

Kal slowed to a stop and let the asteroid's meager gravity drift the sled to ground.

The nearest stack of boxed gold was only meters away. Without a single human on-site and a hacked security system, the mine was wide open.

Kal put her helmet to Daniel's. "It's time we did some serious stealing."

~~~

Still buzzing with elation, Kal slapped the switch to close the ramp. As air rushed back into the cargo bay, she waved an exultant hand at the boxes stacked against the forward bulkhead. "I never thought I'd see a tonne of gold in one place. That's 50 million bucks' worth!"

Daniel patted one of the boxes. "And I never thought sticking the knife into Kolovchenko would feel soooo great."

"And this is only the start. Right, Daniel, it's time for Phase 2."

Daniel picked up one of the one-kilo ingots on the deck by the ramp. "I can't believe you're going to waste these. Time's not a problem; we can go back and find something else to use instead of ingots. That way we would end up with 100 million bucks. Hell! Why not 200?"

Kal sighed. "For someone so smart, you can be a real dumbass, Daniel. First, think shotguns; if you want to destroy a spread-out target, you need lots of projectiles. Even if we spent all day down there, we would never find anything as good as those ingots. They are perfect: small and damn heavy. Second, cashing in one tonne of gold without Kolovchenko finding out will be hard enough; two is just asking for trouble. And third, enough is enough; greed is what gets most criminals caught."

"You'd know, I suppose."

Kal glanced at Daniel. The gold-lust was almost tangible.

~~~

Deepshorne-6455 filled the command holoscreen, a bottomless black shape that gobbled up the stars as the *Wraith* headed stern first for the mine, a speck of intense light.

Kal commed Daniel. "The target datum is confirmed, and our vector is nominal. Ramp opening now."

"Ramp open . . . Okay, I can see the mine."

"Now remember, the ingots only need a gentle push, just like we practiced. Soft hands, Daniel, soft hands. It's critical you keep the cloud really tight."

"It's all under control, thank you."

"Just making sure . . . Okay, off you go."

Five minutes later, Daniel said, "All gone."

ShipCon blipped the thrusters to slow the *Wraith*. Kal watched intently as the cloud of gold bars drifted away, heading right for the mine.

"Ingot vectors are nominal," ShipCon reported. "Time-to-impact 86 seconds. Total energy yield on impact will be 2.2 kilotonnes TNT-equivalent."

Kal smiled, a smile of feral satisfaction. "That will do it."

Daniel erupted onto the bridge, his face flushed with anticipation. "When you told me what you wanted to do, Kal, I thought you were nuts. I hadn't realized how fast we could get the *Wraith* moving."

"It might be the most decrepit shuttle in humanspace, but it's no sluggard. And we have plenty of driver-mass to burn."

The seconds ran off until the mine filled the holoscreen with a blazing sprawl of lights.

Kal glanced at Daniel. He sat hunched forward, eyes on his holoscreen, lips parted in anticipation as the cloud of ingots hurtled towards their target at 750,000 kilometers an hour.

"Yes, yes, yes," he whispered as the ingots carpet-bombed the mine, their massive kinetic energy blossoming into a firestorm punctuated with flares as bots' microtoks failed, flares bleached into oblivion a second later as enormous ball of energy engulfed the entire mine.

The tokomaks powering Deepshorne-6455's separation plant had just lost containment.

Daniel smacked the arms of his seat. "Shiiiiiiiit! I love this!"

As the *Wraith* hurtled across the shattered wreckage of Deepshorne-6455, a stab of regret jabbed at Kal. Leaving all that gold behind hurt.

Daniel wasn't the only one infected by gold-lust. "I want to do more of this. We need to hurt Kolovchenko and go on hurting it."

Kal wagged a finger. "Slow down, sport. This is one of their few bot-operated facilities. Even if we took them all out, Kolovchenko is so huge we'd only hurt their pride."

Daniel's face set in a mulish scowl. "Not if we attacked one of their big facilities, something like a helium-3 plant. As long as we have enough driver-mass, what you did here would work there too."

"No, it won't. The big targets, the valuable ones Kolovchenko cannot afford to lose, are protected by sensor arrays and megajoule pulsed lasers. They would spot us long before we got close enough for you to hack into their AIs. And the *Wraith* is the one thing I don't want Kolovchenko finding out about."

"We can sneak in."

"Space Warfare 101, Daniel. In the cold of space, warm objects stick out like dogs' balls, and ships are warm."

"Ah, yes. I hadn't thought of that. Sorry."

"That's okay. And we would have to do a shitload of jumps getting from system to system. Yes, the *Wraith* has done us proud so far, but it's only a few steps short of a wreck, like every other Garford shuttle. I spend most of my time fixing defects, and that's only going to get worse."

Daniel sighed. "True enough. Do we have enough cash for a new ship?"

"For a second-hand courier, yes, not for one that can look after itself if things turn ugly. Which they will when Kolovchenko finds out about us."

"What would you get if cash was no problem?"

"A Hemmings SpaceTech Viper modified to take the Q-drive."

"And a Viper is what?"

"A system defense vessel," Kal replied, "SDV for short. It has an armored hull, anti-ship missiles, a full quad-layered close-in defense system with missile interceptors, shotguns, cannon, and lasers, a full sensor pack, a combat AI, and a light ground-attack lander."

Daniel's eyebrows shot up. "That sounds impressive . . . and expensive. How much would one cost?"

"Not sure; I've never had to buy an SDV."

"Well guess then."

"Uh . . . Up to a hundred million for a new one, I'd say. Plus the cost of installing the Q-drive."

Daniel frowned. "A hundred million! Where are we ever going to find that sort of money?"

"Not sure yet. But let's not get ahead of ourselves. We cannot do anything until we have sold the gold. Hopefully, Jaden Harafi's bullion dealer is as good a friend as he says she is."

—22—

As the pax transfer drone left Heerat-3 nearspace on vector for its rendezvous with the *Wraith*, Kal was still seething over the way Jaden Harafi's best-buddy bullion dealer had treated them. "That woman was a parasite. 30 million dollars, she paid us. 30 million! That gold was worth 50!"

Daniel dropped his head into his hands. "Oh, for chrissakes, Kal! Stop complaining, please."

"Why would I? That woman—"

"That woman was never, ever going to give us top dollar, and why would she? Two strangers with fake IDs had just rocked up with a thousand ingots of stolen Kolovchenko gold carrying Deepshorne-6455's stamp and a comm from Jaden Harafi telling her she could trust us. She was taking a huge risk; of course she was nervous."

"Bullshit!" Kal snapped. "She told us nobody would ever know they came from Deepshorne-6455, not once she'd melted them down and doped the gold with trace elements. No, no. She was just putting on an act so she could screw us."

"You are such a tightwad; all you do is complain about money."

For a moment, the urge to run almost overwhelmed Kal. 15 million was enough to live out the rest of her days somewhere quiet. With an effort, she forced herself back to reality; running wasn't an option; once the Q-drive genie was out of its bottle; Jo Risell would send SVG to hunt her down. "Fine, I won't mention that bloody woman again, though it's ab—"

"Enough! We have our money. We have fake IDs that work. So, Kal, be happy. Now, what about Marcia Grivak?"

"This is how I see it . . ."

~~~

Kal gave up on sleep. Tonight was one of those nights when the craving for the buzz of vodka ate away at her, a craving made worse by knowing the *Wraith*'s new foodbot—a Jorgenthaler, an engineering marvel that could produce any dish or drink human ingenuity had invented—was just down the passageway.

A very expensive marvel. Daniel had only stopped bitching about its cost when Kal had threatened to beat him to death with it.

She slipped out of her bunk, went to the crew-room, and drew a cup of superb espresso, the last line of defense against her body's incessant demands for alcohol.

She switched the holoscreen to one of Heerat's news channels. It had been a long time since she had paid the rest of humanspace any attention.

She soon turned the holoscreen off, wondering why she bothered. It was all the same garbage.

One story had snagged her attention, though. A terrorist attack had killed the Yttrium Federation's president and 195 others, many of them children. Its security service's AIs had confirmed that the four people believed responsible all spoke with Terran accents. Sadly for the course of justice, the suspects were long gone before their drone-delivered bomb had exploded.

If they were Terrans, they were safe; Terra refused to allow its citizens to be extradited. Friends of Kolovchenko too, as Risell and Diop had proved when Kassafar's war crimes investigators came calling.

It all felt very odd to Kal. Why would four Terrans travel so far to kill so many people? Thanks to Kolovchenko's rapacity, Terra wasn't Yttrium's favorite system; that hardly justified the slaughter of so many innocents.

Still, somebody had thought it worth the effort.

For some reason, an image of Jo Risell crossed her mind. As fast as it had come, Kal dismissed it. The woman might be a psycho, but Kolovchenko would have no interest in a second-rate system with only one asset: the nine gateways that gave the rest of humanspace access to the mineral-rich Andover sector.

Curiosity nagged at Kal until she started to check the knowledgebases, her craving for vodka forgotten.

An hour later and she had a list.

In the previous year, ten systems had suffered terrorist attacks like Yttrium's. All had targeted political leaders. Some opposed to Terra's unwavering support for Kolovchenko. Some volubly pro-Terran.

And nobody had claimed responsibility for any of them, which made no sense. Taking the credit for atrocities was standard operating procedure in the terror business.

Kal gave up trying to make sense of what had happened. She was too tired to go on.

Five minutes later, she was asleep.

—23—

Ensuring Kolovchenko's SVG was not surveilling Grivak had been a tedious business; expensive too. In Kal's experience, it always was.

But she was satisfied, finally.

"The AI confirms Marcia Grivak is clean," she said to Daniel. "No tracktags, no holocams, no microdrones, no uptick in local radio or laser comms traffic as she moves around, no out-of-place wetware. If Kolovchenko's watching her, it's too damn smart for me."

She jabbed a finger at the holoscreen showing 'vid from the microdrone swarm tracking Marcia Grivak as she took her regular early-morning walk through one of Kolomna's parks. "All I see is an ordinary woman doing ordinary things. So, you okay to do this?"

Daniel nodded. "Yeah, yeah. I'll be fine. The Kafe Namoki, as we planned?"

"Yes. She likes her routine; she should be there before her evening classes."

"Which gives me an idea, Kal. Why don't we check out the Keliang Foundation? Moscow's not far and we have the time."

"Why not? Nothing better than a ride on a clapped-out maglev."

~~~

Daniel put his mouth to Kal's ear as the tour of the Keliang Foundation wrapped up. "What a load of horseshit. Nobody here is doing any fundamental research. All they care about is cutting gateway operating costs. I wouldn't piss on any of them."

"Me neither," Kal whispered back. "And I loved it when the research director said, 'I never thought I would live to see the day when we discovered all there is to know about the fabric of space-time, but we have.'. What a total dumbass."

"That she is . . . I'm going to buy one of the Institute's 'We Know Pinchspace!' t-shirts. You want one?"

"Why the hell would I?"

Daniel poked Kal's arm. "You are such a miserable bastard! I'm buying them anyway. And think of it this way: We'll be the only ones telling the truth."

"Fine! Make it three. Grivak would be a size 10, I think. And move yourself; I need a coffee before we head back to Kolomna."

~~~

Daniel walked over to where a slight woman sat at a table, head down, shoulders slumped, hands cradling a mug of coffee, a woman defeated, without hope.

"Marcia?"

Grivak glanced up. "Yes?"

"Can I have a quick word?"

"No, sorry. I need to be back at work. I have a class at six."

"Two minutes. Then, if you want me to leave, I will. You will never see me again."

"Uh . . . Okay, two minutes."

Daniel took a seat. "Thanks . . . Remember the paper you published just before you left the Keliang: A Multi-Band Model of Pinchspace?"

Grivak's head snapped back, eyes darting left and right. "Please go away." Her voice quavered. "I'm not allowed to discuss my research. I'm leaving now, and don't try to follow me. I'll call the police if you do."

As the woman pushed back from the table, Daniel said, "Your paper was right, and I've proved it."

The woman hesitated as curiosity battled fear. Curiosity must have won, and she resumed her seat. "How?"

"We've built a working jump drive."

Grivak's mouth had sagged open. Recovering herself, she said, "Did you just say you'll built a jump drive?"

"I did. Our ship can do 15 light-years a day."

"Which band?"

"Zeta. The next upgrade will let the drive tap into the theta band; that'll give us 30. We call it the Q-drive. The Q is short for quaqua, which means anywhere in Latin."

Grivak stared at Daniel for what seemed like an age, tears flooding her eyes, "The Quaqua-drive! Oh, I like that!"

She fumbled in a pocket for a Kleenex and dabbed her eyes. "That paper was solid," she continued. "The Keliang wasn't interested, so I published without its approval. The director hauled me into his office and gave me two options: Publish a follow-up paper using falsified data to prove everything I'd written was wrong, or . . ." Grivak's voice faded away.

"Or what?"

"He never said; he didn't have to. He had this woman in his office . . . Her eyes had no warmth, no pity, no understanding. Without doing or saying anything, she terrified me. She still does."

Daniel pushed a holopic across the table. "That sounds like Jo Risell. Is that her?"

"Let me see . . . Yes, it is."

"I'm not surprised. Risell and her people do all Kolovchenko's dirty work. After the meeting, what happened?"

"When I refused to publish the retraction, I was fired. That woman, Risell, she sent her people after me. They harassed me for months, trying to pressure me into telling the world my work was flawed. I refused, so the Keliang distributed a retraction notice—in my name, would you believe—agreeing with my critics that I had falsified my research data."

"It sounds like they were trying to provoke you," Daniel said.

"I'm sure they were, probably to give them an excuse to beat the hell out of me. But I kept my mouth shut, and they never bothered me again."

"You were lucky, Marcia."

Grivak rolled her eyes. "I sure as hell don't feel that way."

"No, you were. 19 out of the 33 pinchspace researchers fired from the Keliang in the last 20 years have committed suicide."

"Are you saying that woman had something to do with those deaths?"

"We can't prove it. We think so."

"Maybe I was lucky," Grivak said, "even though they destroyed me along with everything I had done. And everything I might have done too, the bastards . . . I just hoped they couldn't keep the lid on things; truth does have a way of worming its way out into the light."

"You got that right too."

"Not that it's helped me much. I spend my days teaching science to general studies kids; the little swine have raised apathy to a performance art. Not that they're my problem any longer; an AI's replacing me from next semester . . . I couldn't publish of course, but I never stopped my research, mostly on the Herschfeld-Musayoka transition fields."

Daniel smiled. "It's interesting you mention them. I think they're the primary cause of normalspace bubble instability, though I think you meant to say Herschfelden-Musyoka fields."

A grin transformed Grivak's face, the light sparkling off tear-filled eyes. "Herschfelden-Musyoka! None of Risell's thugs would have picked that . . . I think it's time you told me what you want."

"Your help, Marcia. We were wondering if you'd like to come and work with us."

"You keep saying we. Who's us?"

"Me and an AI tech called Kal."

Grivak frowned. "And the two of you built this Q-drive? No, that I don't believe. It's impossible."

"An asteroid, a big one, had taken out Ladaki-6. Kal and I were on one of Ladkai-6's moonlets; we watched the asteroid all the way in; it was horrible. Long story short, we had to find a way to get back to civilization, and we did."

"I remember Ladaki-6. The media talked of nothing else for weeks. It was the first time humanspace had lost an entire planet and its gateways. There was a freighter in transit too; it's still out there somewhere."

"The *Leviathan-VI*, yes. Kal and I were booked on it back to Voronezh-4. Check the casualty lists for Daniel Wei and Kal Kariuki. And you'll find my parents there too: Patriarch Absalom Wei and my mom, Sofija,"

Grivak closed her eyes. "I'll have a look."

A minute later, she reopened her eyes. "I'll be damned; you guys were there. And now you're here, so I guess you must be telling the truth. Let me tell you something. This drive of yours is Kolovchenko's worst nightmare. I know how those scumbags think. They won't be interested in your Q-drive. All they'll want to do is bury it, and you too."

"We won't let that happen. Kal and I want to put our Q-drive in the hands of ordinary people, even if we have to fight Kolovchenko to do that."

Grivak stared at Daniel for an age. "You said you wanted my help. Are you serious?"

"I am."

"Well, I must be mad, but what the hell? It's not like I have much to lose. What do I do?"

"Go home and grab your stuff, just what you'd need if you were going away for a week." Daniel slid a cashcard across the table. "Book an open return ticket on the Pluto Express. When you get to the Charon Research Station, go to the transfers desk; we'll have a pax drone waiting for you. It'll take you a while to reach us; our ship is waiting a long way out. Use the card for anything you need along the way."

For a moment, doubt clouded Grivak's face. Then she smiled. "I can't be any more screwed than I am now, so I'll see you there."

Daniel slid the Keliang t-shirt across the table. "One last thing, Marcia. This is for you. Wear it when you come onboard our ship."

"I don't understand."

"You will when you read what's on it."

—24—

Marcia Grivak put a hand on Daniel's arm. "We're jumping four light-years and some. In one go. Without a gateway."

"We'd not be here without your work," Daniel said.

A faint flush of pink colored the woman's cheeks. "I wish you'd stop saying that."

"Shan't!" Daniel jiggled foot to foot in excitement as they both cackled.

"Focus," Kal growled from the command chair, not that she was feeling grumpy. The opposite, in fact. She was both relieved and happy now that Daniel had his intellectual equal to talk with. Maybe he'd stop bugging her with latest of what Kal called his 'have I told you about . . .' ideas.

The *Wraith* dropped into normalspace. A dull red-orange star splashed on the holoscreen.

Grivak was on her feet. "A red dwarf!"

"Yes, it's—"

"Don't tell me! I need to work this out for myself. Can you give me a full spectrum analysis, Kal?"

"Standby . . . commed to you."

A long silence. Then Grivak spun around, her eyes glistening with tears. "That's Proxima Centauri!"

Kal pointed at the screen. It is. The white dot at bottom left is Kolovchenko's interstellar gateway test facility."

"I spent a year there when I first started at the Keliang. The engineers were great, the management the usual know-nothing assholes, and most of the so-called scientists a joke . . . I cannot believe this. You guys can't imagine what this means to me, not after everything I've been through."

Kal patted Grivak on the back. "I think we have some idea."

"Ah, yes. Sorry. This not the place to talk about how terrible things have been for me."

"It's okay . . . Right, Daniel. I'll leave you to give Marcia the ship tour."

"And you can get back to work, Kal. We can't talk to Hemmings without build-ready specifications for our new SDV, if we ever scrape up the money to buy it."

Kal sighed. "You just want me to use that ridiculously expensive ship-design AI you made me buy."

"Jeez!" Daniel hissed. "You can be such a dick sometimes, Kal. I've sent you the specifications for the Block-2 Q-drive, so just get on and update the design for the SDV, please."

Kal leaned over to Grivak. "Daniel's a bit thin-skinned. Please be gentle with him."

Daniel kissed Kal on the cheek. "And you are an asshole, Ms. Kariuki."

"I certainly am . . . I'll be in the crew-room when you're done. There's something the three of us need to talk about."

Daniel nodded. "Okay . . . Why are you grinning like that? You look like the village idiot . . . Oh, wait one second! I know you. You've worked out how to find the money for our new ship, haven't you? Come on! Let's hear it!"

"When you've shown Marcia around the *Wraith*. I need a break from you both raving on about Herschfelden-Musyoka fields, whatever the hell they are."

~~~

Daniel studied the ship on the holoscreen. "That is a fantastic piece of metal. I love the way the hull has those patterns on it."

Kal checked a media release she had found on the net. "I found a media release that says they're a pure gold inlay, half a centimeter thick."

Grivak pointed at the screen. "Look at those fusion drives; they're huge for such a small ship. I'd have said government courier, but it's way too fancy for that."

"That's no courier. It's Amos Ferruci's private yacht, the *Magellan*."

Grivak's head snapped around. "The Kolovchenko Amos Ferruci?"

"And the richest man in humanspace. Every year, after Kolovchenko's annual general meeting, he heads for a system called Ventura, which he owns outright. He even has his own gateways, and he's not the only one. Most of the Founders group of Kolovchenko shareholders have their own systems, all with private gateways."

"I bet they paid a lot less than the New Xinjiang consortium did for their gateways to Wallenski-7," Daniel said. "Why would we be interested in him?"

"We're going to kidnap Ferruci when the *Magellan* drops into Ventura-3 nearspace," Kal replied. "We'll keep him until the family has paid us a ransom of, umm, let's see . . . How does half-a-billion dollars sound?"

Grivak and Daniel stared at Kal, their eyes wide in shock.

Daniel was the first to recover. "Did you just say half-a-billion dollars?"

A huge grin split Kal's face. "I sure did. That seems like a reasonable price for a man worth over a trillion dollars would pay for his liberty."

"Maybe it is but kidnapping a man like Ferruci can't be that easy. For a start, how would we get past the system defenses?"

"Well, that the thing. There aren't any; Ferruci's gateways provide all the security he needs. And Ventura-3 has no deepspace sensor network; unlike Ladaki-6, it doesn't have an asteroid problem."

Grivak shook her head. "Hold on a second, Kal. The super-rich are paranoid, and I speak from experience. I went out with one for a while, and what a mistake that was. The man was a complete pig. He liked to watch . . ."

Daniel and Kal exchanged smiles.

Pink patches splashed Grivak cheeks. "Uh, sorry . . . Forget that."

Kal forced herself not to laugh. "I'll do my best. You were saying?"

"Ferruci will have a close-protection team; professionals, probably ex-military. People with too much money always do; if they're not paranoid, it's part of their 'look at me, I'm so rich' thing."

"Marcia's right," Daniel said. "And what happens if the Ferruci family don't pay the ransom? I don't care how big an asshole Ferruci is, we can't kill him."

"We're not killing anyone," Kal replied. "We just won't hand Ferruci back until the ransom's paid, not that we'll tell him that."

"We have another problem. We won't be using a gateway to reach Ventura. Unless they are total morons, Kolovchenko's security people won't take long to work out that we jumped in-system to kidnap Ferruci and then jumped back out. They'll know that their precious monopoly is over . . . and that will tell Kolovchenko it has to start developing its own Q-drive," Daniel added.

"After your Deepshorne caper, Kolovchenko probably already has," Grivak said.

Daniel nodded. "They have to. That shouldn't stop us, though."

"If there's another target as easy as Deepshorne, I can't think of one." Kal turned to Grivak. "What do you think?"

"I don't think you should be too worried if Kolovchenko finds out, to be honest. You can buy a ton of protection with half-a-billion in the bank. But you can't do this on our own; you'll need professionals who can take on Ferruci's bodyguard."

"Yes, we do, and I know where to find them."

—25—

Kal walked out of the spaceport and stopped, bludgeoned to a halt by the brutal heat, her eyes watering in the sunlight as she looked around.

Andimeshk-4 was famously chaotic. This was anarchy.

People swarmed, cars threaded, baggagebots wove, cleanerbots swept, vacuumed, and washed down, securitybots fought a losing battle to maintain some semblance of order, and everywhere idlers idled in small, animated groups.

Kal's neuronics directed her to a battered car, shimmering in the blistering heat. A bot had it trapped against a wall.

She pushed through the mob. Collapsing inside the car with a sigh of relief as the air-conditioning washed cold over her, she told the AI where to go, flashed her cashcard at the reader, sat back, and waited for an age until her car was able to barge its way clear and onto the freeway.

An hour later, the car pulled up outside a warehouse. Kal flinched as she stepped out, the heat even more intense.

A lean, wiry man with close-cropped hair, not that tall, stood outside, squinting at her through the glare.

Ex-marine, Kal thought; she could usually tell. "Yannick Labele sent me. You must be Jens Fonseca."

"And you must be Kal Kariuki."

"That's me." Fonseca's smile made Kal wish she was a lot younger.

"Welcome to Andimeshk. Come on, let's get out of this damn heat . . . Yannick told me to plan for a boarding," Fonseca said once inside the cool of the warehouse. "What's the target?"

"I want to kidnap a senior Kolovchenko exec, a wealthy man. He'll be in his private yacht."

"Somewhere out in deepspace, I assume?"

"No. Just after his yacht has dropped from the gateway."

"That changes things. Boarding a ship in planetary nearspace can't be done—and my team won't even try—unless you can bribe the local system-defense force to ignore what's happening. And that will not come cheap."

"There'll be no system-defense assets."

Fonseca frowned. "I didn't know there were any planets with gateways and no SysDef assets to protect them. You sure about that?"

"Absolutely certain. Can you do the job?"

"Assuming there's no SysDef to worry about, the team I've picked can handle it, yes. And ordering a missile cube was the smart thing to do. In my experience, there aren't many starships captains willing to risk a shot up the tailpipes. Is there a close-protection team?"

"Not sure," Kal replied. "We should assume there'll be one. Yannick said eight at the most, probably all ex-marines like your guys."

"That'd be right, but my team can handle a CPT. Can I assume the target is not an Andimeshki VIP?"

"You can. We'll be going out-system."

"Well, that's up to you. I assume you know that getting all our equipment past Kolovchenko's gateway security teams is going to cost you a small fortune."

"That won't be your problem, Jens. When we get to the target system, you will have everything you need. When can you leave?"

"The team is on standby, so two days. You have the money?"

"I'll make the payment after I've seen the equipment, if you don't mind."

"Sure. This way."

Kal followed Fonseca into the warehouse proper, a gloomy space filled with metal racking, the shelves loaded, loadbots bustling back and forth moving boxes around.

They came to a wire cage. Fonseca opened its gate. "This is your stuff, all boxed and ready to go."

Kal stared at floor-to-ceiling shelves loaded with the familiar dun boxes of military equipment. She checked the contents. Everything a ship-assault team needed to board the *Magellan* was there.

"The electronic-warfare system?" she asked.

Fonseca pointed at a plasfiber box. "In there. Its sensors cover the full radio-frequency spectrum. It comes with a library of all emitters in humanspace, cross-referenced to the ships and orbitals they have been installed in."

"And the dentology library? I need to identify ships from the dings and scrapes on their hulls, even if they have gone dark."

"You'll have detailed 3-D models of most of the ships in humanspace, though not for some of those from Outer Rim systems."

Kal nodded her appreciation. She liked knowing which ships the *Wraith* was sharing nearspace with. "Installation?"

"One of the team is a combat-systems technician; he'll fastset the EW system's sensors to the hull. They'll be wired up to the combat AI using your ship's external dataports. It won't be pretty, but it will work. And he can be your tactical officer as well if you want."

"I do want. Okay, I think we are done . . . Right, the payment's gone through."

"Thanks. We'll meet you at Orbital Transfer Station Six, two days from now."

"Add a week to that, Jens. My ship is waiting a long way out. There'll be a pax transfer drone waiting for you and all the gear. It'll know where to find us."

Fonseca grinned. "A week out from OTS-Six, eh? Something tells me this might be an interesting mission."

Kal returned the smile. "I can promise you this, Jens: You've never had one like this."

—26—

As Kal walked into the *Wraith*'s cargo bay, she ran an eye over Jens Fonseca and his team.

Eleven Andimeshk Corps of Marines veterans. One technician, ex-Andimeshk System Defense Force. All with combat experience.

"Before we start, captain," Fonseca said, "I have to ask. What sort of shuttle is this? It looks like a damn hedgehog with all those stumpy masts."

Kal grinned, enjoying the look of baffled confusion on his and everyone else's face. "I'll explain everything in a minute, but first you need to know we're heading for Ventura-3, a private planet 257 light-years from Andimeshk."

Fonseca frowned. "257 light-years? Sorry; we're not doing that. I am not going through godknows how many Kolovchenko gateways in a shuttle carrying illegal ordnance. We'd never—"

Kal held up a hand. "There'll be no gateway transits on this trip. We'll be—"

A chorus of disbelief from Fonseca's team cut her off.

"Calm down, everyone . . . Thank you. This is the hard part, so pay attention. Those masts are part of what we call the Q-drive. It lets us make a pinchspace jump direct to Ventura-3; that'll take us around 17 days, no gateways required."

Fonseca stared at Kal. "What the hell are you talking about? Everybody knows that's impossible."

"So Kolovchenko keeps telling us, only it's wrong. How else do you think the weirdest-looking ship in humanspace got here?"

The sys-tech leaned forward; Kal's neuronics identified him as Nazar Atlassian. "Pinchspace nodes. That's what those masts have on top. Am I right, captain?"

"Yes, you are. They maintain the normalspace bubble that carries the ship through pinchspace. We can do 15 light-years a day."

"Come on!" one of the team called out. "Kolovchenko's gateways do five, and this heap of junk does 15? This is complete bullshit."

Kal's hand shot out to restrain Daniel as he shot to his feet, his face red with anger. "Sit!" she barked.

She turned to the woman. "Wind your fucking neck in, marine. And keep your mouth shut unless you have something worth saying. Is that understood?"

"Uh . . . Yes ma'am. Understood. Sorry."

"That's okay; you'll be able to see it for yourself. Daniel has just upgraded our Q-drive; we'll be making a short jump out past Andimeshsk-14 to make sure that's working okay, and then we'll be on our way. Right, we're done. Jens, with me on the flight-deck, please. The rest of you can patch into our command net to see what's going on."

~~~

Fonseca stood in front of a holoscreen brilliant with stars in their millions, Andimeshk's most distant planet a dark gray circle 150,000 kilometers off the *Wraith*'s port side. He shook his head. "We have just jumped ten billion klicks without using a gateway! I tell you what; this ship of yours is something else. It's going to really shake Kolovchenko up."

Kal smiled. "That is the idea."

"Let me tell you something else, Captain Kariuki. What Kolovchenko did to the Andimeshk Federacy back in '87 nearly destroyed us. We were in the mother of all a recessions, for chrissakes! And what did it do? Hit us with massive penalty fees because we were late paying gateway charges we simply could not afford, and Kolovchenko knew it. Did you know we're still paying off those penalties?"

"I did, yes."

Fonseca put a hand up. "Sorry, I got a bit carried away."

"Don't apologize. What Kolovchenko did was unforgivable. The way I see it, the best way of stopping it is by getting our Q-drive into every freighter and liner out there. I want to use the ransom money to buy an SDV with the armor and weapons to make sure we stay alive while we do that."

Fonseca's eyebrows arched skywards. "Jeezus! You are full of surprises. And I hope you succeed, I really do. We will never forgive Kolovchenko. You give me a shout if you need help shafting it."

"Why do you think you're here?"

Fonseca slapped his forehead. "Of course! Ferruci runs Kolovchenko; okay, I get it . . . I have to say, ma'am. I've never had a client like you."

"The M'bakaa marines never saw fit to promote me to officer, so less of the ma'ams, please."

Fonseca was silent. Kal knew why; he was checking her service record.

"Fuuuuuck!" he breathed at last. "You're Staff-Sergeant Kal Kariuki; the M'bakaans gave you the Marine Cross. The name sounded familiar; I never made the connection."

Kal finger-flicked the words away. "That was another life, Jens. I'd rather not talk about it."

"I've done four VVIP jobs for Jaden Harafi. He told me he'd served with a marine who received the Marine Cross for saving his butt. He also said . . ."

Kal swore under her breath. Jaden Harafi loved to talk.

". . . she ended up with a massive alcohol problem after being beached by some asshole staffer. He never mentioned names, but that was you, am I right?"

Kal swore some more. "Does it matter?"

"I'm afraid it does, captain. What we do is risky enough without working for the drunken captain of a clapped-out shuttle. I'm sorry; you need to turn this ship around. The mission is off."

"Hold on a second." Kal commed Daniel to stop whatever he was doing and get to the flight-deck.

"What's up, Kal?" Daniel asked as he emerged from the hatch.

"When did I last touch alcohol?"

"What?"

"Just answer the damn question."

"Um, let's see . . . It's been five years since Ladaki-6 was trashed, so I'd say four years ago."

"Close enough. Thanks, Daniel. You can go now."

"What the hell is going on?"

Kal waved Daniel away. "Later! Just go."

"I'm not your slave," Daniel muttered as he dropped through the hatch.

Fonseca put a hand up. "I'm sorry. I should've asked before I opened my big mouth."

"It's okay, Jens. If you don't look after your people, nobody else will. And not a day goes by without me wanting a drink; it's like an itch you cannot scratch. But I made a promise to Daniel, a promise I've kept. Which has come as bit of a surprise, to be honest; I didn't think I'd last a week before I was back on the juice."

"As long as you stay dry, we're fine."

"My next drink will be when our Q-drive has bankrupted Kolovchenko. Until then, nothing. That's my promise to you."

"That'll do me."

—27—

Kal flicked up the visor of her helmet to wipe away the sweat stinging her eyes. It had been a long, nervous wait, the part of every mission she had hated the most.

She knew there was no reason to get so wound up. Thus far things had gone well. Thanks to Daniel's malware, the holocams infesting Ventura-3's gateways were never going to see the *Wraith* as it headed into nearspace. And Nazar Atlassian had proved a capable tactical officer, quickly and methodically using the makeshift electronic-warfare system he'd installed to identify every object in the nearspace around Ferruci's private planet.

Not one of which posed any threat to the *Wraith*. Ferruci was defenseless.

"Command, Tactical," Atlassian called out from his makeshift tactical officer's workstation. "Threat plot remains green. Request Buster-Red."

Kal's chest tightened. That code-phrase would tell everyone the first phase of the operation was about to start. Things were about get serious. "Buster-Red, approved."

"Standby . . . Buster-Red . . . now!" Atlassian said as the *Magellan*'s sleek, gold-inlaid hull appeared from the gateway. "Target vector nominal. Target assigned . . . Bruiser away, time-to-target ten seconds."

The bruiser—marinespeak for an anti-ship missile—burst from its cube and streaked away on a thin silver pencil of pure energy, its warhead flaring into a fireball directly ahead of *Magellan*'s bows.

"*Magellan*, this is the *Trader Phoenix* on Emergency," Kal said. "That was one of my anti-ship missiles. The next one goes up your tailpipes unless you shut down your main engines and open an airlock to be boarded."

Silence.

"*Magellan, Trader Phoenix* on Emergency. Respond, or I will disable your ship."

A voice, firm, authoritative. "*Phoenix*, this is Lüderitz, captain of the *Magellan*. A system-defense ship is on its way to deal with you. I demand you stay clear."

Kal's voice hardened. "Demand all you like, Captain Lüderitz. We both know there are no system-defense ships in Ventura. I will fire a missile into your tailpipes if you do not cooperate. Is that understood?"

A long pause. Getting instructions from Ferruci, Kal suspected.

Finally, Lüderitz responded. "Understood, *Phoenix*. What do you want us to do?"

"Shut down main engines. Maintain constant vector. Do not pitch, roll, or yaw ship. Open your port personnel access lock and standby to receive my boarding party. It will respond to any resistance from your crew with lethal force, as will the *Phoenix* if necessary. Is that understood?"

"Yes, yes . . . Engines are shut down; my port airlock is open. Ready to receive."

"Roger. I am on approach to take station off your port side now."

"Command, Tactical," Atlassian said five minutes later. "In station."

Kal gave the order to start the assault. "Buster-Blue, Buster-Blue!"

"Buster-Blue, roger," Fonseca replied.

She patched her neuronics into the feed from Fonseca's helmet-mounted holocam. It was up to him and his team now; she and the *Wraith* could do nothing more.

Except pick up the pieces if things went wrong.

In assault armor over skinsuits and carrying combat shotguns, the assault team crossed to the *Magellan* and disappeared into the open airlock.

Captain Lüderitz waited in the lobby, flanked by two of her crew, standing her ground even in the face of ten combat-suited marines. She was a tall, well-built woman in a uniform of midnight-blue: high-necked; four gold stripes on each shoulder; a gold command starburst above the word 'Lüderitz' in gold thread on her left breast, 'SS Magellan' on the right.

Her pale-gray eyes blazed in anger. "You people have no right to force your way onto my ship. Leave now, or I will—"

Fonseca fired from the hip. His shotgun punched a low-velocity slapdisk into Lüderitz's stomach, smashing the air from her body with a *whoosh*. Doubled over, she crumpled to the deck, mouth working as she fought for breath.

The crew flanking her reached for their needle-guns. Fonseca's team was too fast, their slapdisks dropping them to the deck to lie choking alongside their hapless captain.

"Morons," Fonseca muttered.

Kal had to agree. Needle-guns against marines? Really? Lüderitz's escort were too incompetent to be hired muscle, she decided. That meant Ferruci's close-protection team were somewhere else . . . unless he had decided he did not need one.

Would he be that stupid? Surely not?

Once the trio had been plasticuffed, the team fastset surveillance holocams to monitor the corridors accessing the airlock lobby, then headed for *Magellan*'s saloon.

Where three more crew in high-collared midnight-blue uniforms waited, pale-faced, sweating.

Unarmed, Kal was happy to see. She did not want anyone to end up dead.

Fonseca jabbed his combat shotgun at the nearest man's face. "Where's Ferruci's close-protection team?" His vocoder-masked voice was harsh.

"We don't have one. Mister Ferruci says the dirtside security team is all he needs while he's here."

"You wouldn't lie to me, would you? That would be a big mistake."

"No, no. We only have Mister Ferruci and the *Magellan*'s crew on-board."

Another jab from Fonseca's shotgun. "How many souls? The truth, mind!"

"Ten . . . No, sorry. Twelve. Mister Ferruci has brought a, uh . . . two friends."

"I'm sure hc has. And I do hope you have been honest with me."

"I have, I have."

"You better; I'd hate to spoil that pretty face of yours. Where do I find Ferruci?"

"I can't tell you that."

Fonseca angled the shotgun away and fired a single round that shattered a mirror on the bulkhead, making the man flinch back. "We've already shot your captain and two of the crew. You want to be next?"

"No, please! His suite is down the passageway, last on the right. He's there with his, uh . . . friends."

"It's okay; I get it. All of you, on the deck! Now!"

The men dropped and were plasticuffed as more surveillance cameras were set.

Kal liked what she was seeing. Fonseca and his team were professionals: competent, methodical, alert.

The patrician figure of Amos Ferruci, resplendent in a crimson bathrobe, emerged as the team entered the passageway.

"What do you people want?" he barked, face red and voice thick with outrage. "I insist you leave my ship, or you will regret—"

Krak . . . Krak.

Slapshots smashed into the deckhead, showering Ferruci in shards of shattered plasfiber. "Shut up, old man," one of the marines snapped. "Come here, now!"

"Command, Boxcar," Fonseca commed. "We have the target."

Plasticuffed hand and foot, Ferruci—too shocked to do anything except bleat in protest—was sealed into a crashbag.

"Scram, now!" Fonseca said.

The team dragged Ferruci through the ship and into the airlock. Fonseca paused to slip datasticks around the necks of the captain and the two crew, then cut their hands free.

"These sticks will tell you what to do next. Make sure you check them out . . . Do you understand? Hey, captain! Pay attention; this is important. The datasticks will tell you what to do if you want to see Mister Ferruci again. Understood?"

"Yes, yes. Understood." Captain Lüderitz's voice was a reedy whisper.

"I hope so. Okay, we are out of here. The *Trader Phoenix* and her crew hope you have a wonderful day."

Kal smiled. The moment Lüderitz uploaded the datasticks to *Magellan*'s AI, Daniel's carefully crafted malware would trash the ship's security knowledgebases along with the neuronics of the crew and Mister Ferruci's friends.

Leaving Kolovchenko with no record of what had happened.

—28—

Kal raised her coffee mug. "Your guys did well, Jens. It was good to watch."'

"Ferruci's hubris helped," Fonseca said. "It's amazing how dumb smart people can be sometimes, but it was your ship that made it easy. So, what's next?"

"Nothing's changed. Daniel and I want to use Ferruci's money to get our Q-drive out there. If we can bankrupt Kolovchenko in the process, that will be a bonus. Not that I've worked out how to do either without getting myself killed."

"We are Andimeshki. We hate Kolovchenko and everything it stands for. We want what you want. Any help you need, just ask."

"Thanks for that, Jens. Something tells me I'll be calling on you again. Right, it's time for me to tell Ferruci what's going on."

"Be careful. He's not a happy man."

Kal walked aft to Ferruci's cell, a storeroom not much bigger than a cupboard. One of Fonseca's marines stood outside, shotgun in hand. Without a word, they slipped on ski-masks and vocoders.

"How is he?" Kal asked.

"Being a total asshole." The marine sounded like a C-grade robot. "He likes to spit. We had to gag him . . . When you're ready, captain."

Kal pulled the door open. Ferruci sat on the deck, his back to the outboard bulkhead, one arm tethered to a pipe, gag across his mouth, narrowed eyes wild with fury.

"Are you going to behave yourself?" Kal asked. "I don't like people who spit at my crew."

The man did not respond.

Kal stepped back. "Fine; suit yourself. Tell me when you have decided to rejoin the human race. Until then, you'll get nothing from us. Not food, not water. And you can piss and shit in your pants for all I care."

"Urggh, gaaahhh!"

"Will you behave if I take the gag off?"

Ferruci nodded.

Kal stepped in and pulled the gag down. "I'll take that as a yes."

"What do you want from me?" Ferruci croaked.

"From you? Nothing. From your family? Half-a-billion dollars."

Ferruci shook his head. "Are you mad? My family doesn't like me enough to pay that much. My wife only speaks to me through her goddamn lawyers; she has done for years. And you can forget the Founders; they all hate me too."

The man's labored pathos made Kal laugh. "Okay, okay, nobody likes you, Mister Ferruci. I get it. They'll still pay to bring home the patriarch of Terra's wealthiest family and the chair of the richest corporation in human history. It'd be a bad look not to, wouldn't you say?"

The fear was obvious now, all anger gone. "What will you do if they don't pay?" Ferruci's voice quavered.

"My people really, really hate everyone who works for Kolovchenko, and you most of all. They want to kill you. I do too. Humanspace would be a lot better off without scum like you and the rest of the Founders."

Ferruci's face was dirty white. "Please, don't kill me."

"As long as you cooperate, I won't. So, here's the deal. We have given your family a month to pay us the ransom. As soon as they do, I'll drop you off in Ventura nearspace."

"You haven't thought this through, have you?"

"You're the one who's been kidnapped, Mister Ferruci."

"I'm talking about what happens next. I don't suppose you've heard of a woman called Jo Risell?"

"I have, as it happens. She runs your Security Verification Group. They're the people you use to kill kids on Yttrium and murder any Keliang researchers who step out of line."

Ferruci's eyes widened. "I might have underestimated you."

Kal kicked Ferruci's foot. "Given you're the one flexicuffed to a pipe, you might be right."

"Fair point . . . Listen to me. You're making a terrible mistake. No matter what happens to me, she will come after you. She is a dangerous woman who will do whatever it takes to make you pay for what you've done."

"Guess what, Mister Ferruci? I really don't give a shit. With half-billion dollars from your family, she'll never find me."

"Oh, trust me, she will . . . There is another way to give both of us what we want and keep you safe from Jo Risell and SVG."

"No, there isn't. Right, I'm done. I'll leave you to hope that ransom gets paid. Bad things are going to happen if it isn't."

"Wait, please. There is a better way to do this."

Kal stopped. "You've got one minute to prove that, Mister Ferruci."

"You didn't come through my gateway, did you? And don't bother denying it. The only ships I allow into my nearspace are the ones I authorize, and they are searched by people who know how to do the job. Are there are no exceptions. Ever."

"I think my being here proves there are."

"No, it doesn't. You're here because your ship jumped in-system."

"Are you done?" Kal asked.

"No, not yet. What about the Deepshorne mine? That was you, wasn't it?"

"I've never even heard of it."

Ferruci shook his head. "We'll get on a lot better if you don't treat me like an idiot. You see, I never bought the 'destroyed by an asteroid' story, so I sent a team to investigate. And I was right to. An asteroid impact leaves a very distinctive signature. What my forensics people found instead was a pattern of multiple impact sites rich in residual gold. That told them a kinetic attack using gold ingots moving fast had hit the mine. Which made sense; the mine had plenty of them to use as ammunition. But you stole millions of dollars' worth first, money you have used to finance my kidnapping. We haven't found the bullion dealer who converted those ingots to cash yet; Jo Risell and SVG are working on that."

Kal clenched her fists, driving her fingernails into the palms of her hands. Ferruci was proving how dangerous a man he was. "I already told you I've never heard of Deepshorne. Just like I haven't heard what's better than me getting half-a-billion dollars in exchange for your scrawny carcass."

"Tchah!" Ferruci barked. "Forget the damn ransom; the family will never pay it Let me buy your ship. Its jump-drive is worth twice as much to me."

Kal rocked on her heels. "A trillion dollars! Now that does have a lovely ring to it. I could buy my own system, my own Ventura. Yeah, I think I could agree to that."

Ferruci straightened up. "You'll do it?"

"No, of course I won't; I don't have a jump ship to sell you. And, even if I did, I would not live long enough to spend my trillion dollars. You friend Risell would make sure of that."

"What if I gave you my personal guarantee that you and all your people would be left alone?"

"I'm not interested. All I want is my money."

~~~

"Do you think he's serious about wanting the *Wraith*?" Daniel asked.

"I'm sure he is," Kal said, "As for paying us a trillion dollars for it, that's crap, as is his guarantee of our safety."

"He seems awfully certain nobody's going to pay the ransom. Maybe we sh—"

"Stop! I'm not negotiating with that man. And we will get our money."

Fonseca's head appeared in the crew-room doorway. "Sorry to interrupt. There's a newsvid you need to see."

"Put it on screen, Jens."

". . . and now for the latest on what the new Terran imperial government is calling the Expansion," the immaculately coiffed talking head said, "here is our international affairs correspondent, Zahra Hassani."

A second head appeared, an avatar of such ethereal beauty Kal doubted the real Zahra Hassani could be even remotely as gorgeous.

"Thank you, Xinyi. As we reported yesterday, the Empire has confirmed it has taken control of the 30 systems closest to Terra, with Teshawa the latest to capitulate. And . . ."

"Terran imperial government? Expansion? Empire?" Kal hissed. "What the fuck is that all about?"

". . . in a media briefing today, the Commander-in-Chief of the Imperial Navy told reporters that operations to bring a further 15 systems under Imperial control are now underway. She also confirmed that more systems will follow, though she refused to name any of those systems on operational security grounds. When questioned about eye-witness reports that Imperial marines had killed thousands of civilians during the Empire's attack on Hindenburg-7, she said those reports were fake news concocted by anti-Terran media. Overall, this has been another horrific week for the independent systems of humanspace. And all the analysts we have spoken with agreed that there is a lot more pain to come as the Imps drive the Expansion outwards. Back to you, Xinyi."

"Thank you, Zahra. And now for the reaction from . . ."

Kal had seen enough. "Turn it off, Jens. I have a bad feeling about this . . . I think I need to have another chat with Mister Ferruci."

~~~

Ferruci sniffed disdainfully. "Of course I know about the Empire. I'm the chair of Kolovchenko's board; nobody in the Terran government even farts without my approval. As for the Expansion, what use is an emperor without an empire?"

Kal wanted to punch the man until his ears bled; rich, arrogant assholes always brought out the worst in her. "How long have you been planning this?"

"A decade. Five years from now, every system, every orbital, every habitat in humanspace will be part of the Empire, whether they like it or not. Any idea what that means?"

"I'm sure you're going to tell me."

"You and your crew will have nowhere to hide. Jo Risell will hunt you down; you won't be hard to find . . . Still think you can get away with kidnapping me now?"

"Nothing's changed, Mister Ferruci, so yes, I do."

"Everything's changed, you fool! Kolovchenko's economic muscle and Terra's political authority make the Empire unstoppable. Come on, whoever you are. Be smart. Stop this nonsense. Sell me your ship, and we'll call it quits."

"I'm not the quitting type."

"Maybe it's time you were," Ferruci snapped. "Terra has set up a new ministry, Imperial Security; ImpSec for short. Care to guess who ImpSec's first minister is?"

"Ah, let me see . . . Could it be Jo Risell?"

"Correct. More than anyone else, she has made the Empire a reality and ImpSec is her reward. Think of the enormous power it gives her, power she will use to find you."

"She'll have a whole empire's worth of things to worry about. Why would she waste her time finding your kidnappers?"

"Because finding you is the fastest way to finding this ship, a task SVG started after your Deepshorne stunt and Imperial Security will finish. Now . . ."

"Bully for them." But Ferruci's words had hit Kal hard. She was fucked if ImpSec caught up with her.

"... I am not exactly the most moral of men, but Risell makes me look like a goddammed saint. She will do anything to crush anyone who threatens the Empire, Terra, or Kolovchenko: lie, cheat, steal, blackmail, torture, kill, she doesn't care as long as she gets the results she wants. And your ship threatens all three."

"She won't catch up with me in time to save you."

"That's irrelevant. If you don't sell this ship to me, Risell will make sure ImpSec finds you and your people. And that woman is cruel like nobody else I have ever met; none of you will die well. Listen to me, please. Take my offer, and I will protect you, I promise."

Kal sighed. "You seem to have trouble understanding me, Mister Ferruci, so I'll say this one last time. Even if this ship was jump-capable—which it is not—a slimesucker like you is the last person I'd sell to. So, stop wasting my time telling me I should. What you need to do is get on your knees and start praying that the ransom gets paid."

Ferruci chest was heaving, mouth open, breathing fast, a man panicking, all bravado, all hope gone. "You're going to kill me, aren't you? That's what kidnappers do."

"It is, and my crew are no different. They want to space you without a skinsuit..."

Ferruci started to shake.

"... and I must say I do I like that idea. I've seen it done; it is a truly horrible way to die, and you are a truly horrible person. I'm trying to convince them there is an even nastier option."

"What's worse than being spaced, for chrissakes?"

Kal studied Ferruci. "You look in decent shape. I'd say you have 40 years left in you, maybe more. How would you like to be the most miserable man in humanspace for every one of those years?"

Ferruci flapped his free arm around his makeshift cell. "And I'm not already?"

"Trust me, you're not. Have your neuronics to look up Jaipur Prime."

"Uh, right . . . It's a North Rim system, a long way out past Kirishita. They stopped paying Kolovchenko's fees, so the gateways were dismantled. Nobody's had contact with them for more than a century. But what's it have to do with me?"

"Radio telescopes on Kirishita still pick up their newsfeeds. They tell us that Jaipur Prime is now the worst system in humanspace: poor, corrupt, violent, disease running rampant, technology back to where it was hundreds of years ago, a system run by an endless succession of psychopathic dictators. An absolute shithole, in fact."

"Okay, it's a shithole," Ferruci said. "So what?"

"Jaipur Prime is where I am going to dump you if nobody pays the ransom."

"Ha!" Ferruci snapped. "I was right! You do have a jump ship. I knew it! I knew it! Come on! Be smart. Sell to me."

"I might just be bluffing. If I'm not, the next dirt you'll feel between your toes will be Jaipur Prime's. Which you will; you'll be too poor to buy shoes."

Ferruci stared at Kal, mouth open. "I've never been poor. You can't do that."

"Maybe, maybe not."

—29—

Content to let ShipCon keep an eye on the *Wraith* as it coasted through deepspace five light-minutes and 90 million kilometers out from Ventura-3, Kal was finishing a welcome mug of coffee as she contemplated a long shower.

"My dropbox has just pinged me," Daniel said when he stepped into the crew-room. "Hemmings SpaceTech say they can give us a price on our SDV next week. All we need now is the cash ... if we ever get any."

Kal sighed. "Oh for chrissakes, relax! Ferruci's family will find the money and we'll be long gone before Risell and her thugs can catch us. Not that there's any point worrying about them. All we can do is stick to our plan."

"Hah!" Daniel snorted. "Apart from buying a replacement for the *Wraith*—which we can't do unless we're paid the ransom—what plan is that?"

"I'll tell you once we have our money."

"Assuming the family pays up."

"Jeez, Daniel! Would you stop saying that? Ferruci knows what happens if we don't get paid. If he ... Sorry, hold on a sec," Kal added when her neuronics pinged, "I have a comm ... Interesting; it's a vid from Junana M'danial. I wonder why."

"Who's she?"

"Kolovchenko's chief executive officer."

When the holovid finished, Daniel sat back, his face twisted with despair. "Fuck, fuck, fuck ... What do we do now?"

Kal patted Daniel's arm. "Calm down; this isn't over yet. Let's get Ferruci to the crew-room so he can see the 'vid. We need to hear what he has to say before we all start slashing our wrists."

~~~

". . . not that I care what the kidnappers do to you, Amos," Junana M'danial said. "Nobody here does, not even your own wife and kids. They don't need you, not when the Imperial Supreme Court issues the declaration of your presumed death and all your Kolovchenko stock is transferred to the family trust. That won't take long; the Emperor has already instructed the Attorney-General to lodge the petition along with an Imperial Directive instructing the court to waive the usual five-year waiting period . . ."

"You can't do that," Ferruci wailed. "I'm still alive!"

". . . on Imperial security grounds. Given how much Kolovchenko's stock you control, the Emperor believes this is not the time to destabilize Terra's capital markets, as I'm sure you'll agree.

"Well, there you are. Amos. The Founders have had enough of your endless pontificating, always telling me and the rest of the Founders what we can and cannot do. And, now that the Empire is a reality, a lot of us . . . well, all of us, actually, worry that your ambitions are no longer in the best interests of the Empire. Putting it simply, nobody trusts you anymore.

"One last thing, Amos. The Board has voted unanimously to fire you as chair and appoint me in your place. Right then, that's all from me; I'm off to have lunch with the Founders. We all agree that a situation likes this calls for French champagne and lots of it. Goodbye, Amos. I hope you enjoy what's left of your life."

"No!" the man wailed when the screen blanked out. "I'm family. I'm Kolovchenko's chair. You have to help me."

Kal patted Ferruci's hand. "You were right. They really don't like you. And being declared dead before your five years is up? That's just cruel."

Head down, the man stayed silent.

Kal wondered at the crushed, defeated human slumped in front of her. He really had thought the family would pay.

"You didn't see that coming, did you, Mister Ferruci?" she continued.

"Junana M'danial is a treacherous, back-stabbing scumbag. And my family are too, every last one of them."

"Clearly, but let's move along. Since our plan to ransom you has fallen on its ass, you're going to Jaipur Prime. The transit will take us a few weeks, which is plenty of time for you to contemplate the life of grinding poverty awaiting you."

Kal put her face to Ferruci's. "One of my guys is running a book on you," she went on. "Most of the money's on you topping yourself inside six months. I think you're a bit tougher than that; I put my fifty on you lasting ten months before you blow your brains out."

"How stupid are you?" Ferruci snapped. "I am the richest man in humanspace. I'll pay the damn ransom myself!"

"You can't. The police will have frozen all your assets. They must; it's the law. Terra is a signatory to the Shandong Treaty, remember?"

"Hah!" Ferruci snorted. "You are so naïve. Do you really think Shandong applies to me? It doesn't, and it never did, not to people with my wealth and influence. My assets are my assets, and I'll decide what happens to them, not the police or the courts."

"Even sitting there in flexicuffs?"

"Even here. Look, I'll give you 50 million; I can't be fairer than that. Godknows, giving that much money to thieving scum—"

"Shut your goddammed mouth, Ferruci, or I'll have my guys kick the shit out of you."

"Sorry. Listen, take the money. Flea-ridden shitholes aren't my thing."

Kal slapped Ferruci's face, hard. "You're not listening to me. I will dump you on Jaipur Prime if I do not get my money, every damn cent of it. And you'll rot there until I do, living in squalor and suffering more than you have ever suffered."

"You can't do that."

"I think you'll find I can. We'll check on you now and again, though. It might take a while before you decide to be sensible, but you'll pay up eventually."

Ferruci's face hardened. "I'm not paying a cent, not now, not ever."

Kal slapped her forehead. "Oh, silly me! I almost forgot. I have one more condition. From here on, the ransom goes up 50 million every time you say no to me."

Ferruci blinked. "What? You're kidding!"

"No. I'm not. The price of your freedom is now 550 million."

"Fuck you! You're not getting anything out of me."

"Saying no has consequences, Mister Ferruci . . . It's 600 now."

"I don't care. I'm not paying."

"650 . . . And the next time you say no to me, it'll be 700 . . . Anyway, I'll leave you to think things over. I need to get this ship on its way to Jaipur Prime."

Kal commed two of the marines into the crew-room to take Ferruci back to his cell.

She watched the marines pull Ferruci to his feet. A man abandoned by his family, sacked as Kolovchenko's chair by the Founders, betrayed by the man he had placed on the Imperial throne.

A broken, terrified man condemned to live the rest of his life in abject poverty.

Kal was sure it was only a matter of time before Ferruci paid the ransom. He had to; it was the only way he could make it back to civilization to take his revenge on the great and the good of Terran society for betraying him.

As the man was led out, his voice cut into Kal's thoughts.

"Wait!" he screeched. "I'll pay, I'll pay."

Kal threw her hands in the air. "Finally! And, now that we're friends, let's call it a round 700, shall we? And don't say no. It'll be 750 if you do."

"Okay, okay. Just get me off this stinking ship."

"First things first, Mister Ferruci. Let's set you up with a commlink so you can get me my money."

—30—

Kal pushed open the door. "On your feet, Mister Ferruci. This is as far as you go."

Fear clouded the man's face. "I've paid you what you asked for!"

Kal tossed him a bag. "Your clothes. And relax; your money has arrived, and you're going home."

Relief replaced fear. "Where are we?"

"Ventura-3 nearspace. Where else?"

"What about all that Jaipur Prime stuff?"

Kal chuckled. "A lie. Everybody knows getting there is impossible without a gateway. We never left."

"Oh, right . . . Yes, of course."

Ten minutes later, Ferruci was back in his trademark midnight-blue suit. "How do I look?"

Kal ran an unsympathetic eye over the man. "Crumpled."

Ferruci ran a hand over his sleeve. "You could have taken better care of my suit. It's genuine Terran merino wool, a Giordano Fiorelli, Milan's best tailor. It cost a fortune."

Kal sniffed her contempt for anyone who thought an expensive suit mattered. "Like I give a shit. Come on, let's go. You're not leaving until we've wiped your neuronics."

~~~

Kal patted Ferruci on the back. "Goodbye, Amos. It's been a real pleasure."

Ferruci stopped at the airlock door. "You're taking a bit of a risk meeting up with a transfer drone in a system I own."

"A transfer drone? No, no, no. You're going home the hard way." Kal waved Fonseca over. "Crashbag the sonofabitch."

Ferruci panicked response was immediate. "Wait! Don't do that, for chrissakes. A speck of space debris could punch a hole right through it. I could die out there."

Kal's eyes narrowed, pitiless. "You are so right." She turned to Fonseca. "What are you waiting for? Get this piece of dog shit off my ship."

~~~

Kal sat at the crew-room table, tired, elated. "700 million dollars in untraceable cash! How about that?"

Daniel could not sit still he was so excited. "I still can't believe we pulled it off."

"You and me both. I'll get the money for our new system-defense vessel off to Hemmings as soon as we're back in normalspace."

"Do that. And talking of our SDV, I have sent Tharmaran Shipbuilding the specifications for installing the Q-drive. The construction manager—"

"Maia Okiro, right?"

"Yes . . . She says they can start work as soon as Hemmings delivers the SDV."

"Tharmaran will think we're mad cutting holes in a brand-new armored hull," Kal said.

"That won't stop it taking our money . . . I can't believe how much this is all going to cost us."

"What did you expect? Tharmaran isn't just the best shipbuilder in humanspace, it's also the fastest. And time's what we're short of, not money . . . Tell you what, I can't wait to introduce Kolovchenko and their Terran Empire to humanspace's best warship. It makes me go all shivery just thinking about it."

Daniel rolled his eyes. "What's with you military types? The instant the merchants of death start waving their bright, shiny toys around, you go to custard. And the cost! Those bastards know how to charge."

"It'll be worth every cent."

"I hope so, though I'm still not convinced we need a freighter as well."

Kal sighed. "Come on, we've been through this. Things always go wrong in combat. We need a support ship, and a second-hand freighter with a Q-drive is the best way to get one. And the ship-broker says there are plenty going cheap thanks to the Imps."

"We still need to find money for ordnance, supplies, spares, crew, and godknows what else. We'll be burning cash at one hell of a rate."

"Oh, do stop fussing! We can always steal more if we run short. Now, have you had a think about the names we talked about?"

"I have, and I agree with you: *Stiletto* for the SDV and *Provider* for the freighter."

"Done . . . Right, I need to wrap things up with Jens before we head back to Andimeshk. His team are keen to know when they'll get their slice of Ferruci's money."

"They did well."

"They sure did."

~~~

Kal had turned in as soon as the *Wraith* jumped for Andimeshk, not that she had been able to sleep, more shaken by the Empire's extraordinarily aggressive plans to take over humanspace than she had let on.

Ferruci had been right.

With Kolovchenko's backing, the Empire was unstoppable. So why would she gift the Q-drive to humanspace if Terra controlled every system in it? That would just cement the Imps' hold on power.

Unless she could find a way to use the *Stiletto* and *Provider* to hurt the Empire so badly the Expansion came to a grinding halt.

Kal found it hard to breathe, crushed by the sudden weight of an obligation she hadn't sought, did not want, but had to meet.

Not that she knew how. It was time to get some help and she had an idea where to find it.

—31—

Ten days into the jump back to Andimeshk and Kal was exhausted, so tired her bones ached, the price she had to pay to fix the biowaste reactor yet again. It was struggling to cope with the demands 14 people were putting on it. A coffee, a shower, and then some desperately needed rack time, she decided as she trudged to the crew-room.

Where she found Daniel waiting, fidgeting with excitement. These days, he always was. Keeping him focused was turning into a never-ending chore.

She grabbed her coffee and slumped onto one of the benches. "What now, Daniel? And make it quick; I need my rack."

"A while back, we were talking about the sort of ships you'd need to take on the Imps. I've done some thinking . . ."

Kal wondered if the man-child ever slept.

". . . and this is what I've come up with. Have a look at the screen."

"Is that an orbital habitat?" Kal asked as a sphere appeared.

"Yup. 200 meters in diameter and massing 300 kilotonnes. And it has a Q-drive."

"Sheesh! Can you build a drive that'll jump that much mass into pinchspace?"

"If your tokomaks can supply the power, the science says yes. Because the ship's spherical, the drive is much more efficient than one fitted to an ovoid ship. Fewer nodes, less power, less instability."

"That would make the perfect freighter."

"It's no freighter. Have a look at this."

Hatches opened to release a cloud of black dots. "Those are ground-attack landers," Daniel continued, "like the one the *Stiletto* will carry modified to remove everything they don't need like wing boxes, undercarriage, and so on. I call them space-attack vehicles;

SAVs for short. There'd be 200 of them. Their main armament would be FireSpark anti-ship missiles from Shenwa-Boeing. I have researched everything on the market; they're the best."

Kal whistled softly. "A 300-kilotonne ship with 200 modified ground-attack landers, sorry, SAVs armed with ASMs. Now that is a great idea."

"Not an original one. It's an updated version of the aircraft carriers Terra's navies operated until sub-orbital kinetics and hypersonic missiles made them obsolete."

Kal stood and went over to the holoscreen, the possibilities Daniel's ship offered swirling through her mind. She thought for a good minute, then said, "Building the ship to carry the SAVs wouldn't be too hard; there are hundreds of orbital designs to start from . . . You know what, Daniel? I think this idea of yours has legs. I'm going to ask Okiro if Tharmaran could build one with freighter-class fusion drives."

"She won't think we're completely insane. She'll know."

"As long as Tharmaran takes our money, I don't give a rat's ass. Let's have a look at the nav plan . . . Okay, we can drop into the Buseoksa System. I'll comm Okiro from there."

"Good, but we can't call it a SAV carrier."

"Ah, no, we can't," Kal said. "As far as Tharmaran is concerned, *Provider* is Freighter-01. So, how about Freighter-02?"

"A freighter that can't fit through a Kolovchenko gateway? Maia Okiro's definitely going to have us committed."

—32—

The comm from Maia Okiro popped into Kal's neuronics the moment the *Wraith* arrived back in Tharmaran-4 nearspace after returning Fonseca's team to Andimeshk.

Kal commed Daniel. "I've heard back from Okiro. Flight-deck, now!"

Seconds later, Daniel erupted from the hatch "What's she said?"

"A bureau called Bondarev has a design for a fusion-drive orbital; she thinks it would be ideal for Freighter-02."

"Did Okiro say how long Tharmaran would take to build it?"

"Nine months, plus whatever's needed for the Q-drive and all our extras."

Disbelief flooded Daniel's face. "A 300-kiloton, fusion-powered orbital in nine months? You have to be kidding."

"Tharmaran has invested a fortune in its production AIs and fabrication shops so it can build ships in half the time its competitors take. That's why I chose it. Trust me, Daniel. If Okiro says Tharmaran can do it, it will."

"What would it cost?"

"A billion, give or take. That's without a Q-drive, armor, weapon systems, magazines, additional crew quarters, and so on. And then there'd be the SAVs and their ordnance."

Daniel's face fell. "Forget it then. We can't afford a ship like that, not unless Ferruci lets us shake him down a second time."

"Sadly, he's not that stupid . . . Hold on." Kal held up a hand as an ephemeral thought crystallized into a fully formed idea. "I think there might be a way to get Freighter-02 built."

"Dream on," Daniel said.

"No, hear me out. We set aside enough money to operate *Stiletto* and *Provider*. Then we use what's left to fund the first phase of

Freighter-02's build and pay Hemmings to produce a design for our SAVs. That gives us three months to raise the rest of the money we need to finish the build and buy our SAVs."

"You have to be kidding! 200 SAVs and their ordnance would cost billions, which we will never find. We would end up with no money, a design for SAVs we can't afford, and a half-built orbital we can't finish. Listen, Kal, let's forget this whole SAV carrier thing; it's not like we need it anyway."

"That's what I thought when you first floated the idea," Kal said, "but I've changed my mind. We do need that ship."

"No we don't. We'll use *Stiletto* to keep us safe while we tell the rest of humanspace about the Q-drive. If that woman you've hired, Professor Sharif, can find us a way to hurt the Empire without getting ourselves killed. That's the plan we agreed, a simple plan, one we have the resources to execute, and one that doesn't need Freighter-02. We should stick to it."

Kal felt as if her brain was about to implode; trying to blend all the ideas churning through her mind into a workable strategy was like wrestling snakes covered in oil. "I know that's what we agreed," she said at last, "but Freighter-02 means we have to rethink things."

Daniel sat back and rubbed his eyes. "Oh, for chrissakes . . . Go on then."

"Marcia says it'll take the Imps two years to develop their own Q-drive, right?"

"Because they have killed or marginalized all their best pinchspace researchers, yes."

"And what happens when they do?" Kal asked.

"Who cares? We'll have made sure every system in humanspace can use our Q-drive, Kolovchenko and its gateways are fucked, and the Empire can't afford to pay for the Expansion. Game over, I reckon."

Kal shook her head. "No, it's not, Daniel. Two years out, the Empire will be three times the size it is now. And it will have its own

Q-drive, a drive it will be working frantically to fit it into every warship in the Imperial Navy. Given its economic power, it will not be long before the Empire can jump its warships to crush any system that refuses to surrender."

"Unless Professor Tarif finds a way for us to interdict the money the Empire gets from Kolovchenko. If she can, then the Imps can't pay for the Expansion, and it really is game over."

"That's what I thought. Not anymore. It's not enough. Don't get me wrong though; Sharif a very smart woman. She'll find a weakness in Kolovchenko which we can exploit to slow down the money flow, I'm sure of it."

Daniel's face creased up. "Now I am confused. If you're so sure Sharif will deliver, what's the problem?"

"No matter what she finds, we can't hurt Kolovchenko enough. That didn't bother me when I thought all we needed to destroy the Empire was our Q-drive. Problem is that was just dreaming on my part."

"But—"

"There are no buts, Daniel. Even if we can cut the money Kolovchenko gives the Empire by a quarter—which we'll never do—the Imps can just borrow the money they need."

"So you want 02 as a backup then?"

"I do. It's the only thing I can think of that shifts the odds in our favor."

Daniel was quiet for a long time before responding. "Here's what I think. One: Letting the Empire take over humanspace is unacceptable. Two: Allowing Kolovchenko's gateway monopoly to continue is also unacceptable. Three: There is no point leaving our money in the bank if it could help us beat the Empire and Kolovchenko. Four: We should get Freighter-02 started. And five: Somehow, godknows how, we raise billions of dollars to pay Tharmaran to finish 02, Hemmings for SAVs, and Shenwa-Boeing for FireSpark missiles."

Kal reached over and squeezed Daniel's hand. "You are exactly right. Now, let me give you the good news."

"Is there any?"

"There sure is. I don't think the money's going to be a problem."

"Piss off! Money's never the easiest part of anything."

"This time it will be," Kal said, "It's not how much 02 costs that matters. It's what it's worth."

"And what is it worth?"

"Billions of people are shitting themselves as they watch the Imps roll up system after system, knowing it won't be long before it's their turn. They also know how miserable life in a Terran colony run by ImpAdmin thugs can be. So, imagine you were the president of a system like Tharmaran. How much would you pay to make sure your system stayed out of the Imps' hands?"

Daniel nodded. "Ah, yes. When you put it like that, even a hundred billion dollars seems cheap. I reckon the Andimeshkis would pay twice. They haven't forgotten how Kolovchenko treated them, and they will know the Empire's going to be even worse."

"And they're not alone, which is why we shouldn't waste time worrying about the money. I think we can raise it; I really do. And, if we can't, at least we tried."

Daniel's fist thumped the table. "You know what? I'm beginning to think we can do this."

Kal put a hand up. "Before you get too excited, there is a snag: Tharamaran will never sign a contract for a billion-dollar ship unless it knows we can pay."

Daniel slumped back, his enthusiasm blown away. "Oh, shit. That's that then."

"No, that's a problem the best hacker I have ever met—which is you, Daniel—is going to solve."

"Are you mad? I can't conjure up money out of thin air. Either we have it or we don't. And we never will."

"We don't need money. We just need Tharmaran to think we're working for a business that's financially strong enough to borrow the money to pay for 02."

"And how do I do that?"

"By concocting the best creditworthiness report Tharmaran has ever seen."

Daniel massaged his forehead. "I don't even know what a credit report is."

"You're a smart guy; I'm sure you can find out. Go on! Get started. The future of humanspace is in your hands, Daniel, and time is not our friend."

"I hate you sometimes, Kal Kariuki."

~~~

Daniel burst in as Kal dozed on a crew-room bench and turned on the holoscreen. "You've got to see this . . . Come on, Kal! Wake up."

Kal rolled her face to the bulkhead. "Fuck off. I'm done for the day. Show me another time."

"No way. You have to see this."

Music filled the crew room, soft, almost sensual. Conceding defeat, Kal rolled back and sat up to watch the holovid.

Shot through a gauzy lens, the holocam started in so close it took Kal a moment to work out what she was looking at. It was an eyelid. Slowly, the holocam pulled back to bring a body into view.

A man sprawled out, mouth open, a viscous strand of saliva drooling to the floor.

"This is Terra's choice for the man to rule all humanspace." A woman' voice, soft but authoritative. "His Imperial Majesty, Emperor Michael the First."

The camera pulled back even more. A woman lay beside the emperor. Face down. Arms out. Naked. Vomit pooled around her head.

"And this is not his wife. It's Emperor Michael the First's special friend, Meiying. Like Michael, she is unconscious after an all-nighter bingeing on scrag, their preferred recreational drug. Better than sex, the Emperor always says, not that he would remember; he has been impotent for years . . . I'm Trinh Nguyen for the Fire Ants. Thank you for watching."

"Wow!" Kal said when the vid finished. "That's good. Nguyen needs to be careful, though. Halcyon is only six gateways from Terra. She's screwed if the Imps take over."

"I'm sure she's too smart to let that happen."

Kal forced herself onto her feet. "I hope so, for her sake. Right, I'm done. I'm heading in-system to meet with Okiro tomorrow. You coming?"

"No. Grivak wants to talk with me about Q-drive power supplies."

"Hey! My credit report, remember?"

"Calm down. I'm on it."

"And can you create one that'll convince Tharamaran we can finance Freighter-02?"

"Oh, yeah, an absolute doddle. I've just got to invent a private company with billions in assets, dummy up phony letters of credit, financial statements, statutory accounts, regulatory filings, and audit certificates by inserting malware into at least 30 knowledgebases belonging to banks, media channels, analysts, and—"

"Jeez, Daniel! It's complicated, I get it. All I asked was whether it could be done."

Daniel sighed. "I'm not feeling the trust, Kal."

"Just answer the damn question!"

"In the end it's just a matter of putting the right data in the right knowledgebases. If I can do that without my malware triggering any alarms—which is the hardest part—then yes, it can be done."

"if anyone can do it, you can." And Kal said she meant it. Anyone who could invent the Q-drive should be able to corrupt a bunch of knowledgebases without being noticed.

"Won't Tharmaran send someone to check? I can do a lot of things, Kal, but I cannot make live human beings swear on their mothers' graves that our phony corporation really does exist and is worth billions."

"That is the one risk we cannot eliminate. We just have to pray that Tharmaran doesn't send a forensic team to whichever raggedy-assed jurisdiction your fake company is registered in, preferably one that's got two or three warzones between it and Tharmaran."

Daniel smiled. "I'll just have to give them a credit report that's so good they won't even want to."

"Yes, you will. Do you need any help?"

"From Professor Sharif probably. I'll let you know."

"I'll tell her to expect a call. Right, we're done. As soon as the pax transfer drone arrives, I'm off. Okiro's got me a room at the Orbital Suites. I'll be there if I'm not at the yard. We still have a shitload of work to do before Tharmaran can start work on 02."

"Optimist," Daniel muttered.

—33—

For what had seemed like an eternity, Kal had been waiting for Hemmings to deliver the *Stiletto*.

Finally, it was here. She was home.

It was the smell, an amalgam of high-voltage electricity, electronics, cooling fans, hydraulics, polymer lubricant on hot bearings, missile launch rams, laser, shotgun, and cannon mountings. The scent of a warship, one no environmental management system could ever scrub from the air.

A smell that took her back to her first ride in a M'bakaan ground-attack lander. A smell no marine ever forgot. A smell she never would.

She ran her eyes around *Stiletto*'s bridge.

Command chair in the center. Her chair.

Tactical and ship systems workstations to her left. Two more—threat assessment and weapons—to the right.

Bulkhead-mounted holoscreens. Lots of them.

Damage-control and medibot lockers.

Skinsuit storages.

Helmet racks.

Emergency power and oxygen supply panels.

And the one piece of equipment without which no bridge crew could function: the foodbot. Another Jorgenthaler, fine-tuned to turn out superb espresso coffee in huge quantities, Daniel's bleatings about its cost ignored.

Kal left the bridge, dropped a deck, and walked aft to the cargo bay. Only a day after Hemmings had delivered *Stiletto* to Tharamaran—Kal still seethed at the gateway fees Kolovchenko had charged for the privilege—it was already busy with bots installing power and data cables for the ship's pinchspace nodes.

Maia Okiro waited for her on the ramp.

Kal liked the woman, a no-nonsense engineer who had shown endless patience meeting Daniel's demands, demands which would only make sense to those who knew of the Q-drive.

Demands that were clearly driving her bananas.

Kal put her cheeriest face on. "Hi Maia. How's things?"

Okiro scowled. The woman had stopped pretending she was happy cutting conical wells into *Stiletto*'s pristine armored hull to take the pinchspace node assemblies. "Fine; you'll have the *Stiletto* on schedule. I just wish you'd tell me what the hell you people are up to."

"When the time's right, Maia. You have to be patient until then."

"Like I have any choice . . . Right, I have new. The boss just commed to tell me that Tharmaran's board has approved the contract for Freighter-2; you'll have the formal notice of commencement within the hour. Work starts Monday, and I'm to be the construction manager." Okiro shook her head. "Lucky me. Another ship full of holes."

Suppressing a sigh of relief, Kal just patted the woman on the back.

She had been so sure Tharamaran would see the credit report for the elaborate fake it was. Daniel had told her to stop fussing. Kal had to concede he had a point; the web of lies and misdirection he had spun from almost a hundred adulterated knowledgebases had been a masterpiece of the hacker's art. And she had enjoyed playing the part of a senior vice-president working for a secretive, multi-billion-dollar conglomerate headquartered on Kufrakal-12, an obscure system on the far side of humanspace.

She tried not to think how Tharmaran's board and shareholders were going to feel when they discovered how comprehensively she and Daniel had scammed them.

Not that she cared too much. If they couldn't see that being conned was better than losing their independence to the Empire, they deserved all the pain the Imps would dump on their heads.

"You okay, Kal?" Okiro asked.

"Sorry . . . Yes, I'm fine. We have a lot going on, that's all. My boss will be happy. Genovese Capital has big plans for Freighter-02."

"Care to share them?"

"You know the answer to that question, Maia."

"I should by now. All you ever say to me is wait, be patient."

"And you do patient so well."

Okiro rubbed her eyes. "I'd call you an asshole if you weren't a customer."

Kal laughed. "It's okay, I am an asshole, so feel free. Catch you later."

$$\sim\sim\sim$$

Back in her apartment, Kal fetched herself a coffee and collapsed onto the couch. It had been a brutal few months. Even so, she felt content. For the first time since the asteroid hit Ladaki-6, she had most of her pieces where they needed to be.

Work to install Q-drives into *Stiletto* and *Provider* was on schedule.

Tharmaran was about to start work on Freighter-02.

She had signed off the design for the SAVs; Hemmings would start building them the moment she handed over the 7.9 billion dollars it was asking.

Grivak had turned out to be the perfect foil for Daniel's unruly brilliance.

And Jens Fonseca had recruited the marines and spacers for *Stiletto* and *Provider*.

Which left only one problem unresolved: what she was going to do with her new ships, a problem that was Professor Tarif's to resolve, something Tarif was taking an inordinate amount of time to do.

Maybe this week, Kal thought as she downloaded the latest report from the dropbox she shared with Tarif and started to read.

When she finished, Kal sat back, her body tingling with excitement, her instincts telling her that Tarif had finally found the weakness she had been searching for.

Kal needed to talk with the woman. Pinchcomms would not cut it. Whether she liked it or not, Professor Tarif was going to have to make the nine-day trip to Tharmaran.

—34—

Kal watched the airlock door close behind Tarif. Now that the professor had walked her, step by meticulous step, through her report, she did not have to rely on instinct anymore.

Tarif's conclusions were indisputable.

Five of Kolovchenko's largest shareholders—Tarif called them the Gang of Five—had invested trillions of borrowed dollars to build a criminal empire that now sprawled across most of humanspace. A debt-fueled empire that allowed the Gang of Five to enjoy lifestyles of such shameless extravagance and excess even the Emperor Nero would have been impressed.

Tarif had argued that the Gang of 5's reckless borrowings left them exposed, vulnerable, fragile. Choke off the money they needed to service their debts, and they would go bust, triggering a wave of bankruptcies so enormous Terra's money markets would collapse into panic-driven chaos.

Chaos that spelled the end of the cheap money the Empire depended on to finance its imperial ambitions. Ambitions that were empty boasts without money.

Maybe, Kal thought as threads of unease played with her mind, maybe. No matter how much she wanted it to be true, no matter how confident Tarif was, nothing in life was ever that certain.

One woman with one ship was going to cripple the Empire by bankrupting a criminal gang? That sounded like the delusions of madness.

It might be madness. Tarif's tightly argued logic said it might be possible. Kal knew she would never have a better target than the Gang of Five, a target that offered an astronomical return on her limited assets.

But her time in the marines had taught her that no plan survived contact with the enemy. Why would Professor Tarif's plan be any different?

After much thought, she had realized that she had to have a fallback. And that fallback was Freighter-02: built, tested, operational, the magazines of its 200 SAVs fully loaded with FireSpark missiles.

It was time to bring Tharmaran onboard. They had to do more than just build 02. To do that they needed the right incentive; greed alone would not suffice. It would take fear as well.

And Tharmaran had a lot to be fearful of.

—35—

Okiro had watched the holovid in complete silence, eyes wide, mouth open.

When it ended, she said, "I, uh . . . I don't know what to say, though at least I know why you made us punch all those holes through *Stiletto*'s armor: to take pinchspace nodes, for godssakes! I sure as hell didn't pick that. After being told over and over that jump drives are impossible, it is very hard to believe, which is why I need to see your Q-drive work for myself."

"Well today's the day. Assuming the acceptance trials go to plan, the *Stiletto* will be taking you and Martha Sikong out to Tharmaran-12."

"I can't wait . . . There is one thing I don't understand: Why didn't you sell the Q-drive to Kolovchenko? It would have paid a fortune for this Q-drive of yours, and I mean a fortune as in hundreds of billions of dollars."

"Oh, we were tempted until Daniel and I realized we wouldn't live long enough to spend the money we were paid."

"Ah, yes. Moral rectitude is not exactly Kolovchenko's thing. Tell you what, Kal. I'm glad we're a long way from Terra."

"You won't be, not once the Imps have their own Q-drive."

"Why would they bother?" Okiro said. "They don't need it. As long as the Imps control Kolovchenko and its gateways, they have humanspace by the nuts."

"Our Q-drive isn't a secret anymore; our best guess is the Imps will have a working drive two years from now. If we can't stop them before then, it won't be long before you and everyone else in the Tharmaran system are Imperial citizens, like it or not."

"That will not happen. Humanspace has thousands of systems. The Imps will run short of ships long before they get this far out."

Kal tapped the table for emphasis. "You could not be more wrong. All the Imps need to overrun your system defenses are Q-drive freighters and missile containers. I have checked Tharmaran SysDef's order-of-battle: eight SDVs. They are not going to stop them; they couldn't even stop the *Stiletto*."

Okiro sat back, her arms folded. "You do not know that."

Kal could see the doubt in the woman's eyes. "Listen to me, Maia. This only ends one way. With the Imps picking off every system in humanspace, easy as stripping rotten apples from a tree."

"And you're going to stop them, Kal? One ship, even one as good as *Stiletto*, isn't enough."

"Why do you think you're building Freighter-02?"

"No idea. Why are we building a freighter with a Q-drive?"

"02 is no freighter. It's a warship designed to carry 200 SAVs armed with FireSpark anti-ship missiles."

"And SAVs are what?"

"Space attack vehicles; stripped-down ground-attack landers basically. We've finalized the design with Hemmings."

Okiro sat back. "My, my! You guys are full of surprises. Those SAVs are going to cost, what? 10 billion dollars?"

"7.9 billion to be precise; Hemmings is giving me a volume discount. And another 30 for their ordnance. FireSparks aren't cheap and we need a lot of them."

"That's almost 40 billion! Genovese Capital doesn't have that much money."

Kal's heart thudded. She could not put off telling Okiro that Genovese Capital did not exist, that Tharmaran had been screwed. "You're right, it doesn't . . . Actually, we don't even have enough to finish 02."

Okiro's mouth sagged open. "Sorry . . . What did you say?"

"We can't pay for 02."

"How can that be? Our due diligence confirmed Genovese Capital could cover its contract liabilities."

"I'm sorry, Maia, but your due diligence wasn't diligent enough. Daniel invented Genovese Capital. It doesn't exist; it never did."

"That's not possible! All the knowledgebases confirmed what was in the credit report. Tharmaran's contract people checked."

"Daniel's an exceptional hacker. Your people only saw what he wanted them to see."

"I don't believe this. How much money do you have?"

"About 45 million dollars."

Okiro's tried to speak; for a moment she couldn't. With an effort, she recovered herself. "45 million? Is that all?"

"I'm afraid so."

Okiro's head sagged. "You are so fucked. Tharmaran hates customers who default . . . You understand we'll seize the hull if you can't pay for the contract?"

"I have a better option."

"I really hope so. Our lawyers are horrible people. You guys are so screwed. Goddammit, Kal! What the f—"

"Calm down, Maia. There is a way out of this that works for both of us. All you have to do is listen."

"No, I don't. We trusted you, and you have shafted us. I'm go—'"

Kal's hand smacked the table, hard. "Goddammit! This is important, so just hear me out, please!"

Anger reddened Okiro's face. "I've had enough of you and your bullshit. The next person you'll be talking with will be our general counsel."

"Sorry. Listen, this matters more than anything either of us has ever done. Come on, Maia. Five minutes."

Okiro took a deep breath, then nodded. "Five minutes."

"Thank you . . . Who makes Tharmaran Shipbuilding's big decisions?" Kal asked.

"Martha Sikong, the largest shareholder. She's been our chair for more than 15 years and was CEO for ten before that."

"Is she afraid to take risks?"

"As long as the argument is compelling, not at all."

"Good, because I have a compelling argument for her, but I need you to hold off until I've showed her what the *Stiletto* can do first."

"What? Before I tell her a fake company run by a pair of con-artists doesn't have enough money to finish 02?"

Kal waved around the crew-room, new-ship bright and fresh. "Con-artists? Does this ship look like a con?"

"Maybe it is. All I know for sure is that you and Daniel are as cunning as shithouse rats."

"Not cunning. Desperate. Come on, let me show Sikong that the *Stiletto* is for real. Then you can tell her."

"No," Okiro said. "I work for Martha Sikong, not you. I have to tell her. She's very old-fashioned; she's fired people for less."

"Is that what really matters here? Your job?

"Well, uh . . . Yes, it does. 15 years I've been with Tharmaran, and I've done well. Why would I throw all that away to keep a delinquent customer happy?"

Kal contained a sudden surge of anger-fed frustration with great difficulty. "Let me tell you something, Maia. The Imps are never going to leave Tharmaran alone. If you think then are, then you haven't been paying attention."

"Like I said, we're too far out for the Imps to bother us."

"You sure about that? Sure enough to gamble your life and the lives of everyone you love that the Imps will stay away from Tharmaran, a wealthy system which is home to the best shipbuilder in humanspace? . . . Come on! Don't just stare at me. Are you sure?"

Okiro grimaced. "I'm not sure about anything anymore, Kal. And there are times when the Imps scare the hell out of me."

"They scare the hell out of me all the time, which why I want you to help us stop them. Daniel and I have been alone, right from the day that asteroid destroyed Ladaki-6. If we have to fight the Imps by ourselves, we will. If you don't want to help us, you can tell Sikong she can take Freighter-02. I'm sure she'll make a big fat profit out of it. Not that she'll be able to spend much of it when the Imps kick your front door down because people like you refused to step up."

Kal sat back to let the long silence that followed run on. What else could she say to Okiro? If hours of holovid footage chronicling the Imp's appalling treatment of the systems they had captured, the dead and injured, the ruined cities, and the businesses pillaged by their Terran competitors weren't enough to convince her, there was nothing more she could say.

"You don't mind putting the knife in," Okiro said at last. "You're a hard woman."

"Given what we're faced with, I have to be."

"I must be crazy. Okay, I'll hold off."

"Thank you, Maia. Right, Sikong will be here in an hour. We'll start the trials as soon as she's onboard."

~~~

Kal, Sikong, and Okiro hung on tethers outside *Stiletto*'s airlock, the Tharmaran system's most distant planet visible only as a dark-gray circle cut out of a chaos of stars.

"Get as much data into your neuronics as you can," Kal said. "You should check it against surveys to confirm what you are seeing is real, not a sim. And do a full sweep of the sky; the relative positions of the stars will allow your people to verify our position."

"This is no hoax," Sikong replied, "though we will check anyway."

"I want you guys to be sure."

"Why is it that so important? Why does it matter whether we're convinced?"

"I'll answer that question when we're on our way back, but don't rush. We have time."

"Don't say that. I could stay out here for hours. It's funny; my shipyard builds starships, but these days the only time I'm outside one is in the yard. I'd forgotten how stunning it is out here."

"It makes me feel irrelevant."

"Which we are, I'm afraid," Sikong said. "We should go back. Something tells me we have a lot to talk about."

~~~

Okiro stuck her head out of the crew-room. "Martha's ready for you, Kal."

When Kal walked back in, Sikong sat, slumped against the bulkhead, looking as if she had been sandbagged.

Which she had in a way.

Being told a customer could not pay to complete a billion-dollar contract was bad enough. Kal's dispassionate view of Tharmaran Shipbuilding's future would have knocked Sikong sideways. As the woman had argued that things would not be as bad as forecast, Kal could the uncertainty in her voice, seen the tells betraying her doubts.

Tharmaran Shipbuilding's success would count for nothing when the Imps seized the Tharmaran system. The business would survive; one of the best yards in humanspace was worth the keeping, but the profits would no longer flow to the families who had owned the business from the day it had started. The brutality, corruption, and cronyism that followed the Empire would see to that.

And what was the point of having an empire if you couldn't screw the owners of great businesses like Tharmaran Shipbuilding?

And Martha Sikong knew it. She would have read the reports from the Empire's new colonies. Any that had dared to fight back had been reduced by kinetics strikes to a Golgotha of corpses and ruined cities, those that had surrendered reduced to serfdom by ImpAdmin thugs.

When the woman spoke, her voice was soft, her words deliberate, precise. "I'm sorry, Kal. You cannot beat the Empire before it develops its own Q-drive. Yes, the Empire has its weaknesses; it's too morally degraded not to. I'm sure you've worked out what those weaknesses are and will attack them with *Stiletto*.

"In the end, it is just you and one ship in a fight with an economic and political juggernaut the likes of which humanity has never seen. That is a fight you cannot win."

"That's no argument for sitting back. As Edmund Burke told us: When bad men combine, the good must associate."

"I don't have the time to debate philosophy with you, Captain Kariuki," Sikong said, "so let me tell you where my thinking is up to."

"Please."

"It is in the best long-term interests of my business that the Imps are stopped long before they reach the Tharmaran system, which they will, eventually. But what you have proposed involves substantial financial risk. Building a 300-kiloton orbital does not come cheap. And this design involves much more risk than we are used to. Yes, your Q-drive works in *Stiletto*. Will it work in something as big as Freighter-02? Nobody knows."

"I'm sure Daniel would be happy to debate that with you."

"It's not a matter for debate, Kal. It's a matter of fact: Does it work or not? And you won't know the answer to that question until 02 has finished its acceptance trials."

"True. I'm sorry, I interrupted."

"It's okay. Look, you've given us a lot to think about. Give me a week, and I'll get back to you."

"Let's get you back home then."

~~~

"What do you think?" Daniel asked.

Kal shrugged. "I really rattled Martha Sikong, though that might not be such a good thing. In my experience, fear often pushes people into making bad decisions."

"She didn't argue about what we're offering if we can't finance 02?"

"No."

"I'm not surprised, Kal. Giving Tharmaran exclusive access to our Q-drive technology if we don't raise the money ourselves is the sweetest deal Sikong and Tharmaran Shipbuilding will ever be offered, one worth hundreds of billions of dollars. What's your gut telling you?"

"Sikong will say no."

—36—

Kal waved Okiro into a seat. "You're killing me, Maia. What the hell is going on? It's been ten days and still no decision."

"I know, and I'm sorry about that. Things turned ugly."

Kal's chest tightened. "Ugly? What's that mean?"

"I probably shouldn't be telling you this. Martha Sikong had to call a board meeting to approve her recommendation that Tharmaran underwrites Freighter-02's build. That part was routine, of course. What wasn't routine was when the board overruled her, six votes to five, something that's never happened in the 15 years she's been chair."

Kal's head dropped into her hands. "I don't believe it. We'll all fucked, you do realize that, Maia? You me, Daniel, everybody. All totally fucked."

"Well, we were . . . until the media reports from Anshun-7 arrived yesterday. You've seen them?"

Kal scowled. "We all knew the Imps were bad, but wiping out an entire city and killing over a 148,000 people? That's a war-crime."

"It is, and that's why Martha called an emergency board meeting last night. She put the motion to approve Freighter-02 again, and this time the vote was nine to two in favor."

"What?" Kal barked. "Freighter-02's a go?"

Okiro's smile was ear-to-ear. "Yes, it is. You'll have the contract to sign inside the hour."

Kal slumped back in her seat. "You have no idea how good that sounds . . . When you and Martha left, I was so sure she would turn us down."

Okiro leaned forward. "You want to hear a secret?"

"Of course. Who doesn't love secrets?"

"As we left the *Stiletto* after the jump back from Tharmaran-12, Martha said she was being blackmailed. She wanted to let you default so she could sell Freighter-02 as a mobile habitat. Which wasn't such a bad idea; we'd have made a fortune."

"And what did you say?" Kal asked.

"I asked her how she'd feel when a Terran shipbuilder hijacked the business. Seeing the AIs she has invested billions in stolen. Listening to ImpAdmin apparatchiks tell her she is low-life scum like all the rest of us Rim Rats. Watching what she says every hour of every day. Not knowing whom to trust. Worrying what her kids might do. Watching friends disappear for no reason. Knowing any attempt to fight back will be crushed by orbital kinetics dropped from Imp ships whose captains don't care how many people they kill."

"Woah! I thought I was hard on you guys. You didn't hold back."

"I had to get in Martha's ear before our general counsel did; the older she gets the more she listens to him."

"Let me guess. The two directors who voted against were lawyers?"

Okiro smiled. "I'm surprised you even have to ask."

"The money must have helped. That's a great deal we've given you. Tharmaran stands to make a fortune if we can't find the money to finish 02."

"Of course it will," Okiro said, "not that the lawyers could see that; all they wanted to talk about was our rights under clause this, that, or the other. Though there was always more to it than that. Martha Sikong—and in the end, most of the board—knew they had to do whatever it takes to ensure Tharmaran Shipbuilding survived as a business in an independent system . . . Now, when are you off?"

"As soon as Hemmings delivers *Stiletto*'s lander. Monday, I hope. It's time to start hurting the Empire."

"Which I hope you do, How?"

Kal smiled. "I'll send you the media release."

"You and your secrets . . . How's your crew?"

"The jump to Tharmaran-12 and back came as a bit of a shock to the newbies."

"I'm not surprised. Right, let's get into it. You said you'd seen some instability in the auxiliary . . ."

~~~

Fonseca followed Kal into her stateroom. ""I've been onboard a week, and I still can't get over it. 30 light-years a day in an SDV better than any I have ever seen, and I've seen a lot. I thought the *Wraith* was awesome, but this is . . . whatever's beyond awesome, I guess."

Kal grinned, waving Fonseca to take a seat. The man was right; *Stiletto* was beyond awesome. "Coffee?"

Fonseca returned a brilliant flashing smile that made Kal a bit woozy inside. "Please. Black and strong . . . So, tell me what you want us to do."

"Our first target is the Hardakken Corporation. It's headquartered on Ventas-2, out on the South Rim. It sells slaves to clients in hundreds of systems, 360,000 last year. This year, Hardakken is budgeting sales of 420,000."

Fonseca frowned. "Hmm, that's not what I expected. I had assumed we'd be trying to tear down the Empire. How is trashing a slavery operation going to do that?"

"Hardakken generates billions of dollars for five of Kolovchenko's biggest shareholders. The Gang of Five I call them. They borrowed trillions to set up Hardakken and their other criminal businesses. Gene-tailored psychoactives, extortion, money-laundering, cybercrime, blackmail, assassinations, counterfeit starship and shuttle spares, and all on a huge scale. The Gang of Five uses the money from those operations to service its gigantic debt."

"Ah, right; I think I get it. You want to destabilize Terra's money markets by bankrupting the Gang of Five. Fear and panic and all that."

Kal smiled. "I always knew you weren't just another block-headed grunt."

Fonseca returned the grin. "Thanks for the compliment. So, tell me where does fear and panic gets us."

"Professor Sharif, my finance guru, says they'll make it much harder and more expensive for the Imps to borrow the money they need to finance the Expansion. And the lenders will stop lending altogether if enough of them start to believe the Empire might not be the sure bet they thought it was. If that happens, the Expansion cannot go on . . . Well, that's the plan; I'm not so sure, though. The Empire is not just a powerful idea, it promises to make Terrans even richer and more powerful than they already are."

"It sure is . . . You know something? Things have always gone Terra's way, right from the day Kolovchenko commissioned its first gateway. If we can kick the bastards hard enough to make them realize they are vulnerable just like the rest of us, you might be surprised how quickly their confidence will collapse."

"That's what Sharif thinks, and I hope she's right."

"I reckon she is," Fonseca said with a feral grin. "Now, Hardakken's slave-trading operation on Ventas-2: soft or hard target?"

"Soft. Its security concentrates on keeping slaves inside the wire, not Andimeshki marines out."

"What about the Ventas government? I assume they are all in on it?"

Kal nodded. "Right up to their slimy necks."

"That means we won't just be taking on Hardakken. We will have Ventas's system defense force to deal with. And its ground forces too, obviously."

"All that's in the mission data pack. First walkthrough will be in the crew-room at 20:00."

"I'll be there, captain."

—37—

Kal scanned the faces in front of her. "Any last questions? Comments? Criticisms? Don't hold back. We're not the Andimeshk marines; the Hardakken operation matters."

Laughter filled *Stiletto*'s cargo bay. With an undertone of nerves, Kal thought; not surprising given what she was asking Fonseca's team to do.

A voice called out. "Are you sure the *Pilgrim Abalardi* works?"

"I am, even though it is the crappiest-looking freighter anyone's ever seen, which is the idea, of course. We want Ventas's system defense to think it's not worth worrying about."

"I don't see that being a problem, captain."

More laughter.

"Okay, folks, okay." Kal had to raise her voice to be heard over the cheerful banter. "We still have a lot to do before we jump. Anything else?"

"The mission sim. It's up?"

"It is. You'll take an AI with a copy along with the mission oporder and intel packs with you when you transfer to the *Pilgrim*. Any more questions? . . . Okay, we're done. Thanks, everyone."

Kal waved at Fonseca over as the briefing broke up. "You happy with things?"

"As I can be. Mister Murphy will be there to work us over—he always is—but I think we can pull it off. This is as competent a team as you could hope for. The only thing that bothers me is the pinchspace rendezvous."

"You should have been there when Daniel and I did the first one. We almost lost *Stiletto*, but Daniel tweaked the AI, and it worked fine after that."

Fonseca sighed. "Honestly, captain, I can't believe the shit you guys get up to. You are insane, both of you."

Kal took a deep breath to quell a sudden rush of doubt. "53 of us taking on the entire Terran Empire? Of course we're insane."

"All great enterprises need a pinch of insanity. They wouldn't be great otherwise."

"At least it's not just me, Daniel, and the *Wraith* on our own anymore. That was hard."

"We can do this, captain." Fonseca's voice was firm. "Trust me, we can."

"My brain says we can. My heart keeps telling me we can't."

"Don't underestimate yourself. There are a lot of frightened, angry people out there. When we show that the Empire can be beaten, it won't be just us in the fight. All those billions will be too, and you'll be surprised what they can do."

Kal was touched by the passion and belief in Fonseca's voice. ""I hope you're right. It's still a bizarre thought."

"It sure is. I'll catch you later."

As Fonseca followed the rest of his team out of the cargo bay, Kal found a handy crate to sit on, content to do nothing for the first time in weeks, the weeks of frenetic work it had taken to make all the pieces that made up the Ventas operation fit together.

She watched her new executive officer as he checked the lashings on the mounds of equipment Fonseca's team had brought with them. Liam O'Donnell was a rangy man in his late twenties. Once a command pilot in Andimeshki ground-attack landers, he'd seen combat with the Martens system-defense force in its short and brutal war with the system's Outer Orbital Alliance; he had a cluster of faint white scars across his forearm to prove it. As Fonseca had promised, he knew his stuff. Kal was happy to have him as her second-in-command.

"Captain, Bridge. Comm from *Provider*. Dropped. Nominal. Will be at Point Carbon at 04:55 Standard."

"Roger. Set vector to intercept. And tell Captain Stefanec I'll transfer across as soon as we've rendezvoused."

~~~

Kal took the mug of coffee from Peter Stefanec; a native of a high-g planet, he was squat and muscular with hands like plates. "How was your first pinchspace jump as *Provider*'s captain?" she asked.

"Normally, I can talk the ass off a rock, but right now . . . it's . . . I, uh . . ."

Stefanec's voice trailed off. He waved a hand around *Provider*'s crew-room, new-ship bright. "I've been a professional spacer for over 30 years," he went on when he had recovered his composure. "Flogging through one gateway after another. Paying Kolovchenko's extortionate gateway fees. Putting up with its security teams' arrogance and disrespect. Slipping them a couple of grand not to detain my ship just because they're assholes and they could. And now all that bullshit is over."

Kal raised a cautionary hand. "It'll be a long haul, Peter. And there are no guarantees we'll win. The Empire's not going to be a pushover."

"It must be doable. You're here, Captain Kariuki, because you think it is, and that's enough for me."

Kal raised her mug. "Here's to the Empire's defeat."

Stefanec lifted his. "The Empire's defeat."

"Any issues with *Provider*?"

"None. Tharmaran Shipbuilding are great outfit, and I trust Maia Okiro. I took delivery of a yacht from her six years ago. She is one of the best construction managers I've ever met."

"She and Tharmaran did us proud, for sure. Right, Peter, we'll see you in Ventas nearspace to remass."

"We'll be waiting for you."

~~~

"Comm from the *Pilgrim Abalardi*," ShipCon said.

Piyas Sharma's avatar filled the screen. She had not been too happy when Kal had made her the *Pilgrim*'s captain, quick to point out she had signed up to be the command pilot of *Stiletto*'s assault lander, not to take charge of a geriatric freighter.

She was an experienced marine. Kal knew she would do the job and do it well.

"SITREP," Sharma said. "We've received transit clearance from Taunggyi gateway security and now on vector for gateway for transit to Ventas-2. Jump time 22:27 Standard. *Pilgrim Abalardi*, out."

"I can't believe what we're about to do." Fonseca seemed anxious.

Kal knew how he felt. It had been a long wait for Kolovchenko gateway security to clear the *Pilgrim* for transit to Ventas-2. "Looks like we are. Okay, ShipCon. Let's go."

"ShipCon, roger. All stations, standby pinchspace transition."

—38—

Stiletto hung at the center of an extravagant display of stars, billions of brilliant pinpricks of light patched into darkness by clouds of interstellar dust. As always, Kal marveled at the profligate beauty of it all, wondering how the ancients could have talked of the emptiness of space.

She forced her attention back to her command plot, one eye on the timer counting down the seconds before the *Pilgrim Abalardi* reached the point in pinchspace where it would meet up with the *Stiletto*, the other on the datafeed from the gravitonic sensors as they sampled pinchspace looking for the spacetime distortion the *Pilgrim*'s transit created, a virtual bow-wave detectable one second and three billion kilometers ahead of the ship.

Any moment now, she thought as the counter dropped through a minute.

"Command, Tactical," Atlassian said; Kal was glad the man had agreed to come along again. She like the solid, no-nonsense competence he'd displayed during the Ferruci operation. "Standby intercept."

The counter reached zero. The *Stiletto* jumped, its departure from normalspace timed to the nanosecond.

"ShipCon, roger," the AI replied. "Q-drive AI confirms in gateway tunnel . . . vector stabilizing . . ."

Kal stopped breathing as the tension wrung her stomach into a tangle of knots; this was only the third time a ship had rendezvoused with another inside a gateway tunnel.

". . . vector is nominal . . . *Pilgrim* now at Red-01, 850 meters, closing."

And Kal allowed herself to breathe again, marveling at the sight of the *Pilgrim Abalardi* as it solidified out of the blinding white fog of pinchspace and slid down *Stiletto*'s port side.

"Command, ShipCon. *Stiletto* now is in station, vector locked . . . *Pilgrim* deploying transfer tube . . . tube latched and nominal. Commencing transfer now."

Kal commed Fonseca. "There you are, Jens. You can believe it now."

"No, captain. I still don't think I can. See you when we get to Ventas-2."

As Fonseca and his marines pulled themselves into the tube, taking with them plasfiber boxes of equipment, Kal commed Sharma. "All set?"

Sharma nodded. "We are, captain. You know, when you told me what you wanted me to do, I thought you were batshit crazy, but here we are. I still can't get my head around it."

"Ventas won't know what's hit them. Any problems with gateway security?"

"Nothing my cashcard couldn't handle, though it did take a beating. And they didn't think much of us or the *Pilgrim*. One asked why we were wasting our time looking for minerals in the Ventas system; she said it had been mined out long since. I told her my boss hadn't made his money listening to people like her."

"Hassling freighter crews is what Kolovchenko does best. There are no changes, so we'll be waiting for you as planned. And if system security tries to shake you down, don't argue. Just pay up."

"Will do."

Kal cut the comm. "How much longer?" she asked O'Donnell.

"The last of the equipment's going across now," the XO said. "We'll be ready to drop in five. ETA Ventas 3 hours 25."

~~~

"Command, Combat. Ventas in-gateway has gone active. Traffic control confirms the imminent arrival of the *Pilgrim Abalardi*."

Kal clenched her fists, doing her best to ignore a stomach now in open revolt. Kidnapping Amos Ferruci had been stressful; this was ten times worse. Unlike the *Magellan*, Ventas SysDef's SDVs could shoot back.

Kal patched her neuronics into the datafeed from drone Recon-6. She chuckled at the sight of the battered ship as it popped from the gateway and into normalspace. It really was a wreck.

"Ventas-2 Nearspace Control, this is the *Pilgrim Abalardi*, inbound from Taunggyi. Request clearance direct to Orbital Transfer Station Alpha. I have a problem with my main-engine tokomaks. We need to dock so my engineers can open them up to take a look."

"Standby . . . Okay, *Pilgrim*, you are cleared for vector direct to OTS-Alpha. SysSec will clear you on arrival. Ventas NearCon, out."

"How long before they dock?" Kal asked.

"2 hours 10."

Yet another wait. The M'bakaa marines had taught Kal how to cope with delays, but it wasn't easy. Not when so much rested on her shoulders.

~~~

The comm jolted Kal upright.

It was Fonseca. "Sorry we took so long, captain. The SysSec guys were in no hurry to give us our entry clearance. They wanted to run a full manifest check against our transit certificate. Sharma's cashcard persuaded them that wasn't necessary. Which was the whole point, I guess."

"I'm sure it was. Is Artie Shaw happy with Team 5?"

Fonseca nodded. "It's always hard to tell with cybergeeks, but yes, I think so. They are working on OTS-A's security system. Once they've broken in, they'll dummy up clearances for the team and their gear so we can transfer dirtside. We won't rush things, though. Having a lot of marines wandering around only makes people ask questions."

"No problem; we have time. What about your fake Ventasi IDs?"

"Artie said adding everyone to Ventas's citizenship knowledgebase was the easiest hack he's ever done, probably because nobody in their right mind would want to be a Ventasi . . . Are we going to have any problems with SysDef?"

"Nothing the *Stiletto* can't handle," Kal replied. "The threat AI has identified all seven of their Mirkis-class system defense force vessels."

"What's their status?"

Kal checked the threat plot. "Five are in Clarke orbit. One is boosting out-system on vector for one of Ventas-2's deepspace habitats; we won't see it again any time soon. The seventh is alongside SysDef's orbital support station; holovid from the recon drones show its main-engine tokomaks have been opened up for heavy maintenance."

"Anything else?"

"Apart from confirmed IDs for all Ventas's orbital surveillance arrays, commsats, and gateway pinchcomm nodes, no."

"Doesn't sound like SysDef's ships are going to give us any grief."

"Not once they see our FireSpark missiles heading their way. The biggest threat they've faced was some lunatic in a yacht who wanted to ram an orbital, and that was years ago."

"They must be bored shitless; no wonder SysDef's morale's not the best. Hold on a sec, captain. It's Artie Shaw . . . Okay, Team 5 are into OTS-A's security system; we now have our transfer clearances."

"That was quick."

"You asked for the best, and the best is what you got."

"Given how much I'm paying, I'd hope so," Kal muttered.

"Trust me, captain, you did. Team 1 will start heading dirtside soon. As soon as they have organized vehicles and set up our forward operating base, the rest of us will follow."

"Does Shaw have any feel for Hardakken's systems yet? I'm not risking your team until he's broken in."

"Team 5's not started on them yet, so no. Shaw says they won't be as easy a target as OTS-A. Criminals are too paranoid to let hackers fiddle with their stuff."

—39—

"Ventas-2 Nearspace Control, freighter *Pilgrim Abalardi*, over."

"*Pilgrim Abalardi*, NearCon. Go ahead."

"OTS-Alpha has cleared us to depart. Request vector for Ventas-9."

"NearCon, roger. Standby . . . You are cleared on vector direct to Ventas-9."

"Vector direct Ventas-9, roger."

"Best of luck from everyone here at Ventas NearCon. We think you'll need it. NearCon, out."

"Smartass," Sharma said. "All stations, SITREP. Undocking now. ETA 05:45 Standard at Point Breaker for the RV with *Stiletto*. Captain, out."

~~~

Kal studied the *Pilgrim Abalardi* as it closed in. The freighter was a disgrace, its hull scarred by scratches and scrapes, the marks of carelessness and neglect, not those of an honest, hard-working ship.

Kal turned to her XO. "Are you sure that thing is spaceworthy?"

Liam O'Donnell grinned. "You did tell Sharma to make it look like a wreck."

"I think she's taken her instructions a bit too literally. Still, the Ventasi seem convinced, which is all that matters."

"Captain, ShipCon. Vector matched with the *Pilgrim*. Lander nominal for transfer."

Kal waved O'Donnell over. "You have the ship, Liam. I'm going aft."

"I have the ship, captain."

Kal met Sharma as she left the airlock. "Welcome back. Jens said SysSec were a bit difficult."

"Just doing what they do best: being greedy assholes. They threatened to bring in a full rummaging crew to tear the ship part unless I paid them 20 k, which was bullshit, of course. In the end we settled for half that."

"Greedy assholes is right . . . Oh, before I forget. I hear you've named the lander."

"I have," Sharma said. "Sorry, I should have told you."

"No problem. Why *'Don't Talk'*?"

"My dad was in attack landers. When I was very young, he asked me to think up a name for his first command. I was being grumpy and said, 'Don't talk, don't talk', so that is what he went with, and I have too."

Kal smiled her approval.

"My dad liked the fact it meant something," Sharma continued. "He thought pilots who gave their landers names like *'Deathbringer'*, *'Thunderfire'*, and *'Hammerfall'* were juvenile losers."

"I've seen plenty of them in my time. Now, anything else?"

"I don't think so, captain."

"Good luck then."

Leaving Sharma to move *Don't Talk* across to the *Pilgrim*, Kal headed off to see how the transfer of driver-mass was going. Well, she hoped. *Stiletto* might need every kilo it could take from the *Pilgrim Abalardi*.

Two hours later, the ships parted, *Stiletto* to start the intricate process of working its way in-system without being spotted, the *Pilgrim Abalardi* to throw sand in the eyes of the Ventasi.

~~~

"Ventas-2 Nearspace Control, *Pilgrim Abalardi*. Pan, pan, pan."

Kal thought the tremor in Sharma's voice a neat touch.

"NearCon, *Pilgrim Abalardi*. What's your emergency?"

"Uncontrolled instability on Tokomak-Bravo. Request clearance to return to OTS-Alpha so we can open it up and take a look."

"NearCon, understood. Standby . . . You are cleared on vector direct to OTS- Alpha."

"Pilgrim Abalardi, roger."

"You seem to be having a lot of problems, *Pilgrim*. Do you require any other assistance?"

"Negative, NearCon. We have everything under control."

"We're pretty sure you don't, *Pilgrim*, so best of luck. We think you'll need it."

"You cheeky fucker," Sharma shot back. "The *Pilgrim*'s a great ship."

"Be advised, *Pilgrim*, the use of obscene language on this circuit is prohibited by Ventas law. We have issued you with a Section 458 citation; failure to comply with its terms will result in the impoundment of your ship. Ventas NearCon, out."

—40—

The comm from Fonseca cut through the soft buzz of the bridge crew. "SITREP, captain. Team 5 has broken into Hardakken's systems. They're going through the security knowledgebases now. We'll be ready to go when you are."

Finally, thought Kal. As the days had drifted past, she'd started to think Artie Shaw's cybergeeks might have met a system even they could not defeat. "Roger that. How come a bunch of slave traders have such tight security?"

"Unlike Ventas SysDef, they appreciate the value of their information. Shaw says there'll be some incendiary stuff in their customer knowledgebases."

"I'd be getting nervous if I was one of Hardakken's customers. Give Team 5 a well-done from me, Jens. Wait one . . . Tactical, what are my options for bringing the *Stiletto* in-system without Ventas SysDef seeing me?"

"Standby," Atlassian said, "Okay, we have an inbound helium drone we can intercept 21 million klicks out from Ventas-2. SysDef won't see us that far out. That would give us a transit time to the strike-release datum of 138 hours."

"Timing for the ground assault?"

"Standby . . . Strike-1 away 04:05 Ventas Standard Time, eight days from today. *Don't Talk* will launch from Point Mutton ten minutes after that. That will give Boxcar a go-time of 05:00 local. But the *Pilgrim* will need to come in pretty hot to meet that schedule."

"NearCon will get upset."

"It will have other things to worry about by the time the *Pilgrim* enters the Restricted Maneuvering Zone."

"I'd say so . . . Jens, I'm back. How does a go-time of 05:00 Ventas Standard eight days out sound to you?"

"Wait . . . Okay, that works for us."

"Good. You'll have the updated oporder confirming the details within the hour."

"Roger that."

Kal cut the comm. She did not need sweat trickling down her spine to remind her things were about to get nasty. Nor had she forgotten that combat operations had a bad habit of turning to shit.

Even a bunch of Rim Rats as dopey as the Ventasi might have some surprises tucked away.

—41—

Time had erased much of what the M'bakaan marines had taught Kal, but she had never forgotten one instructor's offhand remark: It was easier, he had said, to hide a beach ball on the floor of an empty warehouse than it was to hide a ship in space.

Which was why she had put *Stiletto* up the ass of the *KryoLifter-636*, a helium tanker inbound from Ventas-6, its aft-facing holocams burned out by one of Kal's combat drones. The tanker was so large that Ventas's surveillance network would only see the *Stiletto* when it broke cover.

If her FireSparks did their job, that would be too late for Ventas SysDef to stop the attack on Hardakken.

With so much depending on surprise, the ride in had shredded Kal's nerves. As always when under pressure, she tended to say too much; she'd forced herself not to talk for sake of talking, not to badger her bridge crew for unnecessary updates, and let them do theirs while she did hers.

Which was to scan bridge holoscreens busy with data streaming in from the recon drones she had sent ahead into Ventas nearspace, checking for any sign Ventas's system-defense force might be expecting an attack.

So far there had been none.

Kal wanted the wait over. With hours to run before *Stiletto* reached the strike-release datum, there was still time for an outbound ship to ask why a helium tanker had a vessel up its butt.

~~~

Fonseca wiped sweat from his face. Night or day, made no difference. It was always hot, the humidity plastering his combat overalls to his body.

Team 1 had set up the forward operating base in a warehouse. It was one of a cluster of concrete boxes built as a technology park on Highway-46, all long abandoned. To the east, the highway crossed the deep, slab-sided canyon cut by the Jalan River and then ran direct to the orange loom on the horizon that marked to position of Ventas-2's capital, Fransass City, its marine base on the city's southern outskirts. Three klicks to the west of Fonseca's FOB, the highway ran past what Hardakken's people called the V-PAC: the Ventas Product Processing Center.

Fonseca's lip curled in utter contempt. Humans were not products.

A single razor-wire fence encompassed the V-PAC's administrative and security buildings. The latter was Fonseca's principal concern; it housed the complex's quick-response force. 50-strong, the QRF was there to suppress any problems the security bots inside the slave compounds could not.

According to the V-PAC's security knowledgebase, the QRF had never been called out, the reason why Fonseca had not been surprised to find it sloppy, ill-disciplined, and bored. Not that he was taking them for granted. Even in the hands of incompetents, 50 guns were still a lot of guns.

A second compound held the Induction and Training Center, a massive, windowless box of a building, 20 stories high and 300 meters square. The ITC was where Hardakken groomed its slaves for sale, where it conditioned them to accept their fate, where it gave them the skills and demeanor Hardakken's customers demanded, cage-fighters and courtesans of all sexes commanding the highest prices, garden slaves the lowest.

The slave-holding pens sprawled away beyond the ITC. Managed by AIs directing hordes of domestic and security bots, they held the tens of thousands of humans waiting to be shipped to for their new owners, each pen a small town with everything needed to keep its inhabitants washed, dressed, fed, and healthy.

At the lowest possible cost.

Even though the complex was three kilometers away, there were times when Fonseca was sure he could smell the sour taint of fear coming from those doomed souls.

~~~

"Command, Lander-1," Sharma commed from *Don't Talk*'s flight-deck. "SITREP. ShipCon has command of the *Pilgrim*. Lander-1 is nominal and at Alert-1 to launch."

"Command, roger," Kal said. "Your crew okay?"

"Equal parts excited and anxious; you know how it is."

"I certainly do. Command, out."

Kal was happy she wasn't riding in *Don't Talk*. It had been years since her last combat drop in an attack lander, an experience she had no desire to relive. Being strapped inside a lightly armored box plummeting to earth while people with surface-to-air missiles tried to destroy you was a bowel-wrenching business.

Kal checked the mission timer. *Stiletto* carried Combat, an AI tasked with managing engagements too fast-moving and complex for human brains to manage. It was time it took over. "Tactical, Command. Assign TACON to Combat AI."

"Standby . . . Combat AI has TACON."

The mission timer reached zero.

"Boxcar, Combat," the AI said. "Execute Granite-Red."

"Combat, Boxcar," Fonseca replied, "Executing Granite-Red . . . Malware now activated . . . All Ventas's SysDef AIs now off-line."

"Combat, roger."

"All stations, captain. Visors down, final suit checks, standby breakaway . . . Systems, are we set?"

"Affirmative," Yasmin Kashani, *Stiletto*'s chief engineer, called out from the workstation where she monitored the SDV's systems. "Hull temperature stable at -170° Celsius. Coolant remaining 15%. Heat pumps at emergency power. Main engines at immediate notice."

Stiletto was ready.

"Command, Combat. Executing Granite-Blue. Standby breakaway . . . Now!"

Thrusters eased *Stiletto* away from the *KryoLifter-636*. Main engines came to full power, the ship's lasers obliterating the helium drone's surviving hull-mounted holocams the instant they had a clear shot.

Armored hatches on *Stiletto*'s flanks swung open. Launchers dumped FireSpark missiles and decoys, their engines spewing flame as they drove for their targets in orbit around Ventas-2.

"Command, Combat. Strike-1 away."

Kal's eyes never left the command plot, a massive holoscreen mounted directly in front of her seat. It was thick with the blue lines tracking the FireSpark ASMs and decoys of Strike-1.

The combat AI commed Fonseca. "Boxcar, Combat. *Stiletto* inbound. Strike-1 nominal."

"Boxcar, roger."

Kal sat back to watch the operation unfold. Until things turned to shit, it was the combat AI's job to manage the frenetic chaos of space-warfare. A task it performed as well as it mishandled the unexpected, a problem that plagued every AI ever built, which was why dealing with Combat's mistakes was the job of the captain and her bridge crew.

With the missiles only minutes from impact, the crews of the five hapless SDVs in orbit around Ventas-2 finally worked out how bad their lives were about to get, a realization marked by the growing cloud of orange strobes that marked the fleeing lifepods, the SDVs' defense left to their onboard combat AIs.

A defense that barely troubled Strike-1.

Stiletto's missiles hit. Their two-stage warheads first tore open the SDVs' hulls, then blasted lethal penetrators of molten metal into the ships. Primary tokomaks lost containment in a blinding flash of energy that transformed the ships into hot plasma expanding into space, cooling fast.

Strike-1 was not done. Across Ventas nearspace, missiles destroyed surveillance arrays, commsats, and gateway pinchcomms modules. More missiles targeted SysDef's orbital support station; set to explode short, their warheads fired blizzards of shrapnel at the station, scouring its hull clean of holocams before a pair of FireSparks destroyed the last SDV in Ventas nearspace.

By now, Kal's attack had tipped Ventas nearspace into utter chaos, ships and shuttles scattering in all directions, NearCon's frantic attempts to keep control overwhelmed by a storm of panicked cries for help.

And not once did an overwhelmed NearCon react to the blatant disregard the *Pilgrim Abalardi* was showing for the Restricted Maneuvering Zone's speed limits.

"Command, Combat. Strike-1. All targets killed. *Pilgrim* approaching Point Mutton . . . Lander-1, Combat. Execute Granite-Yellow."

"Granite-Yellow. Launching. Lander-1, out."

Seconds later, *Don't Talk* erupted from the *Pilgrim*'s cargo bay under full power, incandescent efflux from its main engines flaying the battered ship.

Kal patched her neuronics into the 'vid feed from the recon drone shadowing the *Pilgrim*, whose main engines were at emergency power driving the freighter on vector direct for Fransass City. Kal hated the thought of wasting a perfectly serviceable ship, but she wanted every Ventasi watching the *Pilgrim* as it burned up on reentry, not paying any attention to a hostile ground-attack lander heading dirtside.

The *Pilgrim* wasn't the biggest freighter around, but Kal was hoping some of its heavy machinery might survive long enough to reach the ground; downtown Fransass City would be nice. And then there were the tokomaks; with the main engines redlining, they would release as much energy as small tactical nukes when the incandescent heat of reentry burned through their containment armor.

Kal wanted things to get ugly for the citizens of Fransass City. Every one of them would know about Hardakken. They deserved to suffer as the slaves had suffered.

"Combat, Lander-1," Sharma said. "Tango-1 in 3-0 mike."

"Tango-1, 3-0 mike, Combat, roger. Break . . . Boxcar, you copy?"

"Boxcar copies."

"All stations, Command. SITREP. *Don't Talk* is heading dirtside for Tango-1, the airbase at Cape Yoshana. It'll be there in 30 minutes. Once Yoshana has been destroyed, Boxcar will start the assault on the Hardakken complex. Command, out."

~~~

Fonseca stared up into the night sky over Fransass City, his head back, mouth open in awe.

High above him, the *Pilgrim* had reentered Ventas's atmosphere, a 20,000 tonne mass of metal plunging to earth, fast disintegrating as huge overpressure clawed its hull apart, spalling fragments into lines of white-gold fire.

Lines consumed by an enormous explosion of pure energy, a ball of incandescent light transformed in milliseconds into roiling, flame-shot cloud.

"Waaah," one of Fonseca's marines hissed. "The captain doesn't fuck around."

Fonseca started as the shock wave smacked the warehouse. "No, she does not . . . Command, Boxcar. That was impressive."

"But not much use," Kal replied. "The 'toks lost containment at 22,000 meters, too high to inflict much blast damage to the city. And most of the debris fell outside Fransass City, away from the marine base. That means we can expect the Ventasi can respond."

"Hopefully not. It was worth a shot though. Boxcar out."

~~~

"Weapons free," Sharma called out to her tactical officer.

"Weapons free. Targets designated."

The sprawling Cape Yoshana airbase lay right ahead. The security towers stayed quiet, not that Sharma cared about them. Their quadruple laser mounts were designed to hack thin-skinned aircraft out of the air. They would not trouble *Don't Talk*'s armor.

Not that she was going to leave them alone.

"Engaging," TACCO said as the lander's lasers slashed pulses of pure energy into the towers, reducing them to burning fragments an instant before *Don't Talk* howled across the wire under full power, its 20-mm cannon flicker-stitching red-yellow streams of hypervelocity shells into the line of neatly parked ground-attack aircraft.

Aircraft which had no chance of survival. Designed for low-intensity ground-support operations, they did not have the armor to save themselves from the destruction *Don't Talk*'s cannon was pouring into them.

Leaving Cape Yoshana's inventory of ground-attack aircraft blazing wrecks, the lander cleared the airbase, and reversed course to put the base dead ahead, the turn so tight the wing-overload alarms bleated in protest. Levelling out, Sharma chopped the main engines back to idle and lifted the nose. The lander decelerated hard as belly thrusters erupted into full power, twin pillars of blazing driver-mass taking the lander's weight from fast-retracting wings.

"50 knots," Sharma called out, rotating the nose down, the lander now balanced on twin pillars of fire thundering from the belly thrusters as it crossed the wire again, closing on a sprawl of defenseless buildings disgorging figures running hard from the cataclysm breaking over their heads.

"Engaging," TACCO said.

Don't Talk's cannon shredded buildings, hangars, power-substations, and mass-driver storages, leaving its lasers to deal with the soft targets: maintenance and transport bots, comms towers, and satcomm dishes.

A brutal display of raw power marked by columns of ugly gray-black smoke climbing into the pre-dawn sky.

"Unless you can see something we've missed, skipper, I'd say that's all targets destroyed."

"Roger that," Sharma said. "Let's get out of here."

The main engines to full power, the nose lifted putting the lander into a near-vertical climb.

"Boxcar, Lander-1. Tango-1 killed. Anchored Point Quebec, holding 0-2-0. Playtime 8-0 mike."

~~~

Fonseca had much enjoyed watching *Don't Talk* trash the Cape Yoshana base, the clinical competence of Sharma's brutal attack deeply satisfying. He felt even better now that the lander was orbiting overhead at 2,000 meters, on call if the Ventasi responded.

He would need its firepower if they did.

The clock was running though. Playtime 8-0, Sharma had reported: 80 minutes to complete the operation before lack of driver-mass would force *Don't Talk* to abort-to-orbit and return to *Stiletto* to remass.

"5, Boxcar," Fonseca commed. "Execute Granite-Brown."

"Granite-Brown, 5, roger," Artie Shae responded. "Standby . . . Malware activated . . . Tango-2 is now black. Bugs away."

The satisfaction in his voice was obvious. The cybergeeks of Team 5 had just trashed the V-PAC's commslinks and datanets; Hardakken's QRF would not be calling anyone for help.

Fonseca checked the holovid feed from the swarm of microdrones Team 5 had put into the air over the V-PAC; bugs, the marines called them for their restless jittering. Nothing had changed; the complex slumbered on, its QRF still asleep most likely, he thought.

It was time.

"Alpha-9, Boxcar. Execute Granite-Green."

An untidy assortment of battered vans accelerated out of the warehouse. The five teams tasked to attack the VPCC were on their way.

Positioned on low scrub-covered hillock overlooking the floodlit gate into the admin compound, Fonseca's two snipers started work. A head shot dropped the first guard, leaving his partner gaping in disbelief until the second shot felled her too.

The snipers turned their laser rifles on the gatehouse, shredding it just in case there was anyone inside. That job done, they started on their next targets: the securitybots patrolling outside the wire.

Thin-skinned, they exploded one by one as their microtoks lost containment.

"Boxcar, Sierra. All targets killed. Moving to Point Ballot now."

"Boxcar, roger," Fonseca replied, relieved that the snipers, along, isolated, and with no backup close to hand, were on their way to rejoin to attack force.

The van carrying the first assault team arrived. It speared through the gate and skidded to a halt outside the QRF building. As it disgorged Team 1, the van with Team 2 slid to a stop alongside.

Fonseca patched his neuronics into one of Team 1's helmetcams just as the marine fired a building-buster missile into the two-story concrete box housing the QRF. The warhead's first stage blew a hole through the wall; a millisecond later, the second stage exploded inside, the marine flinching back as the blast blew out the windows, the air shredded by fragments of glass and concrete.

She'll need new combat armor, Fonseca thought.

As dust eddied, a figure fired two grenades into the entrance. A sharp *crack-crack.* Smoke billowed out of the doorway as Team 1 poured inside, hurdling the body of some fool too brave to run away.

Team 2 had split left and right to cover the building's emergency exits, their assault rifles stammering into methodical, disciplined fire that cut down figure after figure fleeing Team 1's frontal attack.

It was slaughter, the attack a rolling wave of gunfire and fragmentation grenades. Fast. Focused. Ferocious. All over in minutes.

"Boxcar, 1. Security building clear. QRF killed."

"Boxcar, roger."

Team 3's leader commed Fonseca. "Boxcar, 3. Admin building clear. 5 is stripping datastores. 4 is sweeping compound for any hostiles."

"Boxcar, roger. Break . . . Lander-1, playtime."

"Playtime 6-2 mike," Sharma said.

Fonseca swore. 18 minutes burned already; the operation was running slow. He buried the urge to tell Artie Shaw and Team 5 to hurry.

He patched his neuronics into the holocam feeds from the bugs covering Highway 46. There was still no sign of any response from the Fransass City marine base.

~~~

"Boxcar, 5," Shaw commed. "All datastores recovered. 3, 4, 5 withdrawing now."

With the operation now six minutes behind schedule, Fonseca's anxiety levels were climbing. Yes, the Ventasi were incompetent and corrupt, but even they had to be mobilizing by now.

It was time to go.

"Roger that, 5. Break . . . Alpha-9, Boxcar. Scram LZ Alpha. Say again, scram LZ Alpha. Acknowledge."

In turn, the five team leaders acknowledged the order to withdraw to landing zone Alpha. Fonseca commed Sharma. "Lander-1, Boxcar. All teams ready for extraction from LZ Alpha in 1-5 mike. Acknowledge."

"LZ Alpha, 1-5 mike, extract all teams. Acknowledged. Playtime now 3-4 mike. Lander-1, out."

Fonseca frowned. *Don't Talk*'s remaining time-on-task was getting short. "Combat, Boxcar. Confirm you are go for kinetics strike on the V-PAC."

"Affirmative," *Stiletto*'s AI replied.

"Boxcar, Command," Kal said. "Advisory. Hostiles now inbound from the Fransass City marine base. They will be turning onto

Highway 46 in five. And they're bringing two Hellcat mobile surface-to-air batteries with them."

"Fuck," Fonseca muttered under his breath. "Boxcar, roger. ETA?"

"30 minutes at the Jalan River bridge, but LZ Alpha will be inside the Hellcat's engagement zone in 15. I won't risk *Don't* Talk, so recommend extraction from LZ Bravo."

"Boxcar, roger. Standby . . . Concur. Extraction now LZ Bravo . . . Break. Lander-1, Boxcar. You copy?'

"Lander-1 copies. Extraction LZ Bravo."

"Alpha-9, Boxcar. Hostiles supported by mobile SAMs are inbound from Fransass City along Highway 46. LZ Alpha compromised. Scram LZ Bravo. Scram LZ Bravo. Acknowledge."

Once again, the five teams acknowledged, turning away to flee from the approaching Ventasi.

"Command, Boxcar," Fonseca said. "We have a problem. If the Ventasi move fast, LZ Bravo will be in range of those Hellcats before we can extract. Request you retask your kinetics strike to interdict. Otherwise we might not make it out."

"Command, Lander-1," Sharma cut in. "We copied Boxcar's previous. As long as the Hellcats are moving, we're safe. If we stay nap-of-the-earth, we can be on top of them before they have time to set up, though there will still be a significant MANPAD activity."

"Command, Lander-1," Kal said. "Noted. Standby."

Much as he wanted *Stiletto*'s kinetics to break up the Ventasi counterattack, Fonseca hated the idea of leaving the V-PAC intact. He was glad he wasn't making the call. He could imagine the tension on *Stiletto*'s bridge as Kal wrestled with the 'either way you're screwed' problem circumstances had dumped on her.

Finally, Kal responded. "Boxcar, Command. *Stiletto* will deal with the V-PAC; we haven't come all this way to leave it intact . . . Break. Lander-1, Command. Standby retasking."

Stiletto's combat AI did not take long. "Lander-1, Combat. Hellcats inbound designated targets Tango-6 and 7. Mission datapack sent. Real-time target data on 66-Bravo. Acknowledge."

"Lander-1, acknowledged. time-to-targets: 7 minutes 15. Lander-1, out."

~~~

"Okay, folks," Fonseca said to his command team. "We're done. Let's get the hell—"

Fonseca's exec cut him off. "Boss! We have a bus inbound."

"Where did that come from?"

"It was parked up overnight five klicks short of the bridge. Assessed no threat."

"Yang, Ricardo, go stop that bus."

Fonseca sent a bug to take a look. As it closed in, he wondered why the vehicle had wire mesh over its windows. And were those people inside?

It was. Small people.

He ran outside as the two marines brought the bus to a brake-screeching stop. The door opened. A man in gray overalls with Hardakken embroidered in red thread on his left breast stepped out, the machine pistol in his hands already swinging up. He was too slow, a double tap from Ricardo sending him staggering back to crumple into a bloody heap on ground, eyes wide, unseeing.

Ricardo pulled the gun away and patting the corpse down for any hidden weapons. "Clear!"

Fonseca ran over and climbed inside the bus. The rank, raw stench of neglected humanity brought him to a stop, retching. He stared through thick wire mesh at the bodies packed tight on long benches running front to back. "Oh, dear god . . . Yang! Get your ass in here!"

The marine's face knotted in disgust. "What the hell do we do now, boss?'

"Talk with Artie. He'll tell you how to get this thing moving."

"Roger that. Where to?"

"LZ Bravo. Where else?"

~~~

Flying low, *Don't Talk* followed the Jalan River, its wingtips barely clear of the rock walls of the gorge, walls that over-topped the lander by 20 meters.

Sharma's faith in the AI that flew the lander was absolute. She still cringed as the lander raced headlong for a cliff before rolling hard to follow the river around to the right. She glanced over at her tactical operator. Behind her visor, the woman's face was drawn tight, hands locked on armrests.

She knew how her tactical operator felt. This was not like shooting up a dozy airbase. The Ventasi marines were expecting trouble, and they'd had more than enough time to get their shit together.

Don't Talk was heading into a shitstorm of missiles and cannon fire.

"10 klicks," TACCO said. "Targets Tango-6, Tango-7 designated."

Sharma closed her eyes for an instant as the lander hauled itself around yet another insanely tight bend in the river. She felt she could reach out and touch the cliff blurring past. "Weapons free."

"Boxcar, Lander-1. 8 klicks."

"Roger. All teams at LZ Bravo."

"Standby pop-up," TACCO said, "Now!"

Don't Talk reared up into a screaming climb out of the gorge, rolling hard to level out over the highway, punching out decoys and flares as it headed for the advancing Ventasi column, its ground-attack missiles dropping clear, whiting out the lander's forward holocams as their engines ignited.

"Banjos away," TACCO called out.

Don't Talk screamed down Highway 46, its hull racketing as its cannon and lasers let rip, chopping lines of death into the convoy of vehicles heading for the V-PAC, the air flaring white as cannon shells tore open microtokomaks.

Sharma only had eyes for the Hellcat surface-to-air missile batteries.

Which vanished, enveloped in violent balls of flame.

"Tango-6, Tango-7 killed," TACCO said. "Scram now!"

Don't Talk was already banking away, main engines at emergency power, fleeing the barrage of fire coming from the Ventasi marines. Ignoring the wandering lines of cannon and small arms fire, *Don't Talk*'s defensive lasers focused instead on the silver-white streaks of incoming MANPADs, slashing them one by one out of the air.

Until, finally, *Don't Talk* was clear, racing away at 500 knots barely 10 meters above the ground, a maelstrom of dust and dirt in its wake.

"Boxcar, Lander-1. Tango-6, Tango-7 killed. Clearing 46 to the north. Command, you copy?"

"Command copies. Nice job, Lander-1."

"Thanks. Break . . . Boxcar, Lander-1. LZ Bravo 5 mike. Advise approach vector and datum."

"Approach 2-2-0 on datum beacon Kilo-6-5," Fonseca answered.

"2-2-0 on Kilo-6-5, roger."

"Lander-1, Boxcar. One more thing. We have a small logistics problem."

"Problem? What sort of problem?"

"We've liberated 45 slaves. We'd like to bring them with us."

"Hold on, Boxcar. Did you say 45 slaves?"

"I did. They're all kids. And they smell terrible."

"Oh, for chrissakes . . . Wait one." Sharma commed her loadmaster. "Did you copy that?"

"Affirmative, skipper. As long as *Don't Talk* can lift them, I can stack them."

"Okay . . . Boxcar, we'll take them. Command, you copy?"

"Affirmative, Lander-1. There is no way we are leaving those poor bastards behind."

~~~

As *Don't Talk* rocketed into orbit, lines of brilliant white slashed down from the dawn sky, lines tracking hypersonic tungsten-iridium slugs as they skewered the V-PAC's massive Induction and Training Center, their kinetic energy transformed into a rippling carpet of explosions that left the enormous building reduced to rubble and the air full of the bitter smell of scorched concrete.

~~~

Kal stood with Daniel at the doorway leading into the *Stiletto*'s cargo bay, the deck beneath her feet trembling as the ship left Ventas-2 nearspace under full power to rendezvous with the waiting *Provider*.

Fonseca and his marines had started the slow process of restoring the lives of 45 damaged humans, stripping off the filthy clothes Hardakken had left them in before taking them to be showered, dressed, and fed.

Daniel's face was ashen with shock. "They're all so young. Some of them are barely teenagers."

"Hardakken knows where the money is. Those poor souls are worth a fortune."

"You're kidding! Who would do that?"

"There are some sick scumbags out there, Daniel."

"No kidding . . . What are we going to do now?"

"Jens has a cousin who works for an anti-slavery group called Hope Reborn. It rehabilitates rescued slaves, and it has branch offices on most of the systems in humanspace, including Andimeshk."

"They sound right. Could we pay something to cover their costs?"

"We will. I rather like the idea of using Ferruci's money to do some good . . . Hold on a sec," Kal said as O'Donnell commed him. "Yes, Liam?"

"I have President Schenk for you on TAC-733, captain."

"Thanks . . . Mister President," Kal said when the Ventasi president's avatar appeared, that of a man in his sixties, saggy-jowled and rheumy-eyed. He reminded Kal of an irritable bloodhound. "I'm Vanda Yang. I hope you've enjoyed the show so far."

Schenk's face had turned a dirty red. "I don't know who you are but by god I'm going to make you pay for what you've done. An unprovoked attack on a peaceful—"

"Shut the fuck up! Have—"

"You can't talk to me—"

"I can. Have you received my demands?"

Schenk sat back and folded his arms. "The Ventas Commonwealth does not negotiate with criminals."

"Any more than I do," Kal snapped. "You have 30 days to comply with my demands. If you don't, I will start destroying your cities, one by one, starting with Fransass City. If you think I can't, take a look at what I did to Hardakken's V-PAC."

"This is outrageous! Transferring all those slaves to Sevastapol-6 would cost the Commonwealth millions of dollars. There are thousands of them."

"Tough. That is the price you have to pay for allowing Hardakken to operate a slave business from Ventas-2."

"Why are you doing this?" Schenk's jowls flapped. "We've done nothing to you, whoever you are."

Kal stabbed a finger at the man's face. "You have 30 days to comply with my demands. 30 days, Mister President, or I will start destroying your cities."

Schenk stared at the screen, mouth working. Words refused to come.

Kal cut the comm, wiping her hands on her shipsuit. "Just talking with that man makes me feel unclean," she said to Daniel.

~~~

Kal sat in her stateroom, mug of coffee in hand as she let the stress of combat leach from her body, the routine business of getting *Stiletto* to its rendezvous with *Provider* in the capable hands of O'Donnell and the bridge crew. She was contemplating a long, hot shower when Artie Shaw appeared. He was a mess, still in dusty, sweat-stained combat overalls.

Kal wrinkled her nose. "I hope this is important, Artie. You smell like an old dumpster."

Shaw bobbed his head in apology. "Oh. Sorry, captain. Conditions were bad dirtside. I'll grab a shower and come back later."

"I was teasing. You wouldn't be here if it wasn't important. What have you got for me?"

"We've broken into Hardakken's knowledgebases. I thought you might like to see what their business looks like from the inside."

"I certainly would," Kal said.

Her holoscreen filled with a data-packed table. "You're looking at the information Hardakken keeps on its customers: personal details, purchases, payment plans, what they demanded from their slaves, what the—"

Kal put a hand up. "Hold on. What do you mean by demanded?"

"Whether they want slaves as household servants, maintenance techs, entertainers, sex partners, or whatever. Here's a typical customer: Markus K. Lerantia, late forties, married, three kids, likes dogs, home system Yendofar, owns a shipping company that operates nine starships, so he's seriously rich, buys slaves for sex, which he likes rough . . . Oh, you slimeball!"

"What?"

"Not you, captain. Mister Lerantia. He's bought 26 slaves over the last 18 years. Look at his purchase history. He orders a new one as soon as his current slave dies."

"So each slave lasts 36 weeks"

"Yeah. And they're all healthy when he gets them, Hardakken guarantees it."

Kal's stomach turned at the thought of what those unfortunate enough to fall into Lerantia's hands must go through. "Are you saying he is killing them?

"I am, captain. He's a psycho, not that Hardakken cares. When one slave dies, it just sells the man another."

"That tells you something about the Yendofar police . . . What else do you have?"

"Financial accounts, staff files, suppliers, files on every slave they've ever handled, logistics, everything really. We can see who buys Hardakken's slaves, who those slaves are, where they came from, and how they were shipped to Ventas, how they were shipped out: names, dates, agents, ground handlers, ships, medical and security escorts, holding points along the way, the lot. We also found an account that records all the money Hardakken paid people to look the other way, starting with Ventas's president and minister for internal security and finishing with almost every one of Kolovchenko's gateway security teams."

"All paid to ignore the consignments of slaves passing through?"

"Exactly."

"What can we do with this information, Artie?" Kal asked.

"My team's been talking about that, captain. Ever heard of an i-bomb?"

"No, I can't say I have."

"It's short for information bomb. It's malware with a difference, a virus bundled with data and programmed to explode. Well, not literally, of course, that would be silly . . ."

Kal forced herself not to roll her eyes.

". . . When it goes off, it releases its payload: smart content bundled with a second piece of malware designed to exploit social media and public news networks."

"Anywhere?"

"Every system and orbital in humanspace," Shaw said, "if you want."

"I do want. So, how do we do this this?"

"Let me talk with Mashalo. He produces 'vids when he's off-watch. He showed me one he did on the early years of interstellar travel. It's quite good."

"Good enough to produce the content for an i-bomb that can destroy Hardakken's backers?"

"Oh, for sure. And everyone who's ever dealt with them. We can package up Hardakken's records to go with the vid."

"Get to it."

"Roger that, captain. I'll keep you posted."

As Shaw fled—Kal knew she made the man nervous for some unfathomable reason—she turned her mind to *Stiletto*'s next target: a habitat in orbit around Narsaq-3 which housed the Gang of Five's second most profitable criminal enterprise: a laboratory and manufacturing plant that produced the gene-tailored psychoactives they exported to hundreds of systems.

Kal had been down the psychoactives road. A few were safe, even enjoyable. Some were living hells. All were destructively addictive.

She had been lucky. Early in her slide into addiction, she had found the money—and the willpower—to buy the neuronics reprogramming she needed to break free. A great deal of money and even more willpower.

She could not begin to imagine why the politicians running the Narsaq system tolerated such an abomination.

—42—

The Imps had the Narsaq system in their sights; Kal was certain of it.

They had no interest in a small empire. Their ambition encompassed every system in humanspace. And it was the job of the Imperial Navy to strong-arm those systems into the Imperial fold.

Task Force 64—commanded by Rear-Admiral Moreno—was now busy wrapping up the capture of the Perezan system. Once done, he would move against Balakken-5. And Kal intended to be there when he did; the opportunity to watch the Imperial Navy in action was too tempting to pass up.

As soon as Moreno had taken Balakken-5, *Stiletto* would head for Narsaq-3, knock over the Gang of Five's drug lab, and be long gone by the time Moreno and the cruisers of Task Force 64 arrived.

A plan O'Donnell had taken exception to. Forget Balakken-5. Forget watching Moreno, he'd said. Focus on the drug lab. Get the job done. Get out fast.

Kal had overruled him.

And not just because she wanted to learn from Moreno's attack. What if she could see a way to take Moreno on and win?

When she'd asked O'Donnell how he felt about that, it was obvious he thought she was mad.

Kal was pretty sure she wasn't.

~~~

"Command, Tactical," Atlassian said. "Task Force 64 now on vector for the Balakken-5 gateway."

"Finally!" Kal glanced at O'Donnell. "I was beginning to think Moreno was putting down roots."

"He underestimated the Perezans, not that the poor bastards had any chance of winning. His orbital kinetics made sure of that."

"Somebody needs to tell the Imps that trashing a planet and killing tens of thousands of non-coms does nothing to help the Empire. It needs friends; it has enough enemies already."

"The Imps don't give a shit, captain. They think they're invincible."

"They're not. Nobody is." Kal checked the red icons that tracked Task Force 64. "Hmm . . . Interesting. Moreno is sending four cargo drones through first . . . Tactical, why he would do that?"

After a moment's thought, Atlassian said, "Balakken-5's defenses are no match for the Imp navy. Its commanders will understand that. That leaves Balakken three options.

"One, close the gateways. Two, surrender. Three, make Moreno pay for his victory by attacking the Imp ships as they leave the gateways. The cargo drones are there in case the Balakken choose Option 3; Moreno is sending them through ahead of his main force to soak up the initial missile salvoes. With the Balakken ships committed, it will be game over once his cruisers turn up."

Kal turned to O'Donnell. "What do you think, Liam?"

"That makes sense to me. Moreno's no fool; he has captured five systems to prove it. Given he has more fighting to do, he's better off sacrificing cargo drones than cruisers. If the Balakken don't fight, then he's lost nothing."

"Do you think they will?"

"They won't close the gateways," O'Donnell said, "not with civilian traffic still in transit."

"Which the Imps can arrange, given they control the gateways."

"Exactly. As for surrender," O'Donnell went on, "I can't see the Balakken just giving up. I'm sure they'll fight. I've met a few, and they are feisty bunch. And they hate Terrans."

Kal chuckled. "Everybody hates Terrans. Anyway, we'll find out soon enough. Okay, let's go . . . All stations, captain. The Imp task force is heading for Balakken-5. As soon as they are through the gateway, we will be on our way too. Captain, out."

Daniel came onto the bridge. "Hey, Kal. Time for a coffee?"

All Kal wanted, all she needed, was a solid night's sleep. "Sure . . . Hey!" she called out as she followed Daniel from the bridge. "The crew-room's not this way. "

"Too crowded. Your stateroom."

Kal smiled; her quarters weren't exactly spacious.

She ushered Daniel inside and sat down. "What's on your mind?"

"Marcia and I both think you've been looking a bit distracted. Tell me what's bothering you. And don't say nothing; I know when something's not right with you."

"I know you do . . . It's the Andimeshki. Fonseca came to see me. Somehow, they found out I'm not going to attack Moreno until he reaches Narsaq. They don't see any point waiting; they want me to hit Task Force 64 when it gets to Balakken-5."

"And what's Fonseca think?"

"He agrees with me. He knows I can't risk this ship attacking Moreno until we've seen the Imperial Navy in combat."

"The success of an operation depends on accurate intelligence. How many times have I heard you say that?"

Kal smiled. "It is a fundamental truth in this business, which some grunts never get it. I didn't. All I wanted to do was kill the bad guys, and Fonseca's Andimeshki are no different."

"Are they going to be a problem?"

"I hope not."

Daniel shook his head. "You hope not? Come on, Kal! This isn't a democracy. Just order Fonseca's marines to do the job you're paying them for, for chrissakes!"

"It's okay; I've been in this situation before. I think I can handle it."

"We're stuffed if you can't."

—43—

The threat AI's assessment had been unequivocal: The Balakken could not defeat Moreno's task force.

As they would have known.

Which made Kal ask why they hadn't shut down the gateways from Perezan-8. Cold, hard logic dictated they should; it was the only certain way of holding back Task Force 64. As callous as it sounded, the ten thousand or so civilians who would die when the tunnels protecting their ships collapsed were a price worth paying. The death and misery that Imperial rule brought with it were no secret. Given time, many more lives would be saved than were lost by closing the gateways.

The Imps had been too smart to give that logic any chance of settling the argument.

Moreno had sent Balakken a written guarantee—in writing and under the Emperor's seal—that the Expansion had stopped at the Perezan system. There would never be an attack on Balakken; it would remain an independent system. Inter-stellar trade would continue making money for everyone. Things would go on as normal.

In case that might not be enough, Moreno also invited Balakken to sign a non-aggression pact with the Empire.

All masterpieces of deceit welcomed with near-hysterical enthusiasm by Balakken's media and everyone living off the ships trading with the system.

Kal cursed their stupidity. Idiots. Greedy, venal, gullible idiots, all of them.

As they were about to find out.

"Command, Combat," the AI said. "The six Balakken SDVs deployed around the gateways from Perezan-8 are confirmed no-threat. Planetary defense surveillance arrays are active. *Stiletto* remains outside maximum detection range for their radar, infra-red, and optronics systems."

Kal allowed herself to relax a fraction. She had been edgy ever since *Stiletto* had dropped into normalspace. Balakken was no sorry-assed Rim system like Ventas; its system-defense force deserved respect.

"SDV status?" she asked.

"Infra-red signatures confirm they are at immediate notice."

Kal turned to O'Donnell. "Even though the Balakken government keeps telling everyone they have nothing to be concerned about, those ships are ready to start shooting. Looks like whoever's running SysDef doesn't believe Moreno's bullshit."

"We can still help stop the Imps. And maybe we shou—"

"Stop right there!" Kal barked. "Even if this isn't a regular navy ship, Mister O'Donnell, I'll not tolerate backchat from anyone, and especially not from my XO. We have a plan, and we're going with it. So, pull your damn head in! Is that understood?"

The ferocity of Kal's response had forced O'Donnell back half a step. "Yes, captain. Sorry; I was out of line."

Kal took a deep breath to check her anger. "It's okay, Liam. I know how hard it must be to sit back and watch after what Kolovchenko did to Andimeshk, but I can't take unnecessary risks with this ship, not when it's the only thing left standing between us and the Empire."

"Understood, captain."

Kal watched the man turn away. She felt for him and the rest of the Andimeshki. Not that sympathy changed anything. She had no feel for how the Imperial Navy fought its ships; its operational security was proving too good even for Artie Shaw and his team.

If she took on the Imp Navy, she had to understand her enemy. Why it had succeeded. Why it had failed. What she needed to do to defeat it.

And Kal really did not care if every Andimeshki onboard thought that was a bad idea.

"Command, Combat. Track 700-886; anomalous emitter profiles detected."

"Talk me through it, Threat."

"886's ID beacon says it's the *Longhauler*," Zana Touré said from the threat desk, "a Class-177 ultra-heavy freighter built by Busanga Heavy Engineering. According to NearCon's movements log, it has main engine problems and is waiting for spares before heading on to the Paradise system."

"And what are the anomalies?"

"886's laser datalinks don't match the ones Busanga installs in their Class-177s; they're the wrong frequency. The collision-avoidance lights have the wrong blink rate. And the main engines are Valdorfs, not Tsaochins."

Kal eyed Zana Touré with new-found respect. "If it's not the *Longhauler*, then what is it?" she asked.

"I've run all its dings and scrapes through our bumpology library; that says it's most likely the *Toa Payoh*, a Class-177 freighter built by Kalwele Industries for Aseradans TransStellar. Same basic design, different systems fit out. And Aseradans is a subsidiary of Kolovchenko Logistics."

"Classify it hostile until we're sure it's not."

"Reclassified," Touré said. "Now hostile track 555-886."

Kal beckoned O'Donnell over. "I have a bad feeling about that freighter. Could it be a q-ship?"

"It's possible. It's one of the oldest tricks in the book, and Moreno can be creative, as he's showed with the drones . . . The Balakken SDVs are screwed if the Imps have loaded that ship with missile containers. Their combat AIs won't be able to handle being caught between two simultaneous missile attacks."

"The Balakken will have more than missiles to worry about," Kal said. "That ship could be carrying marines as well. The Balakken would have no idea; like every other system in humanspace they never check ships in transit . . . I'm sorry, captain. I think we have to warn the Balakken that might be a q-ship."

Kal wanted to punch O'Donnell. Taking a deep breath to control her anger, she said, "We won't know until Moreno starts his attack. And, if I'm right, I cannot afford to have the Imps asking how the Balakken knew about it. No, we will wait."

Silence.

"And that," she added, "was an order, in case you missed it, Mister O'Donnell."

"Aye, aye, captain."

Irritated, Kal waved the man away. She commed Fonseca to the bridge.

She had the q-ship on her command screen when the man arrived. "That's the *Toa Payoh*. It's pretending to be another ship, the *Longhauler*. I think it might be a problem."

Fonseca's face crinkled up, puzzled. "Why do we care about a freighter?"

"Because the *Toa Payoh* is owned by a Kolovchenko subsidiary. I suspect it's an Imp q-ship carrying missile containers and marines. Any idea how many it could carry?"

"A freighter that size? Hmm, let's see . . . It's big enough to carry a marine assault brigade: 5,000-strong with the attack landers to drop them dirtside. That would still leave plenty of room for missile containers."

"They're what I'm worried about. When we get to Narsaq, the last thing we need is a q-ship whose capabilities I do not understand hanging around while we attack the Gang of Five's drug lab. So, go tell your people that finding out what that ship's up to is one of the reasons I do not want to help Balakken, much as everyone wants me to."

"I'll do that, captain," Fonseca said.

But will you convince them? Kal asked herself as the man headed off.

She wasn't at all sure he would.

—44—

The mission timer told Kal that the first of Moreno's four drones was due through the gateway from Perezan in two minutes. If the *Toa Payoh* really was a q-ship, it was time it started to move into position.

Which the freighter did, driver-mass erupting incandescent from its main engines.

"Sheesh!" said O'Donnell. "The sonofabitch has gone right to emergency power. No freighter captain I've ever met would treat his main engines that roughly."

"Command, Combat. Main engine efflux profile confirms track 886 is the *Toa Payoh*, not the *Longhauler*."

"Got you now, you mongrel dog," Kal whispered.

The Imp q-ship accelerated towards the Balakken task group, NearCon's strident instructions to return to its assigned orbital slot ignored.

"Command, Combat. Inbound gateway active. Normalspace transition imminent . . . Gravitonics confirms gateway drop imminent; mass consistent with first Imp cargo drone. Assigned track 750-001, classified no-threat."

The instant the massive drone appeared, the Balakken SDVs reacted, dumping missiles into space, missiles that coalesced into swarms and headed in on pencil-thin lines of fire.

Bait laid; bait taken, Kal thought, hollowed out by guilt.

The second cargo drone appeared, then a third, and a fourth. More missiles rode on spears of light towards them.

The missiles struck. Defenseless, the drones could do nothing to resist the attack, their thin-skinned hulls torn apart. Space filled with an incandescent flare of energy as tokomaks failed.

"Command, Combat. Hostile 555-886, missile containers away . . ."

Kal checked the holovid from the recon drone tracking the *Toa Payoh*. Any second now, those containers would start off-loading their payloads of vampires, the brevity code for the Imps' Eaglehawk anti-ship missiles.

And they did.

"...Vampires away. Targets are the Balakken SDVs...Gravitonics confirms gateway drop imminent; mass consistent with the light cruiser, *Alacrity*. Assigned track 555-001, classified hostile."

"Command, roger." Kal could feel the guilt beginning to tear at her. The Balakken were about to get screwed, and she could have stopped it.

The first of the Imp cruisers appeared, ignored by the Balakken, their missiles busy ripping into the carcasses of the dying drones.

"Command, Combat. Hostile track 555-001 identified light cruiser *Alacrity*."

Kal watched the rest of Task Force 64's cruisers stream through the gateway. Like the *Alacrity*, they too were ignored.

Exploiting the confusion, the Imps had formed into two groups, their launchers spitting missiles into fast-growing swarms.

Trapping the Balakken SDVs between the jaws of a three-pronged attack.

"Command, Combat. Hostile 886 is altering vector to clear the combat zone . . . New vector confirmed, a low-orbital pass over Foundation City."

"The q-ship is sending its marines dirtside," O'Donnell said.

Kal was sure he was right.

"Command, Combat. Hostile 886 is deploying landers...40 in all."

"That's an assault brigade, captain. Foundation City is going to be smashed."

Kal felt sick. She had been a marine; she had seen the damage an assault brigade could do to a soft target.

The Balakken SDVs could do nothing about the landers. They were too busy fending off the clouds of missiles the q-ship and

Moreno's cruisers had sent their way. Their close-in defensive lasers fired, flickering from target to target. Imp missiles started to die, exploding in violent flashes of light. Yet more fell to anti-missile shotguns pumping tight clouds of metal balls down the threat axis.

But not all, and now it was the Balakken's turn to die. Missile after missile slammed into the SDVs until their tokomaks blew, vaporizing them and their crews.

Until nothing remained of the six ships save clouds of plasma. They and their crews might never have existed.

The battle was over. The Imp Navy had control of Balakken-5 nearspace. It had taken ten minutes.

"I think it's over," Kal said to Fonseca, "Balakken is—"

"Command, Combat. Tracks 552 through 557, vampires away . . ."

Kal's heart skipped. Those tracks had been classified no-threat.

". . . Missiles are Balakken ASMs, and they're targeting the Imp task force."

"Numbers?" Kal asked.

"120 from six containers. Stern shots. Those missiles might have chance, captain."

Kal felt like cheering. as the Imp ships reacted, thrusters turning their vulnerable sterns away from the incoming missiles. "Those Imp bastards didn't expect this."

"Command, Combat. Vector analysis confirms missiles are targeting *Regulus* and *Matador*. Time-to-target: 4 minutes 15."

As the missiles closed on their targets, the task force's close-in defenses started to tear the attack apart.

Leaving only one survivor.

The missile had cut through the maelstrom of laser, cannon, and shotgun fire to hit *Matador* at its weakest point: the stern. The warhead exploded, punching its molten-metal penetrator through the engine room, through the armor protecting the ship's primary fusion plants, and into the tokomaks.

Containment loss was instantaneous. A millisecond later and the massive release of energy had consumed the ship and all on board.

Kal broke the stunned silence, her face grim. "The Imps weren't the only ones to miss those containers. We did too. Threat! How that happen?"

"The AI misclassified them," Touré answered. "They had been re-skinned to confuse the Imps' optronics. And they fooled ours too."

"Re-skinned how?"

"Chromaflage programmed so they looked like recon drones."

Kal frowned. "Clever. Talk with the AI. Make sure it knows what to look for next time. We cannot afford to make that mistake again if we want to stay alive."

"Will do, captain."

"All stations, Command. The Imps have destroyed the Balakken SDVs; the entire system is now theirs for the taking. As planned, we will be jumping to Narsaq-3, the Imps' next target. I've scheduled a walkthrough of the Imp attack to go through the lessons learned. 20:00, all hands, cargo bay. Captain, out."

~~~

The mood in the cargo bay felt ugly, the air filled with subdued conversation, a buzz that grew louder as Kal stepped up to the makeshift podium. She scanned the dour faces of Fonseca's marines, every head down, their eyes avoiding hers.

A stab of doubt.

The men and women in front of her were not subject to military law. They were mercenaries under contract; they would not do as they'd been ordered simply because she was paying them. No mercenary in history ever had.

To follow orders, they needed to have confidence in the mission commander. Without it, they would never put their lives at risk.

She lifted her hands. "Okay, everybody, settle down please . . . I need to say something before we look at the lessons we can learn from the Imps, what they did right, what they did wrong . . . I gather some—"

A voice from the back. "We sat back and did nothing. Decent people died, and another independent system is in Imp hands. If we don't stop them, then who will?"

Kal searched out the heckler; Yordalian, a fire-team leader and one of the best marines onboard. If people like him weren't with her, she was screwed.

"Marine Yordalian," Kal called out. "On your feet . . . Now, goddammit!" she snapped when he hesitated.

The man stood, his face burning red. It wasn't anger, Kal realized. It was embarrassment. Mercenary or not, he was still a marine deep down; criticizing his commanding officer was not in his DNA.

Kal locked her eyes on Yordalian's; nobody else mattered now. "You are quite right. We did sit back and watch. Why? Because those were my orders."

A rumble of protest. Kal paused to let it die away.

"You want to stop the Empire," she continued. "I do too, but not as payback for what Kolovchenko did to Andimeshk back in '87. That's revenge, and revenge never solved a—"

The protests overran her voice.

"Quiet!" she barked. "What are you? Marines? Or a fucking rabble? As long as you are under contract to me, you will listen when I have something to say. You can tell me what you think once I have finished. Until then I want silence."

Kal's eyes had never left Yordalian's face. Slowly, reluctantly, the man nodded.

"The Empire controls godknows how many systems with more in its sights," Kal went on, her heart battering at the walls of her chest, horribly aware how close she was to losing control of Fonseca's Andimeshki. "An empire without moral worth. An empire controlled by criminal scum. An empire with thousands of ship, millions of spacers and marines, and trillions of dollars . . . an empire that we have to defeat."

A growl of agreement.

"And what do I have to defeat those thousands of ships and millions of spacers and marines and trillions of dollars?"

Kal stabbed a finger at the deck.

"I have this ship," she continued, "94 spacers and marines, a support ship, and half-a-billion dollars that I'm burning through faster than a wildfire through grass. Compared to the Empire, I am a speck of fly-shit on an elephant's butt. The Imps would laugh if they knew what I want to do.

"But *Stiletto* is no ordinary ship. Thanks to its Q-drive, we can hit the Imps anywhere, anytime, and they will never see us coming. Even so, it is still just one SDV against thousands of warships. If I lose my *Stiletto*, I lose. Andimeshk loses. The rest of humanspace loses . . . And I will not let that happen, not as long as I breathe."

Kal paused for a moment. Her voice soft, she said, "I want what you want, Marine Yordalian. If you think I don't because of what's happened here today, then you are even dumber than I thought . . ."

A soft laugh ran through the cargo bay.

". . . so be in no doubt: I want to destroy the Empire, and Kolovchenko with it. You are Andimeshki; I know that is what you want too. I don't think any of you are here just for the money, not anymore . . . though I guess the money might still have something to do with it."

Another laugh; louder this time, Kal was relieved to hear.

"All of you have seen combat," she went on. "You know how quickly things can turn to shit. And why? Because your commanders did not understand their enemy. Stupidity like that kills spacers. It kills marines. It kills ships. I am not stupid. I am not going to make that mistake. That's why I let the Imps trash Balakken-5 today. Not because I wanted to. Because I had to.

"The *Stiletto* is all I have. Without it, this war is over, and the Imperial Navy will crush every system in humanspace, Andimeshk too. And humanspace will stay crushed, forced to endure centuries of corruption, brutality, death and suffering . . . So, before you tell me I should have done things differently today, think what that means for ordinary Andimeshkis. For your children, your families, your friends."

Kal let her words hang for a moment, then raised her hands, palm out. "These hands hold the future of billions of humans. And I will not risk their futures just to make a bunch of Andimeshki mercenaries feel good . . ."

Heads began to nod. Kal could feel the tension ease.

". . . and I never, ever will. However hard it was for you today, it was a lot harder for me. I had command authority. I could have saved some of the Balakken who died today. I chose not to, and now the blood of those spacers is on my hands. And I will have to live with that until the day I die.

"Today, we saw our enemy for the first time. We learned a lot. And that learning is our first step towards destroying the Empire. Which I am going to do, because this is a war we cannot afford to lose . . . Oh, for chrissakes, Marine Yordalian! You can sit down now."

Laughter filled the cargo bay.

Kal looked into the eyes of each marine in turn. "I've said what I wanted to say. Anyone have something they'd like to tell me?"

Another silence.

As it dragged on, Kal let herself breathe easily again. The crisis was over.

"No? Okay, then. Lessons learned first, and then the changes we are going to make for the Narsaq operation as a result. Liam, over to you."

"Thank you, captain."

—45—

Kal stuck her head into the cyberwar team's makeshift headquarters. She could not help herself; she been waiting a long time for Artie Shaw and his people to break into the Narsaq Foreign Intelligence Service's datanet.

Shaw sat with his geeks, hunched over a holoscreen, heads touching, muttering to themselves. He spotted Kal. "Sorry, captain, I know we're taking too long."

"Not if you find Director Peng for me. Besides, we have plenty of time before the Imps turn up."

"Well, I have some good news. We've discovered that FIS's defenses against the KrystoFac vulnerability aren't up to date. That lets us exploit the—"

"Artie! The simple version, please."

"Sorry, captain. We've found a weakness, and we're running our latest break-in simulation to see if we can exploit it."

"Great stuff. I'll be—"

"Yes!" one of the team shouted. "That will work!"

"Leave it with me, captain." Shaw turned back to his team. "Show me."

"Comm me when you're ready, Artie," Kal said to the man's back.

~~~

Kal was finishing the latest run though the Narsaq ops plan when her neuronics pinged.

"Sorry, guys," she said to O'Donnell and Fonseca. "Yes, Artie?"

"We've broken into the Narsaq FIS's datanet and we've located Director Peng. You can talk with him any time you like. Sorry it's taken us so long."

"No problem . . . Liam, Jens. Artie's got us into FIS. I can talk with Peng. You ready?"

The two men nodded.

"Okay, Artie. Patch me through to Director Peng."

She closed her eyes to let her neuronics take over. For a moment, her mind's eye filled with gray fog, and then Peng's avatar appeared: a man sporting the thin, razor-cut mustache fashionable amongst older Narsaq men, eyes wide in shocked surprise.

"What the hell?" he spluttered. "Who are you? How did you access me?"

"I apologize for hacking into your datanet, Director Peng, but these are desperate times."

"Who are you?"

"Colonel Folau, Imperial Security, though I am no friend of Emperor Michael or his administration."

"Why would I care?"

"The Imp Navy has just captured the Balakken system. Narsaq-3 is next."

Peng sat back and crossed his arms. "That is a lie, Ms. Folau. The Imperial government has advised us that the Balakken system has agreed to join the Empire and that the Expansion will stop there. It has also asked us to send a delegation to finalize a non-aggression pact, an invitation our president has announced he will accept."

"You're being played, Director Peng. The Imperial Navy promised the Balakken the Expansion would stop at Perezan. It didn't, and you're next. And you can tell your president there'll be no pact between Narsaq and the Empire; the ships of Admiral Moreno's Task Force 64 attacked Balakken while its Minister of Interstellar Affairs was on his way to Perezan to negotiate terms."

"That is not our understanding. This discussion is over, Ms. Folau."

"Director Peng, wait! I will send you holovid of the Imp attack on Balakken-5. Det Norsk Veritas has authenticated it as unedited original footage. Perhaps that might help you trust me."

Peng gazed at Kal for an age. "I must be mad. Please go on."

"Standby . . . Okay, you should have it now."

Peng mouth sagged open as he watched the 'vid. By the time it was over, his face had turned a dirty gray. "Those lying ba . . . Who are you, really?"

"A question for another day."

"Okay . . . You said you wanted to help us stop an Imp takeover of Narsaq. How can you do that? We have seen the Imp's order-of-battle. You cannot possibly have enough ships to defeat them; no system in humanspace has. Even if you did, you cannot get your ships here without using the gateways, something Kolovchenko would never allow. I'm sorry. I fail to see how you are in any position to help us."

"I think you might be surprised what your people can do with accurate intelligence and our help."

Silence. As it dragged on, Kal willed the man to make the right decision, to take the best offer he would ever receive.

It was an age before Peng responded. "I'll listen to you, if only because of the Balakken holovid. What do you propose?"

"To provide you with accurate and timely intelligence on Moreno's intentions."

"You'll need to be more specific."

"The precise timing of Task Force 64's attack on Narsaq-3 and the order in which he sends his ships through."

Peng's eyes narrowed. "That's impossible. The Imps control the pinchcomm service from Balakken."

"What KolovComm sells you and everyone else is not the same service it provides to ImpSec. How do you think I was able to get 'vid of the Balakken operation?"

"Hmm . . . Maybe."

"And there is more I can do to assist you, a lot more, the details will have to wait until you've decided whether to accept my offer of help."

"You will have to leave this with me, Ms. Folau."

"Of course. I have attached details of the portal you can use to talk with me. And stop trying to backtrack this comm, director. If my people can break into FIS's commsnet, they can make sure you will never find me. And you should fix your cybersecurity; I will send you details of the hack we used to break in. Goodbye, Director Peng."

Kal cut the comm and opened her eyes. "Did he buy it?"

O'Donnell nodded. "The holovid of the attack on Balakken should convince him the Imps are coming. If he is, logic says he will take all the help he's offered."

"You know what worries me?" Fonseca said. "The Imps are going roll over the Narsaqs if Peng refuses to work with us. That means there is a significant risk any intel we supply will leak out."

"We can't do this without taking risks," Kal replied. "If things go well, we'll not only hurt the Empire—which will play well with your guys, Jens—we . . ."

Fonseca glanced away, his face flushed.

". . . can ramp up the pressure on the Gang of Five by destroying the drug lab they have in orbit around Narsaq-3. Which reminds me; I just had a comm from Professor Sharif. Her contacts on Terra say there are rumors the Gang of Five are having trouble rolling over one of their bonds."

"Losing Hardakken must have hurt them," O'Donnell said.

"It did, and the lenders are getting nervous. That's why we can't ease up now . . . Okay, then. We'll be jumping back to Balakken-5 soon, but before we do, Moreno. Do either of you think he'll do something different when he attacks Narsaq?"

O'Donnell scratched his face. "Hmm . . . No, I don't think so. He'll do what he did at Balakken-5; why would he change a winning formula? And, like us, he won't let his threat AIs be caught out again by the missile-container trick."

"The only unknown is whether Narsaq does the smart thing and closes the gateways with Balakken," Fonseca said.

"Not one system has done that so far," Kal said. "It's too much to expect a government to kill thousands of civilians to save itself. The ship-owners and traders don't help either."

Contempt twisted O'Donnell's face. "Self-serving scum; whatever bullshit the Imps feed them, they believe. And the Imps' disinformation is a work of art. That whole 'send your diplomats to negotiate a non-aggression pact' thing is brilliant. I can't think of a better way to reassure a system it's not a target."

"Brilliant is right. I'm just surprised Kolovchenko's founders have taken so long to work out that the rest of humanspace was theirs for the taking."

"Like you keep saying, captain, that's why we have to stop them."

Kal smiled, a grim, humorless smile. "Here's hoping we will."

—46—

Kal was in her stateroom when Daniel stuck his head in. "You look pleased with yourself."

Daniel flipped out a seat and sat down. "I am, which is why I thought I'd cheer you up."

Kal wondered how much Daniel's new love, Marine Skylar K'hala, had to do with the happiness he radiated. "That'd be good. What have you got?"

"I wanted to tell you about something Marcia and I have been working on for a while . . . well, she did most of the work, though I have been—"

"Daniel! Stop waffling on. I'm butchered; all I want is my rack."

"Ah, sorry. I'll be quick. You know how Kolovchenko piggybacks an interstellar pinchcomms network on its gateways?"

"I also know how much KolovComm charges us suckers for the privilege of using it. So what?"

"How would you like to destroy KolovComm's business?"

"That would really hurt Kolovchenko, so of course I would. How?"

Daniel pointed to the bulkhead-mounted holoscreen where a box had appeared. "With this . . . See the pinchspace node on the nearest face? Let me spin the drone . . . see the second node?"

"Yes, but what I'm looking at?"

"A pinchcomm drone. It will allow point-to-point communications through pinchspace."

"Look, Daniel. This is all terribly exciting, but how do you and Grivak find the time to do this? I would rather have a faster Q-drive. I'm fighting a war here, not running a research lab."

For a moment, Kal thought Daniel was about to start crying, he was so upset.

She stood and pulled Daniel into a hug. "I'm sorry. I'm such an asshole sometimes. Forgive me, please."

Daniel wrapped his arms around Kal. "It's okay," he murmured. "You've got a lot on your plate."

Kal gave Daniel a squeeze, then let him go. "That's no excuse. Come on, let's rewind. Where are you up to?"

"Grivak and I have used *Stiletto*'s microfabs to make two prototypes. We used microfusion modules I pulled out of stores to power them."

Kal threw her hands up. "Daniel! We need those for emergency power if our tokomaks are damaged. Did you ever consider that?"

Daniel blinked, a befuddled owl. "Ah . . . no, can't say I did . . . I guess I got so carried away by what pinchcomm drones could do for us, the damage we could do to Kolovchenko's cash flow, I never stopped to think . . . I'm sorry, Kal."

"It's okay. I'd have told you to go for it if you'd asked, so no harm done, but I need to know everything happening on board . . . and that includes any socialization between my senior Q-drive scientist and a certain marine called Skylar K'hala."

Daniel's face flamed red, his mouth opening and closing without any words coming out.

Kal thought he looked like a goldfish enjoying a feed. A sight so engaging, Kal burst into laughter. "Oh, Daniel! You're the best thing that's ever happened to me."

Daniel glared at Kal through narrowed eyes. "You're teasing me now."

"No way. I meant it."

"Really?"

"Yes, really. Now, I have a shitload of stuff to do before I can crash out, so go tell Yasmin what you have been up to; the chief engineers of warships get grumpy over things like this. When she has calmed down, ask her to order enough feedstock and power modules to build, uh, let's see . . . another 20 of Grivak's drones and more microfabs as well. And talk with Captain Stefanec; the *Provider* has more than enough space to operate as our fabrication shop."

"Got it."

Kal smiled. "Now piss off . . . And well done to you and Grivak. This is fantastic work."

Daniel's face radiated pleasure. "Thanks," he called out as he left.

Given the insanity consuming humankind, Kal wondered where Daniel would end up. Somewhere, she hoped, a decent human being could live the life he deserved.

Wiping away the tears that filled her eyes, she commed O'Donnell. She wanted to see what he thought of the latest development from the Gnomes' Grotto, the crew's name for the cramped space packed with AIs and holoscreens where Daniel and Marcia Grivak spent most of their waking hours.

—47—

"Command, Combat," the AI responsible for fighting the ship said. "New track 777-344, exiting New Hope gateway. Classified freighter, no-threat . . . Narsaq-3 NearCon reports 344 is the *Wujakari Express* in transit to Balakken." "I was so sure Moreno would repeat his q-ship trick," she said, "so where is it?"

She zoomed her holoscreen in on the new arrival. Yet another freighter, the umpteenth since *Stiletto* had returned to Narsaq-3 nearspace.

Her anxiety levels—already high as the wait for Director Peng to respond to her offer of help dragged on—cranked up another notch.

O'Donnell shrugged. "Maybe he's decided not to use one this time around."

"Why would he do that? The tactical advantage it gives him is huge."

"He might have run out of freighters."

"Hmm," grunted Kal, unconvinced. If Moreno needed a freighter, he'd just steal one from the Balakken. She would wait another hour, then have the Threat AI recheck every ship orbiting Narsaq. Moreno's q-ship had to be there somewhere.

"Command, Combat. Track 344 is firing main engines . . . correction, its port main engine only. It's putting in a big vector change."

Now I have you, Kal thought, her every instinct telling her the *Wujakari Express* was not the ship it claimed to be.

"Command, Threat," Atlassian said. "344's main-engine efflux profile does not match the *Wujakari Express*'s. Standby identification . . . Track 344 is the Terran-registered freighter, *Harmony-445*. That's Moreno's q-ship, captain."

Finally, thought Kal, much relieved. She waved O'Donnell over. "I'm sick of waiting for the Narsaqs to get off their fat asses. I'm thinking of telling Peng that Moreno's planning to pull the same q-ship trick he used at Balakken. What do you think?"

O'Donnell tugged an ear. "Hmm . . . I guess it won't hurt. And it does confirm that Moreno's planning an attack. Peng will ask how we know, though."

"I'll worry about that when he does. Okay, I want every emitter on that ship cross-checked against the profile for the real *Wujakari Express*. We cannot afford to mess this up."

"Yes, captain. I'll—"

"Command, Combat. NearCon advisory. 344 is heading for an orbital slot to await repairs to its starboard main-engine tokomak. All ships are reminded that it has not cleared Narsaq system security. No approach within 100 kilometers without prior NearCon approval."

Kal whistled softly. *Nice try, Mister Moreno,* she thought.

"Command, Threat. I have identified anomalies on 344's collision-avoidance radar, ID beacon, and collision-avoidance lights. None match the systems fitted to the real *Wujakari Express*. They do match the *Harmony-445's*."

Kal commed Fonseca to the bridge.

"We've found Moreno's q-ship," she told him as he arrived, "which confirms Narsaq-3 is his next target. But, before Liam talks about that, can you update us both on the drug lab operation?"

"I can, captain. We have confirmed the Gang of Five's operates a psychoactives complex in an orbital, *Narsaq*-6399; not being dirtside makes it a much softer target than the Hardakken facility. Artie and his team have broken into *6399*'s systems, so we know how the orbital's laid out and where its vulnerabilities are. The ops plan has all that detail; you will have the final version shortly. My guys have simmed the operation, and I am confident we can take it. Not without risk though; the habitat has a 60-strong security team, all ex-cops."

"Not exactly the A-team then?" Kal said.

Fonseca chuckled. "Not even the D-team. Their boss should be dirtside playing with her grandkids. She doesn't believe in training: no weapons handling, no compartment-clearance drills, no zero-g work, no physical conditioning. And there's nothing to keep them busy and interested. They mostly deal with lab rats trying their own product and going psycho, and that doesn't happen often. Even so, there are always risks facing that many hostiles, but I think they are manageable. And we'll have *Don't Talk*'s cannon to back us up if things get sticky. Unless something changes, I recommend we go."

"Subject to the Narsaqs agreeing to accept my offer of help, I concur." Kal turned to O'Donnell. "Tell us about Moreno, Liam."

"All our planning has assumed the Imps would use a q-ship, so the arrival of *Harmony-445* doesn't change anything. If the Narsaqs act on the intel we provide, and we can give them missile support without compromising our own security, the sims say we can stop Moreno's attack. If the Narsaqs refuse our help, Moreno will capture the entire system just as he took Balakken and Perezan."

"You sure of that?"

"I am. The Narsaqs only have five old SDVs, and their Musaytir anti-ship missiles are obsolescent. If they get lucky, they might take out one or two of Moreno's cruisers. They can't stop them all."

"Even if they don't fall for Moreno's drone trick?" Kal asked.

"Without our help, Narsaq will run out of ships and ASMs long before the Imps do."

"As every other system Moreno's hit has found out . . . There is one thing before I talk with Peng," Kal went on, "I want to send him our sim package. If that doesn't convince him to work us, nothing will. One change, though. Show us using Musaytirs. I don't want some FIS analyst asking how we got our hands on FireSparks that are only manufactured on the other side of humanspace."

"A good point, captain, given the Empire's embargoed all ordnance shipments to independent systems like Narsaq."

"Which FIS will know," Kal said. "It would take them long to work out the only way we could have acquired them is using a Q-drive ship."

"No problem. I'll make the changes."

"Good. Now, before we wrap up, Daniel says Marcia can give us two prototype pinchcomm drones for testing on the way to Balakken-5. Can you talk to her? We have to decide where to drop them."

"No problem, captain," O'Donnell said. "But will they work?"

"Ever since that asteroid hit Ladaki-6, I have bet my life on Daniel being right more times than I can remember, and I'm still here. As for Marcia, she's as smart as Daniel. If they say the drones will work, I'm not going to argue with them."

"I wouldn't," Fonseca said. "Once those two start with their n-dimensional equations, my brain crashes. Tell you what, though. I really hope they work. I like the idea of sending KolovComm to the wall."

Kal bared her teeth. "Me too. Losing its pinchcomm monopoly will cost Kolovchenko a fortune. Right, we're done. All we can do now is wait to hear from the Narsaqs."

~~~

". . . the Narsaq Security Council has agreed to accept your offer of support," said Director Peng. "We need to work out the details of course, but we'll be in touch on that."

Kal wanted to cheer; it took an effort not to. "I have to say, director, that is a huge relief. We were afraid you'd let mistrust make the call."

"Oh, there's still plenty of that around. In the end, the holovid of Moreno's attack on Balakken settled the matter. That came as huge shock to SysDef, Moreno's use of cargo drones and a q-ship especially. And our SecState was even more upset when she found out about the Imps' non-aggression pact scam . . . I shouldn't tell you this, but she had been very vocal arguing that pact proved the Empire's *bona fides* beyond any doubt."

"You can't blame her. Every system between here and Terra has fallen for it."

"True . . . Now, explain something to me. How did SysDef miss the *Harmony-445* and you didn't?"

"Decades of operating within a benign threat environment would be my guess. As for us, we pay attention to the details; a mistake like that can get us killed."

"Ah, yes . . . I have a question. There was no q-ship in the holovid of Moreno's attack on Balakken you gave us. Didn't he use one?"

"He did. That's what made us look for one here. I didn't want to say anything until I was sure he was going to repeat the trick."

Peng's avatar bored into Kal. "Are you holding anything else back?"

"Nothing important, director, I can assure you."

It was time to change the subject, Kal decided. "I have two requests," she went on. "They will sound odd, but I am hoping you can see your way to meeting them."

"You can ask," Peng said.

"During the Imp attack, I intend tasking my attack lander to carry out an operation against an orbital habitat, *Narsaq-6399*. I'd like SysDef's approval to do that."

Peng stared into the holocam, eyes narrowed. "Why would somebody who says she is on a mission to destroy the Empire attack one of our orbitals?"

Kal sighed; she'd known Peng was never just going to say yes. "It's part of my plan to destroy the Empire."

"I have trouble seeing how."

"Five of Kolovchenko's founding families control humanspace's largest criminal cartel; I call them the Gang of Five. They have borrowed trillions dollars to finance their operations. I plan to bankrupt them. If I can do that, my finance analyst says there is a high probability that will destabilize Terra's money markets to such an extent the Empire runs out of money to fund the Expansion."

"The ultimate asymmetric-warfare strategy," Peng said. "Very smart, Ms. Folau, if it works. But what does this Gang of Five have to do with *6399*?"

Peng's face was the exemplar of bland; he knew. Kal was sure of it. "It's the biggest producer of gene-tailored psychoactives in humanspace, and the Gang of Five own it."

Peng chuckled. "Yes, they do, Ms. Folau. Your intelligence is remarkably sound. Not many people know that."

Kal smiled; she was beginning to warm to Peng. "I had a feeling FIS would."

"It has to. *Narsaq-6399* is a foreign-controlled habitat. FIS keeps an eye on it, even though its authority stops at its airlocks, something many of us take great exception to, me included. Sadly, our politicians refuse to do anything about it; they prefer to take the money instead."

"A position they can't defend anymore," Kal said. "The Gang of Five are Kolovchenko Founders, and the Founders are the driving force behind the Empire that's just about to kick your front door down."

"I would agree."

"Then you'd be happy to persuade Narsaq SysDef to look away while I, uh . . . deal with *6399*?"

Peng was silent for a moment, then said, "One of FIS's agents on Shenzen-4 told us that a terrorist group had hit Ventas-2, destroying a slave-trading business, six SDVs, all of its orbital defense infrastructure, a ground-defense airbase and its aircraft, and the best part of a marine battalion. The terrorists also forced the government to repatriate over ten thousand slaves. A stunning success against a morally repugnant business hosted by a corrupt system government, would you not say?"

Kal swore under her breath; she had underestimated Peng and FIS. "It sounds like it, but what has that to do with the Gang of Five and *6399*?"

"Four things about the attack struck my analysts as odd. The sophistication of the operation. The capability of the attacking ship's weapons; very few SDVs have kinetics and advanced vector-agile ASMs with two-stage warheads. Where that SDV came from. And, oddest of all, nobody has claimed responsibility, something anti-slavery terrorists always do."

"What does a terrorist operation have to do with my wanting to eliminate *6399*?"

"We have a lot of information on the people you call the Gang of Five, Ms. Folau. They not only own *6399*, they also own Hardakken. Persons unknown attacked Hardakken. Persons unknown are about to attack *6399*. Given how far apart the Ventas and Narsaq systems are, that strikes me as an extraordinary coincidence."

Kal shrugged. "Coincidences happen."

"Yes, they do, and perhaps that's all it is . . . But we were talking about *Narsaq-6399*. Given that the Gang of Five are part of the Terran imperial conspiracy, I think I can persuade my government to tell SysDef to give you the okay. As I said, I'm not the only one who'd be happy to see that cesspit drained."

"Thank you. Unless something urgent comes up, the next time we talk will be when I have the Imps' ETA at the Narsaq in-gateway for you. Until then, director."

"Until then, Ms. Folau."

Kal cut the comm and sat back, exhausted, the sweat running down her back.

Day after day, the pressure had mounted. All she wanted was a beach, a beer, and to be left alone.

A fantasy that was never going to happen.

She wasn't sure how more she could take. And, what made things worth was the simple fact that she could not walk away, not now.

—48—

". . . and I say to the people of Balakken, welcome to the Empire of Terra, membership of which will bring enormous economic and social benefits to you and all the systems of humanspace. I thank you for your time. Good night."

The holocam pulled back from a woman dressed in a black suit, the gold aiguillette dropping from her left shoulder marking her as Balakken's new Imperial Governor.

Kal gave the woman the finger; she could not help herself. "You are such a pompous asshole."

Fonseca stepped into the crew-room, grabbing himself a coffee before slumping on a bench. ""Hey, captain. Enjoying more imperial soap opera?"

Kal turned off the screen. "Imperial farce, more like it."

"Makes a change from tragedy. Word is the Imps are having trouble persuading their new subjects to accept the benefits of empire."

"The Imps don't have enough boots and attack landers to fight dirtside. Not that they care. They just drop kinetics on anyone who picks up a weapon, and to hell with the collateral damage. And when they've crushed the resistance, the survivors are left to starve to death until they agree to cooperate."

"Cutting off the Imps' money will put a stop to all that."

"It should," Kal said, "but I worry about how long that will take . . . It makes me feel so damn tired."

"Hey, hey, hey! I have been reading the reports from your Professor Sharif. Ventas was a huge win, out of all proportion to the effort we made."

"Yeah, it was. And, talking of Sharif, I got another update this morning from her. She says the Gang used to be able to borrow money at 5%. They're now having to pay double that. So yes, we are having an effect. Though I feel sorry for the poor bastards who bought their junk bonds; they're worth a lot less than they were before Hardakken."

Fonseca scowled. "My heart bleeds for the bastards. I hope they are screwed; they shouldn't have lent their money to people who think slavery is a fine idea."

Daniel arrived. "Sorry to interrupt, guys. Kal, you asked for an update you on the pinchcomm drones. Long story short, they work."

Kal stood and dragged Daniel into a hug; it would have squeezed the air out of a man twice his size had it gone on much longer. She stepped back, her hands on his shoulders. "I knew you could do it. I knew it."

"I'm glad you did." He leaned forward, his voice a whisper. "Because I didn't, and neither did Marcia. That reef is a bad one."

"Yeah, yeah," Kal whispered back. "And don't forget gravity reefs are our secret; make sure you don't tell anyone else."

~~~

Kal was down deep when a comm dragged her awake.

Atlassian had the watch. "Task Force 64 has broken orbit, captain. Vectors are nominal for the Narsaq gateway."

"On my way."

She forced her unwilling body from its rack, threw on a jumpsuit, and ran for the bridge. She dropped into the command chair, eyes scanning the command and threat plots. "So, what have we got?"

"Same sequence as for Balakken, four drones up front, then the cruisers with the marine transports and support ships bringing up the rear. They'll reach Narsaq three days from now."

"And us?"

"11 hours 24 ... plus any of those unscheduled drops the AI seems to like so much," Atlassian added, scowling.

Kal understood the man's frustration. He was not privy to the secrets of gravity reefs.

"Okay . . . All stations, captain. The Imps are underway. We'll be jumping for Narsaq-3 as soon as they're through the gateway. Final walkthrough the plans for the Narsaq operations will be at 14:00, cargo bay, all hands."

~~~

Kal was watching the Imp ships crawl across her command screen, when a soft cough diverted her attention. It was Artie Shaw.

Kal waved him over. "Hi, Artie. What can I do for you?"

"The team has had an idea. I thought I'd run it past you."

"Please. Watching snails is more exciting than this."

Shaw frowned. "Snails? What have snails got . . . Oh, yes. That's one of your jokes, captain."

Kal chuckled. "Yes, it is. What've you got?"

"Kolovchenko has spent billions making sure the AIs which control its gateways cannot be hacked. Nobody will ever break in."

"Even your guys?"

"Them too, but Kolovchenko didn't bother securing the gateway transit reporting system, the TRS. Which is understandable; all it does is publish arrivals and departures to tell people what's going on. When we poked around the code, we fou—"

Kal put a hand up. "Hang on. You hacked into the TRS?"

"We did, captain. I needed something to keep my team busy. Anyway, we discovered that the gateway AI pushes ship arrival times to the TRS, correct to the microsecond. The TRS then rounds that time off to the nearest minute and sends it out to the public."

"Why would we care?"

"The TRS has all the data we need to calculate a target datum based on a ship's precise drop time and exit vector."

"Wait on! Are you saying we can blind-fire our missiles at a ship before it drops into normalspace?" Kal asked.

Shaw smiled. "I certainly am, captain. You could hit that ship one millisecond after it drops if you wanted to."

Kal got it.

Imp warships would be all but defenseless in the seconds after they dropped through a gateway, before their combat AIs had completed their threat assessment, before they could deploy missiles, decoys and countermeasures, before they had assigned targets to their anti-ship missiles and close-in defenses.

They would only realize they were under attack an instant before the *Stiletto*'s FireSparks ripped their guts out.

"Brief the XO. See what he thinks."

"Will do, captain."

—49—

"Lander-1 for you, captain."

"Patch it through," Kal replied. "Go ahead, Lander-1."

"We've checked in with Narsaq NearCon," Sharma commed from *Don't Talk*'s flight-deck. "They've cleared us into nearspace from Point Batwing direct to orbital *6399*."

"Roger that. How are my marines?"

"Shitting themselves; I am too. The Narsaqs have us by the nuts. We're finished if they are playing games."

"They have too much to lose."

"That's what logic says. I just wish my gut agreed."

"Trust me," Kal said with a confidence she did not feel, "they'll will come through for us."

"I hope so, captain. Lander-1, out."

Kal felt for Sharma. *Don't Talk* was alone and defenseless, its safety secured only by the assurances of Director Peng.

She checked the command plot. The Narsaqs had tasked a freighter, the *Maxwell Pride*, with neutralizing the *Harmony*-445. Loaded with missile containers and the marines of Narsaq SysDef's Special Operations Group 88, it was now heading in-system.

Just another ship transiting Narsaq-3's nearspace, it was on vector to pass close to the Imp q-ship.

It would not be long now.

Kal's whole body was tense, the bands around her chest so tight it was an effort to breathe, the pressure almost physical. What was she even doing here? How had an alcoholic AI tech who had been a highly decorated marine in another life end up with the fate of an entire system in her hands?

It was insanity.

Forcing back the doubts eroding her confidence, she ran her eyes around *Stiletto*'s bridge as if to reassure herself she was not alone.

Which she wasn't.

The four who would fight the ship with her—Atlassian, tactical; Touré, threat assessment; Karcher, weapons; Kashani, engineering—sat hunched over workstations networked into the AIs in the Tank, an armored compartment directly below the *Stiletto*'s bridge. That left O'Donnell free to roam, dealing with whatever crises the Fates threw at them.

All she had to was trust them and the rest of the *Stiletto*'s crew to do their jobs while she did hers.

Kal returned to her command holoscreen. Things were as they should be, the mass of comforting blue friendlies and green no-threats around Narsaq-3 broken by the solitary red icon marking the position of Moreno's q-ship.

And wasn't the *Harmony-445* in for a shock, she thought.

A sudden surge of optimism brushed aside her self-doubt. You can do this, Kal told herself, you can do this.

She flipped her screen to show the ships in the gateway tunnel linking Balakken to Narsaq. She offered up a silent prayer of thanks that Artie Shaw and his cyberwar team were on her side.

If not geniuses, they were close. Like most AI techs, Kal was no slouch when it came to the arcane world of hacking. Shaw's cybergeeks made her look like an amateur.

O'Donnell came up the bridge ladder.

Kal beckoned him over. "I need an answer, Liam. I'm not blind-firing missiles until I'm sure they'll only hit what I want them to hit."

"Artie's walked me through the dataflows from the gateway control system," O'Donnell said. "Data integrity is 100%. You will have valid firing solutions for the missiles."

"Good. What's the target datum?"

"One second after each ship exits the gateway. Against an Empire-class heavy cruiser, a 20-strong FireSpark missile strike screened by decoys has a hard-kill probability of 99.6%."

Kal pumped a clenched fist. "Now that it what I like to hear! Thanks, Liam. Once I've been through the strike profile, I'll update Director Peng. I don't want the Narsaqs fluffing around on this."

"I'll leave it with you then, captain."

~~~

Kal was not surprised to see Director Peng looking so washed out. Stress, she assumed; with the Imperial Navy on its way to trash his home planet, he should look tense.

"... and to be honest, Ms. Folau," Peng was saying, "a lot of us here think what you're proposing is impossible."

"They don't have to believe me, director. All they have to do is watch."

"You cannot keep ducking the one question the Narsaq Security Council keeps asking: Why is Narsaq trusting someone who cannot tell us who she really is, who she works for, what she's trying to achieve?"

"Perhaps you should tell me, director."

"I think it's because you give us hope, Ms. Folau. Our latest sims left us in no doubt: The Narsaq system will fall to the Imps if we tell you to go away. That would leave thousands of our people dead and most of our cities levelled."

"That is right. As for your doubters, you will soon have all the proof you need that we aren't some sort of elaborate plot to screw you over."

Peng rubbed his eyes and sighed, a sigh of resignation. "I'm hoping not. I do have one last request. SysDef wants to avoid any blue-on-blue incidents. We'd like you to liaise with the Commander, Task Force 10, Commodore Zuana. She has been tasked with stopping the Imps; her ship is the *Kuliak*, and she is very competent, I'm happy to say."

"The simplest thing I can do is give Zuana access to my combat AI."

"I hoped you'd say that. You can talk to each other on TAC-554 to set that up."

"TAC-554, got it."

"Thank you, Ms. Folau."

"Tactical," Kal said as soon as Peng had gone, "patch me into TAC-554."

"Standby . . . the link is live."

The avatar popped, a woman in her thirties untroubled by the pressures of command. Looking at her, Kal felt every one of her years. Zuana could have been one of her children, if she'd ever been dumb enough to have any.

"Commodore Zuana," Kal said. "Director Peng suggested I comm you."

"I've been expecting your call, Ms. Folau. What can I do for you?" Zuana's words were clipped, tight.

Kal did not have to be psychic to see the woman was a mass of conflicting emotions, fear of betrayal most of all probably. "I'd like to start with an apology. I hope Director Peng has explained why I cannot be more forthcoming, but I cannot do that without putting my life and the lives of my people at risk."

Zuana's face betrayed not a flicker of emotion. "You must understand how difficult it has been cooperating with a complete unknown on something as critical as the defense of our system."

"The *Harmony-445* will prove we're with you."

"Which should reassure me . . . except it doesn't."

"I'm sorry to hear that, commodore, but I do not have time to massage your bruised ego. For my own reasons, I am here to do as much damage to the Imps as I can. If you don't want my help to stop the Imps, fine. I'll do the job anyway; I have already deployed my strike packages."

"What? Where?"

Kal waved a hand. "Out there somewhere."

The stony face stared back for a moment, then cracked into the faintest of smiles. "Peng told me you were a hard woman."

Kal smiled back. "People tell me that. Look, let's stop tap-dancing around, commodore. I'll patch you into my combat AI. That way you will see all my tactical data. The only thing you won't have is the position and vector of my ship."

"That's works for me . . . I've sent you a security token. You can datalink through on TAC-884."

"Wait one . . . Tactical, set up a combat AI datalink with *Kuliak* on TAC-884. Just make sure the Narsaqs can't see where *Stiletto* or *Provider* are."

"Roger, captain . . . Okay, our positions and vectors have been scrubbed . . . linking . . . *Kuliak* acknowledges . . . security token authenticated . . . datalink is up."

"Okay, commodore. You're in."

"Holy shit! How many recon drones have you deployed?'

"20. I have an aversion to surprises."

Zuana grimaced. "No kidding . . . Okay, I see your strike packages . . . 14 of them. You are putting a lot of metal into space, Ms. Folau."

"I have an even stronger aversion to losing."

"I can see that . . . Let's have a look . . . Jeezus! You've deployed FireSparks; even the Imperial Navy's ASMs are nowhere near as good. I think it might be a bit late not to trust you; your ASMs could have torn my ships apart, any time you wanted."

"That they could, commodore."

"Hold on a second, Ms. Folau . . . My staff have just told me that your strike packages have been configured to hit the Imp cruisers one second after they drop into normalspace. That cannot be right. Nobody can set up the targeting that quickly."

"We've accessed real-time drop data from the gateway AI, accurate to the millisecond. That lets us designate a target datum

1,500 klicks from the gateway; that minimizes the risk of collateral damage if a ship loses containment."

"I'd like to know how you've done that, Ms. Folau."

"You will, commodore, as soon as this is over. Can we talk about how we're going to do this?"

"Well, now that we understand your capabilities, splitting the operation into two phases makes the best sense. First, your FireSparks take out the cruisers. Second, my SDVs deal with any Imps ships that survive your missile strikes before cleaning up the marine transports and support ships. How does that sound?"

"I think that'll work, commodore. We'll need a detailed opsplan to make sure it does. Can your staff work one up?"

"You'll have a first cut inside the hour."

"We should talk again then."

"Agreed," Zuana said, "and, before you ask, yes, we will be leaving Moreno's drones alone. Any problems, you can contact me any time."

"And you me. Folau, out . . . Tactical, Command. Commodore Zuana is giving us tactical control over our strikes, so we are clear to go. Transfer TACON to the combat AI."

"Tactical, roger." Atlassian's voice was calm and measured. "Combat AI has tactical control."

"Weapons. Strike status?"

"Strike-1 through 14 on standby to commit, targets assigned. *Harmony-445* now designated hostile track 555-888, no change."

Kal commed the *Provider*, now loitering beyond the edge of Narsaq nearspace well clear of any threats.

Stefanec's avatar popped. "Yes, captain?"

"Things are about to kick off, Peter. Any questions?"

"None. The *Provider* will be here if things don't go to plan."

"Much as I have great faith in *Stiletto* and its team," Kal said, "that is reassuring. Just don't forget you have the authority to do what you think best if things go pear-shaped. Logan Mwzele is a very competent tactical officer; you can trust his advice."

"Understood, captain."

"Good. *Stiletto*, out."

"Command, Combat," the AI said. "SITREP from Lander-1. At Point Batwing on vector for *6399*. Narsaq SysDef is ignoring them."

"Command, roger. Send to Lander-1. Jackal-Blue. Acknowledge."

"Sent . . . Lander-1 acknowledges Jackal-Blue."

"Roger. Personal for Sharma. Narsaqs are happy. You can relax now."

"Sent . . . From Lander-1. Personal for captain. Too late. Will be indenting for new underwear on completion."

Kal had to laugh, even though she was not entirely sure Sharma was joking.

Don't Talk's journey in-system would have been a gut-wrenchingly lonely business.

~~~

"Command, Combat. Emergency bulletin from Narsaq NearCon. By order of Narsaq System Defense, all pinchcomm links to Balakken are now off-line."

Kal offered up a silent word of thanks. Until the Narsaqs made their first move, there had always been a chance they might not stick to the plan. They'd not be the first people to let paranoia overrule logic.

And the locals had good reason to be paranoid. Ms. Folau and her take-it-or-leave it attitude would have troubled the most relaxed of Narsaqs.

"*Maxwell Pride* now on final approach to hostile 555-888," the Combat AI said.

"Any sign 888's expecting trouble?" Kal asked.

"Negative. Main cargo bays remain closed, vector unchanged."

Kal watched the Narsaq freighter carrying the marines of SOG-88 head for the *Harmony-445*. The Imp q-ship's chances of survival were diminishing fast as the gap closed: 5,000 klicks . . .4,000 . . .3,000 . . .2,000 . . .1,000 . . .

The *Maxwell Pride*'s cargo-bay hatches swung open. Squat containers spilled into space, off-loading their missiles the instant they were clear. Within seconds, the space around the Narsaq freighter had filled with pencil-thin lines of brilliant white light as microfusion engines accelerated missiles towards their target.

The *Harmony-445*'s combat AI was paying attention. Moments later, the Imp q-ship started to spill missile its containers into space.

Giving the Narsaq ASMs their targets. One after another, the Imp containers exploded into violent, fleeting flares of blue-white light as the microtoks powering their missile payloads lost containment.

Kal bobbed her head in approval. Nicely done, she thought, the tension of the long hours waiting for the Imp attack to start beginning to fade.

And then the final blow: a pair of missiles on vector for the *Harmony-445*'s stern. Clouds of shrapnel released by proximity-fused warheads shredded the complex main-engine arrays, nudging the q-ship off-vector, thrusters flaring as it fought to regain control.

Not everything went the Narsaqs' way. A single Imp container, overlooked in the freewheeling chaos, was given enough time off-load its missiles, their engines flaring into life.

"Oh, shit," Kal hissed. The *Maxwell Pride* was defenseless against Imp ASMs.

"Command, Combat. Hostile 555-888, vampires away. Targets confirmed friendly track 888-100."

Kal breathed again. The Imp missiles were heading for Commodore Zuana's flagship, *Kuliak*, an attack too small to trouble the Narsaq SDV.

Kal turned to O'Donnell once *Kuliak*'s close-in defenses—lasers, cannon and shotgun—had hacked the Imp missiles out of space. "*Kuliak* did well."

"You know, all those missile containers have me thinking the days of big ships might be over. Attacks from lots of small ships would be unstoppable."

Kal smiled. Small ships and lots of them. Just as Daniel had foreseen.

"Command, Combat. *Maxwell Pride* is launching its landers . . . Holding clear."

"Roger . . . Waiting to see if the Imps will fight, I'd say . . . Do you think they will?" Kal asked O'Donnell.

"The Narsaq marines are probably outnumbered at least five-to-one, but I'm sure the Imp brigade commander knows what'll happen if he chooses to fight. A single missile strike and there'll be not one Imp marine left alive on that ship."

"I'll bet you—"

"Command, Combat. Flash from CTF-10. Imperial Marine Assault Brigade 25 has surrendered. SOG-88 now boarding *Harmony-445*. Will advise when secure."

Kal patted O'Donnell on the back. "Well, there you go, Liam. I was about to bet you 50 they wouldn't surrender."

O'Donnell chuckled. "I wish you had. That's one bet I'd have taken."

"Command, Combat. Personal from Director Peng. Reads 'Thank you'."

Kal looked at O'Donnell. "Something tells me the Narsaqs trust us now."

"They should. That was very convincing,"

"It was. Let's hope the next act goes off as well."

"It will, captain."

Kal frowned as her stomach tightened up. She had seen far too many guaranteed-to-succeed missions go belly-up.

She checked the Imp task force as it approached the Narsaq gateway. As with the Balakken operation, four cargo drones led the attack, followed by the heavy cruisers: Rear-Admiral Moreno's flagship, *Imperator*, and the *Defiance*, *Dependable*, and *Vengeance*, plus the light cruisers, ten of them.

It still surprised Kal to see the marines in their assault ships and the usual gaggle of support and combat-repair vessels only minutes behind the last of the light cruisers. An attack of hubris, she decided; Moreno must have assumed the cruisers of TF 64 would have no trouble trashing Narsaq-3's defenses. It would also explain why he had elected to lead the attack; at Balakken, he had delegated that task to the more maneuverable light cruisers.

"Command, Combat. First drone drop imminent."

Kal mouth was dust-dry. There would be a lot of dead Imps before the day was out. She had seen too many corpses in her time to want that.

The fat, blunt shape of the first drone dropped into normalspace, its main engines bursting into life once it cleared the gateway. The second popped, then the third and fourth.

"Command, Combat. The Narsaqs are ignoring the drones."

Kal felt a rush of relief. Fat, dumb, and sluggish, the drones were a missileer's dream. She hadn't been confident the Narsaqs would have the self-control to ignore them.

Many system-defense forces wouldn't.

"Command, Combat," the AI said. "Strike-1 away. Target 555-100."

Kal found it hard to believe that she was about to attack an Imperial warship. And not any old ship; the *Imperator*, flagship of Rear-Admiral Moreno.

And she wasn't alone. The air on the bridge was thick with a mix of fear, tension, and anticipation.

Amidst a flare of ultraviolet radiation, the INS *Imperator* filled Kal's command holoscreen.

One second later, flashes rippled across the starboard quarter of the Imp heavy cruiser as the FireSpark missiles of Strike-1 smashed home, the first stages of their warheads blasting pockets out of the armor, pockets through which second stages punched penetrators deep into the ship.

The strike was over in an instant and the *Imperator* had survived. Kal prayed it stayed that.

And then, in a single searing flash, the cruiser was gone, taking with it all souls aboard.

"Command, Combat. Hostile 555-100 killed. No lifepods."

Kal stared at her holoscreen. An Imp heavy cruiser vaporized by her missiles on her orders, killing hundreds of Imp spacers. It was almost impossible to believe.

Stiletto's bridge was quiet. Nobody said a word.

One after another, Imp ships appeared in normalspace only to fall victim to *Stiletto*'s strikes, the heavy cruiser, *Dependable*, following *Imperator* into incandescent oblivion.

The *Defiance* and the *Vengeance* fared better, the missile salvos hitting far enough forward to miss the tokomaks powering their main engines. They were left wrecks, rolling off-vector, bleeding air and smoke and ice from rips in hulls blasted open by secondary explosions as ordnance magazines and auxiliary tokomaks exploded, the space around them fast filling with the firefly-flash of lifepods fleeing the disaster that had engulfed their ships.

By the time *Stiletto*'s missiles had destroyed the *Allegiance*—the fourth of the light cruisers to drop—Kal had had enough. The Imps had now lost three ships with all hands; the way things were going they would not be the last.

"Combat. Flash comm CTF-10," she ordered.

When Zuana's avatar appeared, her face drawn tight with shock.

With the *Alacrity*'s arrival imminent, Kal cut through the formalities. "My FireSparks are turning this into a massacre. I'm aborting my missile strikes. Can you handle the rest of those cruisers?"

"I can, yes. I—"

"Wait!" Kal said. "Combat, abort all strikes."

"Aborting . . . Strike-9 through 14 revectored to Point Jumbo, now on standby."

Kal commed Zuana. "Sorry about that, commodore. You have TACON. My remaining strikes are on standby if you need it."

"I have TACON, roger. We'll take it from here."

"Command, Combat. Tango-9 dropping . . . Confirmed the INS *Alacrity*."

Zuana gave the light cruiser no quarter. The *Kuliak*'s missiles were too many, and the Imp ship's close-in defenses—for some reason strangely ineffective, Kal thought—allowed too many missiles through.

The problem was that the Narsaq missiles were Musaytirs, not FireSparks. The explosively formed penetrators which their single-stage warheads fired were incapable of piercing the *Alacrity*'s armor.

But every ship has its weaknesses, the *Alacrity*'s its massive lander-bay hatch. A single Musaytir hit the hinge line, gifting the warhead's penetrator a path inside the cruiser, tearing open one of the *Alacrity*'s auxiliary power plants and triggering a violent release of energy that gutted the lander bay and blasted great slabs of armor into space.

As brave as she was reckless, the *Alacrity*'s captain ignored the Narsaqs' instructions to strike her colors, responding instead with a stream of Eaglehawk anti-ship missiles.

The instant the first missile showed itself, Zuana ordered the *Kapisillit* and its sister SDV, the *Kummmiit*, to fire a second strike, the missiles targeting the ruptured hull around *Alacrity*'s lander-bay hatch and the main engine clusters, a strike that disemboweled the ship forward and crippled it aft, the cruiser's captain recovering her commonsense and striking her colors.

A light cruiser carried a crew of 245. By Kal's estimate, half them would now be dead. Sacrificed to make a clique of rich Terrans even richer and more powerful.

Like aristos queuing for the guillotine, the rest of Task Force 64 dropped into normalspace. Only the *Adamant* refused Commodore Zuana's order to strike, a decision met with missile swarms from the *Kangaatsiaq* and the *Kullorsuaq*. Swarms that left the Imp ship a gas-bleeding wreck, tumbling through space, out of control, spitting lifepods.

As the last Imp cruiser struck, Kal let out a long sigh of relief. It was over.

Except it wasn't. A jolt of fear shocked Kal.

She had been so focused on the Imps, she had forgotten Fonseca's attack on the Gang of Five's drug lab. Watching over her marines was her job. A job she had not been doing. The thought of what her negligence might have cost turned her stomach.

A quick check of the mission status screen settled fast-mounting panic. Fonseca had the operation in hand, but he had taken casualties.

As if to remind Kal that her people were exposed, Fonseca reported in. "Command, Boxcar. Scram 2 mike."

"Command, roger."

"Uh, there is one more thing," Fonseca added. "We will be bringing some extra bodies back with us."

Kal groaned. "What? Again?"

"Affirmative. Eleven non-coms. Slaves supplied by Hardakken and used to test new drugs."

Kal hoped Fonseca wasn't going to make a habit of rescuing waifs and strays. "Roger that; we'll be ready for them . . . SITREP on the Imp attack: three cruisers destroyed, four combat-ineffective, the rest surrendered."

"Happy to hear that. Boxcar, out."

Without the Imps to worry about, Kal could only watch Fonseca manage the hardest part of any operation: withdrawing without taking unnecessary casualties. Which might not be easy, not with *6399*'s security team largely intact.

A threat Kal need not have worried about, thanks to sustained bursts from *Don't Talk*'s cannon that sent the superannuated ex-cops—helpfully concentrated into a single, large group—bolting for the lifepods, the compartments behind them reduced to a wreck of torn metal and plasfiber.

15 long minutes later, Kal received the report she wanted to hear.

"Command, Boxcar. Withdrawal complete. All lab and support personnel have evacuated the orbital and are now in lifepods; NearCon has confirmed it will organize recovery. Demolition charges will fire once they are clear. Casualties: one Kilo, two Charlie, plus the eleven non-coms, all Bravo. Request CASEVAC soonest."

Kilo! Knowing one of her marines had been killed tore at Kal, though the butcher's bill—two wounded, both assessed Charlie, non-urgent—had not been as bad as Kal had feared. Against a well-trained security team commanded by a competent leader, it would have been much worse.

"Command, roger," Kal said. "We're on our way . . . Combat, jump to Point Backstop, then make vector to intercept *Don't Talk*, expedite."

Kal threw off her harness and slid out of her chair. Her body ached after the hours she had spent immobile. Once she had racked her helmet and stripped off her skinsuit, she put a hand on O'Donnell's shoulder. "You have the ship, Liam. I need to talk with Zuana."

"I have the ship, captain."

As she left the bridge, Kal took a last look at the command screen. Task Force 64's survivors were sad-looking bunch as they headed for their orbital slots.

It was still hard to believe.

~~~

A desperately needed mug of coffee in hand, Kal watched Zuana's avatar pop. "That went well, commodore."

"It did, Ms. Folau, mostly thanks to you and your FireSparks, though some of those Imp ships should never have been in combat. My TechInt people say too many of their mission-critical systems were degraded. One of them, *Alacrity*, only had half its close-in weapons stations operational. Moreno let himself get a bit too comfortable, I'd say."

"Which is understandable. He's had it pretty easy up to now . . . What's your plan from here?"

"The marines are on their way to the Imp ships. As soon as they have taken control, we'll start shipping the PoWs dirtside," Zuana said. "After that, who knows? It'll be up to the politicians to clean up the mess."

"What about the Imp ships?"

"They'll be condemned as prizes of war, and we'll take them into service. My engineers think the yards might be able to save the *Vengeance*, though the *Defiance* is probably a write-off. It's a pity; those Empire-class heavy cruisers are fine ships."

"Apart from needing heavier armor and better close-in defenses, yes, I'd agree."

"They weren't a match for your FireSparks."

Kal paused, wondering for a moment how far she should take the opportunity to hand. All the way, her instincts told her. "Talking of heavy cruisers we think the days of big warships might be over."

Zuana smiled. "Funny you should say that. One of my staff made the same point not five minutes ago. I'm going to ask SysDef to convene a working group to look at it . . . I don't suppose we could persuade you to be part of it?"

"We'll be there. We might even have answers to some of your questions. We've been thinking about this for a while now."

"Thank you, Ms. Folau. I will be in touch . . . I do have something else I would like to discuss, if you have the time."

"Please."

"What you have helped us do today is extraordinary. However, it would be negligent of me if I did not put it into context. With your help, one system has stopped the Imps, but for how long? The Empire will come after us again, and when they do, Narsaq is . . . forgive my language, fucked. You need to think about what that means for you. And one more thing: I have a bright young captain working for me."

"The one who thinks the future of space-warfare doesn't include big ships?" Kal asked.

"The same. René Duvall is his name. He doesn't think what you say stacks up, Ms. Folau. Forget the pinchcomm problem; Duvall says you also want us to believe ImpSec doesn't know about your private navy and its FireSpark missiles, missiles the Imperial Navy itself does not have, missiles Kolovchenko's gateway security teams would never have allowed you to ship to Narsaq from Shenwa-Boeing's plant on Halesowen-5, the only place in humanspace where FireSparks are made . . ."

Kal wondered what she had done to deserve Duvall; the man was too smart, dangerously so.

". . . So, here's what Duvall concluded: To do what you have done, he says your ship must have a jump drive."

Kal forced a laugh. "Yeah, right. Everyone knows the jump drive is impossible."

Zuana sighed. "We both know that's not true. Listen to me, Ms. Folau Everyone needs friends, even you, with your jump ship and FireSpark missiles, which is why you should think about working with us. We both want the same thing: to destroy the Empire. We trusted you; I think it is time you trusted us. Hold on . . . Sorry, I need to talk with my boss. Do you need anything from me?"

"I don't think so. Once I have my lander back, we'll be recovering any hardware we have left over; FireSparks are expensive."

"I'm sure they are, so do that . . . Oh, by the way," Zuana added, "SysDef is reporting an unknown ship on vector to intercept your lander. Would that be you by any chance?"

"Yes, it is. Sorry; we were about to check in with NearCon."

"Do that. I'll tell SysDef you're a friendly; they'll leave you alone. Is there anything else you want to tell me? Let's see . . . How about the UV flare that made spotting your ship so easy?"

Kal wanted to kick herself. She had told Combat to take *Stiletto* in-system without a moment's thought; she might as well have sent the Narsaqs a comm telling them to expect a jump ship. "I'll answer all your questions when the time's right."

"Sooner would be better. Zuana, out."

Kal sat back.

She hated it when people gave her advice she should take.

She hated it even more when she made stupid mistakes.

~~~

O'Donnell commed from the bridge. "Apologies for interrupting, captain. Director Peng's asked to talk with you."

Kal took the comm. "Director Peng. What can I do for you?"

"President Ha'alaafa has asked me to thank you for your assistance. We'd be part of the Empire by now if you hadn't helped us here today."

"That's very kind, though I'm sure you haven't forgotten we did it for our own reasons."

"That is not something I like to talk about. It suits me to paint you in an altruistic light."

"Whatever works, director. What can I help you with?"

"Narsaq and all the systems rimwards from us have agreed to form a defensive alliance. We are calling it the Coalition of Free Systems. All Coalition systems will be transferring their system-defense assets into a unified navy. We will also be funding a substantial warship construction program . . ."

Kal suppressed a sigh; a request for Q-drive technology was coming her way, she knew it.

". . . and we'd like your help with that. Commodore Zuana has briefed me on your last conversation."

"She thinks we should join forces with you."

"That and more," Peng said. "My analysts agree with her that your ship uses jump-drive technology, hard though that is to accept. Giving the Coalition access to that would be of enormous value in our fight against the Imps."

Kal was trapped. The more she denied the truth of what Zuana and Peng were saying, the more foolish she'd look. She needed time to think. "Forgive me, director. I need a minute; something's come up."

She put the comm on hold.

The Imps already knew she had the Q-drive. It would not be long before they had their own. Time was running out. Fast.

And Peng's offer was as unambiguous as it was appealing: accept Narsaq's help defeating the Empire in exchange for her Q-drive.

To keep on pretending her ship didn't have one was pointless. She should take Peng's offer.

Though not until Peng had agreed to a few conditions of her own. Like paying for Freighter-02 and its SAVs. Hell! One SAV carrier was good; two would be even better. Unless absolute morons ran the Coalition, paying a hundred billion dollars was a reasonable price to pay to keep the Imps at bay.

Not that she had any problem joining the Coalition; quite the opposite. The more she thought about it, the more she liked the idea. Her solo fight against the Empire had been crazy and stressful, at times terrifying, the cost of failure almost unbearable, the weight of the responsibility she carried getting heavier by the day.

If she was honest with herself, she had to accept that the time would come when that weight would break her. A time which the tremors afflicting her hands told her might not be so far off.

Kal returned to the comm. "Sorry about that, director. You have given me a lot to think about. Send me a summary of what you propose; I'll get back to you as soon as I can."

"You'll have it within the hour . . . There is one last thing you should know," Peng added. "The Coalition has negotiated an armistice with the Imperial ambassador here on Narsaq-3."

Kal sat bolt upright. "What?" she barked. "I hope you're joking . . . Shit, you're not! Why the hell would the Coalition do that?"

"To bring the pinchcomm links to and from Balakken back online."

"And the gateways?"

"They are staying open."

Kal stared at Peng, eyes wide in disbelief. "Are you people insane? This is Narsaq's only chance to shut down the gateways without killing anyone."

"I know that, and my government does too, but the decision's made."

"The Imps attacked through those gateways, and they will again."

"You can't be sure of that."

Kal threw her arms up. "Oh, dear god! I have spent months making sure I understand the people running the Empire. They will not take kindly to humiliating defeat, I can promise you that. When they attack again—which they sure as hell will—you'll never know they're coming until they start pumping ships through the gateway, and they will keep the ships coming until you're overwhelmed."

Peng had the grace to look embarrassed. "The government doesn't think the Imps will attack us again. And the Coalition's interstellar traders are an influential group, especially here on Narsaq. They have strong links to the ruling Liberal Party."

"None of which will help you when ImpSec direct-action teams start infiltrating your smug, money-grubbing system. Cruisers and drones aren't the only way the Empire can win this war. And, in case you don't know what direct-action teams do, search for terrorist attacks on Yttrium . . . Anything else?"

"No, Ms. Folau. Thanks for your time."

The instant Peng had gone, Kal commed O'Donnell to her stateroom.

~~~

The shock on O'Donnell's face was apparent. "Goddammed traders! All they cared about is money, and money has talked. The oldest story in human history."

"I'm afraid so," Kal said.

"Cretins, all of them. So, what do we do?"

"The best thing we can do: join the Coalition of Free Systems."

"Why? We have our own plans."

"Things have changed. Zuana's staff and Peng have worked out how we and our FireSpark missiles got here."

"Oh, shit," O'Donnell hissed. "That means every Narsaq and their dog will be talking about it soon. They won't be able to contain themselves."

"You're right there. I reckon every system within ten gateways of Narsaq is going to know before the month's out; if that doesn't light a fire under the Imps, nothing will. But, as long we are the only people in humanspace with a working Q-drive—which I am certain we still are—the Coalition will have to give us what we want."

~~~

Fonseca collapsed onto a crew-room bench, his the body of an exhausted man.

Kal handed him a beer "Losing one of your people must be hard, Jens.".

"KIAs are the worst part of this business. At least Chen had no next-of-kin. I was hopeless at writing the letters."

"I was never senior enough. Is there anything you didn't want to talk about in the hot washup?"

"Yeah. My exec says she's worried about one of our guys, Xaabsade. And, if Ushabir is worried, I am too."

Kal frowned. "Xaabsade? I was at the hot washup. It sounded to me like he did well."

"He did, but somehow it wasn't him. I can't really describe it . . . He's one of my regulars; has been for years. He's solid, dependable, a thinker when he needs to be, even in a firefight, and he always stays on mission."

"Not today?"

"He just wasn't the same old Xaabsade. He took risks he never used to take, stupid risks. He's smart and experienced; he knows the difference between bravery and recklessness. Today that line got very blurred."

"People behave oddly for a reason," Kal said. "Any family or money problems? Has he fallen out with any of the team? Is he sick?"

Fonseca ran a hand through his hair. "I wish it was that simple . . . I'm sorry, captain. Maybe I'm overreacting. We were all very twitchy going in. You said the Narsaqs were on side, but none of us knew for sure that they could be trusted. And a lander is a soft target; a couple of anti-ship missiles and we'd have been gone."

Kal grimaced. "One of the reasons I haven't slept too well these past few nights. Do you want me to talk with Xaabsade?"

"No. It's hard to criticize marines for taking risks; it's what we do. Ushabir will let me know if he says anything to the team. We'll keep an eye on him, see how he goes the next time we're in action. I'll have Ushabir talk with him if he looks like he's becoming a liability; Xaabsade's more likely to open up to her."

"One of my company commanders told me that half an exec's job is listening."

Fonseca nodded. "And she's as good an executive officer I could ask for. If the man's got anything to say, he'll say it to her."

—50—

Kal's head ached. Dealing with the Coalition was hard enough. Working through the options for *Stiletto*'s next mission with what seemed like half the ship's company entrenched around the crew-room table had been like trying for a strike with a grease-slathered bowling ball.

But, finally, they were agreed.

"Let me sum up then," Kal said. "Our first mission will be to Teshawa-2 to strip PinchTekk's plant of every pinchspace node we can find before destroying the plant.

"Our second mission. The latest intel from FIS says the Imps are planning to base a new task force on Tongchen-6 with orders to take control of the entire Tongchen sector. Given that's where most of our ordnance suppliers are based, we can't allow that. We are going to stop the Imps by shutting down Tongchen's gateways before the first three cruisers assigned to the task force arrive from Qianshan-2 early next month.

"And finally, Terra's gateways. I don't have to tell you that it's the most dangerous operation we'll ever do, which is why I won't make the final go/no-go decision on it until I am sure we're up to the job. I will not risk my ships and the lives of my people for a heroic failure."

Kal eyed everyone around the table, defying anyone to restart what had been at times a fiery debate, one fueled by Fonseca's insistence that the Tesahwa-2 and Tongchen-6 operations were a waste of time. In a return to his Andimeshki roots, he wanted to go straight to Terra.

Kal sympathized. Fonseca and his team were getting nervous. The Expansion had started its push into the Yoganathan sector; that meant the Imps were heading for Andimeshk.

But *Stiletto* and its crew were too green to take on Terra, the most heavily defended planet in humanspace. She needed the Teshawa and Tongchen operations to prove they were up to that task.

"So, any final questions, thoughts?" she went on. "No? Two last things then. The i-bomb for the *6399* operation will be ready tomorrow. Please watch it and give your feedback to Mashalo. And second, Artie Shaw says the i-bomb for the Ventas operation will explode twelve hours from now. Given it has reached most of humanspace, that is going to make life interesting for the Imps. That's all, so thanks everyone . . . Hang on, Daniel."

"What's up?" Daniel asked once everyone was gone.

Kal had been dreading this moment. "I want you to listen to what I have to say before you say anything."

"Uh . . . Yeah, okay, but wh—"

"Daniel! Listen, don't talk."

"Sorry."

"You and I have been a team ever since Ladaki-6. That has to change. I've decided to let O'Donnell run the Teshawa operation. If he performs as well as he has in the sims, I'll hand over command of *Stiletto* to him."

"Why?"

"We both hope this war ends before the Imps get their own Q-drive ships," Kal said, "but the chances of that happening aren't good. If it doesn't end, the Coalition will need a new generation of officers to carry on the fight, not clapped-out wrecks like me. The last few years have been the hardest thing I have ever done, and I don't think I can do it much longer.

"Which brings me to you. You are too valuable to risk in combat anymore, which is why I have spoken with President Ha'alaafa. She has agreed Narsaq will fund an Institute for Pinchspace Science, and we both want you to be its first research director . . . starting tomorrow."

Daniel stared at Kal. "Tomorrow? No way! I'll miss the Teshawa operation."

"That's the whole point. We can't afford to lose you."

"No way, Kal! I am not leaving *Stiletto* until we have finished off what you and I started. End of discussion."

"The decision's made, Daniel. You and Marcia are going dirtside tonight...and before you start shouting at me," Kal added as Daniel's face hands tightened into white-knuckled fists, "there are no guarantees we can finish off the Empire before it develops its own Q-drive. That means the Coalition is going to need you more than ever. I'm sorry; that's just the way it is."

"What about you? The Coalition needs you too."

"No, it doesn't. I'm expendable. You're not."

Tears flooded Daniel's eyes. "Don't say that."

"First chance I can, I'll quit."

"Promise?"

Kal took Daniel in her arms. "I promise."

She let Daniel go. "You and Marcia need to get all your stuff packed up. The shuttle will take you both dirtside at 22:00; a liaison officer from the president's office will meet you on arrival. And I'll see you for the meeting with SecState on Wednesday."

—51—

Kal and Daniel sat enjoying the gentle warmth of a spring afternoon, their table cluttered with remnants of lunch.

Daniel broke the companionable silence. "Do you think we'll get what we want?" he asked.

"The new carriers and their SAVs will cost a fortune, but I think the Coalition systems have to pay whatever it takes to stop the Imps."

"Better than being a colony, I guess."

"Much better, and they all know it. I just wish we hadn't taken so long to finalize our agreement."

"And what a pain that was. I wish—"

A security bot hissed to a stop, alongside the table. "Excuse me, Mister Wei. I am here to escort you to your meeting with the Secretary for Industry."

Daniel stood. "Sorry, Kal. I'd better go."

As he made to leave, he leaned in, "How about this, Kal? First, a meeting with SecState, and now I'm off for one with SecInd. Not bad for a kid from the butt-end of nowhere."

"That won't stop me from kicking your ass if you let it go to your head."

Daniel swooped in to plant a kiss on Kal's cheek. "Yes, mom."

Kal watched him go. At times Daniel could be infuriating, but she had grown to love him more than anyone since her great-aunt. She smiled; Daniel was fast becoming the son she never had.

It was a comfortable feeling. A feeling of deep contentment. It had been a long time since she had felt so happy.

She started as a man dropped into the seat opposite. "Oh, Jerry, hi. Sorry, I was daydreaming."

Director Peng nodded at the beanpole figure hurrying away. "The more we learn about what you and Daniel did with a pair of wrecked gateways and an old lander, the more incredible it seems. Even now I have idiots telling me you two are part of an Imp conspiracy."

"Worst Imp conspiracy ever if we are. Coffee?"

"No thanks, Kal. I have drunk enough today to float a damn boat. Can you spare a few minutes? I'd like to talk through your upcoming missions. FIS has an office over at State."

"Sure. Let's go."

Together, they walked across the plaza, an intricately tiled space canopied by jacaranda trees in all their extravagant purple glory, the afternoon sun lancing bars gold through the branches.

"Our first president was Brazilian," Peng said as they walked across a carpet of fallen blossom. "She loved jacarandas."

"Who'd have guessed?" Kal murmured.

She followed Peng through security and over to a door marked 'FIS Liaison Staff'.

The access lock opened into an open-plan office. Peng waved a hand at the crowded space, jammed with workstations, all occupied, all busy, the director's arrival ignored. "As you can see, our beloved Secretary of State doesn't believe in doing FIS any favors. My staff call this Forward Operating Base Alpha. Anyone who survives six months here gets a medal."

Kal followed Peng into a room barely big enough for the table and chairs it held. "I guess that makes the State Department enemy territory."

"It feels that way, especially when FIS's intelligence assessments don't support State's latest *cause de jour*. Anyway, I wanted to talk about your next missions."

"What about them? I thought FIS had signed off on the concept of operations?"

"For Teshawa and Tongchen, yes. They're exactly the sort of operation *Stiletto* should be doing. And they have a manageable level of risk."

"And they let me blood my crew without over-exposing *Stiletto*. Lurking on the edge of nearspace while my missiles rip the Imps a new one isn't enough. So, what's the problem with Terra?"

"Listen, Kal. I want your word you'll abort if things get too risky."

"I know how much risk I can accept."

"It's not that simple," Peng said. "An end to all this madness will only be a single missile strike away; if you destroy Terra's gateways, the Empire's finished. You wouldn't be human if you did not let that influence your decisions. And I think you're underestimating how much pressure you're going to be under, pressure from the Coalition, from your Andimeshki, from yourself, pressure to go for it and risk be damned."

Kal shrugged. "We'll have signed our agreement with the Coalition by then. That will make *Stiletto* a navy ship and me a Coalition officer. My orders will tell me what I can and cannot do."

"Tell me, when you were a grunt, did you obey orders?"

Confusion clouded Kal's face. "Uh . . . Yeah, I did."

"You didn't on Kolokaar-5 with the 41st Marine Combat Group."

Kal stared at Peng. "You know about that?"

"Of course. You are critical to this war; I must understand you . . . Listen to me, Kal. When you reach Terra, do what you did then. Forget your agreement with the Coalition. Forget any orders the Coalition navy might give you. Forget what your Andimeshkis want. Forget what you want. Do what you think deep down is right. And, whatever you decide to do, you will have my complete support."

—52—

Kal ran an eye over the throng clustered around the holoscreen: heads of state, senior brass from the Coalition navy and marines, Director Peng, Narsaq's chief scientist, along with their staffers. All stared, open-mouthed, at an unremarkable brown-dwarf close to the Narsaq system.

"Tell me I'm not dreaming," a voice called out.

"You're not, Madam President," Kal replied. "That's Ka'liifa. The *Provider* has just jumped half a light-year . . . Now, if the principals would like to follow me, we have a deal to complete."

~~~

Kal sighed with relief. Finalizing the partnership agreement had been an exhausting process, one not helped by the scrum of politicians and their advisers she had faced across the table, only Daniel, O'Donnell, and Fonseca on her side.

After a great deal of bitching and moaning, the Coalition had agreed to almost everything she had asked for, including paying Tharamaran for the two carriers and their SAVs, a hard-won battle that would return millions of dollars to Kal's and Daniel's bank account.

True to military form, the Coalition Navy had already given the carriers an acronym, CLA: carriers, light, attack. A document of eye-watering complexity now recorded everything, one that had left Daniel muttering about bureaucratic bullshit and Kal trying to shut him up.

Zuana came over as the meeting broke up. "Excuse me, captain. Can I have a word?"

"Of course. Oh, I forgot. Congratulations on your promotion."

"Thank you. Being chief-of-staff to COMFLT is a big job . . . I just wanted to let you know that COMCOMARFOR . . ."

Kal's mind froze for a second; it wasn't easy keeping up with the blizzard of acronyms the Coalition was spawning. COMFLT: Commander, Coalition Fleet. COMCOMARFOR: Commander, Coalition Marine Forces.

". . . has allocated Combat Assault Team 2 to *Provider* for the Teshawa operation. It's 180-strong with four heavy attack landers and commanded by a Major Himaya. He's very competent; I think you'll get on."

"Has CAT-2 seen any combat?"

"None, which is why it's under your TACON, not that the marines liked that. My boss told me the discussion with General Falana was, er . . .. very robust."

Kal had to laugh; her Andimeshkis were a rough lot. "It's the right decision. CAT-2 needs to be blooded; no sim can ever give you that gut-churning certainty that you're about to die. We can review things after Teshawa."

~~~

Daniel took a beer from the foodbot. "That was interesting."

With an effort, Kal passed up a beer in favor of coffee; there were still times—thankfully rare—when the old cravings returned.

She could not help smiling at Daniel's excited enthusiasm. "You look very smug."

"I should," Daniel shot back. "I never wanted the Q-drive to be a secret, and now it's not. It will be where it belongs, out with ordinary people. Kolovchenko cannot stop it now. It's too late."

"Just make sure the cybersecurity is solid. What's inside a Q-drive AI is worth trillions to the Imps."

"Artie Shaw is running the final break-in tests now; he says the Imps will never find out what's inside those boxes. And when we implement the command-key system, the AIs will be useless even if they did."

"How's the Institute coming along?"

"We move in next month." Daniel's grin was huge. "It's going to be awesome."

"Now that is one thing I never doubted. Hold on a sec . . . Jens has just commed me to say Major Himaya is on his way."

"Is he the boss of this CAT-2 outfit?"

Kal winced. "Boss? Try commander."

"Yeah, yeah."

Daniel sank his beer, stood, kissed Kal on the cheek, and then he was gone with 'Don't you dare not come back' shouted over a shoulder.

~~~

Fonseca scanned the faces of his marines. "Any questions? No? Okay, we're done here. *Provider* is embarking the marines of CAT-2 as I speak. I want all team leaders in the lander bay at 22:00 to go across to meet them. Carry on."

Erikk Xaabsade let himself be carried along by his fellow Andimeshki marines as they made their way out of the cargo bay. Unlike the rest, all busy swapping the usual pre-mission bullshit, he was silent.

His fire-team leader put an arm around his shoulders. "You look a bit glum, ZaZa. You okay?"

"Yeah. I've not been sleeping too well, that's all."

"Have the medibot check you over. The Teshawa operation is going to be a bitch, and I need everyone to be on their game."

"Yeah, will do. Sorry. I'll go now."

~~~

Fingers laced behind her head, Kal lay in her bunk. The sleep her body craved just refused to come, her mind too busy churning through the deployment ahead.

The Imps knew they were up against a Q-drive ship. Every Imp system would be looking for the telling flash of ultra-violet radiation that all ships emitted when they dropped into normalspace.

Teshawa-2's defenders would be expecting *Stiletto*.

And if the Imps had sent reinforcements to protect such a high-value target . . .

—53—

"Command, Combat. Recon-22 and 23 have cleared Teshawa-2 nearspace and are now back online. Starting data downloads."

Kal breathed a little easier. Waiting for drones to complete a fly-through hostile nearspace was an anxious business. There was no more compelling way to warn a system commander an attack was heading her way.

Finally, icons started to pop on Kal's command screen as the threat AI matched objects detected by the drones to profiles in the threat knowledgebase, a trickle that fast turned to a flood. Green: civilians, no-threat. Red: hostile. Blue: friendly. Yellow: still unclassified.

"Command, Combat," the AI responsible for fighting the ship said finally. "Threat plot update complete. Threat red. Tracks 555-001 through -006 classified hostile. All identified Hammer-class SDVs. Standby IDs—"

"Stop! Threat red; I've got it. Go to exception reporting," Kal ordered, wondering why AIs found it so hard to be succinct.

"Okay, folks," she said to the group around her. "The threat AI thinks the Imps have deployed six SDVs to defend Teshawa-2, one of the most valuable systems in the Empire. Any thoughts on that assessment?"

Captain René Duvall—Zuana's smart staffer and now the Coalition navy's liaison officer for the Teshawa operation—was the first to speak. "The latest INTSUM from FIS told us to expect Hammer-class SDVs, and there they are. To make sure nobody can miss them, they're radiating every sensor they have."

O'Donnell studied the threat plot. "It's like they're shouting out 'look at me, look at me'. It feels wrong."

"And FIS also said to expect the Imps to send reinforcements," Duvall said. "I think the threat AI has missed something."

A murmur of agreement.

"We're seeing those SDVs because the Imps want us to," Logan Mwzele, *Provider*'s tactical officer, said. "There are more warships waiting for us, I'd bet my life on it."

O'Donnell nodded. "I agree with Logan. I know the Imps are badly overstretched, but the PinchTekk plant is a vital part of Kolovchenko's gateway system. So, where are the reinforcements?"

"The answer will be in the data," Duvall replied. "I think we need to audit the threat AI's assessment."

The sour looks on everyone's faces made it obvious what they thought of that.

Kal half-smiled. Working through the learned logic an AI used to decide what each piece of data meant was a brain-numbing process, but necessary. AIs made mistakes too. "I agree . . . Liam, René, Logan, over to you . . . You seem a bit glum, Peter," she added, waving *Provider*'s skipper to follow her.

"Not unhappy, captain. Confused; this space warfare stuff is new to me. And all the jargon doesn't help."

"Come on, Peter. It's more than that."

Stefanec rubbed his eyes, "Ah . . . Yes, it is. Look at me. I'm a freighter skipper; we are trained to avoid trouble. The thought of my *Provider* getting close to hostile warships makes me . . ." Stefanec's voice faded away.

"We are all scared; we've not attacked a system as well-defended as Teshawa-2. The problem is fear. It's contagious; the more anxious people are, the more unreliable they are under pressure. You cannot let it show; your crew will be worried enough as it is."

"I'm sorry. I'll do better."

Kal put a hand on Stefanec's and squeezed. "You must. When things go to shit, your people will be looking to you. Listen, if it is any consolation, I am going to scrub the operation if I think the risks are too high. I cannot afford to lose *Stiletto* or *Provider*."

"Understood, captain. Is there anything else before I head back?"

"No, I don't think so. We won't have the detailed ops plan until we've confirmed what we are up against. Your tactical officer will brief you when it's done."

"Logan Mwzele is a good man. I'm glad I have him."

~~~

Fett up on her desk, Kal was enjoying a coffee when O'Donnell's comm broke her concentration.

"Captain! We have something."

"Show me," Kal said as she reached the bridge.

"We've found a 2.2 gigahertz radar transmission from one of the contacts close to the PinchTekk plant. It only lasted a second, and we've not seen it again. The AI decided it was an artifact and ignored it."

"What's the threat knowledgebase say?"

"It's a JK-887 radar, obsolete, and only fitted to the Imps' City-class SDVs. Once the AI knew what to look for, it found a second one."

"What else did the AI miss?" Kal asked.

"Three more anomalous contacts, close to those two SDVs," O'Donnell replied. "NearCon's traffic report has them listed as commercial freighters in Clarke orbit awaiting cargo, but their infra-red signatures are too warm."

"All that heat means they're carrying more electronics than any freighter," Duvall added. "Our threat AI hadn't learned that was important; it has now."

"Glad to hear it . . . Combat, classify as hostile."

"Combat, roger. Reclassified. New tracks hostiles 555-007 through 011."

"What do you think?' Kal asked O'Donnell.

"We need to know for sure what those Imps ships are. The Ventas butt stunt is what's called for, I think."

"Agreed ... Tactical," Kal said to Atlassian. "I need a butt that will let us take a good look at the space around the PinchTekk plant. See if you can find me one."

"Standby, captain."

Duvall face had creased with bewilderment. "What's the Ventas butt stunt?"

Kal patted Duvall on the shoulder. "Watch and learn."

—54—

Recon-72 drifted from its layup position deep inside one of the *Arclight-45*'s massive main-engine cones. Taking extreme care not to be seen by the drone's holocams, it threaded a path between the tanker's massive helium-storage spheres, heading for the bows.

Two hours later, Recon-72 came to rest. Screened by a bank of heat dumps, it had an uninterrupted view of Teshawa-2 and everything in orbit around it.

Recon-72 fired a laser databurst back to a distant pinchcomms drone, reporting its safe arrival back to *Stiletto*.

René Duvall had the watch when the message arrived. He read it. Sitting back, he shook his head.

The Ventas butt option.

He had a lot to learn.

~~~

"Command, Combat. We have Recon-72's final data download; it has relocated back to the port main engine cone. Standby . . . *Arclight-45* is adjusting vector to make final approach to orbital Helium Base-2 . . . Recon-72 has dropped off-line."

Kal relaxed a fraction. The massive tanker's deceleration burn had cremated the hapless recon drone. The Imps would never know how close her watcher had been.

"Command, Combat. Threat has analyzed the holovid from Recon-72. We now have positive IDs on hostile tracks 555-007 through 011: two City-class SDVs, *Beijing* and *Jakarta*, one Battle-class auxiliary, the *Majia River*, and two Yankee-class SDVs, *Y-14* and *Y-43*."

"The Imps have transferred those Yankees from Terra," Duvall said. "They were part of the Imperial Navy's training task group, TG 500."

O'Donnell's face was tight with disbelief. "What are the Imps thinking? Yankees are obsolete; they shouldn't be anywhere near a warzone."

"We all knew the Imps were having trouble finding the assets they needed for the Expansion," Kal said, "but deploying training ships where they might get shot at? They must be desperate. Anybody know what a Battle-class auxiliary does?"

"It's a marine unit transport, light; MARUT-L for short," Major Himaya replied. "It carries a mobile assault battalion: 800 marines supported by six heavy ground-attack landers."

They were facing a battalion of marines? Kal did not like the sound of that. "And a MAB does what?"

"Low-intensity, short-duration security operations, both orbital and dirtside. I'd say they are here to stop people like us messing with the PinchTekk plant."

Kal took a breath to calm a sudden rush of nerves. "Okay. Time to finalize the ops plan . . . Liam, a word before you start," Kal added waving O'Donnell aside.

"Yes, captain?"

"I've been thinking. I want you to run the operation; you will be making all the tactical decisions from here on. Any doubts, you talk to me. And if I don't like what you're doing, I'll step in. Otherwise, I will sit at the back of the bridge, saying nothing, and doing less. Okay?"

O'Donnell blinked. "Ah, yes, I guess . . . This is a surprise, captain."

"Can you do it?" Kal asked. "Now's the time to say no, not when things go pear-shaped."

"Yes, I can do it."

"I'm sure you can too, Liam. I have seen you in the sims. I'll push out an update to tell the troops what's happening."

"Okay, captain . . . Hold on; you'll need a personal callsign to make sure our people don't get confused . . . How does Boss sound?"

Kal winced. "Way too mariney."

O'Donnell frowned. "Uh . . . Next thing up from a captain is a commodore. How about that?"

"Bugger off."

A long pause.

"Chief?"

"No!"

"Uh . . . Leader? Top Dog? Head Honcho?"

Kal rolled her eyes. "Give me a break."

"Captains get promoted to commodores. How about that? I'm sorry; I can't think of anything else."

Kal threw up her hands in defeat. "Oh goddammit! I can't think either, so let's go with that."

O'Donnell reached out, grabbed Kal's hand, and shook it. "Congratulations on your promotion, commodore. Well deserved, I must say."

"Just watch it," Kal growled.

"Of course, commodore. Whatever you say, commodore. Will there be anything else, commodore?"

"Kill me now."

"Not before I've had the microfabs run up commodore's shoulder straps," O'Donnell said, vanishing down the bridge hatch an instant before Kal's coffee mug fizzed past his head.

—55—

Chilled by the bitter cold of deepspace, the swarm had coasted in for millions of kilometers, unseen by Teshawa-2's surveillance network.

400,000 kilometers out, a laser databurst from *Stiletto* woke the swarm from its long sleep. Microtoks powered up. Systems warmed and came on-line. Containers disgorged Musaytir anti-ship missiles and decoys. Ship simulators deployed their transmitter arrays: laser, infra-red, ultra-violet, radar, datalink.

The AI controlling the swarm fired off a databurst back to *Stiletto*: Strike-1 nominal.

~~~

"Command, Combat. Executing Catfight-Red . . . now!"

Kal was watching the optronics feed from one of Strike-1's recon drones. A double flash flooded the screen, bursts of ultra-violet radiation given off by ships as they dropped into normalspace.

O'Donnell glanced at Kal. "What do you think, commodore? Will Teshawa SysDef pay any attention those flares?"

"My 50 says it will."

"You and your bets . . . and that's another I am not going to take. The Imps know we have Q-drive ships."

"Command, Combat. Hostile tracks 555-001 through 006 underway; designated target group Tango-Golf-1."

"They've taken the bait," O'Donnell said.

Kal wasn't surprised; there was no way the Q-drive was still a secret and every human alive knew what UV flares meant. It was still demoralizing when the Imps proved they weren't the half-wits she wanted them to be.

"Command, Combat. Tango-Golf-1 on vector to intercept Strike-1. Plume analysis confirms they are redlining their main engines."

She was happy not to be aboard one of the Imp SDVs. As O'Donnell had pointed out, they were second-rate ships. Up against Strike-1's Musaytir anti-ship missiles masked by hundreds of decoys and escorted by ship-sims to bamboozle the Imps' sensor arrays, only a hefty dose of luck would save any of them.

"Command, Combat. Tango-Golf-1, vampires away; 2,000 Eaglehawk anti-ship missiles, no decoys."

O'Donnell frowned. "Combat. ASMs and no decoys? You sure about that?"

"Affirmative."

"Am I missing something, commodore? ASM attacks are a numbers game: the more missiles and decoys, the better."

Kal thought for a moment. "It's inexperience. The Imps' combat AIs have only ever dealt with soft-targets, usually hijackers and psychotic captains."

O'Donnell's face was a feral snarl of anticipation. "I'd like to see their faces when Strike-1 releases its missiles and decoys. Which will be any . . . second . . . now!"

"Command, Combat. Strike-1 away."

"Command, roger," O'Donnell said. "All stations, Command. Teshawa SysDef has sent its six SDVs to intercept our first missile strike, so we will be jumping in-system in five . . . Combat, send to *Provider*. Jumping to Point Clamshell. Be at immediate notice to follow. Ops plan unchanged. Acknowledge."

"Message sent . . . *Provider* acknowledges."

"Command, roger . . . Lander-1, Command. You and your decoys will be launched and on your way to the PinchTekk plant as soon as we drop. The instant one of the Imps locks you up, you turn and run. No asking for orders. Got that?"

"Lander-1, understood," *Don't Talk*'s command pilot replied.

"Combat, Command," O'Donnell said. "Execute Catfight-Blue."

"Command, Combat. Catfight-Blue, roger. Strike-2 through -7 to Alert-0. Lander-1 and decoy escort to Alert-2 for launch. Jumping now."

Stiletto dropped into normalspace 50,000 kilometers from the PinchTekk node plant, at two kilometers across one of the largest orbital structures in humanspace. Predating the development of artgrav plant, the complex had at its center a massive cylinder, the Hub from which radiated six spokes ending in smaller spheres.

One sphere—Sierra-6—was the focus of the operation; the Logistics Management Facility, which stored the finished nodes PinchTekk supplied to hundreds of gateways across humanspace. And, once the Imps had developed their own Q-drive, they would need even more nodes, and lots of them.

The Imps could not afford to lose the contents of the LMF any more than they could the PinchTekk complex.

Which was why doubt picked at Kal's confidence. Why weren't there more defenders? It was bizarre . . . unless *Stiletto*'s threat AI and recon drones had missed something.

Ignoring the metallic grinding of *Stiletto*'s rotary launchers dumping missiles and decoys into space that had filled the bridge, she compelled herself to stand back, to go through the threat plot, searching for any inconsistencies.

Not an easy job. What she saw was chaos. Facing an imminent attack, almost every civilian ship in Teshawa-2 nearspace had panicked; main engines flaring into life, they were heading for the safety of deepspace, all NearCon's attempts to restore order ignored.

And plume analysis had confirmed that not one of them was a warship.

As for the stay-behinds, they were all too cold to be anything other than a civilian ship all but shut down. As best she and the threat AI could tell, the Imps had nothing waiting to ambush her.

"Command, Combat. Strike-2 through -6 away. Hostiles 555-007 through 11 now designated target group Tango-Golf-2. Lander-1 to Alert-0."

Kal still had trouble believing what the Imps had done. *Beijing*, *Jakarta*, *Y-14*, *Y-43*, were warships that should never have been anywhere near Teshawa-2. Which they were about to find out.

As for the *Majia River*, marine standard operating procedures in Kal's day allowed soft-skinned transports in-system only when nearspace had been scoured clean of all hostiles. That ship belonged someplace else.

"Command, Combat. Track 555-007. Vampires away, 140 Eaglehawk ASMs. Zero decoys. Target *Stiletto*."

"Command, roger," O'Donnell said. "Execute Catfight-Yellow."

"Catfight-Yellow," Combat replied. "Lander-1 launched. Nominal. Decoys launched and nominal . . ."

Kal zoomed her holoscreen in. Thanks to *Don't Talk*'s escort of decoys, the Imps would see not one lander but 20, all accelerating hard for the PinchTekk plant.

". . . Strike-7 launched, now on vector for *Majia River*. Final target designation awaiting hostile lander launch."

One after another, the *Beijing*, *Y-14*, and *Y-43* joined the fight, their missiles following those fired by the *Jakarta*. Kal's hands tightened on the armrests of her seat. The Imp missile strike was now 440 Eaglehawk ASMs strong.

O'Donnell pointed at the untidy gaggle of missiles on-screen, all heading for *Stiletto*. "Teshawa SysDef has messed up. It hasn't coordinated the strike. Those ships have just dumped missiles overboard and sent them on their way. And the swarm geometry . . . well, there isn't any. It's all pretty random. And there are no decoys."

Kal stayed silent. If O'Donnell was trying to cheer her up, he had failed. Even a ship as capable and well-armored as *Stiletto* would struggle to fend off the Imp Eaglehawks.

"All stations, Command. SITREP. The Imps have sent 400 or so missiles our way. They will be with us in five, so final suit checks and visors down. The good news is we got our strikes in first. All being well, the ships protecting the PinchTekk plant will soon be history. Command, out."

Kal dragged her eyes off the stream of red icons heading her way. Her job was to look for anything O'Donnell might have missed; she was no use to him if she didn't.

The command plot threw up no surprises. The missiles from the six Imp SDVs were on vector to intercept Strike-1's diversionary attack. Those from the four ships screening the PinchTekk plant would reach the *Stiletto*'s missile-engagement zone any moment. What was odd was the way the Imps were ignoring *Don't Talk* and its protective decoys as they headed under full power for the node plant.

Even odder was the reluctance of the Imp marines embarked in the *Majia River* to show themselves. The SysDef commander must know by now the PinchTekk plant was the Coalition's target. Kal's would have had those marines on their way to protect the most valuable asset the Imps had in Teshawa-2 nearspace, if only to make sure their landers weren't hunted down by hostile ASMs.

Fear and panic, Kal thought. It wouldn't be the first time an untested command team had collapsed in the face of . . .

No, wait.

The *Majia River* had opened its cargo-bay doors. Its assault landers were on their way. Kal bared her teeth. "Too late, boys."

The AI managing the battle was already responding. "Command, Combat. New tracks hostiles 555-012 through 017, identified as hostile landers, now designated target group Tango-Golf-3. Strike-7 assigned to interdict."

They might be Imps, but Kal felt a twinge of sympathy for the marines; she'd been a grunt too. No lander ever built could survive a FireSpark ASM with orders to kill its target. The system commander should have ordered the marines into lifepods with orders to get the hell out. And the *Majia River*'s crew too; designed to operate in low-threat environments, a MARUT-L had minimal armor, its only defenses eight turret-mounted shotgun mounts.

Which might as well toss pebbles at the incoming FireSparks.

Stiletto's missiles closed on the four Imp warships. *Jakarta* and *Beijing* were the first to die, their defenses crushed by the sheer speed and agility of the attack, massive balls of energy consuming ships and crews as FireSparks gutted their tokomaks.

O'Donnell treated the two obsolete training ships, *Y-14*, and *Y-43*, and the *Majia River* more gently by splitting the attack into two waves. The first destroyed their main engines; needing no more encouragement, the crews had abandoned ship with commendable speed. As soon as their lifepods were clear, the second wave of missiles sent them into oblivion after the *Jakarta* and *Beijing*.

The last targets were the all-but defenseless Imp landers. Kal had insisted on only one change to O'Donnell's opsplan: fitting fragmentation warheads to Strike-7's missiles in place of armor-piercing. That would have been cold-blooded murder, she'd said.

And now those warheads exploded, firing cones of shrapnel into the landers' main-engine assemblies, reducing them to tangles of shattered metal spewing hydraulic fluid into space, the landers left to drift through space on vectors to nowhere, their cargoes of marines able to do nothing except wait for rescue.

A quick check.

The first of the chaotic stream of Imp missiles was almost on *Stiletto*, the attack was a disjointed, sprawled-out mess, its leaders a full minute ahead of the laggards. Which made the job of *Stiletto*'s combat AI easier.

But, if Combat overlooked a missile in the freewheeling chaos of attack and defense—one of the inexplicable mistakes all AIs were prone to make—and that missile was on vector for *Stiletto*'s vulnerable stern, then things could get very ugly.

Kal she buried the thought. She pushed herself back into her seat's crashgel lining and tightened her harness.

Stiletto's hull vibrated as its missile interceptors streaked across space to rip holes in the Imp attack.

The metallic racket of autocannon, the *pock-pock-pock* of lasers, the hull-crunching *wham-wham-wham* of shotguns joined the fight. A fight that had too many elements moving too fast for any human brain to process, a fight fought by the ship's combat AI, a fight that reduced Kal and her crew to observers, their lives hostage to a mindless machine.

The counter tracking the attack was a blur as Imp missiles died. It stopped.

At zero.

The attack was over. Not one missile had reached *Stiletto*. Kal started to breathe again; the *Stiletto* had passed its first serious test.

"Fuck," a voice said. "That was scary."

"No small talk, guys," O'Donnell called out. "Combat, Command. To *Provider*. Catfight-Green."

"*Provider*, Catfight Green, roger. Jumping now to Point Jackass."

An ultra-violet flare announced its arrival. Seconds later, Major Himaya's landers had deployed, powering away as the freighter turned end-for-end for its deceleration burn to take station off the PinchTekk plant.

Kal let herself relax a fraction. She loosened her harness and turned to René Duvall. "You okay?" she asked.

The Coalition navy's observer sat hunched forward against his straps, his face pale and sweat-slicked behind the visor of his helmet. "The attack on *Kuliak* was nothing like this. That was a lot of missiles."

Kal knew the sims had warned the man the battle would be brutal, but no sim conveyed the terrifying reality of being the target of missiles intent on killing you. "It could have been worse. If we'd been facing that many FireSparks in a tightly coordinated strike mixed up with decoys, we'd be dead now."

"I thought we were."

Kal patted Duvall's hand. "Welcome to space-warfare, Q-drive style."

Duvall smiled, the rictus smile of a corpse.

"Command, Combat. Tango-Golf-1 vampires time-to-target 5 seconds."

"What a waste of Eaglehawks," O'Donnell said as the missiles fired by the six Imp SDVs met Strike-1, the interception marked by fleeting flares of warheads firing and missiles dying. Kal's eyes never left her command plot, willing Strike-1 to power through.

She wanted those six Imp SDVs killed.

"Command, Combat. Strike-1 is now clear. Loss rate 3.3%. Reconfiguring now."

The strike split into six stream, one for each Imp SDV. Kal selected the holovid feed from a recon drone embedded with the stream targeting the INS *Hammer*. It was soon close enough for her to see the Imp ship's close-in defenses start work. Flashes flickered across its hull as pulsed lasers, cannon, and shotguns poured fire into the incoming attack.

The stream reached its target, its leading edge packed with decoys to overload the close-in defenses and screen the missiles following on behind. Traveling at over a million kph, the decoys shattered on the armor, shrouding the hull in a blazing blanket of exploding microtoks.

An instant later the Musaytirs that had survived the *Hammer*'s close-in defenses hit home. Warheads fired. Hypersonic, molten-metal penetrators slashed through the SDV's armor as if it through paper, eviscerating the ship and consuming its crew.

One missile hit further aft. Its warhead ripped into an auxiliary tokomak. Losing containment, the plant released a massive wave of incandescent energy that blew out the emergency vents before vanishing into space.

The INS *Hammer* was one of the lucky ones. Severely damaged it would never fight again, but it had survived. Three of the Imp SDVs had not. They had vanished, immolated in the flames of failed tokomaks.

That left two Imp ships. In theory, they should not have survived, but they had, thanks to captains who had positioned their ships— probably by accident, Kal thought—close enough to provide mutual support. Together, they raised a wall of defensive fire so thick, so focused, it had destroyed all but a handful of missiles all of which had missed the SDVs' main-engine and auxiliary tokomaks.

"Command, Combat. Hostile tracks 001, 002, 004 killed. 005 combat-ineffective. 003 and 006 combat-degraded."

Kal clenched her fists in frustration; *Destrier* and *Trebuchet* had survived, god only knew how. Not for the first time that day, she wished Strike-1 had been FireSparks and not the less-capable Musaytirs.

Strike-1's missiles had hit *Destrier* hard, tearing great gashes into bows and forward sections, skeins of ice-laden air and hydraulic fluid bleeding into space.

Kal took a long look at the Imp ship. "Looks like the bridge has been wiped out; that means no combat Its ASM launchers seem okay."

"*Trebuchet*'s untouched forward," O'Donnell said, "and that is not good for us. As long as *Destrier*'s emergency control room's working and it can launch its missiles, *Trebuchet*'s combat AI can control the strike."

Kal pointed at the screen. "Just look at the damage *Trebuchet*'s taken amidships. Godknows how it didn't lose a tokomak."

"The usual reason: luck. Looks like we have a fight on our hands, commodore."

"I reckon." Kal took a breath to steady herself as she checked the command holoscreen. No change. *Provider* was taking station off the PinchTekk plant, its landers standing off alongside *Don't Talk*, Himaya's marines already inside.

An hour was all Fonseca's and Himaya's marines needed. Kal wondered if the two surviving SDVs from Tango-Golf-1 would give them that much time.

"Command, Lander-1," Sharma said. "Sitrep."

"Go ahead," O'Donnell replied.

"Boxcar reports Team 1 has secured Sierra-6 and its node inventory. Advises quote 'lots of nodes'. Lander-1 and *Provider* standing off to receive. Teams 2 through 5 have secured the Hub. Plant security is trying to push them out. Though fighting heavy, Boxcar advises unlikely to succeed and expects to empty Sierra-6 of nodes and withdraw on schedule."

Himaya's marines were getting the fight they wanted; Kal hoped they were able to handle their first taste of combat.

"Command, Combat. Hostiles 555-003 and 006 are reversing vector, hostile group now redesignated Tango-Golf-4."

O'Donnell said to Kal, "I was hoping they'd call it quits."

So had Kal; captains who wanted to live long enough to see their grandchildren would have. "Two ASM platforms and a working combat AI means trouble."

"Best we stop them then. Combat, Command. Set vector to intercept Tango-Golf-4. Standby missile strike."

Kal gave a nod of approval. The two Imp SDVs, already damaged, their reaction-control systems and close-in defenses compromised, stood little chance of surviving *Stiletto*'s missiles.

But there were few certainties in space warfare, as the two SDVs had already proved by surviving an attack they should never have. Even wounded, the two Weapon-class SDVs could fire a missile salvo large enough to make the *Stiletto* fight for survival, a fight the gods of war might decide it was *Stiletto*'s day to lose.

She needed to make sure O'Donnell had allowed for that.

"What's your thinking, Liam?"

"The further from the PinchTekk plant we engage those ships, the more time we'll give the marines and *Provider* to clear nearspace. I don't care what happens to the *Destrier*; it's useless on its own. If the *Trebuchet* survives and we don't, it cannot afford to engage the

Provider at long range. Doing that only risks the plant; it must get close before it fires its missiles."

"It does. And that's a safe option against a soft-skinned freighter. What's your plan?"

"*Provider* has to jump out of Teshawa-2 nearspace before an Imp missile salvo can reach it. Stefanec will have orders to abort immediately if we are knocked out and *Trebuchet* remains combat-capable, not that I think that's likely."

"It is possible," Kal said.

"The Imps have seen how lethal our missiles are; they won't be thinking too straight when they see our FireSparks coming their way. But you are right. They might get lucky and we don't make it . . . It might be better if you briefed Himaya and Fonseca," O'Donnell added.

"To tell them *Provider* will have orders to leave them behind if things go to shit?" Kal asked.

O'Donnell's face tightened. "We can afford to lose marines and landers. We cannot afford to lose both our Q-drive ships."

"No, we can't. Okay, I'll tell them. Just make certain that Captain Stefanec and his TACCO understand they do not have the option to disobey orders."

"Aye, aye, commodore."

~~~

Kal flipped up the visor of her combat helmet to wipe the sweat out of her eyes, her gloved hands clumsy and awkward.

For what seemed like an age, she had watched as the two Imp SDVs crawled across the command plot. The range to the *Stiletto*'s FireSparks' missile-engagement zone had reduced at glacial rate, the strain of waiting for the Imps to launch their missiles fraying her already ragged nerves.

Her only consolation was knowing that the crews of the two Imp ships would be feeling a hundred times worse. They would have seen how *Stiletto*'s FireSparks had crushed the ships defending the

PinchTekk plant, the way a fist smashes an egg; their combat AIs would have told them their chances of surviving *Stiletto*'s attack were close to zero.

"Command, Combat. Strike-8 away. Target Tango-Golf-4."

You guys should have stayed home, Kal thought as fusion-powered mass drivers drove *Stiletto*'s missiles and decoys away in a tight cloud on vector for the *Destrier* and *Trebuchet*.

She checked O'Donnell. Even though his face was impassive, the fingers of one hand drummed out a restless, chaotic beat. Kal was glad to see it; any commander who faced an incoming missile attack without being afraid was a danger to himself and his crew.

"Command, Combat. Tango-Golf-4, vampires away. Estimated 500 ASMs, no decoys. Target confirmed *Stiletto*."

Fuuuck, Kal hissed under her breath. Eaglehawks might not be the best ASMs in humanspace, but that was a lot of missiles for one ship to beat back. For all her faith in *Stiletto*, things were not looking good.

She did the only thing she could: wait, doing her best to ignore the metal bands tightening around her chest.

Two minutes in, gimballed engines slewed the swarm into skidding turns, a vector change that fractured the swarm into eight cone-shaped streams, their tips—once again mostly decoys to distract and overload the Imps' defenses—leading the way.

Surely the captains of the two Imp ships must have realized their ships were doomed? Kal willed them to accept reality and send their crews to the lifepods.

The space around the Imps remained empty of the pods' tell-tale orange strobes, and still the SDVs powered on. Their crews were going to die with their ships; nothing was more certain. Kal wanted to scream in protest at the pointless stupidity of it all.

Now the Imps' close-in weapons opened fire, triggering the zig-zagging dance of death the missiles and decoys used to confuse the Imps' combat AIs.

As *Stiletto*'s attack pressed home, missiles and decoys started to die, warheads exploding and microtoks failing in blazing flashes of light. But too few died to make a difference.

Destrier was the first to lose its doomed fight.

As *Stiletto*'s combat AI had intended, four missile streams smashed into the SDV's upper hull, one hitting well forward to finish demolishing the damaged bow, the rest aft targeting the main engine tokomaks. Warheads drove penetrators through the armor and into the ship. Some, checked by heavy machinery, expended their prodigious energy immolating whole compartments and everybody in them. Most passed right through the hull and out into space, killing any of *Destrier*'s crew unfortunate enough to stand in their path. A handful breached the secondary armor around the main-engine tokomaks. With containment lost, *Destrier* vanished in a ball of incandescent gas.

Less than a second later, the *Trebuchet* had followed its sister-ship into oblivion taking with them the souls of almost 200 Imps whose commanders had been too stiff-necked to see the inevitability of their ships' destruction.

The bile rose in Kal's throat.

"Command, Combat. Tango-Golf-4 killed. Remainder of Strike-8 aborted and revectored to Point Malachi for recovery. Main engines to emergency power . . ."

Kal checked the threat plot. The strike fired by the two SDVs was less than a minute out, the missiles packed into a tight stream by the *Trebuchet*'s combat AI, a swarm geometry designed to overload the close-in defenses facing the attack, while leaving the rest of the *Stiletto*'s weapons without targets.

Smart, she thought. *Stiletto* was in trouble.

". . . Active decoys away."

Launchers spit boxy shapes into space. Where there had been one *Stiletto*, now there were many. They filled the space between attackers and attacked with a cacophony of electro-magnetic radiation designed to confuse Imp missile sensorheads, the confusion compounded by sheets of searing white microflares to burn out their optronics.

Forcing some Imp missiles, befuddled into paralysis, to self-destruct. Others, no less bewildered, wandered off into deepspace.

Too few.

"All stations, Command. Vampires inbound. Brace for impact."

Kal's forced herself back in the crashgel seat, hands clamped on the armrest, sweat burning salty in her eyes.

Time ran out and *Stiletto*'s close-in defenses hit the Imp salvo, missile interceptors arcing out, their gimballed engines sending them plunging into the body of the incoming swarm, a storm of laser, cannon, and shotgun fire hosed down the threat axis into the head of the Imp attack

A frenzied, chaotic counterattack that hacked missiles out of space to explode in a violent tapestry of pinprick flares of light.

Kal had stopped breathing as the threat plot tracked the Imp salvo down, the counter blurring as *Stiletto*'s defenses shredded the attack.

Until she allowed herself to believe it was all going to be oka—

With a bone-jarring *wham-wham* that whipped Kal hard against her harness, two Eaglehawk ASMs slammed into *Stiletto*'s hull. The first hit the bows on the port side, a glancing strike that squandered its warhead on the armor, its legacy a shallow, flame-scorched scrape.

The gods of war gifted the second missile a result. It hit the micrometer-wide gap between the hull and the armored cap protecting one of *Stiletto*'s pinchspace nodes, a weakness through which the missile's warhead fired its penetrator, vaporizing the node and trashing the conduit carrying power and control cables before it expended the last of its monstrous kinetic energy ripping apart Shotgun-2's mounting.

Stiletto's bridge filled with the shriek of alarms. Kal's eyes scanned the ship's status board, her concern growing fast as the list of compromised systems grew.

O'Donnell was already out of his chair. "The threat plot is now green, commodore. Damage control team is on its way. Request you take command while I see what needs to be done."

"Do it," Kal said. "All stations, Commodore has command."

She checked and then rechecked the command screen to confirm O'Donnell's assessment that the Imps in Teshawa-2 nearspace no longer posed any threat.

He had been right. Save for a handful of attack landers—which *Don't Talk*'s missiles would destroy if they were stupid enough to make a move—the Imperial Navy no longer posed any threat.

She commed *Provider*.

Stefanec's avatar betrayed his concern. "We've seen the damage report. What can we do?"

"Your priority is to extract the marines as soon as they've finished, but they can take their time now. I want every node they can recover. We need them all."

"Understood. What about *Stiletto*?"

"I don't have a detailed damage report yet. You have our vector out-system. I want you alongside me as soon as you have recovered your marines. One way or another, we're going to fix this ship."

"Roger that, captain."

~~~

Kal stood with Yasmin Kashani amidst the flame- and blast-seared tangle of metal and melted plastic that had once been a shotgun mounting, the air so acrid her eyes watered. She ran her eyes over the damaged node's innards, a mess of heat-blistered cables poking out of the foam sealing the hull.

Her face was sour with frustration. "Talk about bad luck," she said to *Stiletto*'s chief engineer. "We have one weakness in our armor, and that goddammed missile found it. Can you fix this so we can jump?"

Kashani bobbed her head. "I can. The *Provider*'s combat repair team has all the spares we need, including nodes. The problem's going to be recalibrating the node array. The pinchspace drive AI likes everything just so."

Kal swore softly. She knew all about node alignment.

She wished Daniel was here to help.

—56—

O'Donnell shook his head, grim-faced. "I should stay. This is my ship too."

"You and the rest of the crew are the only ones who understand how to use Q-drive ships in combat," Kal said. "The Coalition needs you."

"I could say the same about you, commodore."

"You could. I still want everyone except me and the chief off this ship."

O'Donnell gave a reluctant nod. "Watch yourself, captain."

"Ready?" Kal asked Yasmin Kashani once the crew was off and *Provider* had disconnected the transfer tube.

The *Stiletto*'s chief engineer was haggard with exhaustion, her face drawn and gray. "We are, commodore."

Kal knew she didn't look any better. It had been a long three days.

Her heart raced. Her mouth was dry. Her stomach threatened rebellion. This was how she had felt the first time she and Daniel had jumped the poor old *Wraith*.

"Combat, message to *Provider*. Jump to Point Witless. If *Stiletto* has not been located within 24 hours, *Provider* is to return to Narsaq. Acknowledge."

"*Provider* acknowledges. Personal from captain. Good luck."

"Send to *Provider*. I hope we don't need it." Kal turned to Kashani. "Any reason we shouldn't do this, chief?"

"Plenty, commodore., but none that count."

"Let's do it then . . . ShipCon, Command, execute jump."

"Standby pinchspace transition . . . now!"

With a gentle tremor, *Stiletto* vanished out of normalspace.

Kal stopped breathing.

"Pinchspace transition completed," ShipCon reported. "Vector is nominal."

Kal let herself breathe again, not that the test jump was over; *Stiletto* would not be dropping back into the safety of normalspace until the Q-drive was stable and its AI happy.

A tremor rippled the deck.

Kal's stomach lurched. She scanned the Q-drive status display. A transient instability, the AI reported, now stabilized.

"Command, ShipCon. Standby normalspace transition . . . now! At drop datum . . ."

Shaking, Kal allowed herself to relax as her holoscreen blazed into life with thousands upon thousands of stars. Deep down, she had been sure *Stiletto* would not survive, not without Daniel to work his arcane magic on the Q-drive AI.

". . . drop error 680 klicks. All systems nominal."

"Command, Combat. Threat plot is green. Comms link with *Provider* is up . . . Personal from captain. Welcome back. Lot of cheering. Well done."

"Send to *Provider*. Too tired to cheer over here. Close on me for crew transfer . . . How did it look?" Kal called out to Kashani.

The *Stiletto*'s chief engineer rubbed eyes bloodshot with fatigue. "Good, now that the AI's got the new node under control. You won't believe this, commodore. That's the most accurate jump *Stiletto*'s ever made."

"No way!"

"It's true. We've always had transient instabilities in our Echo and Foxtrot nodes down aft, though not this time, godknows why."

"Being hit by a pair of Imp missile warheads would be my guess. Send a full diagnostic data dump to Daniel as soon as we get back; maybe he can work why. And thanks, chief. You and the *Provider*'s combat repair team did a fantastic job."

"Here to serve," the woman said with a beaming smile that Kal suspected was all relief.

~~~

Kal beckoned O'Donnell over as he led the rest of the crew from the transfer tube. "You did well, Liam, more than well enough to take command of *Stiletto*."

"What? Formally? As captain-in-command?"

"Absolutely."

"What about you? Will you stay on?"

"Only until the Terra operation's over. Then it's retirement for me. So, what now?"

"Uh . . . I assumed we'd abort."

"The chief says *Stiletto* is nominal. And I think we can do without one shotgun mount. It's your call, though."

"Ah, yes . . . In that case we go." O'Donnell grinned. "You know what? In between the flashes of blind terror, I rather enjoyed kicking the shit out of the Imps."

An instant's disquiet; Kal wondered if one hard-fought win had gone to his head. Over-confidence could be—and often was—a killer. She'd need to watch O'Donnell.

"Right then," she went on. "I have an appointment with my rack. The ship's all yours, so get us on the way to our next mission. I want to be in Tongchen-6 nearspace before any Imp heavy cruisers turn up and we're already behind schedule."

—57—

The gods of war had been kind.

Stiletto's reconnaissance of Qianshan-2 had paid off. The three Imp heavy cruisers were still in Clarke orbit loading supplies and ordnance. Even better, the local net had been full of chatter about their imminent departure for Tongchen-6, an egregious breach of Imperial Navy operational security.

All much to Kal's relief; three Imp cruisers were worth 30 SDVs. The *Stiletto* would have had a fight on its hands if they'd already made it to Tongchgen-6 nearspace.

Just that thought set her hands trembling. Teshawa had broken a chunk of the confidence off her, unsure how she'd handle another Teshawa. For the first time in her life, nightmares full of missile attacks, exploding ships and dying spacers had plagued her nights, nightmares her neuronics' PTSD program seemed unable to manage.

But her nerves weren't so shot that she'd missed the opportunity the Imp cruisers' tardy departure for Tongchen-6 had offered up.

An opportunity she and O'Donnell agreed they had to take.

Kal glanced at him. Slingshotting Strike-1 around Tongchen-6's largest moon behind had been his idea and a good one; it was now travelling faster than any missile strike in the history of space warfare.

She smiled. Even faster than the ingots she had used to trash Deepshorne-6455. All that seemed another happier life a million years ago.

She slipped out of her chair to fetch herself another coffee, her third since O'Donnell had launched the attack against Tongchen-6's unsuspecting system defenses. Time had dragged as his first strike clawed its way across space. Not that the delay mattered. This was one attack the Imps did not have the assets to stop.

"Command, Combat. Hostiles 555-001 through 006 are getting underway."

Finally! Kal switched her neuronics to the vid feed from one of the recon drones escorting Strike-1. The Imp SDVs—main engines at emergency power—were accelerating hard.

She wished them luck; the Imps' combat AIs would be struggling to deal with Strike-1, which had now splintered into an unruly cloud of zigzagging missiles and decoys thousands of kilometers across. A system-defense commander's nightmare. Predicting which missiles were heading for which targets would have been impossible.

They are so fucked, O'Donnell had said with a look of savage anticipation as he'd given the order to commit Strike-1 to the attack.

It was soon obvious that the SDV crews had agreed with that assessment. As *Stiletto*'s missiles closed in, they took to the lifepods.

A smart move, Kal thought.

Seconds later, Strike-1 reached its targets. Nearspace filled with the flicker of warheads exploding, a curtain of yellow-red flares, come and gone in milliseconds.

In a single, brutal attack, *Stiletto* had destroyed Tongchen-6's entire system-defense infrastructure: the six hapless SDVs, SysDef orbitals, optronic and radar arrays, commsats, and the system's pinchcomms links back to Terra.

"Command, Combat. All targets killed. Threat plot is now green. I have cleared Assault-1 in direct to the gateway control complex . . . *Provider* confirms landers away . . . Brickyard reports Assault-1 is nominal."

Kal settled down to wait. She didn't expect the Narsaq marines to have any problems. Teshawa-2 had given Himaya and CAT-2 their first taste of combat; they knew how combat felt for real. Not that PinchTekk's security team had been a pushover. Competent, disciplined, and well-trained, they had fought hard. CAT-2 had suffered the casualties to prove it. Even Fonseca had been impressed; the Narsaqs had performed like Andimeshkis, he had said. A rare compliment, Kal suspected.

And O'Donnell had shown a creative side Kal had not expected. The tactics for the Tongchen operation had been his. With the Imps' system defenses destroyed in a single, preemptive strike, *Stiletto* did not have to make a covert approach in-system, always a high-risk exercise even with a passing heavy drone to hide behind.

And the slingshot around a handy moon had been a neat trick, one Kal had not expected from a normally dour O'Donnell, a maneuver that had whipped *Stiletto*'s missiles and decoys in-system at almost a million kph.

The defenders would have been shitting themselves when they saw the attack heading their way.

But, sound though his tactics were, O'Donnell had conceded they would not work against better-defended systems like Terra. With its layered defenses of SDVs, cruisers, missile containers, and planetary-defense stations coordinated by a C^3I system processing data from an extensive network of sensors and expendable recon drones, Terra's defenses were the most capable in all humanspace, and by a massive margin.

A margin which would only grow as the Imps absorbed the lessons of Narsaq, Teshawa, and Tongchen. Lessons they had to learn; if they did not, they would lose control of Terran nearspace and the Empire would collapse like an arch losing its keystone.

Which was why the Imps weren't just adding more warships and planetary-defense stations to Terra's defenses. They were building a second surveillance network. Codenamed BigEye, it relied on optronic arrays capable of discriminating between ships, missiles, and decoys, even at extreme ranges. When BigEye went live, bluffing the Terrans into responding to diversionary attacks rather than the main assault would become a lot harder.

And the latest INSTSUM from Peng's FIS had reported that the Imps were upgrading their cruisers with a new—and more capable—anti-ship missile. The Taipan, it was called.

Kal knew what more capable meant: improved vector-agility and a two-stage warhead neither of which the obsolescent Eaglehawk possessed.

But her FireSparks did.

She shivered as fingers of ice traced a path up her spine.

The business of space-warfare was getting too difficult, tactic and counter-tactic evolving fast. It was time for her to quit, to leave the business of fighting the Empire to people with the energy and resilience to cope with what might become a long and bloody war.

And she would.

As soon as the Terra operation was over.

~~~

"Commodore," O'Donnell called out from the command chair. "CAT-2's at the gateway support complex."

"Roger that," Kal said.

O'Donnell hadn't wanted Himaya's marines to do this the hard way, but he had no better options. The Imps had worked out how *Stiletto* had ambushed Task Force 64 at Narsaq. To make sure that never happened again, they had installed gateway-grade security in their traffic reporting systems.

Artie Shaw had said there was no point even trying to break in.

Which was why O'Donnell had sent Himaya's marines across to the gateways, their job to persuade the duty gateway supervisor to help Artie Shaw tap into the gateway traffic reporting system. Accurate targeting of the three Imp heavy cruisers now making the four-day transit from Qianshan-2 depended on it.

She patched her neuronics into the holovid feed from Himaya's assault lander, *Slapshot*. It hung alongside the gateway support complex as the marines—black dots against the searing white of spherical modules hung on plasteel girders—blasted their way into its cargo lock.

Explosions flared soundlessly, sending the excised patch of hull tumbling away into space.

The marines of CAT-2 vanished inside.

~~~

Thanks to a security team with enough common sense to know a fight they could never win when they saw one, it did not take CAT-2 long to secure the gateway support complex.

The assault leader—callsign Alpha-1—flicked up her visor as she stepped into the control room, the on-watch team corralled in one corner, hands on heads. "Who's in charge here?" she called out. "Come on, the sooner you tell me what I need to know, the sooner we're gone."

A man raised his hand; it trembled. His face was gray, the color of sun-flayed timber, shiny-slick with sweat. "I'm the duty gateway supervisor."

Alpha-1 beckoned him over.

The man stood in front of the marine, shaking bodily. Kal felt for him. A skinsuited marine in assault armor was a daunting sight.

And Alpha-1 was huge. "Okay, sir. Calm down, please. Yes, we are going to do some damage to your gateway, but you'll all be fine as long you answer my questions."

"Damage? What do you mean?"

"Enough to make sure it cannot be used until we let you fix it. Now—"

The supervisor's eyes flared wide in protest. "No! You can't do that."

"Oh? And why not?" Alpha-1 asked.

"We have ships in transit."

"Your traffic reporting system says there are no ships on their way here . . . Oh, wait. Let me guess. Could that be because these ships of yours are Imperial Navy warships?"

The man's face tightened.

"You need to watch your body language, my friend," Alpha-1 said. "I need access to the TRS datafeed with the precise time those ships will drop."

"I can't. I'm not allowed to."

Alpha-1 tilted her massive bulk forward, putting her helmet to the man's forehead. "Don't make the mistake of thinking I'm a kind person, sir. I'm not."

"Don't hurt me."

"Work with me, and I won't have to."

The supervisor's head dropped in defeat. "*Regulus*, *Groombridge*, and *Procyon*," he mumbled. "*Regulus* will drop at 22:20 Standard, the rest at five-minute intervals after that."

"Any other Qianshan traffic, up or down?"

"22 freighters heading to Qianshan; 19 on their way here. Things are quiet, what with the war and all. The navy is sending two support ships through as well, but we won't know their ETA until they depart Qianshan."

"You're doing well, sir. Now show me the raw data."

"I, uh . . . I can't do that." The supervisor's voice was a shaky mumble.

Alpha-1 pushed one of her team forward. Kal zoomed in; it was Artie Shaw. "With this man's help, you can. Now, you either work with him or I'll space you. You have ten seconds to decide . . . nine . . . eight—"

"I'll do it, I'll do it."

Alpha-1 patted the supervisor with a massive gloved hand. "There you are. That wasn't so hard, was it?"

O'Donnell cut in. "We are getting vid from dirtside, commodore. It's on TAC-539."

Kal patched her neuronics across. Amidst the flash of grenades releasing eddying clouds of narcogas, a mob was busy storming a building in Greek-classical style, a seething mass of humanity whose arms rose and fell as they clubbed and clawed their way past security forces in black riot gear. "Is that Tongchen City?" she asked.

"It is; the Imperial Governor's residence. I'd say the locals weren't happy being part of old man Michael's empire."

"I don't blame them . . . Who was the president of this system before the Empire took over?"

"A woman called Velasquez."

"I want to speak with her. I'm hoping the Imps haven't killed her yet; see if you can find her."

"Yes, commodore."

Kal was about to switch back to the feed from Alpha-1's helmet holocam when her neuronics pinged.

What the hell? A comm from her public dropbox?

Kal decrypted the message.

It was short. It was clear. It was what she had prayed for.

COMFLT had postponed the attack on Terra.

As relief overwhelmed Kal, she wondered why.

~~~

"I have President Velazquez for you, commodore."

The woman's avatar popped, eyes, red-rimmed and bloodshot, sunk deep in ashen wells, cheekbones sharp, hair cut short into a rough, ragged crop.

Kal wondered when the woman had last enjoyed a decent feed. "Thanks, Liam . . . Madam President. I'm Commodore Kariuki. We've been watching developments dirtside and were wondering if we can do anything to assist."

"Thank you. The officer who commed me, what was his, uh . . . Sorry, commodore, but this has all been a bit overwhelming. You know, I never thought I'd leave that godawful camp alive . . . Your man; what was his name?"

"O'Donnell. He's the *Stiletto*'s captain."

"He said you represent some sort of anti-Imp alliance."

"Yes, the Coalition of Free Systems. My ships are part of its navy."

"Some ships you have here, commodore. After all the bullshit Kolovchenko has fed us over the years, I find it hard to believe you can jump wherever you like . . . But I have one concern. O'Donnell told me you're cutting our gateways."

"We are, Madam President, as soon as all civilian traffic is out. We've already told Kolovchenko that any new ships allowed through should plan for a long stay in deepspace. And we've made sure every captain thinking of coming to Qianshan knows that."

"Oh . . . That will cause us a lot of pain."

"Not as much pain as the Empire would keep inflicting on you. And I appreciate Tongchen-6 is a big trading hub, but the Coalition cannot let the Imps capture the Tongchen sector. Its mil-tech industries are too important to us. Without them, we cannot buy the weapons and ships we need. But we will let you reopen the gateways as soon as it's safe to do so."

Velazquez was silent for a while, then said, "I'll do my best to make people here understand that. It won't be easy, but I think they will; the Imps have been very hard on them. The imperial governor is an asshole called Shimano; all he ever wanted to do was crush us into the ground. Godknows how many of our people have died since he let his ImpAdmin thugs loose on us."

"You have Shimano in custody?"

"And his senior staff. We'll give them all a fair trial, though I have no doubt what the outcome will be . . . I'm sorry, Ms. Kariuki, I'm wasting your time. Thanks for your offer, but I think we have things under control. As soon as the Imps discovered they had been cut off from the Empire, they couldn't surrender fast enough. Except for the ImpAdmin teams, that is. They knew we would show them no mercy after what they have done to the Tongchen system, so they preferred to stand and fight. We'll have the last of them either killed or prisoner before the week's out."

"We expect to be here for one more day, so if you do need help, make sure you ask."

"Thank you. We will."

~~~

Kal pushed a mug of fresh coffee across to O'Donnell. "I can't say I'm too sorry about the change of plan. The idea of attacking Terra was keeping me awake nights."

"I'm not sorry either, to be honest. We are good at knocking over half-assed systems like Ventas and Tongchen. Teshawa was harder, but we came through. We are not invincible, though. I was worried hitting Terra was going to teach us that lesson the hard way."

"We'll have to take it on one day."

"We will, but COMFLT's right to wait. Our chances of knocking out Terra's defenses are much better with the new carriers. Yes, that gives the Imps more time to upgrade their defenses, but I don't care how solid they are; our carriers will let us put more SAVs into an attack than Terra's defenses can ever handle. And we'll have *Stiletto*'s FireSparks, plus *Provider*'s SAVs and missile containers as well."

"I can't wait." But Kal could; just the thought of entering Terran nearspace twisted her guts into knots.

"We should get up to the bridge, commodore. Our visitors will be here in an hour."

~~~

"Command, Combat, Strike-1 away . . . Standby *Regulus* drop . . . now!"

Amidst a halo of ultra-violet radiation, the lean, black shape of the Imp heavy cruiser popped into normalspace.

Stiletto's forward holocams had locked on the Imp ship, zoomed in so tight Kal could read the red-on-white safety instructions around an airlock. Strike-1—all decoys; impressive but harmless—slammed into the hull just aft of the bows, an area covered by the heavy cruiser's external holocams.

"Command, Combat, Strike-2 away."

"INS *Regulus*, this is Coalition warship *Stiletto* on Emergency. You have ten seconds to strike before my second missile swarm hits, only this time it will be all FireSpark missiles."

With barely three seconds remaining, a voice said, "We're striking."

"Strike-2, abort, abort!" O'Donnell shouted.

"Command, Combat. Strike-2 aborted. Revectored to Point Zumba for recovery."

O'Donnell flipped up his vizor to wipe the sweat from his eyes. "Roger. *Regulus*, *Stiletto*. Request your commanding officer."

An avatar appeared, a woman in a shipsuit, her face chalk-white. A woman who had not been expecting trouble. "What do you want?" she asked.

"Are you the captain?"

"I am. Captain Hafez, Imperial Navy. You?"

"Captain O'Donnell, Coalition of Free Systems Navy. Now, pay attention. *Groombridge* is about to drop. When it does, I want you to order its captain to follow our instructions."

Hafez's face set hard. "I could, but I won't. What Captain Li does with his ship is his business. I have surrendered. I am no longer his superior officer."

"That's not what Article 26 of your Code of Military Justice says, but you already know that. Let's hope Captain Li cares more for the lives of his crew than you do. Shut down sensors, transmitters, and weapons systems, open all external airlock hatches and doors, and prepare to be boarded."

"Understood."

"I hope so, Captain Hafez. If you do not comply, I will destroy your ship without further warning. *Stiletto*, out."

O'Donnell turned to Kal. "I've a bad feeling about this, commodore."

Kal nodded. "Me too. Hafez didn't give the order because she knows *Groombridge* will stand and fight."

"Command, Combat," the AI said four minutes later. "Strike-3 away ... Standby *Groombridge* drop ... now!"

An ultra-violet flare and the second Imp ship was in normalspace, flashes of light flickering across its bows as the decoy swarm hit.

"Command, Combat, Strike-4 away."

Kal sat, hunched forward, body tense as O'Donnell ordered the Imp cruiser to surrender.

As she had feared, the *Groombridge* rejected O'Donnell's order to strike, main engines coming to full power, launchers starting to dump ASMs into space.

"You are a damn fool, Captain Li," O'Donnell said as Strike-4 hit.

FireSparks—save for a few hacked out of space by defensive lasers and shotguns—ripped into the *Groombridge*'s stern, their warheads reaching deep inside to gut the main engines, the explosions blasting the ship into a slow roll to port.

Kal's chest tightened. Firing missiles into a warship was hardly safe. But, by keeping the salvo small and targeting the stern of the ship aft of the tokomaks that powered its main engines, the combat AI had done all it could to ensure the missiles would not destroy the ship and its crew.

Not that even the most precisely designed strike could guarantee that. The tokomaks that powered a warship's main engines sat in an armored compartment immediately forward of the engine room. It took only one warhead to punch through that secondary armor and one of those plants would lose containment, a catastrophic release of energy that would vaporize the ship.

Time slowed to an ooze as *Groombridge* continued its slow tumble away, spewing jets of gas, ice, and smoke into space.

"Damage assessment confirms *Groombridge* has suffered no damage to its main-engine tokomaks," Combat said.

"Roger that. *Groombridge*, *Stiletto*. You have ten seconds to strike your colors or my missiles will destroy you."

"You murderous bastards!"

O'Donnell did not blink. "Five seconds."

"We're striking."

"*Stiletto*, roger. Stand-down all sensors, transmitters, and weapons systems, open all external airlock hatches and doors, and prepare to be boarded. Failure to comply will result in the destruction of your ship and risks the lives of your crew. Contact Tongchen NearCon to request any help you may need. *Stiletto*, out."

"Command, I have Hafez for you."

"Captain Hafez," O'Donnell said. "What can I do for you?"

Hafez's face was engorged with anger. "You'll stand trial for what you've done, I'll make sure of it even if it's the last thing I do."

"This is what war looks like, captain. You refused to order the *Groombridge* to strike, even though you had the authority to do so and knew the consequences of that refusal. What happened is on your head. Now, you going to help me stop *Procyon* going the same way?"

A voice off to one side. "Do it, captain. They'll kill them all if we don't."

Hafez's head dropped a fraction. "I'll give the order, but I will still hold you to account for your actions today."

"My name is Liam Tsing-Tsai O'Donnell, Captain, Coalition of Free States Navy, service number 4777-AK-9816. Got all that? Or would you like me to repeat it for you?"

"I don't understand."

"If I am to be indicted by the most brutal and corrupt polity in humanspace, I'd like you to get my particulars correct. But remember this, captain: Any hesitation on *Procyon*'s part, I will destroy it. *Stiletto*, out."

~~~

Stiletto's bridge crew watched in silence as *Procyon* followed *Regulus* into orbit around Tongchen-6. The *Groombridge* and its escort of salvage vessels trailed behind, the wounded ship still bleeding ice-loaded plumes of air into space.

"Command, Combat. Brickyard reports CAT-2 now in control of all hostiles."

"Command, roger," O'Donnell replied. "I've just had a comm from the Tongchen, commodore. They have confirmed they'll take the Imp ships off our hands and deal with the prisoners."

"You told them we're taking some back to Narsaq to be interrogated?" Kal asked.

"They agreed to that, but only if we give them the Q-drive."

Kal laughed. "Cheeky buggers!"

O'Donnell smiled. "They sure are, but I think we should give it to them. We can't restrict it to Tharmaran Shipbuilding and the Coalition. You and Daniel want it in ships across humanspace, and so do I. And the sooner we do that, the weaker Kolovchenko becomes. Waiting makes no sense."

"You're right. I'll talk with President Velazquez."

"I need to get on, commodore. I have a prisoner transfer to organize."

As O'Donnell walked away, doubts nagged at Kal. Daniel had designed a command-key system to ensure Q-drives were only used for peaceful purposes. Which they would, until somebody built their own drive from scratch.

She had a horrible feeling that she and Daniel had opened the doors of hell for any mean sonofabitch with ambition and money and no scruples to do just that.

Knowing they might go down in history as a pair of well-intentioned bumblers who saved humanity only for it to be screwed over by power-hungry scumbags like Amos Ferruci was almost more than she could bear.

~~~

"They're waiting for you, commodore."

"Thanks, Liam. They've given their parole?" Kal asked.

"They have, but are you sure you can trust them? I mean, this whole parole business is all so, so . . . medieval."

"They're commissioned officers in the Imperial Navy, not slavers or drug-dealers. And I will have Mai alongside me doing his best waiter impression in case they try anything. Relax; I'll be fine."

O'Donnell threw up his hands. "Your call, commodore, but Jens is going to post two of his biggest marines outside in case you have a problem."

"Fine. I'll patch a vid feed from my neuronics to them. Any sign of a problem, they can kick down the door and rescue me."

"That is the first sensible thing you've said, commodore."

"Why, thank you. Now, piss off. I need to make myself presentable."

"Good luck with that," O'Donnell said, shutting the door just in time to intercept the boot Kal hurled at him.

~~~

Dressed in her best shipsuit with the thick gold bar of a commodore on each shoulder, Kal stood as the crew-room door opened to admit two women and a man, the four thin bars on their shoulders marking them as Imperial Navy captains.

"Welcome aboard *Stiletto*," she said. "I am Commodore Kariuki. Captain O'Donnell sends his apologies."

"Hafez, *Regulus*."

"Li, *Groombridge*."

"Klimt, *Procyon*."

Kal waved them into their seats, then put a hand on the shoulder of the man standing beside her, a shoulder solid with corded muscle. "This is Systems Technician Mai. He will be happy to fetch you a drink. The foodbot is a Jorgenthaler, so you can have whatever you like. There is a menu if you need any inspiration."

The three Imp officers stared back. It was obvious they were struggling with the sheer absurdity of it all. Kal was not surprised. One minute they commanded the most potent warships in humanspace, the next an SDV had ambushed them and forced their surrenders.

And now they were sitting down to have dinner with the woman responsible for that humiliation.

Kal turned to Mai. "I'll have the usual, please."

"Yes, ma'am."

Kal raised a glass of pale-yellow, fizzy water; she ached to taste the real thing. "The Jorgenthaler produces a very fine glass of champagne. This is the '96 Pol Roger. For a licensed fake, it's particularly good."

Hafez sat up. "I'm not a champagne person. Can that thing do a Hammerfold cabernet-sauvignon? The '88?"

"Of course, ma'am. An excellent choice." Mai was as smooth as any sommelier. Not that Kal had met many; when she'd run out of money to buy psychoactives, she had always gone for alcohol in quantity, not quality.

When everyone had a glass—in Li's case, his second of over-proof bourbon, his first swallowed in a single, convulsive gulp—Kal lifted her glass. "I would to like to propose a toast, which is not easy given we are enemies, but we all have people we love, and I cannot think of anything better to toast . . . Our loved ones."

"Our loved ones," echoed the three captains.

"Sometimes gone," Li added softly, wiping tears from glistening eyes, "but always with us."

The man's response surprised Kal; it had been many years since she had heard it, a response particular to the M'bakaan military. "I see you know the toast, captain."

"From my father. He joined the M'bakaan system-defense force when he left high school. It was one of the toasts at officers' dining-in nights. He used it when he drank to my mom's health, which he did at sunset, right up to the day he died."

Li. The name was familiar. Kal had her neuronics searching while the man was talking. A name and bio popped. "Was your father Darius Li?" she asked.

"Why, yes. You've met him?"

"I have; he was captain of the *Fort Medellin* when I was a grunt with the M'bakaan 41st Marine Combat Group. We both saw a lot of action during Kolokaar's civil war."

Li lifted his glass to Kal and drained it, waving at Mai for a refill. "It's a very small universe, Commodore Kariuki."

"That it is, Captain Li."

Her glass untouched, Hafez's mouth had tightened during the exchange, her lips thin bloodless slashes. "Tell me something, commodore. The deaths of so many Imperial spacers and marines—at Narsaq, at Teshawa, and now Tongchen—are your responsibility. How do you feel about that?"

"I regret it greatly, captain, but I did ask we not talk politics or service matters tonight. Can we move on?"

"No, we cannot! You are war criminal, Kariuki, and I am going to make sure you face Imperial justice for the crimes you have committed."

"You can try, captain, as is your right, but, since you cannot meet my request to restrict tonight to social matters, perhaps you should leave."

Hafez exploded to her feet, slamming her chair back into the bulkhead. "My pleasure."

Kal sighed. "Oh dear. SysTech Mai. Have security escort Captain Hafez back to her berth."

"Aye, aye, captain."

Hafez's departure left Kal with mixed feelings. Part of her felt for the woman, humiliated by a brutal defeat that condemned her to remain a captain for the rest of her service as an Imperial Navy officer, if she wasn't shot for surrendering her ship without a fight.

But the rest of Kal felt nothing but contempt for the woman's part in the largest criminal enterprise in history.

Once Hafez had gone, Kal said, "My apologies. I should have handled that better. Now, let's eat. Captain Klimt. You have been quiet. Perhaps you'd like to order first?"

~~~

O'Donnell closed the door after the two Imps. "I have to give it to you, commodore. You are one devious sonofabitch, if you'll excuse me saying so. You knew they'd talk, didn't you?"

"Bitter experience," Kal replied. "Shock, humiliation, and an unrestricted supply of alcohol usually make people say things they shouldn't."

"Those two will wake up cursing you, Li especially. He was out of control; he let slip a lot of things he's going to regret as soon as he's sober."

"Given he's just had his ship shot out from under him, not to mention all the bourbon he got through, I'm not surprised. But my invitation was explicit: no politics, no service matters. I stuck to those conditions. They didn't."

"Peng will be happy."

"He ought to be. You don't often get the chance to listen to officers that senior unload about everything that's wrong with the Imperial Navy. Some of the technical stuff is pure intel gold."

"The loss of Moreno's task force has hit them harder than I expected. It's no wonder the navy's morale is non-existent. And Klimt's comments on her family facing bankruptcy were interesting."

"My heart bleeds," Kal spit. "They shouldn't have done business with the Gang of Five."

"Looks like your flea-versus-elephant strategy wasn't such a bad idea . . . I can't justify this, commodore, but I think we might win this war."

"Only if the Imps don't get their Q-drive ships first. We just have to hope Tharmaran delivers our carriers before they do."

—58—

Daniel jumped up as the security bot ushered Kal into his new office. He dragged her into his arms and held her tight. "I am so glad to see you. I've been so worried."

Stepping back, Kal put a hand to Daniel's face, fingers tracing the line of his cheekbone. "And I am glad to see you . . . Sorry, I'm being a bit emotional," she added, wiping her eyes.

Daniel's eyes glistened too. "Just look at us. It's been awful, sitting here behind my fancy desk not knowing what was happening . . . I read the after-action report on Teshawa. You should not have jumped *Stiletto* after the missile strike. That was dumb."

"Why? I trusted my chief engineer, like I always trusted you. Was I wrong?"

"I guess not . . . but I do worry."

"No need; I'm doing enough of that for the two of us. Now, I need a coffee. It was a rough ride down; I thought Ladaki was bad, but that was one hell of a storm."

"One of the joys of living here. They do storms the way drunks do drinking . . . Oh, shit, Kal! What am I saying? I'm sorry."

Kal had to laugh at the remorse on Daniel's face. "It's okay. I'm not the drunk I used to be, though I still miss a hefty slug of vodka over ice more than I can say . . . And, before you ask, no, I haven't started drinking again, but I do need a decent coffee, somewhere we can talk."

"Follow me. The Institute for Pinchspace Science doesn't run to Jorgenthalers, but the coffee in the canteen is okay."

~~~

Kal had watched Daniel as he talked about his work, his face alive, eyes sparkling, hands waving with excitement: driving Tharmaran to finish the carriers, finalizing designs for new courier ships and freighters, upgrading the Q-drive, manufacturing pinchcomm cubes and setting up networks, and more. She smiled. He was one of kind, no doubt about it.

Kal took advantage of a momentary pause in Daniel's flood of words. "Do you realize what we're seeing here?"

"What?"

"A glimpse of the future. What you're describing is what will happen across humanspace as Q-drive technology spreads out."

"No more Kolovchenko. I can't wait."

"Me neither . . . Oh, god! Look at the time. Sorry, Daniel. I need to go; it's time for my meeting with Peng. You take care."

"You're the one who should be careful."

"Don't you worry about me. I'll be fine."

"I've lost one mother, Kal. I do not want to lose another . . . But talking about mothers, I, er . . . We, umm . . ."

"Come on, Daniel. Spit it out!"

"You know about me and Skylar?"

Kal reached across the table to take Daniel's hand. "Everybody knows about you and Skylar."

"Ah, yes . . . Anyway, Tongchen was her last operation. She's pregnant and we're going to get married . . ."

Tears flooding her cheeks, Kal pulled Daniel into hug, her whole being engulfed by unalloyed joy.

". . . and we think that means you are going to be a grandmother."

The embrace lasted a long time.

~~~

Kal had to raise her voice to be heard over the buzz of a crowded crew-room. "Okay, folks, settle down. This is Jerry Peng, Director of the Narsaq Foreign Intelligence Service. Now that COMFLT has postponed the Terra operation, he is here to brief us where we go next, which is Poliak-8. And this—" She nodded at the man sat beside Peng. "—is Kasim Gedaran. He's the FIS's Assistant Director,

Technology Intelligence. He is joining us to see how the sharp end of the business works."

"Happy to be here," Gedaran said, bobbing his head.

"Over to you, director."

Peng stood and went over to the holoscreen. "Thank you, commodore. Right, why Poliak? It's just another Imperial shithole, I hear you say . . ."

A ripple of laughter. Poliak was infamous for being a poverty-stricken dump.

". . . and you would be right, but it's only three gateways from Terra, an advantage its rivals for last place don't share. And that is why Poliak-8 now hosts this place."

An image appeared on the bulkhead-mounted holoscreen. Taken from a drone, it showed rows of huts around an open space speckled with figures, all enclosed by razor-wire fences. Outside the wire were more buildings, more figures, and a vehicle park.

"That's Senucia Prison," Peng went on. "The Imps have around 2,000 high-value political prisoners locked up there; HVPs they call them."

Another pic, a man. "Senucia's commandant is this guy: Colonel Enlai Traavik of the Imperial Prisons Service. To make room for a growing number of new HVPs as the Empire expands, the Minister for Imperial Administration has told Traavik he has to cut Senucia's HVPs by 500 a month."

"And how's he going to do that?" O'Donnell asked. "Repatriating them?"

"No. He's going to execute them . . ."

A hiss of disbelief.

". . . which is a big ask. I don't mean to sound callous but killing that many people takes a lot of organizing. And Traavik's finding it more difficult than he expected. Since he took over as prison commandant two months ago, he's only managed to murder less than a hundred."

"When it comes to the Imps," O'Donnell said, "I can believe anything, even this obscenity, but what's it got to do with us?"

Peng pointed to the next pic: the head of a young woman, long black hair falling glossy to frame a cinnamon-skinned face dominated by piercing gray eyes. "This is Trinh Nguyen, oldest daughter of the president of the Halcyon Commonwealth. She was captured when the Imps took over a month ago."

"Hold on!" O'Donnell protested. "Are you telling me we're going to attack a planet in Terra's front yard to save a politician's daughter?"

Peng put up a hand. "If that was the only reason, you wouldn't be going anywhere near Poliak-8, but it is not. Nguyen is in Senucia because she and her team—they call themselves the Fire Ants—have made a career of humiliating Emperor Michael."

Fonseca leaned forward. "I've seen their i-bombs. One had a segment with old Mikie trying to chat up the family's pet pig while off his face on scrag. It was brilliant."

"All her i-bombs are. That's why they have gone viral, despite ImpSec's best efforts to stop them. More than half the human race can identify her from a holopic and tell you what she stands for, unlike Narsaq's president, for example. Much as we all like and respect Luka Ha'alaafa, not even one percent of humanity even knows who he is.

"Which is why our interest in Poliak is much bigger than Nguyen. Senucia's prisoners come from hundreds of systems, all arrested by ImpSec, interrogated, and then handed over to ImpAdmin. If we leave them there, Traavik will kill them and the thousands of HVPs that follow."

"So Senucia's being turned into a death camp?" Fonseca asked.

"It's hard to believe, but yes. Traavik's still having trouble doing that, but we think he will. The Minister of Imperial Administration is not someone who tolerates failure. Your mission is to free Senucia's prisoners. When you have, we can show humanspace what the Imps do to people like Trinh Nguyen, people they know well."

"Nguyen's a bonus then?" Kal asked.

"A huge bonus. She will get us burn-through on social media. But it won't be just about her. There are a thousand stories to come out of Senucia and we mean to tell them all."

~~~

Kal turned to Peng as the crew-room emptied. "Thanks for your time, director. Let me walk you to your shuttle."

"Thank you."

"The intel you're getting out of Poliak is solid. I just wish I could say the same about Terra."

"Terra is not Poliak. We are not completely blind, though. Like every digital society, some of what people know dribbles out; that gives us a lot of chatter, which ships are going where, for example. The families of the crews leave plenty of clues on social media."

"What about the things that really matter?" Kal asked. "Weapons system performance, ordnance deliveries, and Q-drive development, of course?"

"Only scraps. And, as for the Q-drive, we've not heard anything."

"You know Daniel and I both think they are working on one."

"I need to find their development site to prove it." Peng paused at the passenger airlock, turning to Kal. "One more thing. You are looking very tired. Combat is for youngsters, not people like us. When are you going to hand over?"

For an instant, Kal wanted to deny she had a problem. Then common-sense reasserted itself; Peng was too smart to believe any dissembling.

"After Terra."

—59—

"Command, Combat. Grav-66 intercept. Ship inbound from Perseus-3; provisionally identified *Golden Dawn*."

Kal let slip a sigh of relief. "I wasn't sure the bastard was actually going to turn up."

O'Donnell nodded. "We'd have had trouble getting 2,000 prisoners out of here if he hadn't."

Kal returned her attention to her command plot. Nothing had changed. *Stiletto* was tucked behind Poliak-8's closest moon, Hallakal, screened from SysDef's sensor arrays. Nearspace was busy with civilian traffic, and Poliak-8's two SDVs— the only warships the Imperial Navy had left them—sat in Clarke orbit not doing much.

Peng's man, Gedaran, sat on Kal's left. He leaned over. "You have to wonder why Poliak-8 has so few sys-def assets. Those prisoners are important."

"The Empire doesn't care about them," Kal replied. "I suspect it's assumed that nobody else does either."

"All stations, Command." O'Donnell said. "SITREP. No change to the threat plot, so the plan stands. We will be breaking cover to make a high-g burn in-system as soon as our first strike has destroyed the Imps' two SDVs and disabled the pinchcomm links back to Chusri. We're not expecting any opposition apart from those SDVs but stay sharp; we may have missed something. As soon as they have been dealt with, *Stiletto* will make a kinetics run to neutralize the Imps' ground defenses before we launch *Don't Talk* to take and hold Senucia Spaceport. *Provider* is following astern of us with CAT-2 and its landers; their job is to secure Senucia prison, coordinate the prisoner recovery, and respond to any counterattacks from the Imps. So, faceplates down, final suit checks."

"He looks the part," Duvall whispered to Kal.

"Most people do, until someone jams a blow-torch up their ass."

~~~

For hours, *Stiletto* and *Provider* had headed in-system, tucked behind the Coalition weapons labs' latest innovations: the pancake.

A neat if tactically limited idea. Poliak-8 was a poorly defended planet with a sensor network long past its best-by date. Pancakes—disks of black, radar-absorbent mylar held flat by gas-filled struts, vectored by tiny explosive pop-thrusters—were more than capable of concealing a hostile ship or missile swarm trying to sneak in close without being seen.

A planet like Terra was another matter. Long before an attacker came close enough to pose any threat, its BigEye optronics would detect a pancake as it occulted the stars.

Kal grimaced. Getting close enough to launch an attack before the defenses woke up remained the most intractable problem in space-warfare. And it always would.

Terra was going to be a bastard to attack.

"Are you all right?" Kal asked Gedaran. His fidgeting was beginning to get on her nerves.

Gedaran started. "Oh, sorry. Yes. It's the waiting. It's worse than getting shot at."

"Trust me it's not . . . Okay, here we go," Kal added as *Stiletto*'s bridge filled with the familiar metallic grinding of a missile launch.

"Command, Combat. Strike-1 away. Target tracks 555-001 through 004."

"001 and 002 are the Poliak's SDVs," Kal said to Gedaran. "003 and 004 are the gateway pinchcomm arrays."

Missile tokomaks came to full power, gimballed engines splitting the strike into four streams.

The pancake had done its job; Kal enjoyed the thought of Poliak-8 SysDef's panic as the *Stiletto*'s missile swarm materialized out of the emptiness of space.

Kal was relieved to see the SDVs' crews display an admirable commitment to self-preservation and take to the lifepods. She had never seen ships abandoned so fast.

The lifepods were well clear when the missiles hit, their penetrators slicing through the SDVs' armor, incandescent fingers that speared into their tokomaks, releasing huge balls of energy that consumed the ships they had powered.

An instant later, fragmentation warheads had shredded the gateways' pinchcomm arrays.

"Fuuuuuck!" Gedaran muttered.

"Command, Combat. Tracks 001 through 004 killed. Nearspace threat plot green. Standby Strike-2. Breakaway now."

Kal turned to Gedaran as the pancake collapsed and *Stiletto*'s main engines blazed into life, driving the ship towards Poliak-8, the *Provider* close behind. "Our turn now."

"Command, Combat. *Provider* now on vector to Point Dexter."

"Dexter's a low-orbit geostationary slot, LOG for short," Kal said to Gedaran. "We'll join the *Provider* there as soon as we've launched Strike-2, our kinetics strike to take out Senucia City's ground-defense force base, designated target Tango-1. Low-power main-engine burns will hold us 5,000 klicks directly overhead. That will it make it easier for the assault landers to get back to us."

"There's one a lot to remember, commodore. This isn't a simple business."

Kal felt for Gedaran. The Poliak operation was simple compared to the attack on Teshawa, but there was still plenty going on. "War never is, Mister Gedaran."

Her first combat operation in attack landers had been chaotic mix of fear and adrenaline-pumped excitement; she had struggled to remember everything in the mission brief.

"Brickyard, Boxcar, Combat," the AI said. "Hotdog-Red."

Gedaran whispered in Kal's ear, "Sorry, commodore, but remind me who's talking to whom?"

"Brickyard is Major Himaya, the dirtside assault commander. Jens Fonseca commands *Stiletto*'s Andimeshki marines; his callsign is Boxcar. Hotdog-Red is the code-word authorizing them to launch their landers."

"Command, Combat. *Stiletto, Provider*, landers away."

The planet was closing fast; *Stiletto* soon started to feel Poliak-8's atmosphere. The kinetics' launch window was small; hang on too long and the ship's armored hull would start to burn up.

"Command, Combat. Bugs away."

"Microdrones, commodore?" Gedaran asked.

"Yes, in reentry-hardened capsules. They'll give us eyes on the target before the kinetics strike. Pigs have huge kinetic energy; they kick up a shit-load of dust and smoke."

"Command, Combat. Pigs away. Strike-2 nominal."

The ship's magazines spewed tungsten-iridium bars; their tiny shape-shifting winglets would vector them to their targets on the planet's surface below as soon as the atmosphere thickened enough to allow them to work.

"Command, Combat . . ."

The main engines had come to full power, driving the ship out of Poliak-8's gravity well.

". . . *Stiletto* now on vector for Point Dexter."

Now the bridge crew could only wait as the bugs plunged earthwards with the pigs close behind, a cascading shower of fire as ablative skins burned off.

"Command, Combat. Bugs deploying . . . on-line . . . holovid feed up now."

Kal patched her neuronics into one of the microdrones now orbiting over the Imp base; despite the destruction of Poliak's nearspace defenses the Imps had still not reacted. The few she could see were idling along, just another day on one of humanspace's biggest shitholes.

The Imps must have assumed the attack on SysDef's orbital assets had been yet another hit-and-run operation the Coalition had started to carry out using Daniel's new courier ships and missile containers. Or the command team responsible for protecting Poliak-8 nearspace had imploded into paralysis.

Probably the latter, she decided.

A blizzard of white streaks reached down from the sky, triggering a roiling maelstrom of smoke and flame that engulfed Senucia Base. The pigs' prodigious kinetic energy obliterated buildings, equipment, and people along with SysDef's inventory of ground-attack aircraft, SAM batteries, and vehicles, their passing marked by columns of greasy black smoke that twisted up into the red and gold calm of the evening sky.

"I've never seen anything like it," Gedaran said. "Hundreds of people killed in a few seconds."

Kal shook her head. "Not people. Enemy combatants engaged in a criminal enterprise. We have the moral authority here, Mister Gedaran; think of the innocent men and women we're going to set free today."

"Forgive me, commodore. You sound like a lawyer."

Kal smiled. "A lawyer tucked away in a civilized system keeping an eye on my legal AIs and drinking great coffee? I wish . . . Okay, here we go."

"Command, Combat. Bugs confirm Tango-1 killed. From Brickyard, Hotdog-Blue."

"Himaya's committing the landers to the attack," Kal said to Gedaran. "I'll patch my holoscreen over to the flight-deck of *Don't Talk*. You'll see everything the crew sees."

"Okay . . . *Don't Talk*? An odd name."

"Long story, another time. Any other questions, ask."

Sharma's voice came up. "Brickyard, Lander-1. Down through 0-8-0-0 . . ."

"Altitude 80,000 meters," Kal said.

"... on vector for Tango-2 in 2-2 mike."

"Tango-2 is the spaceport, right?" Gedaran asked.

"It is. And Tango-3 is the prison camp."

"This is a lot more complicated, more intense, than I expected."

"Which is why poor intel doesn't help. It's difficult enough dealing with what we know without having to respond to the unexpected."

With its main engines at full power, *Don't Talk* drove earthwards nose-first, Sharma doing everything she could to land her precious cargo of marines alive.

Even if she appeared to be doing her best to kill them all.

The first tendrils of Poliak-8's atmosphere flickered yellow-red around *Don't Talk*'s hull, the meters unwinding at blinding speed until. Main engines now shut-down, it reared nose-up, its belly flat on to the fast-thickening atmosphere.

The screen went blank, the datafeed blocked by the plume of ionized gas shed by the lander as hyper-compressed air ripped past, its kinetic energy transformed into heat.

And then *Don't Talk* was back. "Tango-2 in 9 mike," Sharma commed as she put the lander back into a steep dive.

"This is where it gets dangerous," Kal said to Gedaran. "The landers will be firing decoys all the way in to confuse any missile systems. MANPADs are the principal threat now."

"I know about MANPADS: man-portable air-defense systems. Nasty things."

"They're the reason *Don't Talk* looks like it's trying to commit suicide. Nose down with the main engines at full power is the fastest way to get dirtside."

Gedaran shook his head. "That is insane."

"Just be thankful the Poliaks don't have any surface-to-orbit missiles. SOMs are a whole new level of crazy."

"Tango-2 in 3 mike," Sharma commed.

Kal's anxiety level went up a couple of notches. Attack landers were most vulnerable as they deployed their wings and flared to shed speed for landing. The decision to commit *Don't Talk* to such a hazardous coup-de-main had provoked a great deal of soul-searching, only ended by O'Donnell's decision to take the risk.

The brutal reality? The Coalition could afford to lose marines and their landers.

"Finals," Sharma called out. "Reapers away."

"Attack drones," Kal said to Gedaran.

Don't Talk pitched up. Fully extended, its wings were massive airbrakes battering a path through the air slashing past as the ramp came down, the loadmaster busy dispatching reapers into the lander's wake.

With a kilometer to run, a stream of cannon shells lanced up from the spaceport, punching into the lander's armor with dull *brrrrrttt*.

Even before the first shell had reached the lander, *Don't Talk*'s combat AI had tracked the stream of shells back to a soft-skinned ATV.

"Dumb bastards," Kal said as *Don't Talk*'s lasers ripped the vehicle apart, its microtok exploding in a searing flash.

Still nose high, *Don't Talk*'s belly thrusters spit twin pillars of ionized driver-mass to take the lander's weight from fast-retracting wings, a savage maneuver known to every marine in humanspace as walking the blowtorch. Approaching the threshold, the landing gear came down, belly thrusters throttled back, the nose rotated forward, and *Don't Talk* thumped onto the runway. Disc-brakes screeching in protest, the lander swung off the runway and came to a stop alongside one of the spaceport's satellite buildings, its arrival screened by the reapers overhead, their lasers flashing to suppress any hostile activity.

As CAT-2's heavy-attack landers howled overhead on vector for Senucia prison, *Don't Talk*'s cargo ramp hit the apron. Fonseca's marines followed their combatbots, ducking for cover as the Imps opened fire. Not for long; *Don't Talk*'s reapers had soon scoured the hostiles from their positions atop the roof of the terminal.

Leaving the reapers to suppress any Imps lurking on the apron, the Andimeshki and their combatbots split into teams. Starting with the terminal building, a small, squat affair that owed nothing to style and everything to cheap, they cleared the spaceport complex with methodical precision, the air filled filed with the *krak-krak* of rifle fire, the *bzzzt* of combatbot lasers, the thudding *crump* of grenades, the screams of wounded Imps.

It was over in 30 minutes.

"Brickyard, Boxcar. Tango-2 cleared of all hostiles. Reapers have secured spaceport perimeter. You are clear to reposition landers when ready."

"Brickyard, roger," Himaya said. "Lander-2 through 5 inbound your position in 2-0 mike. Casualties?"

"Eight Charlie. CASEVAC not required. Prisoner processing team setting up now."

"Brickyard, roger. Out."

"That is how it's done," Kal said, as always impressed by the Andimeshkis' brutal competence. She glanced at Gedaran.

He was sitting with his eyes locked on the screen. "I had no idea."

"Neither did I before I signed up with the marines. And this was a straightforward operation. It's a lot harder when you're facing real marines equipped with MANPADs they have the training and combat experience to use. An Imp paramilitary wouldn't recognize one if it was fired up her ass."

She chopped her holoscreen over to Himaya's command plot. It told her she had misjudged the Imps, some at least. Whilst many had surrendered with indecent haste, a hard core had not. Holed up in their barracks, Himaya's marines were having to dig them out building by building, CAT-2's massive firepower neutralized by the prison's proximity, the inmates protected only by flimsy plasfiber huts.

But, before long the marines and their combatbots had reduced the barracks to ruins, the few survivors stumbling from the rubble, bleeding, dazed, dust-coated, their arms up.

Kal switched her screen to the feed from the first marine to enter the camp. "You poor bastards," she whispered as detainees appeared from their crude huts, some so emaciated the bones of their shoulders showed sharp through the thin fabric of gray uniforms, eyes huge in faces stretched tight by hunger.

The marines split up to search the huts, coaxing the reluctant to join the gray tide flooding through the gates to be triaged.

"This is an obscenity," Gedaran murmured. "What the hell were the Imps thinking?"

Kal slipped off her safety harness and slipped out of her chair. "Winning at any cost. Combat, how's *Golden Dawn* going?"

"Standby . . . *Golden Dawn* has just cleared the gateway from Perseus-3 and is on vector for its assigned orbital slot."

"Can you talk to its captain?" O'Donnell said. "He'll be shitting himself. I want to start lifting the detainees off, and he needs to be ready to receive them."

"I'll calm him down. And while I do, can we get *Stiletto* alongside *Golden Dawn*? I'd like want to be there when the detainees arrive."

"Will be done, commodore."

~~~

Kal and Gedaran stood to one side as the latest lander-load of detainees left *Golden Dawn*'s personnel airlock, some on stretchers, their ravaged bodies testament to the harsh treatment Colonel Traavik had afforded them.

Gedaran nodded at the woman limping past, her arms across the shoulders of two marines, her hair shorn to ragged stubble, clothes patched and worn, feet bare and black with dirt. "If that's what the walking wounded look like, I hate to think what the poor bastards still dirtside look like. How could the Imps do this?"

"Because nobody tried to stop them. The corruption of power and all that."

As Major Himaya left the airlock, Kal motioned him over. "Well done, major. Textbook stuff."

"We shouldn't let it go to our heads. Most of those ImpAdmin paramilitaries weren't worth a pinch of shit. I'm glad they weren't imperial marines."

"Take the credit, major. It was well done. CAT-2's casualties?"

"Two Kilo, two Alpha, five Bravo, one Charlie. The medics say the wounded will all pull through."

Two killed. Kal knew that deaths in combat were inevitable. That did not make them any easier to bear.

"Apart from that," Himaya went on, "nothing much more to report except to say we've freed 2,223 detainees, recovered the prison's knowledgebases, and arrested all the senior Imp staffers left alive." Himaya nodded at the line of hooded prisoners shuffling from the airlock. "That's them."

"Including Traavik?"

"We found him hiding in a cargobot out back of the admin building. The sonofabitch had a pistol though; he wounded one of my people."

"That man has a heap of questions to answer. The extra detainees; what's the story?"

"The freighter *Bonaventure-VI* delivered 319 just before we arrived in-system. A second, the *Harvester,* is due tomorrow with 512 more."

"Oh, for fuck's sake . . . Hold on a second, major."

Kal commed O'Donnell. "The detainees arriving tomorrow. Your intentions?"

"Stay so we can take them out with us. We can't leave them here."

"I'm glad you said that. Okay, talk later." Kal turned back to Himaya. "That prison was already full. Where was Traavik planning to put the new arrivals?"

"I don't think he cared. They weren't going to be around long. His staff told us he was planning to ramp up the executions."

~~~

A soft knock on the door. It was one of the marines. Kal swore; she needed a week's sleep. "Come in."

"Ms. Nguyen, commodore."

Kal had to struggle to keep the shock off her face. The woman was an emaciated parody of the young, vibrant woman she had once been. "Take a seat, Ms. Nguyen. Coffee?"

"Please. The Imps didn't think we deserved any. The bastards seemed determined to make our lives as miserable as they could."

Kal handed Nguyen her mug. "They can't hurt you, not anymore."

"You don't understand what you are up against; they're animals. All you've done is postpone the inevitable."

"We don't agree."

Nguyen's head dropped, her shoulders shaking as sobs racked her body, the mug slipping from her hands, bouncing, splashing coffee across the deck. "I'm a dead woman. You can't stop them; nobody can."

"We can, and we will."

Nguyen wiped eyes red and swimming in tears with the back of a hand. "I wish I could believe that."

"Have a look at this holovid. It shows what happened when the Imps attacked Narsaq-3. It might change your thinking."

Long after the holovid had finished, Kal sat, content to wait for Nguyen to speak. At last, the woman spoke, "Do really think you can beat the Empire?"

"We have a chance. We defeated the Imps at Narsaq-3 because we've made their greatest strategic asset—gateways—redundant."

"Until they build their own Q-drive ships. What happens then?"

"We intend to beat them before they do."

Hope flickered in Nguyen's eyes. "You can do that?"

"With the help of people like you, yes."

"People like me? What can I do?"

Kal leaned forward to look Nguyen right in the face. "Be a Fire Ant again. I want to show humanspace what happened in Senucia Prison Camp. It's time to pay the Imps back for what they've done here."

Nguyen half-smiled. "I'd like that very much."

"I'll transfer you to *Stiletto*. You can talk with one of my crew, Zemin Mashalo. He's been producing our i-bombs. They've been okay, but let's just say there is room for improvement. Please go easy on him though; he's been doing his best."

~~~

Kal watched the *Golden Dawn* head for the gateway. "I'm glad the prisoners are out of here."

"Not as much as they are," O'Donnell said. "And you've got a new best friend in the *Dawn's* captain. He didn't expect a bonus once he's delivered everyone to Perseus-3."

"We've enough on our plate without him screwing us over as well . . . He told me I was the best client he'd ever had."

"That doesn't say much for his business."

"Hey!" Kal protested. "I'm not that bad . . . Talking of prisoners, I've been thinking about those new arrivals."

"They won't be a problem. No freighter captain is going to argue with Major Himaya and his marines. And *Provider* can handle that many extra souls, no problem."

"It's not that. There's something not right about the *Harvester*. I couldn't work out why, so I went looking through the prison knowledgebases. And I think I've found what was looking for."

O'Donnell's face creased into a frown. "Hold on, commodore. It's just another freighter. What's the problem?"

"There was no detailed manifest for the *Harvester's* 512 prisoners. Up to then, ImpAdmin had sent one with every prisoner transfer. And that made Traavik so pissed he sends a stream of comms demanding one so he knows what to expect when the *Harvester* turns up, but ImpAdmin never even replies."

"That could have been a slip-up."

"No. I think it was a deliberate decision by ImpAdmin. Now, does that sound like a routine prisoner transfer?"

"I guess not, but so what?"

"The *Harvester* and its prisoners will arrive the day after we leave. I don't think that's an accident."

"Come on, commodore!" O'Donnell protested. There is no way they could know that."

"The timing of the *Harvester*'s arrival tells me they did. And the reason there's no manifest is because those prisoners aren't HVPs."

"I'm sorry. I just don't buy it."

Kal thought for a moment. "Okay, try this. Someone with access to our plans—a senior COMFLT staffer, say—gives the Imps the timings of the Poliak operation. But the Imps have a problem: Terra is the only planet with the heavy cruisers they need to take on the *Stiletto*, and it's too far to get them here before we arrive. And, even they could, they are reluctant to send ships through the gateways after what we did to them at Narsaq and Tongchen."

O'Donnell rubbed his forehead. "My brain hurts."

Kal chuckled. "Stay with me, Liam . . . What the Imps can do is send a freighter full of prisoners from Chusri, knowing we'd find out that the *Harvester* was on its way from Senucia Prison's knowledgebases."

"Ah, yes. Artie Shaw was surprised how easy it was to break into them. You think that was planned?"

"To make certain we knew about the *Harvester*, yes. And what were we going to do when we did?"

"Rescue the prisoners, like we did at Ventas."

"Yes, because we are caring people," Kal said. "So, we delay our departure to wait for the *Harvester*. The instant it drops, it starts dumping missile containers into space. Within a minute, there are godknows how many missiles coming our way, an attack we didn't expect and aren't prepared for."

O'Donnell sat back, his face suddenly pale and sweaty. "And we can't blow the *Harvester* out of space because that would kill 512 innocent people. That lets it unload missiles until the *Stiletto* and *Provider* are plasma . . . Godddammit, commodore! The bastards have set us up."

"They sure have. Let's see if Gedaran can tell us what we're up against."

The FIS man was not long coming. "You wanted to see me, commodore?"

Kal waved him into a seat. "I have a question. Assume you are an Imp Navy operational planner. You've been given an ultra-high-value target to destroy but you only have a freighter for the job. How would you do it?"

"Only a freighter? Let's see . . . Missile containers are my only option. But why do you ask?"

"You know about the freighter arriving tomorrow?"

"The *Harvester*? Yes, I do."

"I think it's another q-ship tasked to destroy *Stiletto* and *Provider*."

Gedaran stiffened. "How do you know that?"

"Later. What can you tell me about the containers?"

"For an HVT, the Imps would use the new Vulkan-Cs, a missile-launch system packed into a standard Class-5 freight container. All freighters have AI-controlled cargo-handling systems; launching the Vulkan-C would be easy and fast."

"Makes sense," Kal said. "What missiles?"

"The new Taipan anti-ship missile. Their Eaglehawk ASMs aren't just obsolete, they're also a fraction too long to fit into a Class-5 container."

"How many in a container?"

"48."

Kal winced. "Rate of fire?"

"Ten per second. FIS thinks the containers will use compressed-nitrogen rams to eject its missile payloads. That's old technology; geotech surveyors use them to launch their ground penetrators; they have done for years. That mean the *Harvester* could deploy thousands of missiles within minutes. The only thing that might slow things up is designating targets."

"*Stiletto* and *Provider* would be hanging around not expecting an attack," O'Donnell said. "We'd be hard to miss, and Taipans can receive target designations after launch . . . Though there is one problem with your theory, Kasim. To fit the timeline, the freighter has to come from Chusri. Why would the Imps have stockpiled brand-new Vulkan-C containers there?"

Gedaran was quiet for a moment. "I think I know why. We have intel saying the Imps are planning to attack the Zatopek sector. The jump-off point for that is Chusri; that's where they'd be stockpiling ordnance and supplies for an offensive. Knowing how short of cruisers the Imp navy is, it makes sense to use freighters carrying Vulkan-C missile containers as force-multipliers."

A long silence.

"What do we do now, commodore?" O'Donnell asked finally.

Kal shook her head. "That's your call now, Liam."

"Ah, yes . . . Okay, we have to assume the *Harvester* is a missile-armed q-ship. If it's not, lucky us. But in case it is, we need a plan to free those detainees without risking the *Stiletto*."

"A big ask, but there must be a way."

"I'm sure there is, commodore, and we'll find it."

"I hope so. Right, I need my rack. Call me once you have decided how to handle things. And don't take too long; we don't have a lot of time."

With that, Kal left the bridge, leaving O'Donnell and Gedaran tight faced with anxiety.

~~~

"Okay, folks, that's it unless there are any last questions," O'Donnell said. "No? Then we're set."

As spacers and marines from the *Stiletto* and *Provider* pushed back from the crew-room table, filling the air with chatter, Gedaran turned to Kal. "I have a request, commodore."

Kal's eyes narrowed. "Why don't I like the sound of that?"

"I'd like to ride with Sharma. I want to see lander ops close up."

"Why, for chrissakes?"

"A couple of days ago, you told me sims aren't like real combat," Gedaran said. "Yes, I can patch my neuronics through to one of the landers' flight-decks, but my brain knows I'm sat back here onboard *Stiletto*, that I'm not risking my life. To do my job as well as you want me to, I need to understand what it's actually like out here."

"I promised your boss I'd return you intact."

"We all have to take risks, commodore. You, your crew, your marines, you all do."

"Because that is what we're paid for. You're not."

"True, but I am paid to give your people the best chance I can of getting back alive. I can't do that unless I understand what it's like for them."

Gedaran was right, and Kal knew it. Too often sloppy intelligence from rear-echelon seat-polishers had put her and her people at risk.

Kal sighed and put her hands up in defeat. She waved Sharma over.

"Yes, commodore?"

"Mister Gedaran wants to ride with you. Is that okay with you?"

Sharma glanced at Gedaran. "Are you mad? One Taipan is all it takes to blow *Don't Talk* apart, and you're dead. Why would you risk that?"

"To help me do my job."

"If you think it will, then I won't argue. Draw a combat skinsuit, helmet, and survival pack from stores. Final briefing *Don't Talk*'s hangar at 22:30. Anything else, commodore?"

"No."

~~~

Gedaran sat at the back of *Don't Talk*'s cramped flight-deck, questioning his decision to allow bravado to outvote common-sense. He could not get comfortable. His nerves twanged like guitar strings. The jump seat was too small, the crash-gel padding too thin, the harness too tight, his skinsuit pinched in all the wrong places, the combat helmet was too heavy, and his back was perspiration-glued to his shipsuit.

Sharma and her tactical operator did not help either. Their laconic, laid-back style only worsened his sweaty apprehension.

Gedaran breathed in, held the air until his lungs burned in protest, then breathed out in a long, slow hiss. You will be fine, he told himself. *Don't Talk* was the most combat-experienced attack lander crew in humanspace. And the operation had gone well in the sims.

None of that helped. He just wanted to throw up.

"Boxcar, Lander-5," Sharma said. "Brickyard has confirmed no change to drop time for Tango-1 ... Loadmaster, ramp down, Stick 9, Stick 10 to jump stations."

Gedaran checked the screen taking its feed from the forward holocams. Fine on *Don't Talk*'s starboard bow was the sprawling complex of girders that made up the in-gateway from Chusri. It was closing at frightening speed. The four landers of CAT Right were dead ahead. Like *Don't Talk,* their ramps were going down, their cargo bays blobs of red light against the black of space, the marines in their sticks, ready.

Gedaran's stomach churned. He had not forgotten Sharma's 'it only takes one Taipan' comment. And the *Harvester* would be carrying hundreds of them. No, thousands.

A burst of ultra-violet engulfed the gateway and the *Harvester* filled the holovid screen, its massive shape lit by the red flashes of its anti-collision lights.

"Weapons free," Sharma called out to her TACCO. "Stick 9, Stick 10. Tango-1 at 8 klicks, closing. Standby jump."

"Roger. Weapons free . . . Tango-1, containers away!" TACCO called as the *Harvester* started to eject Vulkan-C missile containers.

Not that any survived for long as FireSpark missiles raced past the gateways to obliterate the containers before they managed to launch a single Taipan.

Reacting to *Don't Talk*'s approach, the freighter's pulsed lasers had opened up, the *tack-tack-tack* as they pecked at the armored hull hull drowned out by the *bzzt...bzzzt...bzzt* of the lander's own lasers returning fire, fire that reduced the offending laser turrets to incandescent stumps of molten plasteel spewing ionized gas into space, adding to the clouds of shrapnel generated by FireSpark warheads detonating, Vulkan-Cs exploding, and missile microtok losing containment.

It was chaos.

Ahead of *Don't Talk*, their thrusters flaring, the landers of Himaya's CAT-2 had matched vectors to take station off the forward personnel airlocks, their cannon hosing shells into the yawning maws of the cargo locks as they passed, shells that brought the streams of missile-containers to an abrupt stop.

Himaya commed all his sticks. "Alpha-Alpha, Brickyard. Tango-1 defenses killed. Martinet-Red!"

Lines streaked from lander cargo bays, their fastset pads locking onto the *Harvester*'s hull. Lines tautened. Assault-armored marines clipped in and pushed across to the freighter, *Don't Talk*'s Andimeshki to the after personnel airlocks, Fonseca leading Stick 9 and his exec, Ushabir, Stick 10.

Which had only meters to go when the Imps jettisoned the outer airlock door. Massing hundreds of kilos, the ceramsteel slab ripped through a line of Andimeshki, slapping them aside like dust, jets of ice crystals streaming from ruptured suits, the flight-deck's crew status board lighting up as the casualties mounted.

Sharma did not hesitate. "TACCO, airlock Sierra-10. Cannon, burst fire, now."

What Gedaran saw as *Don't Talk* skidded sideways to take station overhead the airlock justified Sharma's response: black shapes streaming from the airlock, exploding in brilliant flashes.

His gut tightened as icons on the status board turned amber. Stick 10 was being hit hard; fragmentation grenades, he thought as *Don't Talk*'s hyper-velocity cannon shells slammed into the airlock, shells that shredded the Imps and their grenade launchers.

"10, Lander-5," Sharma said. "Airlock Sierra-10 clear, inner door open. CASEVAC bots are recovering your casualties now."

"10, roger," Ushabir replied. "Going in now."

Sharma glanced back at Gedaran, "Stick 10 was lucky the Imps used grenade launchers, not claymores."

Gedaran shivered. Claymores would have killed all the Andimeshki of Stick 10 apart, but the Imp marines were onboard to keep prisoners under control. They weren't there to fight off a boarding they'd never expected.

He checked Stick 9. Luck was with the marines of Fonseca's stick; they had arrived after the airlock door blew into space, the grenade-launcher problem quickly solved by dumping their own grenades on the Imps inside the airlock.

Fonseca commed Himaya. "Brickyard, 9. Airlock Sierra-9 clear. Making entry now. This section has been vented to vacuum, but the artgrav remains on. No sign of any . . . Okay, we are taking heavy fire from aft. My bugs are showing we have hostiles coming up the starboard-side accessway."

"Brickyard, roger. Stick 10 has taken casualties. CASEVAC in progress. Wait where you are for backup, then clear all sections aft of your position. When that's done, secure everything up to the aftermost cargo bay."

"9, roger."

Gedaran's switched his attention to the eight sticks making up CAT-2's assault.

Cannon-fire from CAT-2's landers had crushed the Imps defending the personnel airlocks. Himaya's marines were now inside the *Harvester*, fire-teams from his tactical reserve already skimming across the hull to support the hard-hit Andimeshki.

Gedaran patched his neuronics into the holovid feed from Stick 7's leader, her marines busy disabling the rams that moved containers around the massive cargo bay.

A simple task that only took sustained bursts of fire trashing the hydraulics, clouds of hydraulic fluid under enormous pressure jetting from torn pipes. Job done, Stick 7 started to work its way through a cargo bay stacked high with Vulkan-C missile containers.

Gedaran's breath caught in his throat as the stick leader passed the port cargo lock. Missile containers sat at the head of queues waiting for the cargo-handling system to ram them out into space, queues that filled the *Harvester*'s capacious cargo hold.

He gave up counting the Vulkan-Cs when he reached a hundred, almost 5,000 Taipan anti-ship missiles. And there were more; the *Harvester* was a big ship.

Stiletto was a tough, well-armored ship, but even it could not keep out a missile salvo thousands strong fired from short-range.

He hated to think what would have happened if the commodore had not wondered why ImpAdmin had sent prisoners to Poliak-8 without a detailed manifest.

It would never have occurred to him to question something so mundane.

He patched his neuronics into the feed from a bug covering one of CAT-2's sticks. It had been moving forward up the portside passageway until stubborn resistance from a group of Imp marines stalled its advance.

Himaya's marines had responded with a furious barrage of grenades, their flash-lit smoke writhing in the vacuum. A fire-team took advantage of the chaos to push on, their assault rifles pouring fire into the unseen Imp defenders, a desperate, clawing fight that kept CAT-2's combat medics and their bots busy.

Hopping from holovid feed to holovid feed, Gedaran did his best to make sense of the chaotic battle now raging through the six decks of the *Harvester*'s forward section. He could not imagine how Himaya stayed in control of things. The Imps were losing, that much was clear. The ferocity and momentum of the Coalition assault, its ability to switch the attack from side to side and deck to deck, and the reluctance of the Imps to give up a bad position by withdrawing to a better one, all helped Himaya's marines drive the surviving defenders forward and down, trapping them in the passenger baggage store.

Gedaran had feared the Imps would fight to the death. But, 30 minutes after the first Coalition marine had fought her way into the *Harvester*, the urge to survive prevailed over duty and honor and the battle for the *Harvester*'s forward sections was over, the Imps, bloody and battle-blackened, throwing down their weapons before being pushed to the deck to have their wrists flexicuffed, the decks around them body-littered, slick with blood.

But the Andimeshki's fight down aft had not ended. Compartment by compartment, they flushed Imps out, some deciding that dying in the Empire's service to be a bad idea, too many fighting to the death.

Until common-sense finally prevailed.

"Brickyard, 9," Fonseca commed. "The Imps aft of the cargo bays have called it quits. All sections now clear. Medics are transferring casualties to Lander-5 through Sierra-9 now."

"Brickyard, roger. Prisoners and walking wounded forward to compartment Bravo-3-2. Cargo bays are secure."

Gedaran watched Fonseca's grunts as they hustled their Imps forward. With the smoke gone, the full horror of the battle was all too clear. *Harvester*'s interior was a shambles, rifle fire and fragmentation grenades all but destroying its internal bulkheads along with every cable, pipe, ventilation duct, and fitting, leaving shattered equipment, torn wiring, storerooms ripped open with their contents strewn everywhere, hydraulic fluid dripping down.

The bodies of Coalition and Imp marines lay where death had taken them, some alone, some in small groups, closer than they had ever been in life. Amidst the dead were the living, combat medics and bots from both sides working frantically to save those who might make it, leaving the mortally wounded to slip quietly away.

In the feeble flicker of emergency lighting, it was the stuff of nightmares.

The Andimeshki ignored it all and moved on.

~~~

"Welcome to hell, Mister Gedaran," one of CAT-2's marines said.

"Thank you . . . What is that smell?"

"Extract of shit laced with essence of piss, sweat and fear . . . and let me show you why," the marine added as he pushed open a door marked 'Economy Class Saloon'.

Gedaran stepped through and stopped, the air so rank he did not want to breathe.

Massed faces stared back at him. They packed what once must have been a comfortable and welcoming place.

"How many prisoners are there?"

"511. One died en-route. We're transferring them to *Provider* as fast as we can."

"What happened here?" Gedaran asked.

"Twelve hours before the *Harvester* dropped, the Imps herded the prisoners in here, left them some water, and then locked the doors. The only problem with that was restrooms. They're all outside, and the Imps refused to let anyone use them. They tossed in a few buckets instead."

"Who commanded the Imp marines?"

"A Colonel Murtagh. She was killed during the attack, her exec also. You have to give those Imps bastards their due. They fought hard."

Gedaran took a deep breath to steady himself, then wished he hadn't; the air was so foul, it burned. "I would too if I'd been responsible for this."

"Yeah . . . The major said you were after Ms. Nguyen. She's down back."

"I see her. Thanks."

Gedaran stepped his way through the throng to where Nguyen was talking to one of the prisoners. "You must be Gedaran?" she said once she had finished.

"I am. The commodore said I'd find you here."

Nguyen waved a hand around the room. "This is going to make one hell of an i-bomb."

"Which is what I want to talk with you about. I have holovid footage from the *Harvester*'s security holocams for you plus more from the prison."

"I'll take it all. I'm done here, so I'll head back to *Stiletto* with what I've recorded. You can comm me what you've got on the way."

"Okay, but I need to warn you, Ms. Nguyen: Some of the prison vid is rough stuff."

"Hey! I was there, remember?"

Gedaran winced. "Sorry. That was pretty stupid of me."

Nguyen smiled as she patted Gedaran on the shoulder. "Yes, it was."

~~~

Nguyen walked out of the transfer tube across to *Stiletto*. "You weren't exaggerating when you said it would be rough."

"I wish I had been," Gedaran replied. "The executions were absolutely horrific."

"They were . . . What surprised me was the way Traavik and guards just stood around chatting as prisoners were killed right in front of them, like that was perfectly normal."

"The banality of evil, Hannah Arendt called it. Traavik assured everyone it was okay to murder ordinary people as long as they were doing their duty by following orders."

"Huh!" Nguyen grunted. "I think he's going to find out the rest of humanity does not agree with that."

"It must have been hard, down there in Senucia."

"It was, but I was still proud of what the Fire Ants did. Even when things turned bad, when I thought I only had a few days left to live, part of me was still glad I'd done what I'd done. But what we are going to do now will make all that look like amateur hour. By the time I'm finished, I'm going to make the emperor wish he'd stayed plain old Mister Michael."

~~~

Kal pushed back her chair and stood, planting her hands on the table. "Enough, Governor Chandra! I've had enough of your bullshit, so here is the only deal I'm going to offer you. Even though I am sure you are lying, I will accept you knew nothing of what Colonel Traavik was up to at Senucia Prison."

"I didn't, I promise you," Poliak's former imperial governor said.

"Listen, don't talk, goddammit!" Kal barked. "In return, you will issue a media statement condemning what happened here on Poliak-8 and resigning your governorship in protest. If you refuse, I will take you to Narsaq-3 to stand trial for what happened in Senucia Prison. Now, unless you want me to reopen the matter of what you did and did not know, then I—"

"No, no, no. I'll do it. Just like you want. On my honor."

"You don't have any honor; you never did ... No visitors," Kal said, turning to the marine standing guard, still in a battle-stained shipsuit, stubby combat shotgun in hand. "If that slimy bastard moves from that chair, shoot him in the gut, and that's an order."

"Shoot the slimy bastard in the gut if he moves, aye, aye, commodore."

Feeling unclean, Kal walked forward to the crew-room, relieved to find it empty. She was sitting down, coffee in hand, when Fonseca walked in. "Hey, commodore. You look like I feel."

"Thanks a bunch. I really am getting too old for this shit. What can I do for you?"

"I wanted to tell you myself. We lost Kahiga."

Kal grimaced. "Damn it all to hell. That's five killed and nine wounded. I just hope it's all worth it."

"Of course it is. We are Andimeshki; we all knew what failure would cost us."

"That doesn't make it any easier. Talking of your people, Jens, you wanted to update me on Xaabsade."

"Yes, I do. He was almost out of control today, like he was crazy. How he wasn't killed I will never know. I'm going to talk with him."

"Okay, do that. What about you?"

"Ushabir did well today. She has been a great exec. She is ready to take over whenever I call it quits, but I think the days of an independent Andimeshki marine unit are over. My people will have to transfer to the Coalition marines if they want to go on with it."

"Will they?" Kal asked.

"Some. Not many."

"Because they're an insubordinate bunch who won't take well to Coalition marine discipline?"

Fonseca smiled. "I'd prefer to call it Coalition marine bullshit. My guys are mercenaries for a reason, but it will be up to them. As for me, I think I'll take my back pay and mission bonuses before looking for a quiet place to settle down . . . Hold on . . . Sorry, I'm needed in the cargo bay."

"No problem. One thing before you go, I just got a message from Himaya about the prisoners we took from the *Harvester*. They were just petty criminals from Chusri's prisons. Not that Traavik cared; one of his staff has confirmed he was going to execute them as well."

Fonseca's eyes narrowed. "You were right, commodore. Those prisoners were bait."

"And you only toss bait in the water if there are fish there to be caught."

"What are you saying?"

"We're the fish. If I had any doubts that somebody told the Imps we were coming, I don't now."

—60—

Kal finished reading the single sheet of paper. "That's excellent, Mister Chandra. Well done."

FOR IMMEDIATE PUBLIC RELEASE.

To His Imperial Majesty, Michael the First.

May it please Your Majesty,

I regret to report the capture by Coalition forces of freighter Harvester CHSR-7765227-KZ and its embarked marine battalion after Harvester had launched a missile attack on Coalition ships in Poliak-8 nearspace. I believe the damage to Coalition ships was minor, but the commander of Coalition forces has refused to confirm that.

Harvester had also embarked 512 petty criminals from Chusri. Before Harvester's arrival, I was advised by Colonel Enlai Luis Traavik of Imperial Prisons Service, the commander of Senucia Imperial Prison, that these prisoners were to be executed. When I questioned the legality of such action, Colonel Traavik gave me a certified copy of an order from Zama Ryzaev, Minster of Imperial Administration. The order, of which I had been unaware, instructed Traavik to execute all prisoners held in Senucia prison [quote] at the earliest possible opportunity [end quote]. I have provided the Coalition commander with a certified copy of that order.

I have been advised me that all surviving Senucia Prison staff will stand trial for crimes against humanity.

In light of the above, I hereby lodge the strongest possible protest at the past and intended murders of Senucia Prison detainees by Colonel Traavik and his prison staff, contrary to Imperial and international law.

Accordingly, I hereby submit my resignation effective immediately.

Signed,

JONATHON K. CHANDRA, Imperial Governor, Poliak System.

Chandra's smile was all smug self-satisfaction. "I'm glad you like it, commodore."

Resisting the urge to give the man a good kicking, Kal said, "Hold on a second while I pinchcomm it to the drug-addled asswipe on the Imperial throne along with every media organization in humanspace . . . All done. Thank you."

"Happy to be of assistance, commodore."

"You've been most helpful, governor. I think the people of humanspace are going to impressed you have taken such a principled stand. I just wish I could be there when Michael the Scumbag reads it."

Fear crumpled Chandra's face. "Please don't say that. He won't be happy with me. He's a terrible man. He likes hurting people who upset him."

"So I hear, but I do enjoy thinking about what he would have done to you, you corrupt, venal sonofabitch. You see, I know why you ended up here."

"It's no secret why I'm here, commodore. The Minister for Imperial Administration asked me to be governor. She told me was my duty to improve the lives of the Poliaks, and that I was the best person for the job. I felt it was an honor to be chosen to help the people of one of the poorest systems in humanspace, so of course I agreed."

"How very touching," Kal said. "Pity it's all horseshit. We have interrogated your personal staff. They've all told us the same thing: You wanted the job, really wanted it, so you bribed the minister to gift it to you. And why? To make a shitload of money by screwing the locals. And that's exactly what you did."

"That is not true!" Chandra protested.

"Your people didn't much like you, did they?"

"I wouldn't say that."

"Scumbag was a word they used whenever your name came up. It's amazing how much information they've given us."

"Like what?"

Kal ignored the question. She pushed a sheaf of paper at Chandra. "Have you seen these?"

"No."

"It's a list of grievances attached to a petition signed by 285,000 Poliaks."

"A petition for what?"

"Asking me to return you dirtside to stand trial."

Chandra's face paled to dirty-gray, lips trembling, tears welling up. "But you . . . You promised I wouldn't be tried, you promised!"

"Yes, I did but only for what happened in Senucia Prison. Poliak's another matter together. Its interim government wants you to stand trial for the crimes it alleges you committed as governor. Since those crimes fall in its jurisdiction, I am obliged as a matter of international law to return you dirtside along with the rest of your senior staff."

"No, no, no! Please don't. They'll tear me apart."

Kal shrugged. "Like I care."

Chandra stabbed a finger at Kal. "Fuck you, Kariuki! As soon as you have gone, the Empire will be back, and I will be governor again. Then we'll see how all those knuckle-dragging Poliak scum like Imperial justice. I am going to make every last one of them wish they'd never been born. And that's a fucking promise."

Kal was enjoying herself now. "I'll be sure to give the Poliaks the holovid of this interview so they can see how you feel about them. And you can forget the Empire coming to your rescue. In exchange for closing its gateways to all traffic, Poliak will be given our Q-drive technology. This is a poor system, but it is well able to update the ships it has. Once it has, there'll be no need for Kolovchenko's gateways anymore . . . Not that you'll care; it'll be a long time before you see the outside of a prison again."

Kal turned and walked out. She commed O'Donnell. "I'm finished with Chandra."

"I'll organize his transfer dirtside. How is he?"

"A self-pitying, blubbering mess."

"And so he should be."

"How long before we can head back to Narsaq?"

"Himaya's just commed me. He needs another two hours to finish transferring the last of the Imp POWs to the Poliaks. Add an hour to clean up, and we can go."

"Okay. Do you need me?"

"No, commodore."

Kal sighed with relief. She was exhausted. "In that case, it's a coffee, shower, and my rack for me. And do not disturb me unless I fail to turn up for breakfast."

—61—

The agent's report had taken weeks to cross the 221 light-years from Terra.

The Narsaq Foreign Intelligence Service AI responsible for handling all raw intelligence from Terra considered the report. Studied the agent's profile. Pulled raw data from tens of thousands of sources. Hunted down correlations, connections, confirmations, contradictions. Incorporated the useful. Discarded the irrelevant. Rejected the erroneous. Integrated the totality. Contemplated the result. Made a decision.

The report was credible.

Seconds after the AI had started work, its assessment was on its way to FIS's Terra section marked 'FLASH GENESIS—HUMAN REVIEW REQUIRED'.

~~~

Kal looked skeptical. "A mothballed orbital research facility? Are you sure?"

Director Peng nodded. "I am. Its location well out from Terra, ImpSec transports shuttling back and forth, courier ships berthed alongside doing nothing until they disappear one by one into deepspace never to be seen again, and repeated visits by Jo Risell's ministerial shuttle all tell us that ORF-31 is important. And there is nothing more important to Risell and the Empire than developing a Q-drive."

"Has ImpSec ever said what it is?"

"It did, not long after your attack on Hardakken's slave complex on Ventas-2. It issued a media statement saying that ORF-31 had been requisitioned for use as a processing facility for high-value political prisoners."

"Which you obviously don't believe, Jerry, so tell me why."

A sly grin spread over Peng's face. "Senucia, that's why."

"Senucia? I don't get it."

"Thanks to you, we have the personal files for all the high-value political prisoners who were sent there. Care to guess how many went through ORF-31?"

Kal's eyes narrowed. "None?"

"Correct. All the HVP prisoners arrested by ImpSec—those that weren't shot out of hand—were taken to Complex-99, a Terran processing center on the mainland north of New Hainan. The records confirm that not one of them went anywhere near ORF-31. Two of Colonel Traavik's senior staffers had been with ImpAdmin's HVP prisoner section from Day 1 of the Expansion; neither had heard of it."

"Okay, it's not what ImpSec says it is," Kal conceded, "but it's a stretch to argue that Risell's Q-drive development team is based there."

Peng's mouth tightened. "I don't normally talk sources, but I think I'm going to have to this time . . . FIS has an agent; let's call him Mister X. He works for Terra NearCon and has access to all the raw data in NearCon's traffic knowledgebases."

"By raw you mean classified ship movements as well?" Kal asked.

"Exactly. Every movement by every ship through Terran nearspace, it's all in there along with those ships' passenger and cargo manifests."

Kal whistled softly. "Wow! That's pure gold."

"It is, which is why you are not going to talk about this with anyone."

"Understood."

"Anyway," Peng went on, "Mister X was trawling through the traffic knowledgebases when he noticed the spike in ships visiting ORF-31 and decided to take a closer look. He found that their cargo manifests were full of the hardware needed to support a complex ship design and engineering project, while the passenger lists included physicists from the Keliang Foundation, engineers from Kolovchenko, Jo Risell twice a month, and not one person from any of the Empire's new colonies. If that's a prison for HVPs, I'm a cabbage."

"All right then, it does look like you might be right. Did your Mister X say what he thought the project was?"

"No, he didn't. His job is sending us data, not speculation, and he knows it."

"Well, if what he's given you is true, he deserves a medal," Kal said. "But is it? ImpSec could have faked his report; it must have access to NearCon's traffic knowledgebases. And Jo Risell is a smart woman; she knows her Q-drive development team is a target we cannot ignore. I can't think of a better way to make *Stiletto* pay ORF-31 a visit . . . I'm sorry, but the more I think about it, the more it feels like a trap."

"Risell's focus isn't setting traps for *Stiletto*. It's getting the Q-drive into Imperial Navy ships as soon as she can. As we both know, once she has done that, it's only a matter of time before the Empire crushes the Coalition and all the other independent systems."

Kal shook her head. "If that's true, why hasn't COMSOLSPACE deployed cruisers to protect ORF-31?"

"A good question, the answer to which seems to be Imperial politics. The Kolovchenko Founders hate Risell with a passion; she's not one of them—she's not even Terran—and she is way too ambitious for their liking. Now that Amos Ferruci's been marginalized, she only survives because ImpSec protects the Emperor and the Emperor protects her. We believe she's keeping ORF-31 a secret so her political enemies don't know what she's up to."

"I smell ambition," Kal said. "She wants to use the Q-drive to make her position even more secure."

"That and more. FIS's profilers say Risell is loyal to only one person: herself. We can't know for sure, but none of my analysts would be surprised if she's not setting things up so she can take the imperial throne for herself."

"Nice woman . . . You haven't really answered my question though. Is ORF-31 a trap or not?"

"Given how it's set up, we don't think so," Peng said. "Risell's no fool; she'll know there's always a chance, however slight, we might find out about ORF-31 and send *Stiletto* deep into Terran nearspace to deal with it. If we do, it will be up to SOLSPACE and the Imperial Navy to mobilize every ship they have to make sure it never leaves; the *Stiletto* is the one target they cannot afford to miss. That's why any operation to neutralize ORF-31 must ensure the Imps are busy someplace else. We cannot risk losing the *Stiletto*."

"No we can't . . . Give me a moment, Jerry," Kal added.

She stood and walked to the window of Peng's office to think. She wasn't worried about Imp cruisers; the *Stiletto* would be in and out before they posed any threat. No, it was the thought of ORF-31's cargo hatches spitting Vulkan-C missile containers and their Taipan ASMs. The *Stiletto*'s chances of survival would be slim at best.

But Peng and the FIS had no way of knowing if ImpSec had turned Mister X, using him to make ORF-31 an elaborate trap. Intelligence was an uncertain business. It always had been.

Kal turned back. "I'm sorry, but this is on you. I can stand here, wringing my hands until the end of time, but that won't help anyone. If you tell me Mister X's report justifies the risk of sending the *Stiletto* in to check out ORF-31, then I'll go with that."

"Talk about putting the pressure on, but yes, I believe it does."

"Decision made then. And, talking about spies, have your counter-intelligence people made any progress?"

"COIN have been through all *Stiletto*'s and *Provider*'s comms logs; they're clean. As for FIS and COMFLT, only staffers with ULTRA CHROME security clearance had access to your mission plans. COIN has checked them all, me included; none had the opportunity or means to send a message."

"What about the Coalition marines?"

"COMCOMARFOR and his staff had no need to know the timing of *Stiletto*'s operations."

Kal's stomach fluttered at the thought the Imp spy might be one her own people, someone who had been with her from the start. It did not bear thinking about. "Are you sure it wasn't FIS or COMFLT?" she asked.

"People with ULTRA CHROME security clearances can't take a shit without COIN knowing. And no, I am not exaggerating."

Kal's mouth twisted with distaste. "Yecch . . . How then? Somebody gave the Imps our plans for the Poliak operation. We need to find whoever it was."

"COIN says that leaves only possibility, Kal, one you're not going to like. It thinks . . ."

—62—

Kal sat on the bridge, heart racing, the faces of her people spinning through her mind.

She could not see any of them as an Imp spy. She just couldn't.

"Bridge, cargo bay. Cargo drones have gone."

"What about *Provider*'s?" Kal asked.

O'Donnell frowned. It was an odd question for Kal to ask, and they both knew it. "Standby, commodore, I'll check . . . They left five minutes ago."

Kal kept her face impassive. "Thanks . . . Give me a commlink to Director Peng."

Peng's avatar appeared in Kal's mind's eye. "The cargo drones from both ships are on their way in."

"Standby . . . Okay, we have their vectors."

"Tell me how you go."

20 minutes later, O'Donnell leaned forward to look at his command screen. "What is that Narsaq SDV up to? It's on vector to intercept *Provider*'s cargo drones. And there's another heading for ours. Tactical, patch me over to the bastards. I'm going to rip them a—"

Kal cut O'Donnell off. "Negative. Ignore them."

O'Donnell's face reddened. "They're on vector for our cargo drones, commodore. We can't allow that. Let me speak—"

"Are you deaf? Leave them be, and that's an order, goddammit!"

The man stared, his mouth working in outrage.

Could it be him? Kal asked herself.

Time dragged past, punctuated by another furious outburst from O'Donnell, insisting they do something to stop the Narsaq ships. An outburst she had crushed with anger so brutal it had left O'Donnell sullen with rage and frustration.

~~~

Peng was a long time getting back to Kal. "Bad news. The Imps' spy is one of *Stiletto*'s people. We found the message hidden in one of the cargo drones' maintenance logs. I've commed you its ID."

Kal fought to stay in control even as the deck fell away beneath her. "Got it. Leave it with me."

She closed her eyes, accessed the holovid from the cargo bay, and started to rewind until she found the suspect drone. It was clearly visible as it sat waiting to be sent on its way.

She soon had her suspect: Xaabsade. As he walked past, his left hand had brushed a small object across the drone's maintenance port.

Kal commed Peng. "It's one of our Andimeshki, Erikk Xaabsade."

Peng's mouth tightened. "Xaabsade . . . I remember him from your after-action reports. Maybe this is why he fought like a demon."

"He wanted to die."

"Sounds like it. Do you want to handle this?"

"He's one of mine, so yes."

"We're here you need any help. Just keep me posted."

Kal cut the link and commed Fonseca. "Crew-room, now . . . Liam," she said to O'Donnell, "with me, now."

"What—"

"For chrissakes! Just do it, okay?" Kal snapped, comming Fonseca's exec. "I need you do something, fast, without any questions, and no talking to anyone. Okay?"

"Understood, commodore," Ushabir replied.

"Take four of your people and arrest Xaabsade but be careful. He might resist, and I don't want him or anybody else hurt. Strip-search him, and that includes a full cavity exam. When you're done, bring everything you find and him to the crew-room."

True to her marine roots, Ushabir's face stayed an impassive mask. "Aye, aye, commodore."

Fonseca waited in the crew-room' he looked puzzled. Kal found a seat on one of the benches. "You guys sit either side of me, and, yes, I will explain."

O'Donnell was white-lipped with anger. "That would be nice."

"I'm sorry, Liam. I couldn't tell you any earlier. Looks like we have an Imp spy on board . . ."

The faces of the two men tightened with shock.

". . . It's Xaabsade."

"What? No, it can't be," O'Donnell said.

Fonseca's head dropped into his hands. "Goddamnit to hell . . . Yes, it can. He's not been right ever since Narsaq. My exec talked with him after Poliak; he told her he was just trying to do everything he could to help finish the war so he could go home. And we believed him . . . I'm sorry, commodore. I dropped the ball on this one."

"No, you didn't. You thought the man was being a bit strange, and so he was, but none of us is psychic."

Fonseca started to his feet. "I'll fetch him."

"Sit down. Ushabir will have him here as soon as he's been searched, but the three of us are the only ones onboard who know about what Xaabsade's been up to. I want it to stay that way."

~~~

"It's hard to believe," O'Donnell said as Fonseca followed Xaabsade—now a hunched, remorse-racked wreck of a man—out of the crew-room.

Kal's mind filled with an image of and ImpSec thug, gun in hand, standing over Daniel. "I never want to be in his situation. I'm not sure how I'd handle being told my kids would be killed if I didn't cooperate."

"This will sound harsh, but that man had choices. He could have come clean as soon as he was back aboard the *Stiletto*. With our help, the consequences for his family would not have been as bad as he expected. Instead, he chose to betray us. That decision put our lives and our ships at risk. What he did is unforgivable."

"Yeah, it was," Kal said.

"What do we do with him now?"

"FIS has a team on its way to pick him up. Maybe they can wring enough out of him to let the Andimeshki roll up the Imp team who recruited him."

"Here's hoping. And I'm sorry. I was way out of line earlier."

Kal brushed the apology away. "It's okay. You must have thought I'd gone mad."

"That did cross my mind."

They both laughed, and not because O'Donnell's comment was that funny. More because it was better than crying. One of her Andimeshki was an Imp agent. Kal still struggled to believe it.

O'Donnell stood. "I'd best get back to it, commodore."

Kal commed Peng as soon as O'Donnell left. "I guess that's that then."

"It must be hard, Kal."

"Being betrayed by one of your own? More than you can imagine . . . and he might not be alone."

"Unlikely," Peng said. "Xaabsade told us that the Imp team killed two high-profile brokers before they got to him. The Andimeshk police would have been looking for them. They got what they wanted; they wouldn't have hung around."

Kal wanted to scream. "How did the Imps know to go to Andimeshk?"

"Remember the slaves your marines rescued?"

"I do. A charity called Hope Reborn took them from us."

"Which branch?"

"The Andimeshk . . . Oh, sweet jeezus!" Kal's head dropped into her hands. "I might as well have sent Jo Risell a comm telling her where I'd recruited my marines."

"You couldn't have done what you did without leaving a trail. And Risell's a very smart woman."

"Even so, I feel like a complete idiot."

"Before you start beating yourself up, Kal, let there is some good news. Thanks to Xaabsade, we now have a huge opportunity."

"To do what?"

"My COIN people are sure the Imps trust the messages he sends them, and I agree."

"They won't now, not after what happened at Poliak-8."

"Why would you say that?" Peng asked. "Xaabsade said you'd turn up, and you did, on time too."

Kal frowned. "It can't be that simple."

"Actually, it can. Think about it. The Imps wanted you to wait for *Harvester*, and you obliged. Why? Because you always do the right thing, just like you did with those slaves. The Imps would have seen that as a weakness they could exploit. And the way you fought off *Harvester*'s missile attack? They'd have blamed themselves for underestimating you; they won't be questioning Xaabsade's bona fides. They'll be praying he sends them something even better ... and we are going make sure he does."

"Ah, okay. I get it. You're thinking of turning Xaabsade."

Peng smiled. "Yes, I am. I want to use him to warn the Imps that the *Stiletto* will be mounting an operation against Terra's interstellar gateways, targets so valuable the Imps will have to throw everything they have into its defense. That will be more than enough to take the Imps' attention off ORF-31."

"I can't think of a better decoy."

"And, no matter how much Risell bleats, she'll get no cruisers to look after ORF-31. Whatever else the Empire loses, it cannot lose its gateways. That's an absolute given."

Suddenly, Kal was too tired to go on. It had been a lifetime since the asteroid had hit Ladaki, the longest, hardest years of her life. She wanted to somewhere, anywhere, else.

"Are you okay?" Peng asked, eyes narrowed in concern.

"I'm not sure ... I'm not sure if I can do this anymore."

"For what it's worth, I don't how anyone could do what you've done. It's beyond remarkable. Everyone will understand if you've reached the end of your road."

"How can I walk away now? Xaabsade gives us the best chance we will ever have of destroying any hopes the Empire might have of developing a Q-drive. Take out their gateways as well, and the Imps are finished. We will never have a better chance. We must take it . . . I must take it."

"And we will, but you don't have to, not in person. You trust O'Donnell; why else would you have made him captain of *Stiletto*?"

"I do trust him," Kal said.

"And you should. He's learned from you, and he's done well under pressure. He will do as well next time and the time after. You do not need to go to Terra, Kal, you really don't. It's enough for you to help with the planning."

"You think so?"

"I think so."

~~~

Sleep refused to come.

Swearing, Kal gave up the struggle, switched on the light, and slid out of her bunk, leaving it a tangled mess.

Showered, she slipped into a fresh shipsuit and headed for the bridge. With *Stiletto* safe in Narsaq nearspace, it was empty. Out of habit, she still scanned the array of screens that curtained the forward bulkhead, looking for any anomalies the AIs might have missed.

There were none.

She helped herself to a coffee and found her seat.

Not that it would be her seat for much longer. It and all the seats in all the Coalition ships that would follow *Stiletto* into combat belonged to younger officers, officers with the training and emotional resilience to endure what lay ahead: a war that threatened to degenerate into a grinding fight that stretched over years.

Logic told her she should leave all that to René Duvall, now a commodore and commander of humanspace's first space-attack vehicle carrier task force, Task Force 100.

And that logic was sound. Kal Kariuki—ex-marine, ex-AI tech, ex-alcoholic—had done more than anyone could have ever asked. More than she had ever thought she could do.

But, but, but.

All her life, she had left a trail of debris in her wake: friendships betrayed; relationships destroyed; debts unpaid; promises broken; commitments dishonored; opportunities squandered.

All with utter disregard for consequences that bordered on contempt for everyone she had ever met.

Even the redemption she had found in the M'bakaa marines had proved ephemeral. Instead of building on what she had achieved, she had pissed away all the marines had taught her, allowing alcohol and drugs to destroy any hope of making a success of her second life as an AI tech.

But now she had one last chance to amount to something. Her last chance to show that she was not an old, washed-up wreck who got lucky. Her last chance to show she could achieve something that mattered. Her last chance to leave behind something that would endure.

For once, she wanted to finish what she had started. More than she'd ever wanted anything in her life. And she would.

—63—

Kal found herself a seat in the flag officer's station, an alcove set back amidships. Complete with its own screens and workstations, it had an unobstructed view of the *Iron Lance*'s bridge.

It was still hard to believe she was on board the Coalition's first SAV carrier. A lifetime ago it had been a notion born of Daniel's fertile imagination. Now Tharmaran Shipbuilding—in an extraordinary display of industrial power—had made the idea reality months ahead of schedule, hounded and harried every step of the way by a relentless Maia Okiro.

I know what failure means for humanspace, she had told Kal.

Sipping her coffee, Kal watched Commodore Duvall as he wrapped up the briefing for the *Iron Lance*'s next exercise. The man's face betrayed the pressure he was under as the Commander, Task Force 100: two SAV carriers, the *Iron Lance* and the yet-to-be-delivered *Iron Sword,* plus *Stiletto* and *Provider*, along with the *Star Crosser*, *Star Jumper*, and *Star Blazer*, three Coalition courier ships Kal had coopted into the role of deepspace recon ships.

Add new missions, new crews, new ships, new AIs, a new style of warfare on a scale nobody had ever experienced, and an Empire fast waking up to the ugly truth that it had a fight on its hands, an enemy unlike any Coalition officer had ever faced, and it was no wonder Duvall looked so stressed.

Not that Kal doubted him. He was as promising an officer as she had ever met. Inexperienced but steady under pressure. And he had seen combat in a Q-drive warship, combat which was a radical departure from the glorified police operations all system-defense force officers spent their entire careers carrying out.

The *Iron Lance*'s combat AI broke into her thoughts. "Flag, Combat. Slammer-Red. Dropping now . . . at drop datum, launching landers now. Threat plot is red."

"30 seconds faster than last time," said Duvall as the last of *Iron Lance*'s SAVs cleared the ship, "but still too slow."

Kal shared Duvall's concern. All the missions carried out in the Coalition's new fleet simulation facility had shown that warships to be most vulnerable in the seconds after they dropped.

As the *Stiletto* had proved at Narsaq and Tongchen.

"Flag, Combat. Recon-01 through 20 off-line . . . Hostile heavy cruisers *Surger*, *Superior* and *Sagacity* no longer in parking orbit. Final departure vector not known."

Kal wanted to see what Duvall would do now. Those missing Imp ships were going to make his life difficult; her brief to the sim designers that they kill all Duvall's recon drones even more so.

~~~

Duvall slumped into a chair beside Kal, running a hand through sweat-matted hair. "That was brutal. All my recon drones trashed, for chrissakes! And cruisers aren't supposed to touch down on moons."

"No reason why they can't as long as the moon's small enough," Kal said. "The reaction-control system of an Imp S-class cruiser is rated to 0.15 g."

"Something I'd overlooked."

"That's why we're here. But you and your people did well overall."

"Given we've not had a lot of time to bring a bunch of rookies crewing a new ship up to combat readiness, yeah, they did. I worry about the combat AIs though; none of them have fought a battle like the ones they're going into. I'd be a lot happier if my task force had some combat experience before we take on Terra."

"We all would, but COMFLT's already delayed the Terra operation enough waiting for Tharmaran to deliver the *Iron Sword*. We can't afford to wait much longer; using courier ships with containers to harass the Imps by firing missile salvos from deepspace makes us all feel good, but that's never going to be enough, not now the Imps are giving their SDVs the new Mamba missile interceptors. And the moment the Imps have a working Q-drive, the advantage swings back to them."

Duvall sighed. "I know, I know. I think we could pull off an attack on Terra just with the *Iron Lance*, but I'll sleep a lot better putting two full wings of SAVs into the attack rather than one."

"As long you can convince the Imps that Terra's interstellar gateways are our primary target, *Stiletto* and *Provider*'s SAVs won't have any problem with ORF-31. If you can knock out those gateways as well, I'll be even happier."

—64—

Kal had not enjoyed reading the latest INTSUM from COMFLT.

Backed by the Empire's prodigious economic power, the Imperial Navy was fast evolving into a new and more deadly force. More warships but smaller. Obsolescent Eaglehawk ASMs replaced by vector-agile Taipans with two-stage warheads, Mamushi missile interceptors by Mambas. A new plant to manufacture the Vulkan-C missile containers that would turn every Imp freighter into a potential missile carrier. Better planetary-defense sensor arrays. Containerized missile defenses for gateways. A brutal purge of incompetent officers, starting with the Commander-in-Chief herself along with most of her senior staff.

The days of *Stiletto* waltzing in-system to kick the shit out of a high-value planet like Teshawa-2 were over.

And it was only a matter of time before the Imperial Navy had ships fitted with Q-drives. When that day came, the Empire would be invincible. With the Coalition forced to fight for its very survival—a fight Kal knew it could never win—there would be no more talk of saving humanspace, no more plans to attack Terra.

A head appeared around the door of Kal's stateroom. "Sorry to interrupt, commodore, but Director Peng's shuttle will be alongside in five."

"I'm on my way."

~~~

Coffee and small talk over, Peng reached into his briefcase and pulled out a single sheet of paper, sliding it across to Kal. "Read this. Sorry, it's taken so long. We had to be sure there weren't any trigger words in there."

"And are you?"

"Oh, yes. Xaabsade knew what would happen to him if he tried anything."

"I'll never forgive that sonofabitch," Kal muttered as she started to read.

TOP SECRET — ULTRA CORAL

JESTER from DREAMER.

STILETTO now operational after Poliak battle damage repairs. MARDET STILETTO briefed today on next mission, a missile swarm targeting Terran interstellar gateways fired from deepspace to ensure STILETTO and PROVIDER not put at risk. Swarm will be quote << biggest missile attack ever seen >>. PROVIDER will offload its MARDET to maximize missile container payload. Swarm to go active 48 hours after STILETTO and PROVIDER arrival in Terra deepspace scheduled for 2311-06-26-23:00 UST. Will advise if any ETA change.

MARDET STILETTO not briefed on missile numbers and launch datum as quote << grunts have no need to know>>. Post-briefing STILETTO XO heard saying to CO that Imperial Navy is quote << very strong, maybe even enough to stop our attack >>. CO reply << We cannot wait until they have their own Q-drive ships. This war is over if we don't kill those gateways and soon >>.

View amongst MARDET STILETTO is that CO and XO are not confident about outcome of this operation.

TOD 2311-06-04-07:34 UST.

TOP SECRET — ULTRA CORAL

"Woah," Kal said when she was done. "That'll get the Imps' juices flowing. I assume Jester is Xaabsade's handler?"

"In ImpSec, yes. That message was sent four hours ago."

Kal's face betrayed her concern. "It feels all wrong to tell the Imps we're coming."

"It's the only way to make Jo Risell believe ORF-31 and her Q-drive program are still a secret."

"Let's hope it works. Any more FIS goodies for me, director?"

Peng nodded. "Just one. Amos Ferruci. The reports we're getting from Terra tell us he's up to something."

"Given the way the Founders reacted to his kidnapping, I can't say I'm surprised, but he's just one man. What can he do?"

"Your attacks on the Gang of Five have destabilized financial markets, driving risk premiums up," Peng said. "Thanks to the war, gateway traffic is down a third, which has flushed Kolovchenko's stock into the sewers. Nobody has much faith in the Imperial Navy after Narsaq, Teshawa, Tongchen, and Poliak; the missile attacks our courier ships are carrying out are chipping away at what little confidence people do have left."

"Nothing like a container load of FireSpark missiles up the Empire's ass to remind the Imps how vulnerable they are," Kal said.

"True enough. And all of that is why the Imps have been forced to introduce the Imperial Security Levy to bankroll the Expansion. Understandably, that is something ordinary Terrans are seriously pissed off about. The Imps are going to find life very difficult if Ferruci can bring those people onto the streets."

"Can he?" Kal asked.

"FIS's Terran desk thinks so, though predicting how a society as big and diverse as Terra's reacts to extreme stress is difficult, especially if that stress comes from an external threat. Even so, we believe Ferruci has the money and connections to trigger a popular uprising."

"You know, I talked a lot with Ferruci while I was waiting for his ransom to get paid," Kal said. "Power was his thing, not money. That was why he drove Terra's imperial project, only to lose everything when the Founders used the kidnapping to sideline him. A Coalition attack on Terra's gateways would give him his best opportunity to recover the power he lost, an opportunity he will take, I'm sure of it. And when he does, it'll be absolute chaos."

Peng nodded. "With a bit of luck, Ferruci will give us a full-blown civil war. I can't see how the Empire could survive that."

Kal felt a sudden burst of confidence. For all its massive surveillance arrays, warships, and shipyards, maybe the Empire could be beaten.

Even if the Coalition needed Amos Ferruci's unwitting help to do so.

—65—

For the tenth time since the *Stiletto* had dropped into normalspace a billion kilometers out from Terra, Kal forced herself to breathe, bottoming her lungs in a long, shaky sigh.

The wait for the Coalition attack to start had left her with nerves twanging and stomach churning. All unnecessary, of course, and Kal knew it. The recon drones surveilling Terran nearspace had seen nothing unexpected, and why would they? The Imps only had enough ships to defend Terra's gateways, not mount patrols into deepspace.

All that reasoning had not helped. No matter how hard she had tried to reassure herself everything was going to turn out fine, a kernel of doubt had refused to capitulate, its jeremiads a relentless stream warning of impending disaster.

She was done. A one more day and she would be on her way back to Narsaq and retirement, leaving the Empire and its ambitions smoking ruins. Not that she cared if the Coalition attack failed. Dealing with the Imps was going to be somebody else's problem.

"Command, Combat. Flag confirms threat assessment complete. Terran threat plot is red. ORF-31 no change."

Kal had seen some ugly threat plots in her time with the M'bakaan marines but never anything like this.

228 cruisers. 113 SDVs. More Vulkan-C missile containers than she could count. Two space battle stations mounting Taipan ASM batteries. A surveillance network bigger than any in humanspace, its cloud of Big Eye optronics drones capable of detecting a cruiser bows on as it occluded the stars a million kilometers out from Terra, a target barely a millionth of a degree wide.

Duvall and Task Force 100 had a fight on their hands.

"Command, Combat. From Flag. Strike swarm away."

"Command, roger," O'Donnell said over the soft buzz of excitement that filled the *Stiletto*'s bridge "All stations, captain. Our first strikes now heading into Terran nearspace. The Imps' sensor arrays won't have picked it up yet, so we're not expecting any reaction from them for a while. So far, the operation's running to schedule, which means we should be jumping in-system at 22:30, but that of course depends on Commodore Duvall's SAVs getting their job done first. If anything changes, I'll let you know. Captain, out."

O'Donnell glanced at Kal. "I still can't believe we're doing this."

"I can't either." Like everyone involved, Kal had found it hard to come to terms with the idea of attacking Terra, the mother planet and the birthplace of humanity. It just felt all wrong.

How had the human race ever allowed it to come to this?

She could only hope a better future grew out of the wreckage of a defeated empire. A future not controlled by the likes of Amos Ferruci and Kolovchenko. A future not terrorized by Ferruci's murderous acolyte, Jo Risell, and her Imperial Security thugs.

She went to get herself a coffee. The strikes had a lot of space to cover before they ran into Terra's defenses; it would be hours before anything happened.

Kal had studied everything FIS knew about Rear-Admiral Aquino, SOLSPACE's commander and the woman responsible for protecting Terra. Unlike her better-connected Imperial Navy peers, Aquino owed her climb up the ranks of the Imperial Navy to hard work, self-discipline, and talent.

But was she tough enough? She needed to be; Terra's politicians would be piling on the pressure, demanding Aquino do something, anything, and do it fast. Like sending out the SDVs to destroy the incoming attack long before it got anywhere close to Terra and its gateways.

A mistake that would have reduced Aquino's already slim chances of saving her gateways to nil.

~~~

Hours after Duvall had launched the attack and much to Kal's surprise—she had suffered at the hands of marine commanders doing what politicians demanded rather than what was tactically smart—Aquino had refused to be drawn. Her cruisers and SDVs still sat unmoving, waiting as the swarm did what Xaabsade had told his handler it would.

The woman would have known that the missiles and decoys in the Coalition swarm would have responded to a premature counterattack by splintering into hundreds of small strikes, forcing Aquino to send her ships chasing after too many missiles too fast and too vector-agile to be caught, shifting the odds in the Coalition's favor and all but guaranteeing the loss of Terra's gateways.

More importantly she had proved herself tough enough to tell the politicians to fuck off.

Stiletto's bridge was silent, all attention on the single blue line tracking Swarm-1 as it ran for Terra, the end of its days-long, 100-million-kilometer journey from deepspace.

Kal checked the mission counter. Any second now.

"Command, Combat. Standby swarm breakup . . . now!"

And, where there had been one blue line tracking the loose cloud of missiles and their escort of decoys and recon drones, now there were five tightly grouped strikes on vectors for the gateways.

"Command, Combat," the AI said. "Strike-1 through 5 now active. Standby target designation."

Kal checked the mission counter. Aquino must have nerves like iron cables. Even though the five strikes were on vector to hit their targets in less than 15 minutes, SOLSPACE's commander had still not committed her ships to the counterattack.

Kal smiled. The politicians would be apoplectic by now.

Just as she was beginning to think Aquino was never going respond, the Imp admiral did. With the Coalition's missile strikes only 75,000 kilometers and six minutes from their targets, Aquino committed her first line of defense: 113 SDVs in five task groups, one to cover each gateway.

"Command, Combat. Hostile SDVs underway, now designated target groups Tango-Golf-1 through 5. On vectors to intercept Strike-1 through 5."

"Finally," O'Donnell said. "I thought she was—"

"Command, Combat. Tango-Golf-1 through 5, containers away. Positively identified Vulkan-Cs."

O'Donnell's head snapped around. "What the fuck . . . Threat! Confirm."

"Confirmed," Zana Touré said from the threat desk. "Standby . . . This is not good, captain. We're seeing 226 Vulkan-Cs."

O'Donnell looked at Kal. "Why would the Imps waste Taipans on our FireSparks? Everybody knows ASMs are useless against missiles. This makes no sense."

Kal wondered why a clever woman like Aquino was doing something so pointless. "No, it doesn't." And then, suddenly, it made sense. "Hold on, Liam . . . Threat, can the Vulkan-C deploy any other missiles? Mambas missile interceptors, for example?"

"No reason not, commodore. You'd need to modify them, of course, but that's just engineering."

Kal turned to O'Donnell. "How the hell did we miss this?" she asked. "As far as Aquino's concerned, the *Stiletto* and *Provider* have done their job putting the swarm together and won't be coming back. Thanks to Xaabsade, she thinks she's facing a missile attack targeting Terra's interstellar gateways. She'd be an idiot not to modify her Vulkan-Cs to carry Mambas, and that woman is not an idiot."

Tight lines of concern framed O'Donnell's eyes. "I think you're right, commodore."

The optimism Kal had felt as the attack on Terra had developed was fading. The Imps' new Mamba missile interceptors would be lethal against FireSparks; the Coalition strikes were going to lose a lot of missiles. "Duvall's SAVs have a shitload of work to do."

"It's not all bad. A Vulkan-C is just an empty metal box once it has dumped its payload of Mambas. So what if some of the Imp SDVs survive? Or even all of them? Duvall's SAVs can deal with them."

"Jeez, I hope so. We're fucked if they can't."

"Command, Combat. Tango-Golf-1 through 5. Missile interceptors away, mix of Mamba and Mamushi MIs. Targets Strike-1 through 5. Standby updated threat assessment . . . On-screen now."

O'Donnell studied the assessment. "That's interesting. Mamushis are nowhere as good as Mambas."

"The Imps must have run short," Kal said. "I'm glad the Coalition didn't delay this operation any longer; godknows how many we'd have been facing a month from now."

"Maybe the Imps' SDVs won't be such a problem."

"We'll see. The Vulkan-Cs around the gateways, the ones we assumed carried Taipans? Their payloads will be all Mambas."

O'Donnell grimaced. "Not that close to the gateways, for sure. Duvall will have to rework his ops plan."

"Command, Combat. Strike-1 through 5, standby starburst . . . Now!"

In an instant, the five incoming Coalition strikes, until now tight, coherent packages, had dissolved into a shambles as missiles and decoys, engines flaring, massive vector changes sending them skidding left and right, up and down.

Vector changes that had the Imps' missile interceptors struggling to stay locked on their targets.

A challenge most of the Mamushis failed to meet. Most of the Mambas did not and space filled with the searing white flares of dying missiles and decoys, all come and gone in less than a second.

"Command, Combat. Strike-1 through 5 now 54% combat effective."

Better than she'd expected, Kal thought, and more than enough to finish off the SDVs. Maybe a few cruisers as well.

She was right. The SDVs' close-in defenses did their best, but numbers counted in missile attacks. Despite the damage done by the Mambas, the five Coalition strikes were left with too many missiles and decoys for the SDVs' combat AIs to target or defenses to defeat, AIs whose failure was celebrated with Imp warships buried beneath a blazing carpet of exploding warheads.

The attack was over in seconds. Not one SDV remained combat effective. Most—their armor incapable of keeping out a FireSpark's two-stage warhead—had simply ceased to exist, transformed into clouds of hot gas by the failure of their tokomaks. The rest, a lucky few, tumbled away amidst clouds of ice-laden gas, spitting lifepods into space.

"Command, Combat. Tango-Golf-1 through 5 killed. Strike-1 through 5 now 4% combat effective. New targets assigned: gateway cruiser screens, designated Tango-Golf-6 through 10."

O'Donnell frowned as he studied the threat plot. "4% doesn't leave us enough missiles to do much damage, commodore"

"Don't be so sure. The only combat experience those Imp ships have—if they any at all—is beating up system-defense SDVs."

Kal patched her neuronics into the holovid feed from one of the recon drones running in with Strike-4, whose targets were the cruisers protecting the Chalawan-6 gateways. The most valuable of all Terra's links to the rest of humanspace, they handled a third of all its interstellar trade.

Whose value Aquino obviously understood. Of her 228 cruisers, she had deployed 62 to protect the Chalawan-6 gateways, a defensive screen augmented by Vulkan-C missile containers.

The containers Duvall's staff had thought a waste of Taipans now started to spit their payloads of Mamba MIs into space, a cloud of missiles that streaked away on thin pillars of fire to rip into the remnants of Strike-4. Again space flared white as Strike-4's missiles and decoys died, those that survived plunging headlong into the wall of fire thrown up by the cruisers protecting the Chalawan-6 gateways.

Strike-4 had started the day with over a thousand FireSparks and as many decoys. Just four missiles reached their final target, the heavy cruiser, *Poseidon*, their warheads' first stages opening craters in its armored hull, through which second stages punched penetrators deep into the ship, immolating crew and machinery, a failed auxiliary tokomak adding an explosive release of energy to the orgy of destruction and blasting a hole in the hull big enough to take a lander.

"And there's more of that to come, guys," Kal murmured as the cruiser fell off station, bleeding great clouds of ice-laden air.

"Command, Combat. Final strike assessments on-screen now."

"Six cruisers destroyed, three combat-ineffective," O'Donnell said. "That's better than I expected."

"Don't get too excited, Liam. That still leaves 219."

"It does, but Aquino's fucked now. She's blown all her Vulkan-Cs stopping the attack Xaabsade told her to expect. I reckon SOLSPACE's staff will be breaking out the champagne right about now, though I think we're the ones who should be doing that."

"Hubris is a dangerous thing, Liam. This isn't over."

"Sorry, commodore."

As she waited for Duvall and his ships to arrive, Kal checked ORF-31 again. Nothing had changed. As it always had, the orbital sat alone and unprotected.

Kal couldn't understand why Risell hadn't forced the navy to deploy missile containers defend ORF-31.

An icy hand took her guts and twisted them, hard.

Maybe Risell had.

"Command, Combat. Task Force 100 dropping . . . now!"

Ultra-violet flares broadcast the arrival of the two Coalition carriers, *Iron Lance* and *Iron Sword*, their hatches already spewing SAVs.

Kal watched the SAVs accelerate away under full power on vectors choreographed to leave the Imps facing five strikes, each broken into multiple streams coming from different directions to overload the Imp ship's combat AIs.

She was sure of one thing. As SOLSPACE's staffers watched the attack develop, they'd not be drinking champagne anymore.

"Command, Combat. Strike-6 through 10 away. Targets Tango-Golf-11 through 15."

The Imp cruisers protecting the gateways now faced ten times as many missiles as the first strike Aquino had successfully fended off.

And there'd be more. The SAVs were already on their way back to their carriers to replenish their magazines.

Kal could imagine the panic ripping through SOLSPACE's staff. They'd just beaten off the attack they'd expected, and now this: the arrival of two massive ships the likes of which the Imps had never seen deploying hundreds of FireSpark-armed SAVs capable of lunching missile strikes tens of thousands strong.

She would not be surprised if Aquino was thinking of shooting herself right now.

The seconds dragged past, the wait doing Kal's long-suffering guts no favors. She'd had enough. She just wanted this over.

"Command, Combat. Tango-Golf-6 through 10, vampires away . . ."

Kal glanced at the threat plot. It was not a pretty sight. Aquino might have expended all her Vulkan-Cs stopping the Coalition's first strikes, but she hadn't given up. The Imp cruisers protecting the Chalawan-6 gateways had fired a lot of Mambas to intercept Strike-9 and even more Taipans to attack the carriers and their SAVs.

Time slowed to ooze, Kal willing the FireSparks and their escort of decoys to move faster, to get this over, to consign the Empire to the dung heap of history.

"Command, Combat. Strike-6 through 10, standby starburst . . . Now!"

Like its predecessors, the strikes now dissolved into a carefully choreographed illusion of chaos. A minute later, the Imp and

Coalition missiles smashed into each other. In an instant, the flares of dying missiles and decoys had come and gone. The engagement was over.

"Command, Combat. Strike-6 through 10. 83% combat effective."

Kal resisted the urge to cheer. The Imps were all but finished, and she was one step closer to retirement. She could almost taste her first beer.

Kal patched into the holovid feed from one of Strike-9's drones. Order was fast coalescing out of chaos as the surviving FireSparks and their escort of decoys reformed into cones, each targeting a single Imp cruiser.

As the Imp cruisers sent a second salvo of Mamba MIs to meet Strike-9, Kal could see that the Imps had lost control of the battle. As Duvall and his ops planners had intended, fragmentating Strike-9 into 61 separate cone-shaped attacks had overwhelmed the Imps' combat AIs. Now their counterattack collapsed into a shambles of missiles hunting for their targets, some locking on only seconds before they hit, most never.

That wasn't the Imps' only problem.

Kal's bared her teeth in anticipation. Aquino's cruisers had been suckered into expending all their Mamba MIs on the decoys packed into the cones' heads. Disregarded, the FireSparks trailing behind slipped past the desperate, flailing blizzard of fire thrown up by the cruisers' close-in defenses.

A blizzard that left Strike-9 almost untouched, thanks to combat AIs optimized to destroy targets coming right at them, not ones that were past and gone in seconds, their sensor heads locked on their actual targets: the gateways.

Gateways whose defensive lasers did their best to hack the missiles out of space, but it was an impossible task, hundreds of missiles overwhelming fire-control AIs designed to deal with lumps of incoming space debris, not vector-agile FireSpark ASMs.

With less than two kilometers to run, the missiles' fragmentation warheads exploded, blasting clouds of shrapnel into the gateways, thousands of razor-edged fragments of hardened ceramsteel that flayed the control, power and support modules, and thigh-thick cable runs off the kilometer-wide structures.

Leaving shattered wrecks bleeding hydraulic fluid into space, wrecks Kal knew would take months to repair.

"Command, Combat. Flag reports all gateways INOP."

"Focus!" O'Donnell roared as cheers filled *Stiletto*'s bridge.

At which point, the crisis overwhelming SOLSPACE collapsed into catastrophe.

The carriers' SAVs had not been idle while their first attack trashed the gateways. Duvall had already sent a second wave of strikes to destroy the Imps' cruisers. The Empire would only be dead, he had said, when a stake had been driven through the Imperial Navy's heart.

And drive a stake through its heart was what Duvall's second attack did.

Despite the cruisers' desperate, scrambling defense, enough FireSparks survived to blast most of the Imp warships into oblivion. The few that escaped annihilation now tumbled through space spitting lifepods, venting clouds of ice-laden through great gashes in their hulls.

Kal checked the ship status board. *Iron Lance* and *Iron Sword* had thrown almost 400 SAVs into the attack; almost all the Taipan ASMs fired by the Imp cruisers had targeted them, destroying 36 along with their crews. A handful of Taipans had attacked the carriers instead; only one had made it through the *Iron Sword's* close-in defenses, its two-stage warhead blasting its explosively formed penetrators through the carrier's armor and into the ship.

Luck was on the *Sword*'s side that bloody day, the hypersonic slug of molten metal blazing a path across one of the SAV hanger decks before punching a hole in the hull to vanish into space.

With the hangar's complement of SAVs deployed, it was a serendipitous result. If the penetrator's trajectory had been five meters to the right, it would have passed through one of the FireSpark ready-use magazines, its crew waiting to rearm the returning SAVs.

Kal felt sick at the thought.

She cut the holovid feed, stunned by the insanity of it all, the attacks and counterattacks minutes-long lifetimes of inconceivable violence, the only comfort knowing that Terra's days as an imperial power were over.

Only one task remained: to make sure no maggots emerged from the Empire's corpse. Maggots like Jo Risell.

Director Peng's assessment had been unequivocal. Risell was the most dangerous person spawned by Terra's imperial experiment, an obsessive woman driven by unseen demons, a woman trapped in an endless search for power recorded in the blood and suffering of millions.

Peng's prediction?

The Empire's collapse would not stop Risell. She was resilient, not the sort of woman who gave up just because things did not work out the first time; as she always done, she would have allowed for failure just as obsessively as she planned for success. She would treat it as just another lost battle in a personal war for power, a war she had no intention of losing, a war she would use Q-drive technology to win.

Kal had thought Peng's prediction farfetched, but time had washed away her skepticism. The man was right. Destroying Terra's gateways was only a battle won.

The Coalition had not won the war, not yet.

It was ironic, thought Kal. Destroying the Imps' Q-drive program was no longer about stopping the Empire; there was no empire anymore. Now it was about stopping just one woman.

ORF-31 had to be neutralized, not to keep the Q-drive out of the Empire's hands but out of Risell's.

"Command, Combat. Message from Flag. *Stiletto* clear to jump to Point Cobalt. Acknowledge."

"Acknowledged," O'Donnell replied. "All stations, Command. We're on our way in, so standby to jump . . . Combat. Send to *Iron Lance*. Jumping now."

Stiletto covered the billion kilometers to the drop datum in a fraction of a second. Kal let the familiar post-drop routine flow over her, her focus locked on the threat plot.

"Command, Combat. Threat plot within 2 million klicks of ORF-31 remains green."

Kal still could not shake the feeling she was walking into a trap.

"Boxcar, Command," O'Donnell said. "Fanfare-Blue."

"Boxcar, Fanfare-Blue." Fonseca's voice was flat, unemotional. "Launching Lander-1 now."

Kal commed Fonseca once *Don't Talk* was on its way to ORF-31. "All set?" she asked.

"Yeah, we are, though my gut is telling me to be extra careful today."

"My gut hasn't stopped telling me that, Jens, not since we dropped into the Sol system."

—66—

The Andimeshkis' capture of ORF-31 was short, brutal, and efficient.

The orbital's ImpSec paramilitary security detail proved no match for Fonseca's battle-hardened fire-teams. Compartment by compartment, deck by deck, they had driven the Imps back, the survivors thrown face down on the deck to be strip-searched and flexicuffed.

"Command, Boxcar," Fonseca said 30 minutes after his marines had blasted their way in. "ORF-31 now secure. Zero Kilo, six Charlie. We've found the project AIs and datastores and are ready to start processing the prisoners."

"Roger, Boxcar," O'Donnell replied. "How long do you need?"

"An hour, if we can have it."

"You can have your hour; so far, the Imps are ignoring us. But that might change, so I'll berth *Stiletto* on ORF-31 to speed things up."

Kal's instincts urged her to override O'Donnell. If things went pear-shaped, unberthing *Stiletto* would be an unnecessary complication that risked delaying their departure.

No, she decided. *Stiletto* was his ship now. He was captain-in-command. It was his call.

She stayed silent.

"Command, Boxcar. Cargo lock 2 is clear. Suggest you berth on that."

"Will do . . . Combat, Command. Berth on ORF-31, cargo lock 2 . . . I'll be happy when we're out of here," O'Donnell added, turning to Kal.

"Me too," Kal said, her nerves jittering. This was all beginning to feel a bit too straightforward. Jo Risell was not the sort of woman who made things easy for her enemies.

A comm from Duvall cracked the silence that followed.

"*Stiletto*, Flag. SITREP. All mission targets killed exempt the space battle stations, and they'll be history soon. You are looking . . . Uh, standby . . . Okay, we have a problem, *Stiletto*. The space battle stations have launched a missile strike, Taipans ASMs. Looks like it is coming for you. Someone in SOLSPACE must have been briefed on how important ORF-31 is. Don't leave your departure too late."

"*Stiletto*, roger," O'Donnell said. "We see them."

"We'll have recovered our SAVs in ten," Duvall went on. "The *Sword* has completed emergency repairs. TF 100 exempt *Stiletto* will jump to Point Legacy. Advise your drop time when known. *Iron Lance*, out."

"Combat, advise Boxcar . . . No, cancel that," O'Donnell said as Fonseca appeared on the bridge. "How are we doing?"

"The first AI is coming aboard now. We'll need 20 minutes to get the rest of them across and another ten to set demolition charges."

O'Donnell studied the command plot for a moment. "Forget the demolition charges; I'll send a couple of FireSparks to destroy ORF-31. I'll give you 15 minutes."

"15 minutes, roger."

"And don't even think of asking for more. Any longer and we can't get to our jump datum before those Taipans reach us. Anything and anybody not onboard by then are staying behind."

"Roger that." Fonseca turned to Kal. "We've talked with a couple of ORF-31's staff. You were right. They did have a Q-drive development program here, though it's not been going too well. They keep losing ships, three last month alone. They haven't been able to work out why."

Kal knew why: gravity reefs, a secret known only to her, Daniel, and Grivak. "Do we have any of the senior people?"

"Negative. They all bailed out in one of the couriers they were using as Q-drive test ships when our carriers dropped. Everyone left behind is pissed at being abandoned."

"I don't blame them; I would be . . . Did that test ship have a Q-drive?" Kal asked.

"No. Work to install one was due to start next week."

"That won't be happening now . . . Sorry, Jens. I'll let you get on."

But where the hell was Risell? Kal asked herself as Fonseca rushed off. And what was she up to?

Things really were going too well.

~~~

With two of his 15 minutes left, Fonseca returned to the bridge. "The last AI is on onboard and all my people are accounted for. ORF-31's personnel are in the lifepods; they'll be on their way any second. We're okay to go, captain."

"I'm pleased to hear it," O'Donnell said. "All stations, captain. Visors down, final suit checks, standby breakaway." He turned to Kal. "I think we're done, commodore."

Kal could see the relief on O'Donnell's face. She flipped her helmet visor down. "I think we are, thank fuck. I can't wait—"

A searing flash of white engulfed her whole being. Shock ripped her chair from the deck, flinging it and her into an emergency cabinet, the impact smashing her helmeted head to one side.

Blackness.

Pain brought her back to dull, thick-headed consciousness.

Pain that flared into a searing mass of agony that consumed her entire left side.

Nanomeds flooded her system. As they eased the pain and shock, Kal moved her legs, relieved to find they still worked. Not that she could shift them more than a couple of centimeters.

She was trapped.

Her battered brain took a moment to process what that meant.

When it had, the prognosis wasn't encouraging. *Stiletto*'s damage-control team—if there was one left—would need hours to cut her free, if any were still alive.

She did not have hours. The Imps would be here in . . . in . . .

She gave up, unable to recall the command plot. But her instincts had been right. ORF-31 was a trap, and now the Imps would be coming for her.

With a start, she realized that her neuronics had been asking for a response. She accepted the comm.

Yasmin Kashani's avatar appeared, her face drawn tight, anxious, bloody. "You okay, commodore?"

Fighting to put the right words in the right order, Kal mumbled, "I'm . . . okay, chief . . . Crew . . . Anyone hurt?"

""We have at least 13 dead and three times that many injured, a lot of them critical. The bridge crew and AI techs are all dead; you're the only survivor."

"How long . . . to reach me?"

"Can't say. *Stiletto* has suffered a lot of damage up forward; everything from the bows back to frame 18 has been trashed and is open to vacuum. There are only three of us uninjured, so it'll take us a while."

Even in her confusion, Kal did not need to ask any more questions. Recovery work in a battle-damaged ship open to hard vacuum was difficult, slow, and dangerous. Three people would need a month to recover her.

She felt exhausted, drained, empty. Her eyes closed. "Too difficult. No time . . . so tired . . . Lifepods . . . any left?"

"Amidships, yes. And *Don't Talk* has shock damage, but its main engines and tokomaks are nominal."

"All survivors . . . in *Don't Talk* . . . abandon ship . . . go, now. Understood?"

"We can't just leave you."

"You can . . . Listen, chief. Direct order . . . no arguments. Tell Duvall . . . no rescue. Too many dead . . . Also . . . direct order . . . understood?'

"Yes."

"Wipe neuronics . . . everyone staying."

"I can't. I don't have the command codes."

With a huge effort, Kal commed Kashani the codes; they would authorize the chief to burn out the neuronics of anyone left onboard the *Stiletto*, alive or dead. "Do it."

The woman stared at Kal in horror. "You as well?"

"Me too."

"Yes, ma'am . . . Good luck."

"Luck no good. Need . . . miracle now . . . Go. Now . . . I, uh . . ."

Darkness returned, closing down until only small, fuzzy circles of light remained.

Circles that her neuronics filled with flashing red light and a disembodied voice. "Warning. Neuronics burnout in progress. You cannot abort this process. Neur—"

Oblivion reclaimed her, her neuronics reduced to scrap, a lifetime's worth of information lost.

~~~

"*Stiletto*'s lander on TAC-599, sir."

"Patch me in," Duvall said.

Sharma's face appeared, green woundfoam slathered over ugly gashes across her cheek and forehead. "Sharma, sir, Lander-1 command pilot. We have just cleared *Stiletto* and are headed out of Terra nearspace. Request recovery soonest. I know the Imps' first missile strike aborted when *Stiletto* was hit, but nothing's stopping them sending more Taipans our way."

"Relax, Sharma. They haven't, and they won't. The Imps don't have any ASM-capable ships left in Terran nearspace. And we've killed the two space-battle stations."

"Ah, okay . . . What about that recovery, sir? We have a lot of casualties and my lander is not in the best of shapes."

"I've tasked *Star Blazer* to jump back to intercept you. All you have to do is stay on vector. Now, tell me what happened."

Sharma wiped a trickle of blood from one eye. "The *Stiletto* was alongside ORF-31 when there was a massive explosion. The chief says it was probably two demolition charges firing penetrators. They had to be to get through into *Stiletto*'s armor so easily."

"Was it a trap?"

"That's what I think, sir."

"Shit . . . How bad is the damage?"

"The charges had been positioned to disable, not to destroy. One was right forward, the other right aft so it didn't matter which side-to we berthed. That's why the tokomaks stayed intact, otherwise we'd not be here, but the main engines are finished. There was a secondary explosion in the port forward LOX storage. The hull, jump nodes, and external systems between frames 6 and 18 have been trashed; all the compartments are open to vacuum, including the bridge. The AI tank has been destroyed along with all classified knowledgebases, which is something, I guess. All combat-related and life-support system are INOP."

"What about casualties?" Duvall asked.

"13 Kilo, 9 Alpha, 12 Bravo, 16 Charlie."

"Jeezus! Is the commodore okay?"

"She was trapped in what was left of the bridge. We . . ." Sharma's voice broke. "We didn't have the people or the time to get her out. She gave the chief a direct order to abandon ship."

"Goddammit," Duvall said. "This was her last mission. Is there anything we can do?"

"Nothing, sir. *Stiletto* is a total loss. And my combat AI is tracking three civilian ships squawking emergency-responder IDs. They're red-lining it for ORF-31 and *Stiletto*, but the commodore said to tell you there was to be no rescue, sir. Another direct order."

"I didn't hear that. Flag, out."

—67—

Kal was trying to work out how long she'd been in hospital. A week maybe? With her neuronics burned out, she wasn't sure; early on, the days had been a blur and she'd slept a lot. Not that she was complaining. The staff had been caring and kind, the food bearable. A vast improvement on an ImpSec prison, she was sure.

Which was where she was heading. Having a wrist flexicuffed to the bed told her that much.

She lifted her head as the door banged open and a red-haired woman walked in. "Oh, dear god!" she called out. "If it isn't Jo Risell . . . Hey, Jo. I hear things aren't going so well for you."

Risell pulled up a chair and sat down. "Let me tell you something, Kariuki, I—"

Kal jabbed a finger at Risell. "It's Commodore Kariuki to you. I earned that rank kicking your navy's ass, so show some damn respect."

Risell stared at Kal for a moment, her face impassive, then nodded, "Commodore Kariuki? Sure, if it makes you happy . . . So, finally we meet. I've had ImpSec chasing you ever since you pulled your Deepshorne stunt."

Kal smiled. "You've left it a bit late to get your hands on me, wouldn't you say? How does it feel having an alcoholic AI tech fuck you and your whole bullshit empire over?"

"Not as bad as I expected, to be honest. Thanks you and the Coalition, Emperor Michael and his cronies have been flushed down the crapper, something that hasn't exactly come as a surprise. I and most of the people on the streets think is exactly what they deserve."

"Let me guess: Amos Ferruci has made his move and you're screwed because he hates you and everyone else in the Imperial administration for not paying his ransom?"

"Oh, my! Aren't you well-informed?"

"I try to be . . . Listen, I'm tired of this bullshit." Kal rolled her body away. "I'm a prisoner-of-war. I don't have to talk to you, so go away."

"Prisoner-of-war?" Risell shook her head. "I don't think so. You're a prisoner of ImpSec, and ImpSec doesn't give a pinch of shit for the Geneva Conventions, though that won't be a problem not as long as you help me out."

Kal rolled back. "And why would I help you?"

Risell pulled a pic from a pocket and held it out. "Cute couple, don't you think?"

Kal stared at the image of Daniel and Skylar; she could almost feel the happiness radiating from them. Not that Risell was trying to cheer her up; Kal knew now how Marine Xaabsade must have felt when ImpSec's goons threatened the lives of his family.

"I have been hunting you long enough to know how stubborn you are," Risell went on. "That is why I've had one of my direct-action teams holed up on Narsaq-3 for two months now. If I was ever lucky enough to get my hands on you, I knew you'd refuse to talk unless I gave you a good reason to. So, Commodore Kariuki, understand this: if you refuse to help me, Daniel Wei and Skylar K'hala will die. Their baby too; GestationTech's Narsaq clinic is looking after the fetus, and their security won't stop one of my DATs."

"You wouldn't do that."

Risell laughed. "I'm not a saint; I've done a lot worse than killing babies to get what I want. And I will again if I have to. All I have to do is give the word."

"You're bluffing."

"Maybe, but you'll never have to put me to the test. My profilers say you'll do anything to protect the only family a sad, burned-out wreck of a human will ever have."

Kal knew Risell was right. "What do you want from me?"

"The answer to a question only you can answer: Why do my jump-drive ships keep disappearing?"

Kal blinked, astonished. "A question only I can answer? Your people just tried to kill me! And they almost did; by rights I should be dead."

"Ah, yes, they did. That was a mistake. My orders were to disable the *Stiletto* so it could not leave Terran nearspace; that only needed one demolition charge to take out the main engines, not two. The people responsible fired both; they said things were very confusing, what with the Coalition attacks and Mister Ferruci's coup. They had a point, but I had them shot anyway . . . Now, are you going to answer my question?"

"How can I? I'm a sad, burned-out wreck of a human, remember?"

"Hah!" Risell snorted. "Spare me the bullshit. You and Daniel Wei designed and built the first jump drive."

"He did. All that pinchspace stuff is way too complicated for me."

"You need to understand something. Getting information out of people like you is something ImpSec does well. You will resist, of course. Most people do, but they always give us what we want in the end. Always. So best you tell me quickly. Your family will live if you do . . . Ah, what the hell! I'm feeling generous; I'll let you live as well. Take too long to talk and your family dies. You will too, but not until I've showed you holovid of Daniel and Skylar having their brains blown out. I won't show you what my DAT does to the fetus, though. I'm not a monster."

"Go away!" Kal spit.

"You might as well tell me now. You will eventually."

"You deaf? I just told you to go away."

"Yes, you did. A mistake, as you're about to find out."

The door opened.

A man walked in, lean, wiry, in a black shipsuit, the gold starburst of Imperial Security on his left breast above the letters 'COMPLEX-99' in yellow thread.

"This is Zhedong Nanmen," Risell said. "His job is prisoner assessment. That's Orwellspeak for what Complex-99 really does, which is to break people like you." She glanced at Nanmen. "How many this week?"

"Over 50."

Risell turned back to Kal. "They all thought they could keep their secrets secret no matter what Mister Nanmen and his team did to them. They were wrong. They talked. Afterwards, they must have wondered why they'd put themselves through so much unnecessary suffering."

"Go screw yourself," Kal snarled, near panic at the thought of what would happen—to her, to Daniel, to Skylar, to their baby—if she refused to cooperate.

"Once a foul-mouthed grunt, always a foul-mouth grunt, eh? Not that it'll do you any good. Mister Nanmen will not stop until you have answered my question."

Kal shot a quick glance up at Nanmen. The man glowered back at her from dead eyes set deep and unreadable under hooded brows, his face expressionless.

Two black-shipsuited ImpSec troopers followed, shepherding a mobichair.

Risell turned and patted Nanmen on the shoulder. "All yours. Try not to kill the bitch before she's talked."

As Risell left, Nanmen's troopers stepped forward. Hands ripped drips and sensors off Kal's body, ignoring her cries of pain. Cutting the flexicuffs off her wrist, they dragged her from the bed and pushed her into the chair, her feeble efforts to resist ignored.

A figure in a white coat rushed in. "I'm Doctor Morizar. What the hell—"

Nanmen spun around. His hand closed around the woman's throat, choking her off. He pushed her back hard into the wall, squeezing until her eyes bulged and face turned a dirty red, arms flailing in a desperate fight to work free.

One of the troopers tightened the last of the cable-ties locking Kal's arms and legs to the chair before putting a hood over her head. "Ready, boss."

Nanmen released the doctor.

The woman massaged the ugly weal on her neck. "You're ImpSec. My patient is not fit to be moved. You'll be reported for this."

She was talking to herself. Nanmen and his troopers had gone, Kal with them.

~~~

The van stopped. A door banged open. The mobichair rolled down and ramp and set off. It turned, seemingly at random. Another door opened. The air was acrid with the burned-rock smell of fresh concrete overlaid with the bitterness of industrial cleaner.

Kal remembered that smell. The smell of prison. She'd been in a few.

More doors. More turns.

They stopped.

A voice. "Here we are."

The whine of servos. A dull thud. The mobichair moved a couple of meters, then stopped. Hands cut Kal free, lifted her out, dumped her on something hard. The hood was ripped off.

She was at a metal table across from Nanmen, the tabletop splashed with what looked like dried blood. The two troopers watched, stunners in hand.

Nanmen leaned across the table and took both of her hands in his. "Such strong hands." He let her go and sat back. "The hands of a woman responsible for the deaths of thousands of Imperial citizens. I hope you realize you'll be held to account for those deaths."

Kal stared at the man. Say nothing. Do not react. Make the bastard fight every centimeter of the way. Buy as much time as you can.

"Talk or not, it doesn't matter to me." Nanmen reached into a pocket and pulled out an injector. "This contains a psychoactive drug called Servalix. Get caught with it on any system in humanspace, and you'll do 20 years in the slammer, but ImpSec loves Servalix. We use it a lot. Why? Because it makes people tell us what we want to know, even if they really, really don't want to . . ."

Kal could not contain herself. "You are such a fucking asshole."

Nanmen ignored her. "That is why we call Servalix the nightmare drug," he continued, "though nightmare doesn't even begin to describe what this drug does to your brain. So, here's what's going to happen, commodore. Once a day, you will receive a shot of Servalix. The first is tiny; it wears off quickly. The tenth dose is big; the effects last hours . . . And nobody gets to the tenth, nobody. I can promise you that."

"So you say," Kal said with a show of bravado she did not feel. "Everyone has nightmares. They aren't enough to stop me lying."

Nanmen smiled. A thin-lipped, reptilian smile. "When we catch you out, and we always do, the dose goes up until the thought of the next day's nightmare is so awful no human being alive will risk it. But there is a way out: the truth . . . Any questions before we start? No? Okay, let's do it."

Troopers secured her wrists and ankles to the chair. "She's set, boss."

Nanmen's hand flashed across, jamming the injector into Kal's arm.

Kal felt a short, sharp sting.

Nanmen patted her hand. "Enjoy the ride."

Slowly, Kal's vision sharpened the details of Nanmen's face. Soon she could see every pore, every wrinkle, every blemish.

She stared in fascination, eyes skipping across Nanmen's face . . . until tendrils of unease started to infiltrate her mind. Tenuous to start with. Then came apprehension and a growing conviction that something bad was about to happen, something she could do nothing to stop.

With a rush, anxiety turned to fear, and with it an absolute certainty that the Thing was coming to tear her apart, its massive, slavering jaws driving huge teeth, razor-edged and needle-tipped deep into her skull to rip out her brain. Frantic, her head thrashed left and right, up and down, looking for the Thing; it was close, its breath hot and foul, the smell of an agonizing death.

Her mind imploded into terror distilled to its quintessence, terror that turned her bowels to water that ran hot under her buttocks, her stomach vomiting up the little it had inside in body-racking of spasms that continued on and on, even when she had nothing left to throw up.

The nightmare was never going to end. A nightmare that stripped her psyche back to a primeval state where only one thing existed: an absolute certainty she was about to die.

With the tiny scrap of sanity Kal had left, she prayed for it to end even though she knew, as surely as she had known anything in her entire life, that it never would.

An eon later, it did end. The terror ebbed away, leaving her a stinking, befouled wreck, head slumped forward, exhausted, her tortured stomach screaming in pain.

Masked and gloved figures in white suits cut her free, stood her up, stripped her, holding her arms up and her legs apart.

A pair of cleanerbots worked with mindless precision to clean the filth off her body and chair. Job done, they left.

Kal stood, dripping, naked, shaking. But not broken, she told herself. Not yet. Nanmen would have to try a lot harder.

A trooper threw a red shipsuit at her.

Kal pulled it on with shaking hands before slumping into her chair.

"So," Nanmen said, "how was that?"

"You're animals."

"And proud of it. So, are you ready to talk now?"

"Not a chance."

"You sure? You've seen how a five-minute shot of Servalix feels. Imagine what an hour's like. Our neurochemists tell me it's the worst thing you can do to a human."

"Five minutes?" Kal rasped. "That's all it was?"

"Hard to believe, eh? So, are you ready to answer Minister Risell's question?"

"No, I am not."

"Your call. Right, we're done for now. I'll leave you to look forward to your second dose."

"Go for it, pal. I'm not talking."

Nanmen leaned forward, again taking Kal's hands in his. "This only ends one way: You will tell us what we want to know. That's nothing to be ashamed of; Servalix makes everyone talk."

"Not me."

"You could be the first, I guess. But Jo Risell is not a patient woman. She will have Daniel and his family killed if she thinks you're taking too long to tell her what she wants to know. And you too. Come on, don't be a fool. Tell me why we're losing our jump-drive ships."

"No."

But Kal knew that she would never be able to hold out. If the Servalix didn't do it, the threats would.

—68—

Kal had been through some terrible times in her life, losing her mom and dad and then her great-aunt worst of all.

Even they had not been as bad as her days in Complex-99.

She glanced up at the countdown timer set high on the wall of her cell. Three hours to go before her next Servalix session.

Hold on, she told herself. The nightmares aren't real. You can do this.

Giving the ceiling mounted holocams the finger, she was finishing a long-overdue pee when the door banged open and a trooper walked in.

"You scumbag," she screamed, scrambling to her feet and pulling up her shipsuit. "You couldn't wait?"

"Watch your goddammed mouth."

"Go fuck—"

The man backhanded Kal across the face with enormous force, splitting her lip, the blow driving her sideways, her head hitting the wall with a sullen thud.

Kal slid to the floor. Blood flowed from the gash on her head as she drifted in and out of consciousness.

Dazed, pain hammering at her head, Kal sat unmoving as chaos erupted around her. Hands reached down, lifted her on a gurney, medibots fixing sensors and lines.

Not that Kal cared. Postponing a Servalix session was worth the mother of all headaches.

~~~

Nanmen walked into her cell. "Well, commodore, I am happy to say your head's going to be fine."

"Hoo-fucking-ray," Kal spit. "You think my damn head bothers me when I know what'll happen as soon as I'm okay?"

"Well, since you ask, the medical AI says we don't need to delay your next session."

Kal stared, unwilling to believe what she was hearing. "What?"

"You heard me." Nanmen waved a hand at the wall-mounted timer; an hour left. "Not long to wait . . . Unless you want to tell me why our jump-drive isn't working?"

"The answer was no the last time. It'll be no the next time. And it's no this time."

"Fine. As long as you're ready for what comes next."

Something in the man's voice caught Kal's attention. "For what comes next? What do you mean?"

"I warned you that Ms. Risell wasn't a patient woman. She wants me to accelerate things, which is why I've scheduled you for a two-hour session."

Fear turned roiled Kal's bowels. "An extra hour? You can't!"

"I can. I'll see you in—"

Without a second's thought, Kal exploded off her bunk, her fist driving right at Nanmen's face.

Except the man had swayed back a fraction to let Kal's fist skim past and clear, momentum spinning her around to dump her on the floor.

Nanmen took Kal's hair in his hand and pulled her head back. "I've been kind to you so far. Nothing physical. Decent food. Exercise. Fresh air. Don't push me, or you will regret it."

With a violent shove, he pushed Kal away.

"I'm sure you thought your last session was bad," Nanmen went on, "but wait until you try a two-hour dose of Servalix. Very few people get that far. You can tell me how you went afterwards . . . Or I should tell Ms. Risell this is taking too long and she should have her people to kill Daniel Wei and the rest of his family?"

Kal cracked, her mental collapse unstoppable. "Stop! I'll tell you what you want to know."

"Your next session will be three hours if you lie to me."

"I won't lie, I promise."

"Go on then. I'm listening."

"Gravity reefs.

Nanmen's eyes narrowed. "What are they?"

"The answer to Risell's question . . . Gravity reefs! Got it?"

"No, but it doesn't matter. You can explain it to the jump-drive team. They'll tell me if you're lying. And don't forget what will happen if you are."

Kal wanted to fight back. She could not find the will.

She closed her eyes and wept.

Nanmen had broken her.

It had only taken him five days.

~~~

Kal lay on her bunk, fingers laced behind her head, staring at the seamless white ceiling of her cell.

Despite the defeat Nanmen and Risell had inflicted on her, she didn't feel too bad. She and the Coalition had defeated the Empire. The civil war Amos Ferruci had triggered would leave Terra a smoking ruin, a fate it richly deserved after the death and misery its people had heaped on humanspace.

That still left the problem of Jo Risell. The Coalition had made clear its intentions to bring her and the rest of the Imperial leadership to trial for crimes against humanity. Logic dictated she should be looking for somewhere to hide, except she wasn't. Peng had been right; the woman was up to someth—

A thump.

Kal sat up and swung her legs to the floor. Earthquake? No, it didn't feel like one. She had lived through a few in her time on M'bakaa, Ladaki too; the tremor was too sharp-edged.

As she stood, more tremors shivered the cell, stronger than the first, followed by distinct, heavy thuds that soon flowed into a wave of rumbling noise Kal could feel through her bare feet.

The light went out.

Shouts, too faint to decipher. Boots pounded along the corridor outside. Silence for a minute, then more shouts.

The next tremor was nothing like its predecessors. It picked the cell up and shook it bodily, the air shredded by a crash that left her half-deafened and her ears ringing, the dust from stress-shattered concrete biting in her nose.

Kal had been on the receiving of enough high explosive to know that what was happening. Somebody was attacking the prison with heavy ordnance.

Insurgents backing Ferruci. It had to be.

Fumbling in the dusty darkness, she worked her way along the wall to the door.

Hope surged, then died. A gap between door and wall had opened, but only big enough for a fist. She peered through. Nothing but darkness. She drove her shoulder into the door.

It did not move. She gave up. That door was never going to open.

For a while, all was quiet.

Without warning, a sustained series of violent crashes hammered the cell around her, opening a crack in the wall opposite the door; it let in a thin gray light all but defeated by the dust-laden air. The wall had split from top to bottom, one half pushed out to leave a crack half-a-meter wide, razor-edged. She might have been able to squeeze through, but that would have cost most of her skin and a liter of blood as well.

Overwhelmed by disappointment, she waited for whatever came next, flinching as more explosions shook the cell.

Voices. Lights. The door was heaved open. Flashlights waved. Figures armed with assault rifles. Their shipsuits were black: ImpSec troopers.

Nanmen appeared. He stepped forward and ran his torch over her. "She's okay. Let's go."

Hands lifted Kal to her feet and spun her around. Body armor was slipped over her head and cinched tight. Helmet and boots followed, her wrists flexicuffed. The troopers hustled her away, down the corridor through a doorway into a rain-swept courtyard strewn with rubble from the eviscerated wreck of a building to her left. A direct hit from something big; probably a two-stage blast-bomb, Kal thought. The sky overhead was thick with tangled skeins of black smoke hounded away by a blustery wind, the air full of the sound of distant combat: the crump of artillery, the sharp crack of rifles and machine guns, the heavy thud of cannon, the snap of grenades.

Sounds she had hoped she would never hear again.

Kal turned to the ImpSec trooper holding her left arm. "Where are we going?" she asked. "What's happening?"

The woman stayed silent, her face impassive.

Anger flared. Kal let herself collapse, pulling her escorts down, sending one stumbling into a jagged block of concrete with a satisfying scream of pain.

To no effect.

Without a word, a new pair of hands took over, and they were moving again, the air thick with the harsh smells of seared concrete and high-explosive. Smells that took Kal back to places she would rather forget.

The troopers hustled her past a shattered security post to emerge on a broad avenue, its trees stripped back to bare branches, where any remained, an avenue littered with bodies, its surface scarred and blackened by sustained cannon fire.

Kal ran a marine's eye over the scene. Ground-attack landers had caught the Imps in the open, their vehicles, soft-skinned trucks with a sprinkling of light armor, left gutted, flaming wrecks, the smoke twisting skywards.

She spotted ideograms on a street sign. She was in China, somewhere in the south, given how warm and wet it was. New Hainan?

It had to be, she decided. Where else would Risell be if not the Empire's capital?

A van screeched to a halt beside her. The back doors opened, Kal was pushed inside, the escort piled in after her, the doors slammed shut, and the van took off, accelerating hard.

Kal looked at Nanmen. "Are you going to tell me what's going on?" she asked.

He just stared back at her from empty, dead eyes. Risell's eyes, Kal thought.

Kal sighed. "Fine. I'll take a stab. The smart ones amongst you . . . I'm assuming smart Terrans do actually exist . . . have decided they've had enough of your pissant empire and all its imperial bullshit. Urged on by Amos Ferruci, they've taken to the streets to kick rats like you back into the sewers—"

Nanmen's rifle rose from nowhere, giving Kal only a fraction of a second to react. She twisted away. Too slow. The butt smashed into the side of her helmet with sickening force, snapping her jaws shut on her lips, blood filling her mouth.

Nanmen leaned forward. "Next time, you won't be wearing a helmet, so keep your damn mouth shut."

Kal was past caring. "And what will Jo Risell say when she sees what you've done? You think she'll be happy?"

The man's eyes narrowed, and for an instant Kal thought she'd pushed him too far. Instead, he just sat back. "You've been warned."

Kal spit blood on Nanmen's boots. "I wasn't listening,"

The man ignored her.

Kal eased her head back, wincing as a bruised neck warned her to take it easy. She glanced out of the window as a sign flash past in a blur of gold ideograms on a scarlet background, below them the word 'Guangdong' . . . the rest of the letters gone in a blur before her brain could process them.

Guangdong . . . Guangdong . . . Wasn't that the mainland, across the straits from New Hainan?

Yes, it was. That meant Guangdong was under attack, New Hainan as well, probably. Maybe Amos Ferruci was winning. Maybe his people would rescue her.

Dulled by pain, fatigue, stress, and the after-effects of repeated doses of Servalix, she closed her eyes as she tried to work through her options.

After a while, she gave up. She had no options worth pissing on. All she could do was wait.

The troopers flanking her stiffened. They were nervous, Nanmen's head swiveling side-to-side.

Something was going on; from the body-language of her escort, that much was obvious to Kal. But what?

"Take Minzekai and Weihou," Nanmen called out.

The van swung back the way it had come. It did not go far before turning, twisting through a maze of narrow streets between time-worn buildings.

Where were they? Kal tried to remember her Terran geography lessons. Without her neuronics to fill the gaps in her memory, she couldn't. She gave up.

A straight road now.

The van picked up speed, accelerating hard.

A searing white flash, a crunching thud, and a giant fist flipped the van onto its roof, sending it sliding down the road amidst the awful shriek of tortured plasfiber. A bang, and now it started to tumble, the inside of the van a chaotic mess of bodies, heads, arms, legs, and rifles, a succession of blows hammering at Kal's body until the van screeched to a brutal stop, its side caved in.

Stunned and hurting, Kal lay there, the only sound the soft ticking of the van's power plant shutting down. It took a racking scream of pure pain from one of the troopers crushed into her seat to galvanize Kal into action. As she tried to wriggle free of the jam of dazed and bleeding bodies, her hand fell on a laser pistol holstered on the upper thigh of one of the troopers alongside her. The man was unconscious, laboring to breathe, face bloody behind his visor. She dragged the pistol out and resumed her fight, thrashing and squirming until finally she was able to roll free, her mouth open, lungs heaving, heart pounding.

She eyed the Boschian horror around her, all color bleached out by harsh white light from the streetlight that had brought the van to such a disastrous stop.

But she wasn't the only one recovering. One of the troopers, fighting to free an arm, had his eyes locked on hers, eyes burning with hate. Or was it fear?

Kal did what she had to do. Raising the pistol, she shot the man in the face. His head sagged back, and the air left his lungs in a long, slow sigh. Kal tried to find even a shred of remorse for what she had just done.

She failed.

The man was ImpSec. All her captors were ImpSec. None of them had the right to live, not after what they had put her through.

Kal did not hesitate. Trooper after trooper, she dispatched the rest of her escort until only Nanmen remained. The light pole had trapped his legs, an arm a crooked, blood-stained wreck across his stomach.

The man lifted a hand. "Please. You don't have to do this."

"You think not, Mister Nanmen? You treat me worse than a dog. You fill me with Servalix. You threaten my family. And now you expect mercy? Well, none's coming your way, sport. You are scum . . . and I am going to kill you," she added, raising the pistol.

Fear twisted Nanmen's face into a grotesquerie, the face of a man dangling over the pits of hell. "Please, no. Don't. Do—"

Kal fired into the man's face, again and again. She felt nothing as Nanmen died, her mind numb, disconnected from reality.

She twisted the pistol around. Steadying it, she used it to cut the flexicuffs off her wrists, the air, already fetid with the stench of death, turning even fouler with the bitter stink of her laser-scorched skin.

She took a medikit from one of the dead troopers. As she slathered woundfoam on her wrists, she forced herself to think. She had to reach the people attacking Guangdong, she decided, and hope they were friends of Ferruci's.

Not the best outcome, she conceded, but she'd rather be talking with Ferruci than Jo Risell. Maybe he'd overlook the fact she'd extorted 700 million dollars from him. That she had threatened to dump him on Jaipur Prime, condemned to a life of grinding poverty. That she had pushed him out of an airlock protected only by a crashbag. That she had been the agent of his catastrophic descent from power into irrelevance.

The more she thought about it, the less Kal fancied her chances. She just hoped the man's insurrection was going well.

The sounds of combat shook the van: the sustained rumbling crack-crash of large-caliber rounds exploding.

They were close.

It was time to go.

Having stripped Nanmen of his equipment, water bottle, and assault rifle, she squirmed her way to the back of the van, shouldered the doors open, and tumbled out onto the ground.

She had forgotten the rain. It slashed through her shipsuit like it wasn't there. Within seconds, her body started to shake with cold and shock. She wanted to give up, to hide until this was all over.

Except she couldn't, not unless she wanted to meet Ferruci again.

The problem was getting away. Her left ankle was agony; walking was out of the question. Something had slashed a deep cut into her right thigh, releasing so much blood her trouser leg was black with it. Blinding shards of pain filled her head. Her body ached, her ribs most of all. And her mouth was a blood-leaking wreck, thanks to Nanmen.

One meter at a time, Kal Kariuki, she told herself, using the wrecked van to drag herself upright. You have to if you want to live long enough to hug Daniel again.

All too aware of the sounds of a major battle approaching from her left, she broke into a shambling run that only lasted a couple of steps before excruciating pain forced her first into a one-legged, sliding hop. That didn't last long either. Collapsing onto hands and knees, she started to crawl.

Four agony-filled blocks later and her bid for freedom was over. Wet, cold, and suffering, she shot open the nearest door, and dragged herself inside. Closing the door, she flicked on her helmet light. She was in a workshop of sorts. It was filled with microfabs, raw-material hoppers, and crates of stuffed toys.

Kal picked one up, a big fluffy dog. A lurid orange, it was being cute, sitting on its haunches, paws up, head cocked to one side, a winning smile on its face.

She dropped it to the floor. "Glad you're so fucking happy."

Out back, she found a small kitchen with a washroom off. No supplies. No foodbot. No running water. A toilet, cistern half-empty. Kal did not hesitate, gulping down all the water she could drink. She crawled back into the workshop and pulled herself into a battered armchair.

This was it.

This was where Kal Kariuki would make her last stand, in a crappy workshop turning out bad-taste stuffed toys.

The first Imp through the door would get a laser shot in the head, and Kal would keep shooting until they stopped coming.

Or they killed her.

After everything she'd been through, the banality of it all seemed appropriate.

~~~

A thunderous boom dragged Kal from a fractured doze, sending her in a bleary-eyed scramble behind an overturned table, stifling a scream of pain as her ankle reminded her to be more considerate.

The building trembled as ground-attack aircraft shredded the air overhead, the ripping sound of cannon fire broken up with the thud-crump of heavy rounds.

Shouts.

They were close. Really close.

Please, please, please, Kal begged, keep walking, whoever you are.

An explosion battered the walls, spalling razor-edged fragments of concrete that slashed the air around her, slicing gashes into her forearm and temple. The blood flowed warm, sticky.

Kal let it run, too tired to worry about it.

More shouts. Right outside.

Bursts of machine gun and rifle fire. The crack of grenades. The thump of heavy cannon. The song of combat, the bass line carried by the distinctive rumbling of tankbots.

Silence.

She slithered across to the door. With a quick prayer that any bugs or combatbots covering the fighting outside had better things to do than worry about her, she cracked the door open a fraction and peeped out.

What once had been a city street was now a demolition site. The buildings opposite were smoking rubble, the air full of the smell of high explosive, the road littered with debris.

A road down which combat-armored figures ran with a desperate intensity Kal remembered all too well from the bad times with the M'bakaa marines.

The figures streaming past wore dark-green combat fatigues, Imperial marines, all discipline gone. Those who could ran hard; the rest, slowed by wounds or half-carrying a buddy, followed. She would have called what she was looking at a fighting retreat if she had been feeling charitable. She wasn't. It was a rout.

It was not long before the street was empty save for the combatbots screening the Imps' retreat, their lasers flicker-flashing at unseen targets, their mindless bravery rewarded by slow, methodical counter-fire that picked them off, some grinding to a halt spewing smoke, some exploding in the searing white flashes as their microtoks lost containment, the survivors fleeing after their charges.

Kal must have moved. The bulbous turret atop one slewed around. An instant after she had pulled back, a burst of laser fire ripped into the door, punching gobbets of molten plasfiber across the floor.

She swore at her stupidity; making any sort of movement in sight of a bot was a rookie mistake. She could only wait and pray the damn thing decided she wasn't a threat.

The seconds dragged past and Kal let herself relax. Covering the retreating marines must have had higher priority.

She slithered back to the wrecked door to risk another peek. The street was empty now, the only sounds the distant rattle and bang of combat.

The Imp marines and their bots had gone.

Not that she was safe. Ferruci's rebels—she assumed they were the ones pushing the Imps back—would be here soon. They would be edgy. Even screened by bugs and escorted by combatbots, street fighting was a dangerous business, against Imperial marines, even more so. She would pay for being too close to a running firefight if she wasn't careful.

She looked around for something, anything to show the rebels she was a friendly.

A white flag was what she needed. A huge one.

She could see nothing white, but she did have the large fluffy dog with lurid orange fur and a big, cheerful grin.

It was the least threatening thing Kal had ever seen.

It would have to do. Jamming the muzzle of Nanmen's rifle up its ass, she pushed the door open a crack and shoved the dog out, propping it up on a handy lump of concrete.

The effort overwhelmed her. Past caring what happened, she slid to the floor, feet out, head back, eyes closed.

~~~

The soft buzz of a bug woke Kal.

Instincts from another life took over. Keeping her body still, she eased her eyelids apart. A holocam lens, a cold, black circle of glass, gazed through the laser-cut hole in the door. With infinite care, she raised her arms above her head, the palms of her hands open and facing out.

The bug backed off.

Footsteps. A pause, then an unseen boot kicked the door open.

A helmet appeared, the face invisible behind its visor. "You have any ID?"

"Not that I can comm you. My neuronics have been wiped. I'm Kal Kariuki."

The visor went up. "Did you say Kal Kariuki?"

"I did."

"Shit! Yes, I recognize you now."

"I think I need a medic."

"Stay there. Help's on its way."

~~~

"Commodore Kariuki, ma'am. Can you talk?"

Kal forced her eyes open. It was a struggle to focus on the blur of a face leaning over her. "Think so."

"I'm Major Reynolds, 223rd Combat Casualty Unit, Coalition Marines. How are you feeling?"

"Tired. Sore."

"I'm not surprised. You've been through a lot, but none of the trauma is too serious. Given time and proper medical care, you'll be fine."

Even through the haze of nanomeds, Kal sensed more was to come. "But?"

"When we ran the blood tests, we picked up some anomalies. Did the Imps give you any meds?"

"Uh . . . Yes, something called server . . . savva . . . Sorry, I can't remember."

"Servalix?"

"Yeah. Bastard stuff."

"All the prisoners we have rescued from Complex-99 are showing traces of it," Reynolds said. "Using it on prisoners is a war crime; the investigators will want to talk to you. They'll need specifics: staff, names, places, times, what they did, that sort of thing."

Kal smiled. "It's way too late for that, major. My ImpSec interrogator was a man called Nanmen. I shot the sonofabitch like you'd shoot a rabid dog. And all his team."

The major's eyes widened. "Oh."

"They had nothing to complain about; they were going to kill me as soon as I told them what they wanted to know. So, what's the plan?"

"Casevac shuttle up to *Iron Sword* tonight some time."

"That sounds just fine."

"I'll let you catch some sleep, ma'am. If you need anything, comm the duty medic . . . Oh, sorry. You can't. Just shout, okay?"

Kal lay back as the man left the ward, a white plasfiber shell busy with medics and bots dealing with the trickle of casualties.

As she slipped back into sleep, a medic brought her a tablet. "Comm for you, ma'am."

It was Duvall. "Commodore! I so glad to see you. The medics say you'll pull through okay."

"I feel like I've been trampled by a herd of elephants."

"Well, you'll be pleased to hear that we have scooped up the people responsible for what happened to you."

Kal frowned. "I killed—"

"No, not them. The commandant of Complex-99 and his senior staff. The war-crimes people are interrogating them now; they say it won't be hard to make to make charges stick., not with testimony from the people we've rescued. And our snatch teams have arrested of lot of the ImpSec's senior people as well."

"Is that why you came to Terra? Please tell me it wasn't about me."

"Officially, no," Duvall said. "The mission objectives were to rescue all the politicals from Complex-99, to pick up as many of the Imp apparatchiks on our blacklist as we could, and generally screw the Imps over while we were at it. Not that that was too hard. Amos Ferruci's people are doing a fantastic job all on their own; Terra's turning into a bloodbath. But, once the cyberwarfare techs told us you were still alive, it added a certain urgency to the operation."

"Please tell me you have Risell."

"I wish but no," Duvall said. "We last saw her with some of her senior staffers heading north off Hainan Island escorted by a direct-action team. We don't know where there are now, but we're looking."

"Risell was the one Imp we really needed."

"She was. Sorry, I need to go. I'm told I'll see you soon."

"You can depend on it."

"You need anything?"

Kal shook her head. "No, I'm fine. I'm right where I want to be."

~~~

Escorted by drones and lead by a tankbot through the gloom of a vile, rain-slashed night, the convoy—a line of trucks splashed with red-on-white crosses and carrying a shuttle's worth of stretchers for the ride up to *Iron Sword*—swung onto the highway.

Not that Kal cared. She was even more tired than she had been when the marines handed her over to the 223rd CCU.

It wasn't all fatigue, though. It was also her mind and body shedding the accumulated weight of the years since she and Daniel had fought their way free of Ladaki, the weight of care and responsibility and obligation.

Tired or not, she felt fine. The Empire was finished, and her war was over.

With the help of a combat trauma program, she would soon be well enough to look after herself. Thanks to the Coalition buying out the contract for the *Iron Lance*, money was not going to be a problem; she'd have more than enough to buy her own Q-drive ship and the rights to the Wallenski system. And there she would build a house and live out her days drinking beer with Hemed Biteko.

Though she would visit with Daniel, Skylar, and the baby. She liked the idea of being a grandmother.

A marine appeared. "The convoy commander asked me to update you, commodore. As you may have noticed, we've had to stop . . ."

Absorbed in her own thoughts, Kal hadn't.

". . . thanks to the Imps opening the flood-control gates. For some reason That's put the bridge up ahead under water. The engineers are on their way to close the gates; as soon as the water goes down, we can move on. An hour at the most, they say."

Kal couldn't work out why the Imps had bothered. What they had done would only hurt their own people.

Resigning herself to the wait, she closed her eyes and went to sleep.

~~~

The crack of high explosive dragged Kal awake. Grenades. Then the sound of small-arms fire.

Close. Too close.

Ignoring the protests from her abused body, she slid from her stretcher and hopped over to the medic peering out of the back of the truck.

"What's going on?" she asked.

"I'm not sure . . . Please, commodore, go back to your stretcher. I'm sure this is nothing."

"And I'm sure it's not." But she did as she was told, too tired to follow instincts screaming at her to get the hell away.

She had barely turned away when a voice brought her to a stop. "Hold it, Kariuki. You are coming with us. And if you mess with me, I will shoot everyone in this truck, starting with the medic here."

Kal swung around. A trooper in ImpSec black had the woman in a headlock. A second held a pistol to her head.

Despair flooded Kal's system. For a moment, she was tempted to tell the Imps to piss off, to let them kill her and everyone else, to end the madness here and now.

A shred of commonsense prevailed. "I'm coming, I'm coming."

The Imps hustled Kal away into the darkness, the rain biting cold through her gown, her ankle agony even in its plasfiber boot, the night flaring red and yellow and white as the marine escort fought back.

Long pain-filled minutes later, Kal was pushed into a van. It took off before she even found her seat, its violent thrashing left and right forcing her to clamp her mouth shut to contain her screams of pain.

How long it was before the van slammed to a halt, she had no idea, but it had been a long ride to godknows where. Not that she cared, not anymore. She did not have the energy to cope with a setback of almost exquisite cruelty.

One of the Imps snapped his fingers. "Out!"

A big man, he looked familiar; without her neuronics, Kal couldn't place him. She flinched as she stepped into rain falling in wind-lashed, icy sheets that lashed her body like shards of glass.

The van had stopped under a protective chromaflage net set up in a grove of trees. A second waited, a battered wreck of a vehicle, rocking on its springs as the storm battered its sides. Its door slid open. The big man followed Kal in, slamming the door behind him.

The light came on as the van accelerated away.

Risell sat opposite.

Kal stared at her. "Oh, for fuck's sake! Don't you ever give up?"

"No, never. It's one of my strengths ... I see you've met my deputy, Harto Diop. He is a very dangerous man. Best you do as he says."

Kal remembered him now. She slumped into a seat, a sodden heap of utter misery. "Come on, Risell. Your empire is finished. Terra's finished. ImpSec's finished. You're finished." She pointed at Diop. "Your pet goon here, he's finished too. All of you. Finished. I don't even care what happens to you, not anymore. Just stop this nonsense and let me go."

"No, I don't think I will. And this not over, despite what you say .. . Like to guess how we found you?"

Kal turned away. She didn't care.

Risell leaned over and tapped a finger on Kal's left wrist. "Ever wonder why that feels a bit tender?"

"I had more important things to think about."

"I suppose you did," Risell said. "That's where we put a tracking chip. All ImpSec's high-value prisoners have them. I sent a team to bring you back in after you killed Nanmen. Your marines put a stop to that, but we knew the medics would CASEVAC you out on a shuttle at some point, and the highway to the spaceport was the obvious place to intercept you. All we had to do was wait until you were on your way and flood the road where it crossed the Yingxiong canal."

"You're insane."

"Me? Insane? No, not at all. I know what I want and how to get it. And you've taught me a valuable lesson."

"Oh, really?"

"Give a smart, focused woman a shit-load of money and chances are she can do whatever she wants. As you did."

Kal's mouth tightened into a sneer of contempt. "Smart? You? You're not smart. You're just a fucking psycho surrounded by fu—"

Kal never saw Diop's hand coming. It hit the side of her head, hard. "You fucking asshole!" she yelled, blinking back tears of pain. "What is wrong with you?"

Diop leaned forward. "If you don't like it, shut your damn mouth."

"Thank you, Harto," Risell said. "She'll learn . . . Now, where was I? Oh yes, smart women with money. You used the ransom you extorted from Amos Ferruci to defeat the Terran Empire. Now that is impressive, and no, I'm not pissing in your pocket. What you did was remarkable."

"Hah!" Kal snorted. "What I did was finish you, Jo Risell, so accept what has happened and go find a rathole to live out the rest of your life. Doing anything else is just stupid."

"You underestimate me."

"Seeing as Terra's being torn apart around us, I don't think I am."

Risell tapped a datastick dangling from a chain around her neck. "See this? It lets me access more money than you can ever imagine. Like you, that money will get me what I want."

"Dream on. The Coalition is coming for you, and no amount of money is going to save you."

"We'll see . . . Ah, looks like we've arrived."

Diop flicked the light off and opened the door. Nothing but blackness. "Clear."

"You can beat the crap out of her if she moves," Risell said to Diop as she climbed out, "but stop before you kill the bitch. I need her alive and able to talk."

"Yes, ma'am."

It was half an hour before Risell returned. Kal did not like the cheerful smile on her face as she reclaimed her seat.

"You'll be pleased to hear that your friends are pulling out. My people think the Coalition will be gone soon."

That hit Kal hard. Without Coalition boots dirtside, she knew her chances of being rescued were zero.

"Come on, Kal. Chin up and all that."

"Why are you doing this?"

Risell patted Kal's arm. "You'll find out."

~~~

Kal had dozed as they drove through the storm-shot night. It was hours before they stopped, Risell up and out the moment they came to a halt.

One of Kal's guards jabbed the barrel of her rifle into Kal's side. "Let's go."

Kal sat back and folded her arms. "Go screw yourself."

The two Imps didn't waste their time negotiating. They dragged her out and dropped her to the ground, now centimeters deep in water as the rain poured from a sky beginning to lighten as morning arrived.

Kal no long cared about the cold and the wet and the pain.

All that mattered now was destroying any chance Risell had of digging her way out of the shit.

That meant trashing the datastick. Without it, Risell was screwed. She would be another psycho with no money, no friends, and hunted by every law-enforcement agency in humanspace. The bitch wouldn't last a week.

A feral smile flitted across Kal's face. Given even the slimmest of chances, she would do her best to destroy the 'stick. And to hell with the consequences.

Risell reappeared. "Take her to the boat. We're going."

"Did you say boat?" Kal asked as she was pulled to her feet.

"I did."

"Jeezus. A fucking boat won't get you far."

"Oh but it will. You see, I always knew things might not go to plan . . ."

"You got that one right, sport," Kal muttered under her breath.

". . . . and a boat's the safest way to get clear. It'll take us two hours to reach Beihai Port. As soon as it's safe, we'll head for Nanning spaceport to take a shuttle off this godforsaken ball of rock; two ships are waiting for us in Clarke orbit. That's when you'll meet my Q-drive development team."

"I still can't understand why you're bothering. You have money. Use it to find somewhere to hide. If you don't, the Coalition will hunt you down, and you will die in prison."

"That will never happen. I have much bigger plans."

"What plans? More chaos, more killing, more destruction?"

Risell laughed. "Of course! They've always worked for me."

"Oh, terrific. Just what humanspace needs."

"It's not what humanspace needs. It's what Jo Risell needs. And sitting on my ass waiting to be scooped up by a Coalition snatch-squad is not what I need."

"Whatever you end up doing, you'll be doing it without my help."

"Nanmen wasn't my only Servalix operator. And don't forget the direct-action team waiting on Narsaq. No, I am totally confident you are going to tell me why our drive doesn't work."

"I already did!" protested Kal. "Gravity reefs, that's why!"

"Knowing you, I'd say that's probably a lie, but we'll find out soon enough . . . Get her aboard. We need to go."

Consumed by dread at the thought of more Servalix, Kal was dragged aboard a sleek cruiser; it rocked in the swell coming from the Gulf of Tonkin. Pushed down a ladder and into a saloon, she was dumped on a bench.

"Don't move," one of her escorts said.

Even if she'd wanted to, Kal couldn't. The random swings in her fortunes had left her crushed to a point where she had decided to do whatever Risell wanted.

Her head fell back against the bulkhead. A minute later, she was asleep.

~~~

". . . Hey, hey, hey! Wake up!"

Kal's head jerked forward. She stared around, wiping crud from her eyes and mouth.

Risell was standing over her, swaying as the boat lifted and fell beneath her. "You snore worse than anyone I've ever met."

"Fuck off."

Risell offered Kal a mug of coffee. ""Now, now, play nice. Drink this."

A sudden craving for caffeine flooded Kal's system. "Thanks . . . Where are we?"

"A few minutes from Beihai Port, then we'll head for Nanning spaceport. But you and I still have some unfinished business."

"No, we don't. You've been losing your ships because of gravity reefs! How many times do I have to say it?"

"You gave Nanmen a glib, two-word answer. He thought you were lying, and so do I."

"Okay, okay. Gravity reefs have nothing to do with anything. I just made that shit up because your so-called experts are too fucking stupid to work it out for themselves."

Risell sighed. She turned to Diop. "Get O'Brian down here, Harto. Tell her she has work to do. She'll know what I mean."

"Yes, ma'am."

"Who's O'Brian?" Kal asked, even though she could guess.

"I told you I had another Servalix operator," Risell said. "I'm sick of all your crap, so I'm going to teach you a lesson you'll never forget. This time you're getting the full three-hour dose."

The thought was more than Kal could bear. "Please, no. It is gravity reefs, it is. I promise."

Risell's face was hard, emotionless. "No more chances, Kariuki. My jump-drive development team are meeting us at Beihai. I'll stand O'Brian down if you can convince them. Otherwise, I will tell her to inject that damn stuff into your body. And she will, no matter how much you beg her not to. You'll get no second chances, understood?"

"Like I care. But I don't understand why you are bothering. You don't have a Q-drive ship. You lost three last month. And the last one to leave ORF-31 wasn't fitted with any nodes."

Risell smiled. "Once again you underestimate me. I have the *Logan Creek*."

"Which is what?"

"Just another hardworking freighter, except it's jump-capable. As soon as you tell us why we are having problems, we will modify the *Creek*'s AI, and then we're good."

"Good for what? You are Jo Risell, the woman who was once Minister for Imperial Security, the woman responsible for the death of thousands, one of the most wanted people in humanspace, and you will be until the day you die."

Again, the smile. Kal hated its smugness, its arrogant self-confidence.

Risell tapped the datastick. "You are so wrong."

"I don't care how much money you've got. It'll never be enough to save your ass, never."

"When you have enough to buy entire systems, I think you'll find it will . . . Ah, good. We're here. Time for you to talk, and don't forget what happens if you don't."

~~~

Martin Xianyu, the Q-drive development project manager was a cadaverous man with great splashes of black around his eyes, a zombie in a low-budget horror vid. Kal hated to think how miserable Risell must have made his life.

Xianyu stared across the table at Kal. "You keep saying that gravity reefs destroyed my test ships, but my team don't believe you."

Kal glared back, her face twisted into a mask of contempt. "I don't care. It's a fact. Gravity shear collapses the normalspace bubble and destroys the ship if you do not drop before you hit one. Like I said, it almost happened to us, but Daniel figured it out. One man. Alone. No support. No resources apart from what we had on our ship. When Daniel had fixed the drive AI, our ship, a beaten-up, clapped out wreck of a shuttle, jumped 876 light-years to Wallenski-7. And what have you and your pack of useless losers done? Jack shit is what. A grad student could have done a better job with her fucking eyes shut."

Risell's hand squeezed Kal's arm. Hard. "Stick to the facts, Kariuki, or I will turn you over to O'Brian."

"Okay, okay . . . I can't tell you anymore. Daniel did the detailed work. But gravity reefs are why you keep losing your ships."

Xianyu turned to one of his team, a woman. "Doctor Kisembi, I know you're my pinchspace expert, but are you sure Kariuki's lying? Now that I've heard her for myself, I'm not sure she is."

The woman's embarrassment was all too obvious. "Ah, yes. I did think it was a lie. But I've done some more research; it turns out a man called Keneally predicted these gravitational anomalies. And he did call them gravity reefs."

"That doesn't mean anything," Risell snapped.

Kisembi ignored her. "I think she might be telling the truth, Martin."

"What do we do?" Xianyu asked.

"Upgrade the AI to detect gravity shear, then see if that stops the jump-drive failing . . . which I think it will."

"Like you would have any idea." Kal stabbed a contemptuous finger at Xianyu. "Your boss says you're his pinchspace expert. Based on how well you've done so far, doctor, I think you should find another line of work."

"Keep it professional," Risell snarled, "or there will be consequences."

Kal glared back at her. "Consequences? What consequences? I have betrayed everything I care for. You can do what you like with me now. I've told you what you need to know, and I'm not saying another word." She leaned back, arms folded, mouth clamped shut.

Risell waved O'Brian over, then turned back to Kal. "Tell me the truth, and we won't need Ms. O'Brian. Lie to me, and—"

"Oh, for chrissakes! It's the truth." Kal nodded at Xianyu and his team. "Not that it matters; I wouldn't trust that rabble to piss in a ditch. No matter what I tell them, they'll still mess it up, you'll end up dead, and humanity will be the better for it."

"If anyone's going to end up dead, it's you."

"Me?"

"You'll be going along for the test jumps. That should focus your mind on giving me what I want, rather than being an such obnoxious asshole."

"Says one," Kal muttered under her breath.

Diop appeared. "Excuse me, boss. Our transport's waiting."

"The spaceport?" Risell asked.

"Secure, though not for long. But we need to get moving; fighting's broken out in Nanning. And we have reports of a PubSafe armored column moving up from Hanoi."

"To do what, for chrissakes?"

"Who knows? To settle old scores, probably. The Vietnamese and Chinese are old enemies; like elephants, they never forget an insult."

Risell stood. "I've had enough of Terra. Let's go."

—69—

"All stations, standby . . . dropping now."

Sighs of relief filled the bridge of the *Logan Creek* as it dropped into normalspace. Kal couldn't blame them; the freighter's crew had every right to be nervous. She hadn't realized how many ships and crews Risell had sacrificed in the struggle to give her the Q-drive she demanded.

Xianyu walked over to where she sat, one wrist cuffed to her seat. "I owe you a big apology, Ms. Kariuki. The problem was just as you described."

"Sorry I was so rude. What you've done is impressive, especially given how many pinchspace researchers Risell's people killed off."

"What are you saying?"

"Anyone who challenged the Keliang Foundation's view of pinchspace, was sacked, discredited, and then killed if they didn't stay quiet."

Xianyu stared at Kal for a moment. "Why do I find that so easy to believe? Emma Kisembi—who is extremely bright, by the way, just very young and not tough enough—told me that two of her co-researchers committed suicide."

"They were murders dressed up as suicides to protect Kolovchenko, Risell's specialty . . . Which makes me ask why you keep working for the bitch. She doesn't care whether you survive this or not. Come on, be smart, Martin. Jump this ship to Narsaq. You'll be safe, and I'll be very, very appreciative."

Xianyu's face twisted in despair. "I would, but Risell has our families with her."

"What? Like hostages?"

"Yes. She didn't actually say they'd suffer if we didn't follow orders. She didn't have to."

"You know she's going to space me, don't you?"

"She wouldn't . . . No, what am I saying?" Xianyu went on, shaking his head. "Yes, she would. She has a lot of blood on her hands, that woman. A bit more won't trouble her."

"Gee, thanks for the reassurance."

Xianyu lifted a hand in apology. "Forgive me, please. That was thoughtless."

"Put in me in a lifepod then. You can tell Risell I escaped."

"I'm sorry, I can't risk it. She'd space me and my family."

Kal sighed. "Yeah, she would . . . Okay, what's the plan?"

"We rendezvous with Risell's ship to transfer everyone across to the *Logan Creek*. Once we've remassed, we're heading for the Ironbolt system. Risell says we'll all be safe there."

"Doing what?"

"She's never said. But, given she's a homicidal megalomaniac, you don't have to be a genius to guess it's something to do with total domination of the human race."

Kal sighed. "That's our Jo Risell. Nothing if not a big thinker."

~~~

Flanked by two of Diop's thugs, Kal sat in the *Logan Creek*'s forward cargo bay, flexicuffed to a pipe. A lot of people had crowded in: Diop's team, ImpSec staffers, Xianyu's scientists and engineers, those of the crew not on watch, all with their families.

Kal scanned the faces. None seemed too sorry to be leaving Terra. She sure as shit wasn't.

Risell walked in, followed by Diop,

"Everyone's here," Xianyu said, "stand fast the crew on watch."

"Thanks, Martin. Okay folks, I will be quick so you can all settle in. First, we will be leaving tonight. We have our clearance from NearCon, and now that those Coalition scumbags have finally jumped out-system, they won't be bothering us."

"More's the pity." That earned Kal a savage cuff to the side of her head.

If Risell had noticed, she did not let on. "And I have the funds for the commitment bonuses you were promised . . . Markus, where are you?"

A lugubrious-looking man standing off to one side stepped forward. "Here, ma'am."

"Markus will arrange the money transfers with the heads-of-family before we lose comms with Terra. That will put the money you're owed into your Ironbolt accounts. Once we arrive there, what you do next is up to you. I will reward those who wish to continue with me with handsome contracts. Those who do not can take their money and do whatever they wish . . . except talk about me."

A nervous laugh ran across through the cargo bay. Risell smiled, a smile that was all threat and no humor.

Kal sensed they all knew how dangerous the woman was.

"Any questions?" Risell went on. "No? Okay, thank—"

"Hey, shit-for-brains!" Kal called out. "What about me?"

Face mottled red with sudden anger, Risell waved a hand at Diop. "Get that woman out of here."

"Yes, boss."

Diop dragged Kal from the cargo bay, down a ladder, and along a passageway. He opened a door into a storeroom, empty save for a thin bedroll on the deck, a bucket, and a bottle of water, and pushed her inside. "Your new home. Have fun."

"What's going to happen to me?"

"Not my call."

"Bullshit. You spend most of your time with your nose jammed up Risell's ass. You must know."

Diop's fist flashed at Kal's face. It stopped short and fell away. "I am the last friend you have onboard, Commodore Kariuki. It'll pay you to be polite."

"You? My friend? After what you and your thugs have put me through?"

"Things are not what they seem."

"Prove it, starting with what Risell has planned for me."

Diop was silent for a few seconds, then said, "I don't think she'll space you."

Kal studied the man for a moment, wondering how what his words were worth. Not much, she decided. The man was no better than Risell in the amorality stakes. "Why wouldn't she?" she asked. "I'm no friend of hers."

"She always has a backup plan. If I was her, you would be part of it."

"I thought bolting from Terra was her backup plan?"

Diop nodded. "It is, but she will have a backup to that backup. She always does."

"And how would I fit in? I'm not worth anything, not anymore."

"Ah, right . . . You don't know, do you?"

"Know what?"

"You're famous, Kal Kariuki, a superstar, the woman who destroyed the Empire. The Liberator, people are calling you."

"You . . . are . . . joking!" Kal hissed.

"Nope," Diop said. "As soon as Terra's pinchcomms came back online, the newsvids from Narsaq were full of you. And that is what's going to keep you alive."

"How? I'm done. What I did is history."

"The rest of humanspace owes you their independence. Over and over, you hear people asking how they can ever repay the woman who risked her life for them. That proves to Risell that you have enormous value. If I was her, I'd sell you in exchange for her life."

Kal felt a cautious flutter of hope. "Jeez, I hope so. I'm way too young to die."

"I wouldn't go that far."

"Bastard."

~~~

Unable to sleep. Kal lay on her bedroll. She only knew Risell from FIS's file, but Kal could believe the woman had a fallback for everything. And, if she was Risell's, then that was fine by her.

Calmed by a sudden wave of optimism, she had fallen asleep when the door banged open, dragging her awake. Two ImpSec troopers.

Fear overwhelmed Kal. She had been wrong; Risell did not need her. She was going to be spaced. "Why? What do you want? What's happening?"

Hands dragged her into the passageway.

"Come on! Talk to me."

The men ignored her.

Kal had hoped she would be brave, noble even, when facing death. Now that the moment was on her, all she wanted to do was throw up.

The men stopped outside a door marked 'Owner's Suite'.

Kal stared at the words. The Owner's Suite? What was going on?

The door opened. Kal's confusion deepened. Two ImpSec troopers had Risell pinned against the bulkhead, a thick ribbon of blood running from a gash above her left ear, staining her shoulder black, her left eye swollen shut, her mouth a bleeding ruin.

Diop stood to one side, laser pistol in hand. He waved her in with a bloody hand. "Commodore Kariuki. Perfect timing."

"What the hell is going on? I thought she was your boss?"

"Not anymore, so shut up and watch."

Struggling to adjust to the bizarre turn of events, Kal was happy to say silent. None of what she saw made any sense. FIS's analysts had commented on the bond between Risell and Diop; the man been by her side since the two of them fled Kassafar, ever the loyal, trustworthy deputy.

Diop put his face to Risell's. "Spare yourself an awful lot of pain, Jo. Give me the access code for that datastick."

"Why would I do that? You're going to kill me, no matter what."

"Not if you give me the code for that datastick. I might even leave you enough money to retire somewhere safe. Don't tell me, and I'll hand you over to O'Brian. Either way you'll end up giving me what I want. The only unknown is how much Servalix you can take before you break."

"I trusted you," Risell shouted, "ever since we started with Kolovchenko. Why are you doing this to me?"

"I don't like using clichés, but this time I will."

A flash of anger. "Get on with it, Harto!"

"Revenge is a dish best served cold. Only in my case what you'll be eating today is ice-cold. Remember a small town called Yakeen?"

"Yes, I do. The Freedom Militia were using it as a base. They hit us hard; the 56th took a lot of casualties."

"Which you took personally. I have never seen anyone so enraged; I thought the veins in your neck were going to burst. And then you ordered Charlie company to kill everyone in the place and bury them under the rubble. My CO refused; you shot him. Then you put your pistol in the XO's face and said you would shoot him too if he refused your orders. He did not want to die, so in we went. By the time we pulled out, we had killed hundreds civilians. And then you had the 56th demolish the town to bury the bodies."

Risell dismissed Diop's words with a flick of her wrist. "That was years ago. It's ancient history."

"Not to me. It only seems like yesterday."

"Come on, Harto. It was a civil war. Shit like that happened all the time."

"Yeah, it did, except Yakeen was the worst of the worst. The brigade commander wanted to court-martial you. Luckily for you the war ended before he could, and you left. The militia would have hung you from a tree if you hadn't."

"That's what this is all about? Some dead civilians?"

Diop swayed forward, his huge hands bunching into fists; for a moment, Kal thought he was going beat the woman to death. "No, it's not . . . It's about my sister. She didn't tell me she'd taken the kids to Yakeen; she must have thought it safer than Foundation City. I only found out what happened to them four years ago when the war-crimes teams finished with Yakeen; godknows, they had no shortage of atrocities to investigate. They sent me the casualty list, hoping to get me back to Kassafar to testify against you. That was when I promised I would make you pay for those deaths. I had to be patient, though; you have always been very well protected . . . until today,"

"Look, Harto," Risell said. "I'm sorry about the Yakeen business, I really am. But it was just one of those things that happens in a war. You can't blame me for it."

"You gave the orders, Jo, so now you can pay for what you did, starting with that datastick. In case you're tempted to screw with me, I will be checking I can access the accounts that 'stick controls before we leave Terran nearspace."

Risell's mouth set hard.

Diop sighed, then beckoned O'Brian over. "I want the biggest dose she can take without her dying on me."

"A two-hour session will be safe enough, boss. Will that do?"

"As long as you can do the same tomorrow and every day for a week. I want the bitch to hurt like she's never hurt before."

O'Brian pulled an autoject from her bag. "She will, I can promise you that . . . I hope you're ready for this, Ms. Risell," she went on, pulling up Risell's sleeve, "not that anybody ever is."

"Last chance, Jo," Diop said.

No response.

"Do it."

An instant before O'Brian stabbed the autoject home, Risell shrieked, "Wait! For chrissakes! Wait!"

Diop pushed O'Brian back. "This better be worth it."

"Harto, please. The datastick controls Imperial Treasury accounts that hold a trillion dollars. Why don't we split that 50-50?"

"When did I say that was an option?"

"But—"

"Do it, O'Brian."

"No!" Risell screamed. "Please, no. You can have it all, every cent, but you have to promise to let me live."

Diop clamped a giant fist around Risell's throat. He squeezed until her eyes bulged and face went red, then an ugly purple. When she began to sag, he pushed her away and stepped back. "You don't understand, do you? This is not a negotiation. Give me what I want, or you suffer. This is your last chance, so decide."

"Okay, okay," Risell croaked, "take it. I've commed you the master code. As long as you have that datastick, the accounts it controls are all yours."

"Let's see if you've been lying to me . . . Fuuuuuck. You weren't, Jo. Those accounts really do hold almost a trillion dollars." Diop jabbed the datastick at Risell's face. "How did you do this?"

"Come on, Harto! ImpSec has the best hackers in humanspace. All I did was point them in the right direction and tell them what I wanted. And they delivered, not that they lived long enough to enjoy their success. Pity. I liked those guys."

"I'm not sure you're human."

"I did what I had to."

"Crap! Everything you did was to feed your psychopathic ego. And you will pay for that."

"I've given you everything you wanted. Now let me go."

"The most dangerous woman in humanspace?" Diop shook his head. "No, I don't think so. The first gravity reef we cross, you'll be spaced."

The color drained from Risell's face. "You can't do that! You promised you wouldn't kill me! You gave me your word."

Diop mouth was a twisted sneer. "My word? Like that's worth a damn, but I'm not heartless. I'll give you a skinsuit. You can admire the glory of the cosmos as you wait for its oxygen to run out . . . Lock the bitch in the storeroom," he said to the two ImpSec troopers holding Risell, "the one forward on Deck 4. Do not leave her until you're relieved, not for one second. And she's not to talk with anyone. Understood?"

"Yes, boss."

Kal broke the stunned silence that followed Risell's departure. "That was impressive, Mister Diop, but why am I here?"

"I wanted you to see what happens to people who do not cooperate with me."

"I don't understand."

"The Coalition's after me. I'll spend the rest of my life in jail if I'm caught. You are going to make sure that doesn't happen."

"How, for chrissakes? What do you think I am? Some sort of magician?"

Diop mimed the sign of the cross. ""You are the sainted Kal Kariuki, the Liberator of All Humanspace and Destroyer of Empires."

"That doesn't mean I can help you."

"If you give me a written guarantee that nobody on this ship will be prosecuted, the Coalition will honor that. To sweeten the deal, I'll return most of the money Risell planned to steal. I don't think it's in anyone's interests for Terra to collapse, do you? I am not a greedy man; I never have been. A couple of billion will do. That's enough for me and the rest of the people onboard. Terra won't mind paying that much to avoid financial Armageddon."

Kal knew Diop was right. Terra's economy was the glue that held humanspace together. Its collapse would trigger a catastrophe. And he was also right about the guarantee; the Coalition would honor it because it came from her hand.

A head appeared around the door. "Captain's compliments, Mister Diop. We've remassed, all stores and pax are onboard,

SOLSPACE reports Terran nearspace clear of hostiles, so we're getting underway."

"Time to the jump datum?"

"2 hours 20."

"Thank you . . . So, Commodore Kariuki. Do we have a deal?"

"What happens if I tell you to piss off?"

"You'll be joining Jo Risell on her spacewalk, the war's biggest winner and biggest loser, together for all eternity. And I'll take all Risell's money. Terra and the rest of humanspace can fuck themselves."

"The Coalition will still come after you."

"For sure, but I'd much rather they didn't; I don't want to spend the rest of my life looking over my shoulder. But, if you give me your personal guarantee, I won't have to. You'll be my quality of life insurance."

"Let me think about it," Kal said.

"You have half an hour. If you turn me down, I'll need time to clean out all those accounts out before we leave, but understand this, commodore: Refuse me, and there'll be no more talking. You will die alongside Risell, and that would be a real shame. She deserves to die; you do not. Unlike her, you are a decent human being."

"Coming from you I'm not sure that's much of a compliment . . . I have one more question," Kal added.

"Sure."

"Why did you wait so long before moving against Risell?"

"Her security detail was the best of ImpSec's best. I'd have needed at least two of my direct-action teams to get past them. With that many people involved, keeping the planning a secret would have been impossible. I just had to be patient; I knew I would get my chance to take her out."

"You couldn't have known that. Amos Ferruci told me few people in the Empire had her power and influence."

"He was absolutely right," Diop said, "but let me tell you a secret: I never, ever believed in the Empire. It was a con, right from the start. Just look at the people running it. They were a criminal rabble: greedy for money, hungry for power, arrogant, full of hubris, lazy, more interested in stabbing each other in the back than making the Empire work. How were they ever going sustain something so ambitious, so complex?"

"They would have if Daniel and I hadn't turned up."

Diop shook his head. "No, they wouldn't. Right from the start, I was at the heart of the Imperial machine; I could see how unstable the Empire was. With or without you and the Ferrucis of this world, the Empire was doomed. It was only a matter of time before the whole corrupt charade imploded. All you did was bring forward the inevitable."

"Which gave you the opportunity you'd been waiting for."

"Yes, because chaos always brings opportunities. Risell had to run, and I was always going to go with her. Of all ImpSec's people, I was the only one she really trusted. That mistake created me the opportunity I had been waiting for."

"What about her security detail?"

"The off-watch teams were on their way to the *Logan Creek* when their shuttle blew up. A terrible tragedy; they were fine, loyal, and dedicated people. Pity about their families, but there you are. The team she brought with her were no match for my people, as you've seen. Living or dead, they were all spaced ten minutes ago."

"You ImpSec guys something else, Mister Diop. Maybe we should dump you and every other Imp apparatchik on an asteroid until you are fit to rejoin the rest of humanity."

"I won't argue with you on that."

"Maybe you're the smart one."

Diop sighed. "I'd have stayed well away from Risell if I was. Right from the start, back when the two of us were in the 56th, I knew she was trouble. It took Yakeen to show me how much. Right, back to your cell. You have some thinking to do."

~~~

In the end, the decision made itself. Kal refused to die making a pointless gesture of defiance. She could not stop Diop. The best she could do was to make sure he did not bankrupt Terra and the rest of humanspace along the way.

Which meant upsetting the Coalition by letting one of the Empire's worst killers go free. So what? Every system in humanspace owed her. Without her, they would all have ended up Terran colonies.

Instinct told her she could trust Diop to keep his word, that she would make it to Ironbolt alive. Then she would be free, Risell would be dead, and humanspace could start the long, slow process of recovering from the damage inflicted on it by Terra's delusions of imperial greatness.

Maybe now, finally, it was all over, and she would buy the Wallenski system and live out her days, happy to be a grandmother . . . She missed Daniel. He was . . .

She sat up.

The main engines had shut down. Why would they do that? Until the *Logan Creek* reached jump speed, nobody was going anywhere.

Something was wrong.

She forced her aching body to its feet and banged on the door. "Hey, hey! What's going on? Hey! Talk to me, you assholes."

No answer, the only sounds the soft hiss of the air-con.

The deck trembled. More of a twitch, come and gone in a second.

She started to worry. She had spent enough of her life in spaceships to have a feel for things. And things did not feel right.

A second tremor. Stronger. A metallic screech.

She pounded on the door until her fists ached.

Still no response.

Then came a sound she knew well: the flat *tokk-tokk . . . tokk-tokk . . . tokk-tokk* of combat shotguns in the hands of professionals.

With sudden, sickening certainty, she understood. Somehow, Risell had mustered enough support to break free and was fighting to take back control.

Kal knew she was dead if Risell won that fight.

The door to her cell burst open. Two troopers, shotguns in hand, bulky in combat armor—reached in and pulled her out in the passageway.

"What's going on?" Kal shouted. "Come on, tell me. What's g—"

A black-gloved hand slashed into the side of her face with terrible force, a blow that jolted her head back so hard she lost consciousness for a second, slumping down to hang between the men as they dragged her away.

When she recovered, she was on a box in an empty storeroom, one wrist flexicuffed to a pipe. The troopers had vanished, leaving her confused and frightened.

The gunfire intensified.

Somewhere aboard the *Logan Creek*, one hell of a fight was going on, but who was fighting whom?

She thrashed at her cuffs in a desperate attempt to work free. She had to get away. She wanted to live. She wanted all this pointless stupidity finished.

Despairing, her wrist scarified into a bloody mess, she gave up.

She was screwed.

There would be no house on Wallenski-7. No watching Daniel's extraordinary talent flourish and his love for Skylar grow. No being a grandmother.

Nothing.

She was sitting back, eyes closed, doing her best to ignore the growing sound of a full-blown battle getting ever closer, when the storeroom door opened. It was Diop, the left side of his face sporting an ugly red cut that ran across his cheek and up into his hair.

Kal had seen that injury before. A slapdisk from a shotgun had hit Diop a glancing blow. He had been lucky. A couple of centimeters to the right, and he would be dead.

"What the hell is going on?" she asked.

Diop slashed a knife through the cuffs and dragged Kal to her feet. "Your Coalition friends have turned up, and I don't feel like surrendering. It's time to play the last card I have left."

"I don't understand."

"You live if I live. Come on, let's go. And do exactly what I say. Mess me around, and I will kill you."

Kal did not care. She was too tired and too hurt to.

Diop hustled her away, stepping through an airlock with the words 'CARGO BAY - AUTHORIZED ACESS ONLY'.

Kal found herself in a vaulting space stacked with shipping containers. What was left of Diop's team waited either side of the three-meter-wide aisle down the center. Most wounded, the faces of all betraying the shock of their shocking reversal of fortune.

"We're so fucked, boss," one said.

Diop spit on the deck. "Not yet we're not."

He threw Kal at the nearest trooper. "Truce," he yelled. "Truce. Let's talk."

A voice boomed back. "Step into the open, no weapons, hands out, palms forward, and I'll do the same."

"Mess with me and Kariuki's dead. Understood?"

"Understood."

Diop handed his rifle to one of the team and stepped out. "Here's the deal. I'll hand over Kariuki, unhurt, and you give me and my people safe passage to the Ironbolt system. And you don't touch any of us at any time, not now, not in the future."

"We need to see that Kariuki's okay."

"She's fine. I give you my word."

"Why would I trust an ImpSec thug? Show us she's alive, or you can forget any deal."

Diop turned to where Kal stood wedged between two of Diop's team. "Bring her here."

Rough hands pushed Kal out beside Diop. A Coalition marine in assault armor stood 30 meters away.

"I'm Lieutenant Kham, Coalition marines," the woman called out. "Are you okay, ma'am?"

"I will be when you've killed this fucking asshole."

Diop shoved her back behind the containers. "As you can see, the mouthy bitch is fine, but she won't be for long. You have five minutes to accept my offer. Refuse, and the next thing you'll see is her body."

"Do that, and you'll all end up dead too."

"Maybe so, but we'll take a lot of your marines with us. It's not like we have much to lose."

"Give up, Diop," Kham shouted. "It's over."

"Fuck off! You've heard my offer. Whether you accept is up to you."

Kal glanced at her guards. The one nearest was looking at Diop, her hand on Kal's shoulder.

Kal moved a fraction. The woman did not react, too focused on Diop. A fraction more and the heel of Kal's hand rested on the thigh-mounted holster all Diop's team wore, a holster holding a laser pistol.

Some things a marine never forgot. Kal could work the spring-loaded release with her eyes shut and brain switched off.

"My orders were to take this ship," Kham called out. "I don't have the authority to negotiate anything with you."

"As long as I have Kariuki, you have to."

Kal's left hand crept higher.

"Who says we care what happens to her? We've got bigger things to worry about."

Diop spit on the deck. "That is bullshit! We all know what Kariuki means to you. She's dead if you don't accept my offer. So, cut the crap."

Kal's hand closed on the butt, one finger on the release.

And still the woman's eyes stayed locked on Diop. As they should. Their owner's life was in his hands.

"Let me check with my boss," Kham said. "I need her okay."

"She is where?" Diop asked.

"Back on *Iron Sword*."

"And she has the authority to okay the deal?"

"Why else would I talk to her?"

"I'll give you two minutes . . . and stay where I can see you, you sonofabitch."

"Calm down, Diop. You'll get your answer."

Diop's shoulders relaxed a fraction.

Kal knew now was her best, her last, her only chance to save herself. She exploded forward, ripping the pistol free as she twisted her battered body to take the shot.

All she needed was a few seconds.

Distracted, slow to react, confused by the unexpected, Diop's people gifted her those seconds.

Kal brought the gun up and fired on instinct, Diop so close she could not miss.

And she didn't.

The shot took Diop as he turned to see what was happening, the intense pulse of energy driving into his cheek below the open visor and up into his brain.

For one awful moment, Diop did not move. Kal thought she had missed. Then he crumpled to the deck, falling back, his head thumping down with a sickening crack.

Her guards' response was brutal. As they tore the gun from her hand, blow after blow after blow pounded her defenseless body.

Barely conscious, Kal collapsed, uncaring, her body consumed by waves of pain, her vision collapsing down to tiny circle of light amidst an ocean of black.

Shots.

Tokk-tokk . . . tokk-tokk . . . tokk-tokk . . . tokk-tokk . . . tokk-tokk.

Silence.

Shouting.

Words but not words. Sounds without meaning.

Silence.

Shouting.

Movement.

Bulky shapes, dark and blurred.

Metallic clattering.

Hands reaching down.

Voices, not harsh, soft.

Kal gave up the fight.

Consciousness faded away.

And the darkness crept in to claim her.

—70—

Kal watched the shuttle come to a stop in front of Wallenski-7's refurbished terminal building. She pushed through the soundproof doors and walked across to it, the residual heat of its re-entry warm on her face. The access lock door swung open, and Daniel was in her arms.

A long embrace only broken by a soft cough.

Kal pulled a face as she stepped away. "Sorry, Skylar. Old marines like me have no manners at—"

The breath caught in her throat at the sight of the white bundle in Skylar K'hala's arms. "Is that . . ."

"Yes, it is. Big Kal meet Tiny Kal."

"But she wasn't due for another three weeks!"

"Teekay had other plans, so we thought we'd save you trip back to Narsaq. Want to hold her?"

Kal thought her heart was going to explode it was pounding so hard. She took Tiny Kal from Skylar. The little form was warm. She smelled of her mother's milk. She was asleep, her button-nosed face wrinkled.

Tiny Kal was most beautiful thing Kal ever seen.

Kal wiped the tears from her eyes with the back of a hand. ""Let's go. I have my new house on the best swimming lake in humanspace to show you. And Hemed is looking forward to catching up with the man who gave him my foodbot."

Daniel leaned over. "You're never going to forgive me for that, are you?"

"After months eating emergency rations and drinking shit coffee, why would I?"

~~~

Daniel dropped into a chair. "When Teekay doesn't want to sleep, she doesn't want to sleep."

Skylar gave Daniel a peck on the cheek and handed him a beer. "You'll learn, darling."

"I'm sure I will; I'm getting plenty of practice . . . Did Skylar tell you about Risell?"

Kal nodded. "That she's pleaded guilty to all charges, yes. Though it's not like her to give up like that."

"Risell's no fool," Skylar said. "She knows the evidence against her is overwhelming. A guilty plea is to make getting parole easier."

"She'll still be inside for what? 50 years?"

"That's what the media are predicting."

"I'm glad to hear it."

Kal sat back to enjoy the thought of Risell rotting in goal while the rest of humanspace forgot the woman's crimes and moved on.